BOOK·ONE

Shadows of the Dracore

Stolen Child
THE BEGINNING

A Tale by Adele DeGirolamo

FriesenPress

Suite 300 - 990 Fort St
Victoria, BC, Canada, V8V 3K2
www.friesenpress.com

Copyright © 2015 by Adele DeGirolamo
First Edition —2015

**Final edit of the 2015 copyright edition
of the Stolen Child Series, was done by
Caspian Hunter Pembroke**

All rights reserved.

No part of this publication may be reproduced in any form, or by any means, electronic or mechanical, including photocopying, recording, or any information browsing, storage, or retrieval system, without permission in writing from the publisher.

ISBN
978-1-4602-6586-4 (Hardcover)
978-1-4602-6587-1 (Paperback)
978-1-4602-6588-8 (eBook)

1. Fiction, Fantasy

Distributed to the trade by The Ingram Book Company

Shadows of the Dracore Chronicles is a work of fantasy. Names, places, and incidences, either are a product of the author's imagination, or used from a historical publication fictitiously. Any resemblance to actual persons, living or dead, including time-lines and events is entirely coincidental.

This book also contains an excerpt from the upcoming second shadow called, *In-between*. It is a continuation of this first novel of the Dracore series; one that had been split into three separate books, primarily for print edition only, for those who wish an updated version of the original novel.

The book *Stolen Child* is the first of the series of the *Shadow of the Dracore Chronicles* and will be followed by consecutive novels — in future writings, to complete the original series. The novels following will be directly linked to the series and create what is to be the Shadow Scrolls of the entire writings of the Faden Corpeous Galaxy's race of Fey, which are now living in the Star System of the Goddess Sopdet.

MESSAGE FROM THE AUTHOR

I would like to thank the cover illustrator for his rendition of our Dragon. His name is Fernando Cortes de Pablo. Also equally I would like to thank the artist Roger Dean, for giving us the imagination that lets us soar, and to Loreena McKennitt for allowing us to hear those images in song. All of which after reading the great adventures of the writer Edgar Rice Burroughs as a child, allowed me to create this tale from the illusions of my own dreams. So, enjoy what is set before you, and laugh at the audacity of the personalities from the unique creatures of this world. They are lightly coaxed from across the galaxy of my imagination, and landing in the pages of this — albeit strangely engrossing, but nonetheless what appears to be a true interpretation of what their historical scrolls would look like...

For all of those other Acknowledgments that I might have missed, I haven't forgotten who they are, what they are, and to whom I need to use as characters in my future books...

Visit the Author's Website at **www.adeledegirolamo.com**.

DEDICATION

Dedicated to my best friend Jan Stevens, and her current service dog Orbie; for without both of them this story may never have been written. Also, I dedicate this book to her previous dog Romeo, who was with her when I first met her, giving me a million hilarious memories of the two of us running around the shores of some beach, like bonafide idiots.

Dear Jan; I know this book has been a long time in coming. Thank-you for everything you have done to keep me writing. You are truley my hero. I will always be with you, and now we have it in print... finally.
your friend forever

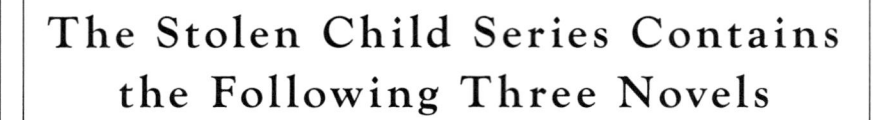

The Stolen Child Series Contains the Following Three Novels

The Beginning
In-Between
Transcending

ANONYMOUS CRITIQUE

This manuscript contains a truly epic story. I was engrossed from the beginning pages, finding the storyline engaging, exciting, fast-paced and gripping in its entirety. A well-plotted story is made even more palatable with the very compelling prose it is told in. The author's characters and creatures come to life with her phenomenal verbal illustrations. Each world, each location, each persona is so intricately relayed to the reader through the author's words that you are simply transported into the Fey worlds within the book with no effort at all. This book will leave anyone wanting to read the next book, in order to continue to lose themselves in the realms the author has created.

...An editorial review...

TABLE OF CONTENTS

Message from the Author i

Dedication iii

Anonymous Critique v

Prologue 3

Chapter One 10
   Sombreia Village, Home of the Shapeshifters

Chapter Two 33
   Escape through the Majikal Forest of Lypurnen Woods

Chapter Three 48
   Soren and the Wood Sprite

Chapter Four 86
   Sibrey's Dream

Chapter Five 92
   A meeting of Minds

Chapter Six 129
   The Leviathan of Leberone

Chapter Seven 147
   Dreamscape of Ancient Tameron

Chapter Eight...176
  Dyareius and the Dragons

Chapter Nine 183
  Llyach Clan of Sylmoor

Chapter Ten 188
  Travel to Kilren

Chapter Eleven 201
  The Caretakers of the Scared Grove

Chapter Twelve 205
  The Realm of the Cloud People

Chapter Thirteen 218
  Symin and the Hidden Army of Leberone

Chapter Fourteen 226
  Ryyaan, the White Dragon, and the Tuatha De`Danann

Chapter Fifteen 235
  Aggulf Elkcum Mound

Chapter Sixteen... 268
  The Village of the old Fomorian King

Chapter Seventeen... 281
  Unexpected Departure

Chapter Eighteen 297
  The Witch called Kashandarhh

Chapter Nineteen... 309
  Entity

Chapter Twenty 325
Arrival of a Dragonlord

Chapter Twenty-One 347
Tameronian Switch

Chapter Twenty-Two 367
The Shadow of Aperthan

Chapter Twenty-Three 390
Assha and the Water Elemental

Chapter Twenty-Four 413
The Unexpected Meeting of Lugh and the Fire Elemental

Book-Two of this Tale 429
A brief glimpse, into that first Chapter.

Special Note 434
from the Author to the Readers

Fey Dictionary 436

List of Characters in This Novel so Far 452

About the Author 467

STOLEN CHILD
THE BEGINNING

Stolen Child

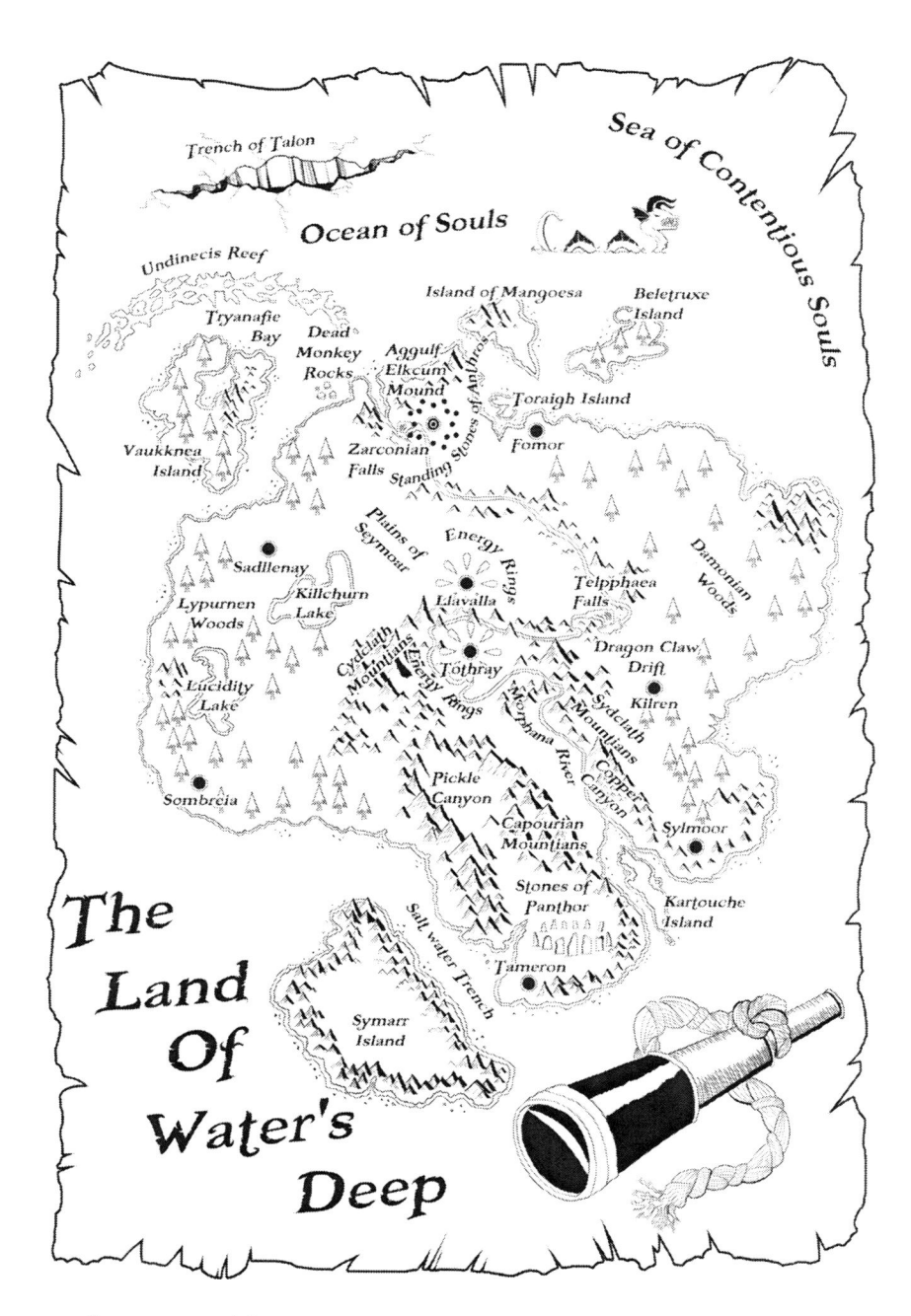

The Land Of Water's Deep

Original Map compilation by Adele DeGirolamo
Illustration by David Carey

PROLOGUE

It's never easy dying, but we all do it eventually. There was a time, long ago, that I truly believed I would have welcomed it without any reservation. But now, I cannot think of a worse time for that to actually proceed in its execution, in this very unique world of my Shapeshifter life. We all have that one silent moment, that quintessential space in a fractured timeline, where we all know, without a shadow of a doubt that the time of our death has arrived and we can go no further in this life. There should be, at that moment, nothing left to do but breathe that last luxurious breath as our lungs expand outwards and then, without so much as a 'by your leave'... simply flipping, croak.

Seriously, humorous as it may sound, I mean to actually fall down, roll around on the ground a bit as my heart slows down to a snail's pace until, with a small little twitch, it's all over without the singer having formed words in her operatic throat. That is, of course, until I rise again like the phoenix from the ashes of another world. While life folds up around you, resetting itself in the space you occupied within this arena of your death, swallows you whole, and leaves no trace of you having been there.

It's funny now, how those words seem to ring true at this moment, as the time is drawing nearer to my demise. Nonetheless, as I laugh at the actuality of it happening, it was not what I expected to happen. We are still one full turn of the revolution of our star, which we Fey call the Mauntra, before this should actually be occurring. However, time seems to have a way of being interrupted by disasters, many of which seem to happen on and off during this rather exceptional occurrence in the time-line of the Fey race, so, I shall have to adjust somewhat before we can figure out just what the hel has happened!

Nevertheless, it would have been wondrous, the true Fey send off for the old Panther clan's matriarchal Elder-Kat, which had been frothed with legend and myth, as it ran off course, pissing off those who had been planning the lovely send off in the first place, only to be knocked sideways, as one final enchantment was put in its place. Their shocked faces would have been enough for me to laugh out loud, as I was left to be hunted and chased through the valley of the Goddesses and back again; as I ran with absolute perfection, to the very end of my bloody life kicking and screaming into the damn wind. That is, before they had time to shove me into the great beyond like a piece of dirt scraped off the bottom of their leather slippers after walking into a steaming pile of Cauper dog-poop!

So, with that sliding off my lips in sheer luxury I will start another journey, and this one must also include that truth of my nature and the absolute genius that I am. That fact alone makes me a fanatical expert on the subjects that I do know about. For this, I may be able to find a way to let you see into our unusual world, which some of your kind knew little about before this day; or for the very least before the Goddesses are able to reach out and find a way to stop me.

You see, as of the moment of this writing my age has been somewhat of an unusual affair. For those of you who have begun this quest alongside the running of the races of the Fey, I am by all accounts what is best described as more of an immortal, by the standards of your metaphysical time-shift. However, to us Fey, a mere nine hundred and ninety eight years old is a slightly elevated time shift in this linear plane of existence that I still, with much reservation, reside within.

However, that too is changing from moment to moment, and does not mean by any fit of the imagination, that I cannot at any time meet my demise; it just means that I have, in centuries past, been able to without too much trouble, scrape through most of my ordeals without the actual process of being bloody dead. However, much to my surprise, I have my doubts about being able to make it through this one, and have a bit of knowledge on the scientific properties of actually making it out alive this time. Nevertheless, that too is running desperately low in its origins, as my signature quantum's fall is rising to the elements and beginning its final disappearance into the winds of Sopdet's skies.

This ability you have as a Human race to actually get dead in a reasonably short period of time still amuses me, and has been a topic of discussion amongst those that have been included within these few hundred pages of written historical reference of my clan and their acquaintances. Therefore, you must know the parameters that have been set before me that have given me the opportunity to explain to you that there are many of us much older than what I and my own kind have a tendency to live.

In fact, there is one creature that lives within these pages which has outlived everything within this universe and I can honestly say, it is one of the oldest living creatures in the creation of the Fey worlds. It will, in time be introduced throughout the pages of these manuscripts, and hopefully will intrigue you enough as the story goes along to hold that interest − or my job has not been correctly accomplished in what I have tried to achieve in this tale.

First, you need to know that we do live well outside the boundaries of your catatonic time of linear existence. Truth be told, we live well outside most things that seem to go bump in the night. But, in comparison to your world, the parameters that are set for us allow us to live to be much older and exist in more than one place and time, through doorways that have been around even longer than our own race.

So as the tale unfolds around you, I feel that within this strange and fairly exciting new world, which has just opened up to you and tried to open up a vast network of threads that are just beginning to infiltrate your imagination that time now has let me follow its dimensions to give you a glimpse into how this all began. I should probably start by introducing myself; how rude of me not to think of that. I am the one that they call The Sibrey; strange title, but it is not one that I have chosen, nor have picked from this side of the veil. But, I do belong, or at least I thought I had to this Togernaut clan of Shapeshifters that lives in the Sombreia village, alongside an eclectic collection of Shifters from different walks of life, which have been more or less left alone for going on a thousand of your years: That is until about halfway through this first chapter in the story, but we shall get to that in a moment.

For now let's begin by saying, sometimes it appears, I do write in my sleep and wake up to discover an entire chapter has arrived, with no memory of the words actually being written by me. I seem to be moving faster through this time shift, as time begins to get shorter, with end days beginning to all blend into the one final push towards my imminent demise. To which, I would hope you can see through this rambling of paraphrases, how my mind needs to work faster than my words, and will throughout the entirety of this story, causing some of you to cringe at my audacity to stretch things out to the farthest reaches of sentence formation.

Bear with the formula; it has to be set for everything to work out that way. Facts are pushed and shoved into larger and larger sentences along the pages of this manuscript, until I am seemingly unable to produce even the smallest of sentences from my Shapeshifter mouth without them sounding like they are not finished. I hope, in time, you will understand the urgency. It is because of this, I'm afraid, you will undoubtedly find mistakes with the wording of a few things spelled differently than those you have understood in the past. However, you will find their meaning of their individuality to come together as the story transforms and comes to life in front of eyes that have borne witness to the story.

Anyways, I am bubbling along, which I tend to do with no thought to how it is that you have taken the time to put aside other things in order to listen to a tale which, as of yet, you have your doubts on its authenticity. A tale, shall we say, about a Shapeshifter's world seen through my eyes that was folded into the history of one such as me. In doing so, you will also see, you are truly not the only one that lives within the boundaries of your time and space, and now since you have stayed with the introductions, I shall give you the last bit you need to help you through this tale of majikal encounters.

The tellings say I was named by my mother, though she is someone that I have never met or, at the very least, not till recently. She, I am told, is incredibly beautiful, as well as coming from a family who is very important in the Tuatha De'Danann world. I have my doubts on that subject; for who could this mother be, that would leave me without ever allowing me even a moment of her time? But, to that we shall let the Goddesses find the reason for her suffering tale; for me, I am disappointed that it took me dying for her to come forth out of the shadows of her world.

There are so many parts of my life that I have not the like of reliving, but as time finds me within this storyline these hiccups will probably make you Humans laugh and may be added in for amusement status simply to give me reverence. Then again, I find taste can be a fleeting gesture in this world you live in, so I shall try to do my best to entertain your literary nuances to the best of my ability.

For lack of a better title, you need to understand, I am also Fey. Do you know the name Fey? Most of you do, if you have spent any time reading books on Trolls or faeries, the latter being rather nasty creatures, despite the lovely photographs and depictions that you Humans have fixated on. But I, on the other hand, have actually spent time with them and had to deal with some of the not so pretty aspects of their so-called personalities, but that also in due time, and another chapter.

Therefore, I will tell you, as it was lived by me, the essence of a fable that now stands before you, lived and directed by all that seek the pages that lay within, after the Goddess Danu went into the night sky and left us alone, leaving the Goddess Sopdet to step into our skies to take her place.

To be of a majikal species, which the Fey represent, is one of the most exhilarating of feelings that floats within the recesses of every brain that lives within this galaxy. I cannot, for the life of me, understand the Human complexity and the gravitational restrictions that keep you earthbound upon your planet, within an atmosphere that cannot allow you to take to air. How does one seize the moment to challenge the winds, if one cannot take to flight? It would be a death sentence to any Fey should they be stranded upon your planet and be unable to fly with the currents that move about within the silence of the sometimes-volatile refractions of what you think is simply nothing more than wind. I choose to stay here, although at one time in my life I have been to your planet and almost got myself killed. That too is another chapter, in a following book inside this series, which you will be presented with in the coming years.

But for now, we of Fey could never find the truth of what we are if we were to stay to soil and never fly again. How awful for you, as a race of beings who should be reaching out for the stars, to have only gone to the moon with no name. Truly, why do you not let it live, and give it its rightful voice? Is having no identity all that you are able to truly find for it, seeing nothing more than a lunar shifting of rocks? That saddens me greatly — the loss of its identity, as it floats above you, giving you light within the nighttime sky while you lay awake on those sleepless nights, reading a manuscript that is, in itself, something of an enigma to others of your kind.

You see these words that you hold in your hands as they come alive in your mind while your fingers slide across the parchment and allow you to turn the pages of the story that you read with your artistic mind; they can only come alive with life that you allow me to create. Does not the tale within give you names for even the smallest of creatures, including many which, in your world, never seen more than a simple water-drop inside a stagnant pond that rests along a forgotten trail, inside the mountains of a grand backdrop of simple rocks? Does your mind not listen to a tale of a species which you are really still unsure is really alive and well, living somewhere out there in that bright sky you see full of stars? Will it even allow your mind to think it is possible? It is, after all, just a collection of thoughts inside a moment placed in time that gives it its sense of purpose as it creates and winds its way around your mind, giving you an opportunity to visit a place that you ordinarily wouldn't be able to find without having been handed the directions by one that lives there.

That is what a name can do to excite and stimulate the brain neurons into believing it is real. For at least the time you have your nose buried in that book, and the world around you is moving in slow-motion away from your internal senses, allowing you to rest inside that thought, it is a glorious and simple ostentatious pleasure to find your mind working for your well-being, instead of against everything your heart wants you to believe.

Simply put, I would ask of you this one thing, as I lay lost within a realm I have never seen before, waiting to rise again to fight another day. Please name the damn moon! It will work…trust me. Believe me, it will give your sense of purpose a new meaning inside the lives of what is yet to arrive within your tiny realm of little remembrance, of how our worlds are linked. There will come a time when you will see us coming out of the shadows, on a moment that is not of your choosing, and if you can do anything for me after I am gone, that would give me pleasure in my long awaited rest, it would be this.

It would be my dying wish for your race which, coincidentally, I have long since given up on as a species, from lack of understanding of how you wish to survive within the stars if you choose not to participate in this simple pleasure of continuous life restructure that is presented to all of us. We cannot come, if you do not believe. It is a simple thing, and your moon plays a big part of who we are in the grand scheme of life, as you have yet to discover.

A name brings substance to what is, at the moment, simple non-sentient flora, and opens a vast array of possibilities to breathe life inside a stagnant mind that will blossom and grow beyond anything you have yet to achieve. As it is, it would appear that you have lived within the shell of blood and bone within your own bodies, and are prisoners restricting the confines of that to which you were born. I, on the other hand, do not and cannot allow that to happen to me. For I shall always live freely among the elements, flying freely among the winds that let us be on the edges of that rim that is locked inside one's mind. Even they have names to follow through, allowing me to move from place to place, moment to moment, at will without the confines of solid form that would be holding me planet-bound.

It is a vanity that accompanies all Fey, which you could say has got me into a lot of trouble; it never occurs to me that I can also be fallible, and caught within the reality of the gravity with which you live. However, that may be true, and it makes no never mind to me that you cannot find peace in the confines of yourselves, even if you cannot fly, or name a moon! At least when I lived I did so with all the majik and essence of every living atom that surrounds the heart that beats within this body. I, at least, will let the blood flow to change my atoms into whatever I want, and transform into the Shapeshifter that hides within the shadows of what is about to come my way. So my darlings, without further adieu I shall give you this... It was one of those days which began a series of events that led me into this tale, and far from what I thought my life would be; that is before, I became a little bit on the dead side of my life.

Damn, something's coming.....I feel it's twist beginning to form; I'm going to have to hurry!

CHAPTER ONE

Sombreia Village, Home of the Shapeshifters

It was on one of those beautiful lazy summer days that the story I'm about to tell, begins to take shape above the shoreline of a lake called Lucidity. The creature broke the surface, from the underwater world of another species, and climbed upwards onto the rock to warm herself within the rays of the surface world's much beloved heat. The rocks against her feet were up against the shallows of one of the many small islands which rest their bones within these warmer mountain waters. She blew the extra air bubbles out of her nostrils with exaggerated flare — daring the air-world to chastise her for daring to come to close to a stray Dragonfly whom had landed a little too close to her arrival. It flew away with barely a whisper, while she simply ignored it and continued to look over her webbed hands with a face still glistening with small water droplets, having just spent the morning swimming and floating among the Naiads; the very ones who have lived here for centuries, making this lake their home.

They had always lived within this lake, which moved about the currents of another, much deeper, and one which lay at the foot of the Cydclath Mountain range, out along the bottom of the Telpphaea falls, where it could be seen winding its way around the cliff edges of the deep ravines, back out to where she now swam today. She waved goodbye and, with a fond farewell, promised she would return at a future date; one not planned as of yet, but always in the forefront of her mind. She was happy to be finally away from the confines of what she probably should have been doing, and was feeling luxurious in the warmer environment, shaking the previous form from her skin to allow the heat to penetrate further into its outer core.

She blinked and slid the underwater lids of her eyes sideways to reveal the lenses that she would need to be another creature, one that breathed through nostrils and wouldn't be able to filter the light with such dim underwater sight. She transformed once and then shimmered in the heat, revealing the partial scales of a Firefox lizard as it came forth, giving her the added texture she craved. She would need these to bring the heat down deep into the places within her blood that had not received warmth in the three arns she had been in the underwater world. Once her core temperature met its desired reading, she would finish the shift, and fall back into her purer form, sliding her lenses back to their original position. But, for now she just wanted to drift in relative solitude, within the creature that held her safely in its aquatic embrace.

The freshwater inside this lake was something that always made her feel alive. This morning, as the warm rays of the Mauntra started to warm her spine, she felt exceptionally high in the environment, with her latest choice of transformation. Diving deeply within the warm waters of the lake's aquiline environment, and giving herself over to its crystalline sounds, which, next to the water breathers, only a Shapeshifter can truly begin to understand its structured clarity; she felt at home. Sibrey had many of these hidden days of late, drifting within the confines of her own mind, finding time away from her lessons and chores. When she did return to their required conductivity, sometime much later than when she had been required to have gotten them done, they could always be found exactly there, where she had left them, with no one the wiser for her deviancy.

Her mind liked to spend these days, believing in this other world. One that had risen deep within her own mind, and deeply frothed with its unusual visions, which she had dreamed about so very many times at various points in her young life. She always found them to attain a fascination in their lucidness, and not anything resembling the current world that existed in front of her eyes. Soon, she knew, time would be exhausted from her morning escape, knowing fair well she was long overdue. Her teachers would be inquiring about her whereabouts, and sending word to her caretaker family in whatever context they liked to fit into the verb of the day, and chastising her for her latest truanted actions. Naughty child, she smiled in her deviousness and continued to climb higher onto the stone's surface, away from the actual touch of the lake, and the voices of those who would undoubtedly be angry. She cared little for their song; there would be plenty of that in the latter hours of her day.

She licked long claws clean of their recent dunking, and stretched her long form to release the hidden pockets where the water might hide. Finding none substantially active, she then followed by shaking the water droplets off her head, in a last ditch effort of final transformation. She had only just begun to enjoy the air breather's world when, looking downwards, she noticed a single feather perched precariously on its end, staring at her with slanted quills smack dab in the middle of the rock. Her heart sank. She would need to find solace somewhere else in the coming days. Just as she feared, her younger brother had found her in her seclusion, through his relentless searching for her continuous whereabouts. The perfectly balanced feather now held the only clue she would be given. Vermodious brothers, always trying to wreck her day.

Enjoying the absolute solitude that only comes from total quiet and rest within one's own brain would have to wait. Nevertheless, even a single feather along the edges of their calling would only make her more resistant to their inquiries. She sighed with a little hiccup of disappointment, sending air towards the underside of her belly. Her lizard lungs then burped, sending additional water molecules into the air in the form of bubbles. Immediately, with one last breath, she turned to face the beautiful mauntrated orb in the sky, fully ignoring her brother's warning, choosing instead to begin her final stages of freedom without him.

But that was not to be. Instead she fumed, finding satisfaction in her thoughts. How was it that they could not seek her out among the waterfalls and fallen stumps which littered their little village on the outskirts of town, instead of driving her nuts with obsolete inquiries she wished not to answer; or at least be forthcoming in her times of civil disobedience. She did agree, she'd had more than her share of times to play, and could be found more often than not out among the lakes where she had been swimming, over in the deeper sections away from the edge. However, truth be known, she had little interest in the things that must be taught, and the sooner they realized that she would not change her ways anytime soon in this little endeavour, the better. Besides, something else was going on in her brain that they were not aware of, and at that moment in time she could not for the life of her begin to tear that apart in front of herself, let alone anyone else. This time she wouldn't let it happen; she had other things on her agenda than brothers or schooling, and before the day was out she would find that peace and solitude she craved, and then return home satisfied in its completion.

It was this, during her final transmogrification of becoming a partly scaled lizard, what she spotted in the reflection of the lake, and not her dear old brother's ugly face, that actually finally stopped her from completing the final transformation into a fully developed amphibian. It seemed that more than just her little Shapeshifter body was out and about in this remote location; all thrashing around in the middle of a lake, deep in the middle of bloody nowhere. This was ridiculous; how many other creatures had he decided to enlist to disturb her? She was going to kill him. Seriously, what was this, a main thoroughfare into the 'let's piss off the reclusive Narcan' and make her day just a little bit more difficult?

What she had seen, finally broke through along the furthest ridge of the Shapeshifters' woods flying in formation and darkening her face from the very direction the Mauntra had been warming her body. She opened one eye and looked skywards as their shadows darkened her face, cocking her head to expose the proper angle of her sight, watching them come. The creatures that arrived within her line of sight had huge black wings accompanied by a body that was fairly strange in colour for any flying creature, let alone what appeared to belong to a dark coloured Dragon. Nevertheless, Dragons they definitely were, and not from anywhere near these parts of the woods. They continued to move towards her while she sunned herself on a little old rock in the middle of the lake.

The name Dragon was synonymous with the wild greens that played along the edges of where she currently found herself to be, and for some apparent reason the latter had chosen to abandon her to her own devices, the moment the others darkened the skyline from high above.

"Crap the little stinkers," she growled low, in her throat. However, that was not unusual for their behaviour this time of year, as anything larger than a bat would have sent them scurrying into the trees, begging the resident Tree Morrigans for some kind of obscure shelter. This was common knowledge, and one of the more familiar aspects of their wilder nature; something Sibrey would have expected of their kind. For who knows what terror would have come into their little minds the moment the others came barrelling into view? They were such skittish little things, looking to the entire world like big, brave Firedrakes floating along the upper air currents. But, Firedrake or not, they had scattered to places unknown the moment the others had come into view, letting their wings take them away from the midst of what appeared to be a really big Dragonistic cousin, suddenly paying a visit to collect whatever debt they had decided their species had incurred as a whole.

Sibrey shook the image out of her head. This had nothing to do with her brothers; any self-respecting Dragon would have better things to do than play games with a Shapeshifter, when their own kind was annoying enough. Instead, she tried to concentrate on what she was seeing. But each time she did it was not the actual Dragon she questioned having come into view, but more the appearance of these unusual creatures near her woods that had her stumped. The Dragons that belonged to their current skies would not have reflected in this manner out on the surface of their lake. The newcomer's sheen was something spectacular in its unusual differences, being as black as they were, as it shimmered in the reflection of the surface without having anything brilliantly coloured to infuse or amplify it.

Truth be known, as she looked from her vantage point from the rocks in the middle of the lake, they all looked to be rather oddly out of sync with most things that were around them. It became even more apparent when they got closer and flew by, reflecting their images along the ripples left by their wake in the lake. It was here she watched several tendrils of majikal dust floating behind them, drifting along in the airwaves like some majikal steed following its nostrils to the scene of the crime. Definitely not her brothers; they weren't that clever.

She watched it drift in the windshear of their wings, moving the air around the circumference of their bodies as it played like little Dragonflies in some form of majikal fog. The ones she was now seeing were not simply floating in play within the thermals above, but were gliding with determination like Caubertian warriors deflecting the rays of some far away threat she could not yet see, far overhead of the area where she was currently sitting, further complicating things inside her head with visions of a clan-war on the rise. However, clan war or not, as they passed her position overhead she began to see how truly striking they really were. Although they were unusual to most that lived on this planet in times of peace, their allure of things to come brought her back to the present. Hum, she thought, she really needed to get out of changing into these amphibians. Their minds always drifted with the tidal fluxes associated with the lake molecules, leaving her, at times, somewhat befuddled in her thoughts. Perfect for days when nothing ever happens, but today it was not really her best choice of pickings; especially with war Dragons descending from out of thin air, right over her damn head!

She watched them as they moved in perfect symmetry, as if their wings were forming some kind of majikal bond with their riders and were more than a simple appendage of their bodies. The word riders hadn't been expected, and once again she sent air bubbles to escape out of her nasal passages, which had not completed their final transformation. Instead, she farted out the backside of her gills, sending some form of gaseous odour out into the air, almost knocking her out. She really needed to stop eating the resident aquatic life inside these lakes, every time she visited the Naiads. It never ended well, and she usually had some form of indigestion, resulting in days of lethargy while her molecules reverted back into her landbound formulation. Nonetheless, as her stomach turned upside-down and inside out, and the occasional regurgitation of a wayward frog leg arrived at the edges of her lips to dangle unannounced without fanfare, the Dragons were there following whatever quest they had been sent out upon, allowing her to see the blackened feathers along the scales of their spines, which perfectly matched the onyx coloured belly armour along their upper-chests.

Shit, poop, bloody, and one freaking damn; body armour only meant one thing...clan conflict! She scurried for a better view with dread rising in her wattle. It was then she realized that corporeal worry was spreading through the marrow of her Firefox bones, and not the tendrils of what she had momentarily thought she had become. With that in mind, and a whole lot of trying to rebalance her weight to reflect the counterpoint of her body's newest configuration, she lost the struggle and fell headlong into the lake.

There were thirteen shadows that darkened the sky when she emerged from the underwater world; each soared just barely above the treetops when she came up, spitting and shaking her little body clean of the water molecules saturating her outer-core. They glided along ignoring her, and passed by overhead, continuing to fly just above the foliage of the next set of treelines, unaware of what had transpired below them. The vast energy produced by those huge blackened wings created movement in the vegetation, sending waves of wind to violently shake the leaves they passed from high above. She watched them for a moment, with embarrassment while, once again, she tried to drag herself back on dry land, concentrating on the Shapeshifter molecules that momentarily refused to morph into another form.

She knew it had something to do with the molecules of the black Dragons themselves. To come into this realm they would have had to pass through the Stones of Panthor, which could only be found on the outskirts of the city of Tameron. Knowing the majik that followed the Dragons was interfering with her ability to change, she struggled to fight its threads while she waited for it to emerge from inside of her and reset itself into the correct formulation. She concentrated on improving her chances, and failed once again in its delivery. The process, however unsuccessful, almost killed her. She had no patience for waiting for anything; everyone knew that, living within their small village. This time was no different and she almost drowned in her attempt; she screamed in disgust as she came back up to the surface spitting Firefox molecules out into the open air. The salamander was not accustomed to such dunking in its current state; she would have to try and hang on until her majik could replace theirs.

She tread water until she made it back onto dry land, just as she heard others out near the treeline experiencing similar manifestations. As soon as she situated herself, she looked around to place the noises that continued to shriek their annoyances. She spotted several small creatures that had been living in those trees hanging on for dear life, as Dragon wings knocked their little bodies into and around the small wind-tsunami they had created, while they passed overhead, heading for the trees in the distance.

THE BEGINNING

At least she was not in the direct line of fire, for the moment; the majik seemed to release its hold over her while the Dragons carried on to the far side of the lake. However, that was short lived. The energy mass from the downdraft moved within the trees, shifting direction, then sent several shock waves down the trunks, and hit the energy the lake had absorbed from the majik of the stones, which was still dripping off their wings as they continued on unaware of the chaos they had left behind. Then, as if that wasn't enough, for reasons only known to itself, and maybe for no other motive than to simply piss her off further, it seem to pick up speed the moment it hit the lake. With horror, she watched as it began roaring downwards in her general direction. She watched it suddenly change course, as if judging her current position, then, finding what it wanted, run straight towards the very rocks on which she was sitting. Damn majikal nuances; why was everybody out to pick off the Shapeshifter? She braced for the impact and ducked into the wave like a body surfer, pushing her body into the flat surface of the rocks, where she could find some form of protection from the wall of water rushing towards her like it truly had sought her out and meant to kill her.

Looking back as I now write, it would have seemed absurd from their standpoint, had they been inclined to watch this thing basking on the rocks in mid-transformation, with parts from several different animals all fused together, clucking away at the sight far above them. After seeing all that, they would have seen her hanging on for dear life, while the waves crashed into the rock sending spray in all directions pushing the body of the creature she had only just become, back into the very lake she had just crawled out from.

Sibrey coughed and snorted the water from her partly transformed lungs, expelling the liquid into tiny mist out the sides of her nasal passages. Then immediately, once getting her bearings, she transformed back into the creature that resided most days inside her true-form. She was, after all, a Shapeshifter, and what she saw above her made her feel like these little games were very small in comparison to what may be going on in the real world. For really, standing on a rock in the middle of nowhere while watching a Dragon that should have been in the written pages of a Time-Shifter's paradox was seriously not conducive to finding the reason they had arrived back from the Island of Symarr, where they were rumoured to have gone after the old Dragon wars.

But fantasy does have a way of coming to life when the Fey become too complacent within their own skins. Or, truth to be told, the skin of any other creature, as it would appear to have happened. Knowing that the original black Dragons hadn't been seen in these parts along the Lypurnen Woods, near the old growth trees of the Shapeshifter village, or even on this continent, in well over a thousand years, something must be terribly wrong for them to have come this far south to the Shapeshifters' small village instead of heading directly to the Tuatha De' Danann stronghold in the north, as they had done in the past.

The huge Dragons, now well past her, headed for the very place she had not more than a moment ago wanted nothing to do with, and picked up speed, gliding meticulously towards Sombreia. She had seen them through the haze of Firefox molecules, as she broke through the water, holding a rider sitting high abreast their upper necks. As she had choked her way into life she had sworn loudly at them, noticing the warriors that each Dragon carried were securely strapped into what appeared to be some kind of leather harness. She remembered something else that momentarily had escaped her thoughts while they flew by, and that image came into view, flooding her memory cells, and then pulled itself out of her visual cortex with her spitting lake water out of her nose. That memory was full of ceremonial colours of the Syann-Clan tribe, and instantly put her Shapeshifter molecules into motion, making her change faster than she would have liked.

This time it worked, and whatever had prevented it before was quietly dissipating into the ozone of the lake molecules, making her somewhat stoned. Her reaction time wasn't quite up to standard as of yet, and the Mauntra's light still made her blink with its brightness, but she could still remember the colours reflecting along the lake waters, as they made their way over the distant trees, disappearing from her sight. She could well envision that the Dragon-riders' muscles were probably in bear-lined leather boots, with leather strips holding the metal of Mercorian swords high along their backs as in the days of true Dragonlord fashion, which had once set the standards of another time in a not too distant past. Her village made those swords and their meaning had definite symbolism to who she was.

She morphed into one of the Princesses from the old city, deciding that it would be more appropriate to look like royalty rather than a simple village Shifter. She caught her reflection in the water and changed her mind; she tried several others with the exact same response as the first, still looking rather foolish in all her stupid splendour. She really needed to have her head examined. Seriously, nothing would have suited her needs in the long run; if she had her way she should have just come as one of the Dragons themselves. That would have been far better than anything she could have thought up herself. Then it would have been fun to see the village folk try and distinguish who was real, and who was not. Now that she would pay good-coin to see.

These legendary warriors of the black Dragons were still considered to be a myth born of fantasy; one that held tales long since gone from the galaxy of their home world. Sibrey had dreamed of their arrival and eventual rescue, as had all the females that lived within their realm, on restless nights deep within places no female should be. Yet here they were, flying above the lake that she no longer held an interest in, far from any dream world, as they headed towards the very village that nothing ever happens in.

That was the reason, more to the point, why she had decided to move, and not the actuality of the Dragons themselves carrying some kind of village saviour bent on rescue. She suddenly realized, with abject horror, that if she was going to continue to play she wouldn't make it in time for them to land. Furthermore, when they did land, no matter who she imitated and changed into, she'd never find something fierce enough to wear in order to receive them. Seriously, she was worried about damn clothes, what was wrong with her? She was never worried about clothes; a new form yes, but clothes never. The lake waters were definitely interfering with her mind.

That got her moving, more than any other thing as she smacked her head to clear out the cobwebs, dislodging a wayward frog that seemed to have gotten stuck. It splashed down into the water and disappeared beneath its depths as she made the first attempt at shifting away. She did her best to arrive before the riders could glide into position to land, but the time spent watching them, and the little parade of images she had decided to visualize in the lake waters, made it quite clear that she would not do so with any such dignity composed of some female gentry from the skies. Right, that would make her a ladey! That made her almost lose it all over again, as her stoned reaction to that description made her start to hoot with laughter, producing a funnier picture than the one she had conjured up in her head. Sometimes she was just too bloody funny for her own good. Damn brothers, she'd show them; they started all of this stupid girl stuff. 'Ok, you little mutant, you are one freaken stoned Shifter,' she whispered. 'If this carries on, I'll never make it in time.' She shook any last remaining pond scum out of her brain and morphed into a bird, which instantly dropped to the ground and flew head first into the rocks....

By the time she arrived, she was mostly sober. At least she thought she was? So, when she came out of her shift in full flight, picking out a few leaves that still remained lodged within her hair from the woods behind, she hadn't thought to check what had arrived with her. Several pieces of twig that were visibly wedged inside the edges of her curls decided now was the time they would gain their freedom. They whirled around in the air, and took off in a haze of rapid migration, heading straight for the airspace the Dragons themselves were currently occupying. Several made it through the other side of their wings and missed several talons sharpened to within the breadth of a razor. While others simply disappeared in a haze of fire, as the Dragons made fast work of the creatures that had been nothing more than a few simple stiff branches a moment ago. The few that did get away with parts of their leaves intact were now rendered a mass of cinders, and fell among the Togernaut clan as the Dragons screeched their heads off in defiance to the creatures that had dared fly too close.

Yep, our lovely discombobulated Sibrey had arrived, in all her glory. If she had wanted to come into the village with molecules a swinging she had achieved that order of business in cosmos. She had really tried to be quiet as she made her entrance, but that was not to be; she had phased in motion, and when she arrived she was still moving in a somewhat forward direction, which made her stumble into the crowd. Her aim was off, and she tried once again to move to the left midway through her shift. She collided with a particular female who was none too happy with her sudden appearance, taking her view of the Dragon-riders and their mounts momentarily out of the picture. She shoved Sibrey out of her way just before Sibrey had been able to fully come through the molecules, and it pushed her further along into the village's center-core. In doing so, she shifted into the middle of the frenzied arrival of the Dragons, not where she would have liked to have arrived, out on the edge. They circled the village one last time and started to land, giving her no time to move back along the fringes of the village wards, to safety.

She had only started to arrange various pieces of clothing, while spotting her father and brothers standing on the outcropping that the village used as a lookout, when the riders and their mythical mounts began landing in the newest foray of wind and wings, scanning the horizon for Goddess only knew what. Humph, maybe her luck had changed. However, something was not as it had appeared to be in her dreams. The males of the village started gathering their swords and arms, looking a lot more serious than what she had anticipated the arrival of the Dragons to be here for, and immediately she morphed into a field mouse and scurried out of the way. Their shouts and excitement could be heard deep into the farthest sections of the village inner thickets, as they quickly ran in long strides to stand alongside each other with a show of armed intent, bringing her mythical dream to a rather abrupt majikal end, and causing the creatures of that glen to flee for their little lives, as she did her best to not be drawn into the rampaging exodus of that rather frantic wave.

Her heart sank; there would be no rescuing today and, if she wasn't careful, she could very well be served up as the entree for whatever dish they had come in search of, if the female she had almost knocked over had anything to say about it. Sibrey stared at the female who pushed her, and she glared at Sibrey for a moment, not blinking, then turned away, dismissing her completely as Sibrey let out a short hiss in her direction. The Dragons continued to find their feet on solid ground, and land amongst them.

Dyareius was surprised all was not well inside the village walls, as he had been first led to believe. The Dragons, picking up the tension, proved his point as they pranced uneasily, snorting their displeasure at the surrounding energy that was beginning to build. All he knew was they had come to extract one Shapeshifter ahead of the scheduled time of her departure. He now watched the commotion escalate, quickly getting out of hand as throngs of Shapeshifters from the village ran with their swords towards the very area they had just landed in. Strange behaviour for a village he thought had been expecting them.

Dyareius signalled some of the other riders in his herd to go back into the air with their Dragons. He needed to strike some semblance of order; to get out of the commotion that was fast getting out of hand. It would be the only way to lessen that confusion without the use of majik; forcing himself, Markus, and two others to stay land-bound until the pandemonium between the resident Shifters and Dragons alike settled down. The rest would not be allowed to land again until necessity demanded it, preventing further damage to the land inside and around the small hamlet. That took precedence over his needs, at all cost. From there they would remain more vigilant inside the airwaves of their recent shift. Should this turn ugly, it would only take a few moments to return to their shift, after they retrieved the female. From there they could take the lead as they directed the majikal flow inside the Dragon rift, instead of placing their boots on the ground. Unfortunately, that was not how it went down.

Someone shouted above the chaos and nodded their head, directing one of the riders towards a lone warrior standing away from the others. Sibrey looked to where they were pointing, and was surprised to see that it was her father they were referring to. It soon became apparent to her that he had long and secretly expected the arrival of these strange warriors, but did not like that their timing had come sooner than was expected. How odd. He appeared angry. No, more like furious; shouts between both him and the apparent leader, called Dyareius, became heated as each side reached for their swords in a show of unyielding defiance.

Each stood their ground. In the coming onslaught of angry words accompanying the insane posturing of their male tantrums, it would only prove to be harder to control the insanity of others all around them, as each would try to prove the validity of the situation to each other. Their responses shortly became more futile and, in the next few minutes, they would fail to either attain, or receive, each other's formal ultimatums.

Still, Sibrey did not run. Instead, she watched, somewhat fascinated by the father she had never really seen before in this light. Earlier today she had expected a far different response to her truanted behaviour. Now, he was literally sticking up for her, as he shouted his head off in what she surmised was her apparent Faery-tale rescue. Though, at that time she did not hear the words in their entirety. When they became clear, and the air became still, she finally heard the meaning behind what they were shouting, though not completely about the little vain part about some long lost Princess, whom they had decided to rescue and abscond with, back to their island castle in the clouds. She was mortified; they had, come for her. But why?

"It's not fair; you told us we would have more time! There is still two more Mauntra cycles before she is to be honor-bound." Her father said with ferocity, at having their arrival come sooner, than what was deemed to be foretold. "This was not, how it was to be completed with our kind Sir Dyareius; it was one of our contingencies, when we took on this role." And with those words her life would change forever; locked in a single moment that became stopped in a time of black Dragons and bloody rites that she had no part of understanding in this early stage in the game of her life.

The beginning of some form of negotiations seem to take effect, as tears ran down her face at the prospect of being traded in some kind of game, much to the glee of one of her former best friends. She did not hear the correct language of what they were trying to get her father to understand, as Sibrey had turned around to glare in her friend's direction and missed several key words. The Aelven warrior continued to shake his head as he shouted back and forth between his warriors and her father. Both did their best to shout above the enormous noise that was coming from a few of the Dragons, as they started getting restless along the village edge, calling to the others in the air, and creating another form of chaos of their own making.

"It is of Fey decree and cannot be undone, as with others in times of crises. We will take the girl; she is needed for things that urgency has dictated, and we shall not leave without her. Follow as you see fit, but we have to go now!" He turned away, moving to signal one of his riders, and that's when things started happening faster than Sibrey thought was Feyly possible, in a village of Shifters that normally remained lethargically composed.

It was at this time that her former friend started to hop with glee, and her father used his ability to cross-reference his own senses, and found Sibrey silently within the large crowd that had gathered behind her. He had tracked her easily, following the recent energy flow that billowed behind her signature matrix when she had first arrived on scene. He knew her chaos, and had been instantly alerted when she had appeared out of the trees. He had placed her the moment she had showed him her entrance wave in their midst, and now found her standing slightly away from the others, beside that female who was a little too happy with the current events, as she sat along the upper-banks in a state of silent shock. He silently lowered his eyes away from her, indicating a destination; which she instantly took, nodding, and then moved to join with the creature that would prove to be the most elusive for them to find.

The moment she ran the female beside her screamed at the Dragonlords, of her escape. One of her brothers, who had been slower at arriving than the others, had only just reached Sibrey's side and in an instant dispatched the apparently mean friend by knocking her flat on her ass, as she squealed like a rat. Sibrey ran as fast as her legs would take her, literally blinking out from their line of sight and hitting the woods in record time, to shift into the one creature that would take her away, and the very hardest to detect — even for a Syann-Clan Aelf with the ability to belong to this exclusive troop of black Dragons. She did not have time to listen as she moved, hearing the last of the shouts and angry words that were exchanged between the father of her needs, and the Dragonlords of her apparent nightmare. Her brother used his shirt to gag the female deviant, who at one time, had been her friend, as she continued to kick him in the shins. They continued to struggle with each other, even after she had been rendered incapacitated, while her father created the diversion needed to out-shout each other in such a precise manner that everyone present had not the knowledge it was done to allow her to escape into the woods. She had to admire the sheer will of his fortitude, and the guts of said brother who, in the future, she would have to pay more attention to.

This day shall remain the last of my life, within the memory of happier times. For, as I disappeared into the trees, the actual words that were sent flying through the air were no longer present in the range of what my ears could hear. To the others of the Togernaut tribe of Shifters, it was heard loud and clear, bringing the attention of every clan member within the direct vicinity to the center of the fight, and far away from the vicinity of the trees and one wayward female Shifter hel-bent on making my life a living hel.

Then the image changed; the Dragons from up above began to land, one by one, into the middle of the chaos, causing something to be born out of a bad dream as the whole village not previously in the fight now came out to watch. Had Sibrey witnessed the next events, she would have been amazed. For, standing beside her brothers and their mates, her own clan-mother had silently joined the men, fully armed to the bloody teeth. Sibrey had never seen her father's mate in any other light than what she had portrayed to her, as the calm nurturing female of her father's house. This would have made her smile, had she seen the transformation of such a dignified figurehead. But she had not witnessed its birth, and flew silently into her Shifter realm, away from the chaos of the village walls, unaware of what the others had sacrificed just to protect the one that she thought they might now consider being an outsider.

The moment all the Dragons had landed, nothing could be heard past a village seemingly under siege, alongside some very big Dragons becoming caught in the crosshairs. As the huge beasts struggled to retain their footing along the inner walls of the village grounds, the warriors focused on the villagers beneath their feet, who ran in all directions, coming dangerously close to Dragon talons attached to paws the size of tree trunks. It was a spectacle, to those Fey watching from their positions out along the sidelines and living in the trees. They watched as the balanced became lost then found again, gaining some slight momentum for the Shapeshifters who, in turn, shoved it sideways and all bets moved to another conclusion. Then, just as they thought one side might have the upper hand, it lost its footing once again in the chaos, and it began all over again. All the while the riders did their best to stop the great beasts from both taking flight, and crushing those that were within range of their massive bodies, sending village Cauper dogs and Fringusha swallows scattering in all directions.

Sibrey didn't hear the shouts of her clan, as they rang out in the open air of the afternoon and the protection of the village grounds seemed to go by the wayside. Instead, she was preoccupied by what stood before her, and the chaos that was about to erupt and fill the morning air. This was no ordinary sleepy village of innocent Fey that just happened to be the landing post of the current Dragon Herders; all of the Dragonlords might have come armed for a possible battle, but those within the village closest to the foray were also carrying weapons, and bore witness to the event with the Mercorian swords of their own armoury. These were the blades known to the founders of the specialized steel, as the Mercorian death blades, and were famous throughout the Fey worlds as some of the deadliest to wield. Each of the males of the Togernauts may have been simple farmers, but that is as far as it went in looking like they were nothing more than an innocent tribe, ripe for the picking. No, on the contrary, nothing could be farther from the truth. This little village of Sombreia was where you didn't want to be in a close range fight with anyone, including a very large herd of black war Dragons, readying themselves for a conflict with a deceptive clan of innocent shapers hel-bent for blood.

Sibrey's father Daniel shook his head, releasing the leather strap that held his hair in place, and watched the others through its strategically set release, who had been waiting for this gesticulation. This could very easily have ended in the deaths of those pushing their way into his sleepy village with nothing more than large, overgrown Firedrakes who sharpened their own scaly hides with razor sharp teeth and called themselves War-Rats. However, the Dragonlords had come prepared for this eventuality, and had instilled a slight deviation from their gathering of tales inside this particular clan, than their normal telling of fantasy, and the legend was about to show itself in its purest form as the signal was given then hesitated upon. They withdrew for only a moment, while Daniel looked to see the truth behind the movement with a short vibration that was released inside the leather that had been instilled by another, more wise in the ways of things than them.

It was said that the Dragons, being still very much wild, and able to cut out a Fey heart with just a single look, held together through a bonding with the essence of the Dragonlords themselves; a fact that should make them rethink their next move. It was told, during the great Aelven Wars, of their power to hold one's mind from finding the means to control their own weapons, allowing the great beasts the opportunity to cleave the Fey within. The only thing keeping the Dragons from killing everything in sight, as far as the Shapeshifter clan understood — and most of them had not the knowledge to find anything different in the telling, were the Aelven warriors riding on their backs, deeply embedded within their own armaments, and the Mercorian death blade that these villagers were led to believe could stop it.

Only half of that was true of course, however intentional as it appeared. For, this day had been foretold by others not directly related to the current reigning royal family and the warriors themselves never got around to stopping the misinformation from actually getting out. So, in keeping with the legend that gave them that fear, and a sword that would undoubtedly be needed in the near future for a very different cause, the Dragons and their masters landed amongst a Shapeshifter clan who, had they been told the truth, would have undoubtedly taken a different approach than hostile posturing, and the story would have taken another turn — and I just might not be telling the tale that stands before you, in its current form. However, their deception was discovered only barely through the leather string, and although it really wasn't completely trusted by his current Shapeshifter body, Daniel decided to not give them the whole truth until he discovered the reason for their deception first hand.

Dyareius watched, shaking his head at the insanity of it all, as one male of the Togernaut clan grabbed a red hot piece of steel, one that was in the process of being rendered into one of those sought after pieces of deadly craftsmanship. The majik was old and didn't belong to this world. The Shifter moved with a new majik that Dyareius had not seen before on this planet, as the blade began to cool slightly in his hands, turning harder than previously forged. He would need to watch what his warriors were doing amongst this tribe, for this new sense of power was not one that had been born into the Shapeshifter's recent tutelage. The Togernaut warrior then took that flame and shifted it from the hot coals of molten metal back down the shaft of the blade, until it was covered in a rich fire, giving it more energy to withstand another sword's edge should it come to be in contact with any weapon unlucky enough to take the challenge. Damn, that made him take notice; it could go either way now. Someone had been here that did not belong to this world. How else would they have learned that, if not for someone else who had been travelling abroad amongst the doorways? As far as he knew, the Shifters never moved off planet. The Tuatha would need to be warned.

Before his mental note could go any further everyone started yelling at once as each rider struggled to keep their Dragon, and the villagers within the ranks, from killing each other. It was another that found Sibrey's father within the crowd, watching her as she began to make her plans of escape. Symin was next in line to Markus in rank, and Markus was second in command to their head drover Dyareius. He watched the squirmish from the back of his Dragon Quist, alongside the other warriors of their caste, in case they all needed to move quickly and fly their Dragons to another position further away from the crowds advancing up the hill where most of them had landed. However, it was for another purpose he was there amongst the advancing crowds, near Soren's Dragon. It would be him, and him alone, that directed the lone Dragon skyward, away from the others the moment his friend found her signature in the crowd. They had prepared for her eventual flight, and Soren was trained in dealing with that very probable course of Shapeshifter reaction to their arrival, before their time was up and they needed to make a hasty departure.

Dyareius decided it was time to take the fight into his own hands and render a situation more of his own choosing. He slid to the ground, placing his sword around the back of his sling before gliding it backwards overhead into his scabbard, showing he had not come to fight. Both leaders would need to have cooler heads to return some semblance of peace to the Sombreian village. The Dragons still snorted and growled, showing how their lungs had an inexhaustible supply of force in their blood fire. Sibrey's father stepped forward and met Dyareius halfway, with the same goal in mind, shouting above the foot stamping and low range growl of the Dragon closest to him, as its tail sideswiped to the left, nearly hitting him in the progress. He watched it come at him with incredible speed, while he vaulted away from it, landing gently out of reach. Unfortunately, one of his sons was not so lucky. He had been standing in the direct line of fire, and had not anticipated this reaction to his father's closeness, especially with one of the riders in its vicinity. It came at him like a Sylph on steroids, and took the wind right out of him, as it hit his foot and trapped him within one of the Dragon's unusually large scales along the upper boney spines, sending him crashing into a boulder left behind from a recent slide.

Daniel made sure his son was not seriously hurt with his mind, and, given the signal he was ok, moved forward to formally greet the Aelven soldier with his sword not so easily placed out of reach and an eyebrow raised in instant query about the incident.

"Why have you come? It's too soon for the girl; she has not finished her training." Dyareius nodded in agreement, and drew a piece of parchment out of his shirt as a tail came crashing in their midst once again. This time the Dragonlord grabbed Daniel by the shoulder, and yanked him out of its way, yelling at his Dragon to knock it off. The Dragon, named Baelf, simply growled at him in a show of defiance, as Dyareius gave it a look of annoyance, dismissing its bad behaviour. Baelf flicked his tail out of their range, just as several villagers started to hurl rocks at his head. He in turn, shifted his attention to their position, while Daniel glared at the offending duo to also knock it off, and all three looked on, waiting for both leaders to move their attention away so they could get on with the fight.

Both complied for the moment, without further argument, while Dyareius glared at Baelf and held up a finger at the flattened response Baelf made with his ears.

"Don't even think about it!" Dyareius admonished. Baelf lightly growled, knowing he had been spotted slowly approaching the duo again, who stood smiling, waiting for him to get within range. Dyareius grinned at the scowling Shifters, who had been found out too soon. "He really can be such a shit. If I were you, I'd wait until he's got his back turned, and approach him along his left flank. He's got a sore talon on that side; if you hit it just right, I'm sure you'll get a better reaction than the one you are currently heading towards." With that being said, he passed the parchment over to Daniel, and silently allowed him time to read what had been written so long ago, while the duo looked from one to another, perplexed at Dyareius's behaviour.

He grinned at their reaction to his comments, watching the crowd grow larger with each passing moment, as the Shapeshifter male continued to read in silence.

"It's not fair, I know we had more time," Daniel pointed out, "and we agreed, back when she arrived, it wasn't supposed to be done this way or we wouldn't have offered her sanctuary." Daniel again looked through the fading parchment, turning it over to see if something else was written on the opposite side that would explain the sudden shift in the decree, fidgeting with his fingers and scratching his neck in frustration.

Dyareius felt sorry for Sibrey's father, but needed to get things under control much faster than the crowd was willing to allow him. He knew he hadn't a lot of time, and spoke quickly, with a sense of renewed urgency, before things began to fall into complete anarchy within the close quarters of the tiny hamlets' walls. He could see the position that a few of the villagers had taken up near the growling Dragons, was slowly becoming less and less under the riders' control, and it wouldn't be long before him and the other riders would have to end this current ceasefire, and be forced into a fight they didn't want.

"As you can see, it's out of my hands," he shouted above the maelstrom starting to rise up to toxic levels. "It's Fey decree, Daniel, you know that, and it cannot be undone by either you or me, no matter how much I would have liked to have accommodated it...truly." He offered both of his hands to Daniel, with his palms exposed upwards, bringing the attention to his softer side. "If I had anything to say about it, I would have done this another way; one that was not so volatile for both our clans. Anything set in this kind of majikal oath must be followed to the exact letter. If not, things will begin to happen that will pale in comparison to what had been agreed upon when this was written." He turned to look at the crowd approaching the Dragons. "Follow if you see fit, but we have to go now before someone gets hurt. Please, can you at least give us that much?" He pointed to the villagers, who were beginning to advance much further up the incline where they were currently talking.

"Sir," Symin could be heard calling him.

Symin, who still was on his Dragon's back, whispered to his mount and urged him forward. He turned briefly to face Dyareius nodding. Then as an afterthought he shouted again, this time with more urgency, pointing to a surge of warriors starting to breach the path up to their position.

"Sir, now would be better than later!" he shouted. As the first Shifters arrived at the rise of the pathway, coming into their line of sight, Daniel briefly held them back with a wave of his hand. They nodded and stayed put while Dyareius signalled his riders to move, watching one of his own not part of the conversation at hand.

Soren had been watching for the arrival of the girl, from his own Dragon, during the entire conversation. He was the tracker of his warrior clan. As he watched what the others could not see, he was finally rewarded when a movement to the left brought his full attention to her position. He smiled and fought back the need to show his success. There would be plenty of time for that in later days, and Dyareius needed only to see his slight grin at the successful achievement of the acquisition of her departed molecules.

The moment the father had turned his attention to another not within sight of what was actually going on in front of him, Soren had seen the beginning of her shift, and tracked her movements along his to the edge of the far trees. With not a moment to lose he made preparations to slide off the back right side of his Dragon, nodding at Symin, and then melted away from the crowds, making for the edge of the tree-line just as Sibrey changed her form. He did not see the animal she had become. Once on the ground, he moved swiftly towards her departure point, thinking he could catch her off guard.

As soon as Sibrey shifted, leaving no trace of her whereabouts, Dyareius heard Soren go; then shouted to Daniel.

"Meet us two days hence, at the Stones of Panthor. Bring as many as you trust, and no less than those who will be of service to your needs," he shouted to the Shifter and then turned to go. But Daniel's hand went to his arm, and the Aelf turned once again to face him.

"She is still so young," Daniel said, looking into Dyareius's face, seeing knowledge of the other, who had taken advantage of their conversation to make his way into the trees. He looked horrified at the discovery, as Dyareius took Daniel's hand off his arm and placed it above his own heart.

"She will be well cared for, I promise you. She will not be harmed," he said, bowing his head to Daniel in respect, and pointing above at the Dragons who were starting to take flight. "We haven't any more time, my friend. I had no choice. The Humans are coming, and we need her. Follow as best you can on foot, or whatever you Shapeshifters do. It makes no difference. But if you travel with us, it will mean certain death for your child. Now go, before your village turns this into a conflict!" He moved off without a backwards glance, striding quickly to his Dragon. The only Dragon now, which was still land bound and roaring impatiently to follow his own kind, was the one that belonged to him. The others had already begun their shift, and were well on their way to where they would meet Soren and their little runaway.

Dyareius moved to join them, taking flight away from the village before Daniel could intercept him. He moved quickly to the jump point, directing Baelf towards the wave of pressure that they needed to begin the drop, as they made preparations to travel through their shift. He would follow his men towards the meeting place they had agreed upon, allowing just enough time for Soren to find the Shapeshifter quickly before anyone else realized they had gone after her. He didn't need a bunch of Shifters morphing into their versions of fire breathing Dragons and coming after his ass if Daniel was unable to stop them. It would be bad enough when the news got out that they had sent in a tracker to retrieve her, and deceived the village, without having gotten involved in any kind of hand-to-hand skirmish.

Baelf, still itching for a fight, growled low in his throat and sent puffs of fire out into the rift, following the pressure field without any guidance. Dyareius patted his head, trying to calm the great beast.

"I know, my friend, we'll get them next time. As for your head, it's only a scratch, trust me," he said. Baelf whined in disagreement, sending another puff of blood fire out into the morning air. It scorched a few air molecules along the way. Dyareius ducked the moment they flew through the debris field of scorched particles, letting them settle along the induction field as he moved fluidly with the Dragon beneath him. They would be lost in the electric currents of the air waves, dissipating within their own fire molecules almost immediately. He hoped fervently that Sibrey would be found swiftly, before anything else started to go wrong and Baelf went back on his own to finish the fight.

He hadn't the slightest doubt in Soren's abilities, but he wasn't so sure how far along Sibrey's teachings had informed her of her own nature. If it had awakened prematurely, without the Elemental Herders in attendance, this was going to be a long night for him and his riders. He sincerely hoped it hadn't.

CHAPTER TWO

Escape through the Majikal Forest of Lypurnen Woods

Sibrey came out of her shift; straight into another quantum's occupied body without setting her Shapeshifter footprint upon the ground. She landed on four soft pads, muscles straining to move between fallen logs and water, transferring her Fey molecules onto its paws as she moved into the beast waiting for her along the treeline. It had come into contact with one of the many streambeds weaving in and out of the forest floor, leaving a single muddied print along the soft edges as she had entered; then nothing more. This was the only trace of her passage, and one that would never be traced back to her. Transformation is never easy, as you need first to find your centre of gravity, and then get used to the oxygen intake of the animal you've become before you're able to actually finalize the transfer. The bigger the animal, the more difficult it is to push the air flow and move stiff, unaccustomed muscles which belonged not two seconds before to a four-legged feline with only one brain, and not the two who were currently occupying it at this moment in time.

The choice had been a simple one and he had welcomed her without any resistance: it was much easier on four legs than on two, and this particular creature happened to be a favourite of hers; one that was used specifically for stealth. Actually moving through the forest as an animal, and not Fey, would give her added time not easily available when on the run in any other form she had been taught to shift into. Shapeshifters have always been able to claim the visual spirit of any animals they become; she, on the other hand, had found another way. Her circumstances had always taken her further in her lessons than what she was actually being taught, and as no one knew of this ability she had attained, she had been able to pull it off easily the moment no one was looking without so much as a single footprint fading into her daunt.

The creature that was called Panther was her speciality. Not only had she been able to change its very structure when she shifted, she had found a way to use the real feline to go within. It was relatively easy, and completely undetectable to the outside world; the one thing her teachers had not yet discovered she had achieved. This made her smile; having this hidden within the confines of her own brain would undoubtedly help her movement through this difficult passage through the woods to freedom. How the idea in the first place had arrived within her line of sight was anyone's guess. It had not been of her own making. However, it had been relatively easy once it had, and the only thing that would keep her alive and ahead of the Dragon runner who hunted her ruthlessly through the trees, was something she wasn't about to question: Neither the whereabouts of its origins, nor the Panther that had given her that gift.

She recalled loosely, as she ran, that there had been a family of these beautiful sleek creatures living deep within the woods near Sombreia's larger creeks. As a child she would often escape the confines of her teacher's lessons to have peace and quiet away from the others with ones that were to become her coven mates, within this world predominately occupied by those of blackened fur. The monotony that was associated with becoming an elder within the Shapeshifter clan only bored her, and she had accidentally discovered the ability to shift in this very unusual manner through sheer luck alone, taking her path into a very different future, full of dangerous excursions that would lead her over the abyss on more than one occasion. This was a gift the others would never share and she revelled in its exclusivity. For their abilities were far different than the ones she inherited. If fact she was more unusual within its arrival than she actually knew, and until just recently it had never occurred to her that it had been exclusively designed to her unique physiology. She was reluctant to share this knowledge with the others, for they would have only found a way to halt her visits into the woods. Instead, she found herself travelling deeper within their depths for the sheer joy of discovery, and away from the detection of the others who sought her out.

It was during one of these times spent running that she had come across one of these gorgeous cats, who at the time had been more fascinated with a kill than another meal made out of her skinny hide. She could still feel the energy he had produced, and marvelled in its complexity as he shone with exuberance somewhere through the trees she had been drawn to. She hadn't been sure of what she had been running towards; however, the moment he came into view, she knew without a shadow of a doubt the reason why. The energy quivered inside the small glen, and everywhere she looked Panther molecules could be seen floating within the air, mixing in with the dense particles of the living forest itself, and creating a different kind of Fey existence for those who witnessed its birth.

When the Panther finished his morning meal he sat up and grinned, looking directly at her and producing a strange kind of seductive growl, beckoning her in. A small shiver of fear ran through her, sending her further away from him. The fragments from the molecules of the glen reacted in kind, following her actions, parting to let her through while the Panther ignored her presence and simply began to clean himself. She had only just begun to back away while he was busy licking his bloody paws, when the particles flowed out of the air and followed her, invading her space. They seemed to be everywhere at once; circling her body, and creating a temporary ward of solidified molecules that prevented her from leaving the area. She marvelled at their complexity, and duality of purpose that was not unlike the majik of the old clan of Tree Morrigans that lived in the area. She tasted their essence the moment they touched her skin, and they followed her as she made her way around different plants and foliage that littered the forest floor. She let her body feel the energy of the unfamiliar molecules that surrounded every pore of her body, all the way up to the tips of her tongue. The Panther whimpered lightly, disturbed by the lightshow, as the molecules danced and played along the edges of where he sat. When they moved off he looked at Sibrey, and watched her move around the Rokh, within range of his hunting grounds. He didn't appear upset, or unusually freaked out about the particles and their behaviour; however, it became apparently clear that he was bothered, by her leaving.

Then, something strange happened. The moment she went to step away from the particles, as she brushed the molecules away from her skin to release their touch, he started to lightly call out to her with a strange pitiful wailing noise. The sound was very much like her younger brother, when he was a young shippel, producing a whine that made her stop moving and look up. The purring continued out into the upper reaches of the trees overhead, heard by others that made these places their homes. Each time she tried to leave he began again, producing a comedy of errors hyphenated by exaggerated vocal responses from the echoes felt across the meadow, as other species, stopped by its rareness, looked up towards her to watch the show. She started to giggle as he watched her watching him, as he cocked his head, looking slightly affronted with her snuffling snorts. When next she looked up at him, after embarrassing herself, he was even funnier than the last time she looked at him. Somewhere in the previous seconds, he had managed to hook one of his fangs along the edge of his bottom lip, where it could be seen stuck in this perpetual scowl of total insulted thought.

Well, that did it; the giggling stopped, and the laughter started. However, she was not the only one to witness the craziness of the situation. Just as she thought it couldn't get any better, the mewing prompted a few winged Fey to abandon their lofty ship in the trees. They screamed several well formulated, indecent words at the two of them, and abandoned their perches for quieter pastures. Both looked at the retreating Fey, then back at each other and grinned. It was comical in nature to see this big cat apparently holding some form of conversation with her that, as of yet, she had not the means to decipher the nuances of.

Astonishingly, the behaviour continued; each time she tried to leave the cat would call her back. Finally, he had had enough of her trying to bail, and picked up the nearest bone of the animal he had killed, and hucked it at her head in a kind of feline peace offering. She was startled; however, she had been able to duck as it landed mere inches from her head, making her shout at him with the hysterics of the situation as it whizzed on by. As soon as the bone had come into the vicinity of where her body had stood, it shoved the Shifter molecules that had been lightly sitting on her skin upwards. They began to dance along the rest of her body, as the bone now past her came to a stop. It seemed to just hang there balancing in midair, wobbling in some kind of magnetic field unable to decide how next to proceed. It tickled the hairs on her arm as the frequency moved around her, then surged towards the bone, picking it up higher in the air and presenting it to her at chest level. She looked on with amazement, watching the particles shimmer in the afternoon rays, showing the partial remains of the muscle and sinew of the now very dead creature. She accepted the bone from them bowing her head in thanks, feeling somewhere between fascinated and seriously creeped out.

But it was short-lived in its timing. No sooner had she touched it, the bone began to show signs of what she could only describe as life. The moment it moved, she almost dropped it in shock, as it began to pulsate in her hands; she blinked, thinking her eyes had deceived her, and it must be part of the illusion created by the Panther to fool her. But she held her ground, watching what it wanted her to see even though she wanted to throw it back at the Panther and hit him in the head, simply for no other reason than because she could. Thankfully, she resisted the urge, and before long the forest particles from the surrounding Rokh moved from her skin to the full length of the bone, multiplying the genetic material of the animal that had died, molding it with that of her Shapeshifter prism and melding the molecules all into one consistent formula. She watched it transform and begin to grow other appendages along the previously severed parts where the Panther had torn it apart, until the animal he had taken as a meal was whole again.

Seeing that she was no longer able to hold its weight, Sibrey moved the creature down to the ground, where it lay limp in its death still transforming. Stunned at what was transpiring right in front of her eyes, and feeling somewhat sick at the thought of this dear creature having been fed on by the brute of a cat grinning away before her, she looked up and glared at him.

"How could you?" she asked as she tried to smooth down the beautiful hide of the once majestic creature, while he sat blinking long lashes in her direction and ignoring her feelings of horror. Instead he tried once again, to bring her emotions back towards seeing him as the creature that had intrigued her. She ignored his attempts, even though she had only recently laughed alongside him, at the grand exodus of the Fey in the trees. But she was distracted from the situation at hand for only a moment. For, just when she felt she was physically going to go over there and punch him in the head, something alongside of her began to change.

The particles in the Rokh circled the creature as Sibrey watched fascinated by the proceedings. It continued to grow alongside the original section of bone the Panther had chucked at her, diving within like fish swimming upstream to spawn. Soon there were so many molecules surrounding the creature that it limited her ability to see it; the creature vanished inside their apparently active hive. She watched as the particles began to spin wildly, changing colour and sending electrical charges out of their nuclei into the centre of where the creature had been laying on the forest floor. She moved backwards, feeling the energy from the electricity that lived inside the charge trickling along the ground as it stretched out to the bottom of her feet, overextending its fingers along the fissures of the rocks at her side.

She moved towards some of the smaller boulders, away from the main vibration they were sending out, giving her body and feet more protection from the stream of energy produced by the forest elements engaged in this new phenomenon. Their mass in singular patterns was exhilarating; their mass duplicated, was far more disturbing. Whatever mountain they had fallen from during the planet's constant upheaval, led the energy to trickle towards the larger surfaces, where it heightened the sensation that was moving everywhere around her, sending the hair follicles along her arms standing straight up in the air. Then the beginnings of change started to manifest as they circled the body of the dead mammal in its entirety, all blending into one. Once this happened, the particles morphed into a new colour almost identical to the fur of the creature, then slowly began to move away fading from her sight.

When the area cleared, in place of the creature that had been a meal for the Panther, was a live breathing deer curled up in a foetal position with its eyes shut, apparently sound asleep, with its antlers intact and resting along the edges of the rocks at her feet. Nothing of its former trauma was visible, except for a tiny drop of majikal molecules where the transference of ritualistic majik could still be seen exiting its body through the ground beneath it. Sibrey gasped at the sight, sending her breath into the open air waking the mature buck; he opened his eyes, and looked at her in bewilderment, slightly startled.

Immediately, the Panther got up and headed into the trees, his job complete, while the deer got to its feet, doing its best to move away from the area in the opposite direction away from the both of them. Eventually, he wasn't sticking around to see what the hel just happened, and which of the two involved, were more dangerous. His legs, although somewhat wobbly, allowed him to make it to the dense trees without falling, as his old body had been transmorphed into a much younger animal, then he too was gone before she could blink, leaving Sibrey alone with just the sound of the wind. Sibrey was confused by what had just happened. Unfortunately, there was nothing she could base it on; so instead she followed suit, removing herself from the area where the uncertainty of it really having happened left her with more questions than she had had before.

She decided the Panther must have come from a renegade clan of probable Shapeshifters who had been living out and around the Sadllenay village lands; part of the relatives of the Kyafth clan of Dryads that had lived there at one time. There could be no other explanation for what had just happened. She had heard whispers of this clan, including tales of their having disappeared one dark and moonless night, around the time of her birthing, when the Dragon wars had been at their peak. The tales told of a coterie of healing Dryads that belonged to a certain secret coven who had been banished out of their home village by the Seelies that had surged over that land, killing many of them as they had lain asleep in their beds.

She had heard whispers that it had caused quite a stir for those that had lived out near any of the villages within walking distance of their lands. It would have undoubtedly been frothed with nightmarish visions of a surge of Seelies moving into the area, for many of the closest settlements. Defenses, she had heard, had included placing a secret ward stacked on top of and along the edges of their own village wards. However, these particular ones from the Sombreia village contained a certain component that the Seelies would not have been too happy about — iron would have been that main ingredient, which would explain a lot of things to Sibrey, who had accidentally stumbled on its molecular strain one dark and stormy evening spent running.

This main component had been used to intercept any stray Seelies hell-bent on further destruction of those Fey that lay claim to be affiliated with the Kyafth clan. It wasn't meant for one delinquent Shapeshifter who had tried to sneak back into the village wards during one of her forays into the woods at night. She had almost swallowed the damn thing as it sent out poisonous threads in her direction, when she had accidentally showed up in her Seelie form; a form she had forgotten to remove after visiting that village on one of the more curious days of her youth. That attention to detail had almost got her killed; however, she had been able to move through its brightly coloured formations when she had frozen the molecules in their places, bending herself from one awkward position to another to move through the threads that had been set to kill her.

When she had arrived with nothing more than a few burned patches on her arms, she had vowed to try and remember. Others might not have been overly excited to see her stupid little games coming to life inside their village walls either. It was one thing to use her gift to watch another species of Fey in their homeland for learning purposes, but to bring it back would only cause more problems for her with her truanted wanderings at night without a damn escort.

She did have her moments; she wondered how it was that her family had not acquired more grey hairs on their poor Shifter-heads. She smiled at that reflection, deciding she had stayed long enough in the glen now that the floor show had ended, and all participants but her were gone. She proceeded with a bit more caution than nights previously spent exploring in the woods, now that she had seen the inhabitants and what their little abilities could do with certain molecular particles. In future, she would remain vigilant when it came to playing with others she was not accustomed to. Instead, she went in search of the Shapeshifter Panther, and others of his pride, to see if the energy they produced was intrinsic to the species or just particular to the one.

It took her a while to find them, but they suddenly were just there above her and all around the area she had entered. She heard them long before her eyes spotted them, finding them sleeping within one of the larger trees snoring away without a care in the world. It had seemed strange to see them sleeping at night; she had always thought the cats were nocturnal creatures, and spent their energy hunting game. However, these ones looked simply played out, as if they had been chasing game for hours already. She would find out much later that the clan had actually participated in the molecular transfer needed to fully animate the forest particles, and when she had found them they were recharging their energy levels so they could finish off the night hunting as a group.

Sibrey had spotted the massive felines out towards one of the trails that lead to the village of Sadllenay along one of the less travelled paths, far away from the main thoroughfare of Fey foot traffic; further augmenting her visions of the long lost race of Dryads. She had once remained within sight of these beautiful creatures for almost a full rotational phase of the ancient Leberonion's lunar mansions. But that wouldn't be until Leberone moved through each of its pinnacles again after the initial sighting, and only after she became lodged in a bitter quarrel with one of her older brothers, and refused to return to the village come nightfall. The village had sent out a rather substantial search party upon the edge of darkness, only to discover she was simply gone. It was at this time, after many fascinating hours silently watching and waiting alongside the movements of this pride, that they seemed to accept her unusual arrival. To them, it became quite clear she was nothing more than another member of their pride; albeit one not formally initiated, but that would come later. For now they seem to tolerate her nearness, as they continued to recharge themselves giving her sanctuary from the dangers of the darkened woods and her own clan; one that continued to hunt for her out along another doorway that the Sombreia hunters still could not see.

She had been an adept student in their pride, following the rules of their pecking order and watching the nuances of their individual personalities; all the while, the Shapeshifters searched for her along the edges of Togernaut territory. She had seen several hunting parties out near the north end of the Lypurnen Woods, but they never found the doorway where the Panthers lay hidden, so she had continued to remain with the pride until she had learned what she had come for.

One day, without much surprise, the Alpha male walked up to her and nuzzled her outstretched hand, which she had extended more out of curiosity than anything else, and the rest was history. She had stayed frozen in time hoping she wouldn't get bitten, as the minutes ticked on leaving her breathless. But fear hadn't played a part in it. She was more afraid that if she moved the big cat would hesitate and she would lose her time with them. The very time she had spent on those long nights slipping out travelling into the forest just to be accepted into their living domain among the trees, away from the stagnant atmosphere of village life.

Anyway, getting back to the Alpha male: He had turned his head away from her, sat down upon the nearest clump of grass and started to preen himself, ignoring her completely. It wasn't until one of the larger beasts had tried to put his body into position between the two of them that she realized just what had transpired, and the fight began. However it was short-lived and the smaller of the two had won the quarrel, and appointed himself her personal protector. Turns out he was the one that had originally found her in the glen and had already laid claimed to her as his own. These events seemed like a lifetime ago, and it was during this time that she became a full-fledged member of the Pantherous family of Fey. They did not, at that time, consent to her actually becoming part of their inner circle; that particular achievement would come even later than the first.

Back in the real world, Sibrey needed to pay attention to what she was doing, by staying ahead of the Aelf that continuously moved about a full mile behind her. Soon, the Panther would take over her senses. Until this actually happened she needed to be perfectly sure she was far enough away from where the Aelf could find her, without prompting her feline host to keep moving before he circled back and started to hunt him. How the Aelf had spotted her as she fled into the woods, was anyone's guess. Surely it was simply an accident, and nothing she had misstepped in her rush to get to the tree-line, away from the village. Either way, she needed to move faster, or at least stay hidden from his sight until she could reach safety. If by some odd chance he caught up to her, and she actually could put visual sight on the rider, she had a better chance remaining safely hidden inside this creature than anything else she had become in the past.

Nevertheless, something told her that being a Dragonlord had given him more of an advantage over an ordinary hunter. Those damn dark Dragons had more abilities than anyone gave them credit for. If she didn't know better, she would think they weren't freaken Dragons at all, but something entirely different lurking deep inside that outer sharpened Dragonistic shell.

She sniffed, trying to hold back a sneeze, responding to the cat finding its whiskers near parts of a certain sneezing lichen bush. His paws moved, and he lightly scratched his face along the bark of another moss filled branch to remove the particles; they fell without incident. They carried on without having any run-in with another of his species. Looking back as she moved off, in the centre of her friend the Panther, she realized her lessons were about to either pay off in Rathskeller gold or come crashing down to a violent conclusion. For, coming into play at this moment when she literally ran for her life from something she could not understand, she was about to expose the very place she hoped to stay hidden, just because of a misplaced nose.

She mentally crossed her fingers that she had learned everything necessary to stay out of harm's way, and that the lessons she learned would keep her hidden from the warrior that came to take her away from the only home she had ever known. If she played it right, and played it long enough, she could escape and return back someday to the family that she knew and loved. Between now and then she hoped that the cat didn't come into contact with anything else that might give both of them away, as she slipped closer to becoming unconscious, and the tracker behind her gained ground.

The forest floor was damp with the recent rains, and although there had been wonderful days of lovely warmth, the upper canopy was far above where the tree roots maintained their sustenance in the richness of the forest floor. It was here that they stayed hidden, in a shadowed world far removed from the heat of another realm, where most winged creatures played and collected their food; occasionally joined by other Fey that crawled and basked in its unobstructed views. The foliage far above prevented the ground from permanently drying out, and didn't give much warmth to the dampness that permeated each standing giant, away from the busy overhead traffic of the trees.

She did her best to visualize where the Panther was taking her, but it proved harder than it looked. He moved so quickly, jumping among the fallen logs covered with thick green layers of cat-tailed mosses, continuing past various moulded nurseries of fallen fruit that littered a speckling of silver Faery grass permeating the layers beneath the bog. The latter moved lightly together as they traversed over their edges, continuing to sway in the wind with their passage, winding themselves along the sturdier stalks. Several that had become caught beneath the Panther's paws could be found bent and broken along the backside of the logs, where they quickly twisted around to find a better location. Finding one not too far from their current spot, they pulled up stake, moving with tiny centipede legs that had been folded beneath the fronds and set themselves back upright, returning to their former shapes as if nothing had disturbed their passage. The woods were full of creatures like these; she only hoped they were as benevolent as these ones were, or they were going to find themselves in a heap of trouble when the Aelf discovered their whereabouts.

The sneezing influence of the lichen bush long past did little to ease her tension. All along the hidden path through the old growth trees huge boulders could be seen lying in their final positions, set off from a slide that must have happened a long time ago. She must have passed through here hundreds of times, but not once had she spotted these rather large mounds of rolling rock. The grounds were literally covered with them. Preoccupied, she moved around them, not really noticing their massive size as she traversed their girth, moving through the meadow covered with ancient volcanic ash. Had she more time it would have fascinated her, the thought that a million years ago all this could have been in the middle of an ancient volcano, while time stood still and the planet ran with true Elemental molecules of another form of life. But she had no time, and the time she did have was almost up, and closing fast on her consciousness.

Both stopped and sniffed the air where a higher density of feline molecules scented the small stream bed that was thickly coated with mare's tail along its edges. They took a short drink to sustain muscles and tissue alike, nourishing both Shapeshifter and feline equally. They didn't stay long; the cat was always watching his surroundings as he moved them deeper within the woods, only stopping for short moments when a rabbit foolish enough to stray within range quickly reversed its decision mid-stride, when the shadow of the big cat crossed its path. But the Panther wasn't hunting, and didn't stay; he continued on without having anything on his mind but the possibility that bigger prey was not too far away, in the shape of something Aelfish.

Sibrey snickered, thinking of earlier attempts on other animals that she had tried to find herself within, one of which had just run out in front of both of them. She thought that maybe she was lucky that this was not the one that had let her stay; it would surely have been a lesson cut short in its entirety, with the encounter this little one would have had if the Panther had decided to stay and give chase.

She sniffed and thought of something else as the rabbit disappeared down its warren, missing the cat by the hairs of a cross-eyed firefly living on a grain of sand. The cat lightly snarled, carrying his passenger to their secret destination, looking for larger game would come later, once she had arrived and he could hunt in peace. Mimicry was one of the Shapeshifter's greatest accomplishments but, truth be known, she found that she could no more become one of them in that capacity than change into a rock that had audible sound, and even at that with no great accuracy.

She remembered the long hours and incredible patience the entire clan had upon her arrival. Unusual thought patterns, and the sudden and unexpected transfer of affection from one of their own towards her were among the long list of things they had to get used to. Then, once again, patience paid off and the lessons began with the clan of the Panthers she had lived within, instead of her Shapeshifter teachers; only this time she stayed in school, didn't deviate from her duties, and remained alongside without the side trips she had been known to take back home.

She watched these great animals over the space of many months, and it soon became apparent that they were also keeping an eye on her, even when she wasn't in their actual denning area. She eventually had to return to the Shapeshifter village, and never told a soul what she had learned; feeling honoured by the gift they had bestowed upon her spirit, then taking that time and rearranging her life to better suit her new gift. The changes in behaviour toward her studies had not gone unnoticed. She began to show great strides forward in everything they wanted her to achieve, but it would take many years before the clan of her village had allowed her another outing without supervision. However, she had on one occasion stayed much later than normal on one such outing, accompanied by several

Shapeshifter teachers and students who had needed to stretch tired muscles and minds away from lessons they received inside the village walls. Long after they had fallen asleep on the outside of the Panther denning grounds, she had heard the Panthers calling her, and she crept back to the great sleeping tree in the vicinity of their dens. Her arrival into their midst once again offered her the opportunity to return the kindness they offered her as a child. This time Sibrey had brought them food, taking the stag the others had killed for the village and presenting it in its entirety to the clan as a formal Thank-You.

While they had feasted, not having been able to find enough food with the Shapeshifters so close, she had fallen asleep there. When she woke, finding the threads of her conscious mind, she had found herself actually transmogrified within one of the stronger males of the group. She was stunned and a little unsettled in the beginning of this new kind of lesson, but soon discovered she could do it at will without hurting the animal or causing it distress. The best of it all came weeks later during an unexpected discovery, as it happened again but with much more intensity. This time it allowed her to stay hidden from anything tracking her amongst the trees, while it had gone on a kill. The next thing she remembered was waking up alongside her feline protector, miles away from where she had previously gone within his body, with absolutely no knowledge of where they had been. Perfect, she had a new hobby, one her old friend could be a part of while they hunted together without leaving the other behind.

It had been the beginning of her next journey into their world, bringing on a new flourishment of activity for her to enjoy and explore. But with each creature she became, none ever allowed her the joining like that of her friend the Panther. Right then and there, she made a promise to the Pantherous clan that she would only use this ability when needed, or when the Panther world itself had use of her in its own world of shadows. Either way, she became part of a new world not previously open to her as a Shifter, as it came and went through the summers of her teens, when everyone else had something more important to do with their days. It had proven easier to hide than she first thought; keeping them busy and away from her training had prevented anyone else from noticing how her ability had progressed far beyond where she should have been, in those long lessons spread out over the years.

Now, she needed to move on and put away her thoughts deep inside her feline companion, as she made her way towards the middle of the forest, away from the tracker and his keen sense of smell.

CHAPTER THREE

Soren and the Wood Sprite

Soren jumped from the side of his Dragon and quietly slipped from the battle, disappearing immediately from the sight of the Shapeshifters going up the ridge. He could ill afford anyone coming after him as Sibrey ran within these trees, if he was going to be able to catch her before nightfall. Furthermore, if Dyareius had not distracted the Shapeshifters who had been closest to Soren, as he slid away from his Dragon, he would have lost a great majority of time going around them. It was something they had discussed before they left the ground. They knew her kind and, despite the precautions they had put in place she had escaped into the woods, regardless. Assha had used his majik to let them focus on the fight that was about to erupt, while Dyareius had hoped common sense would prevail. Both had worked; without either of them, it would have cost him valuable time. All he needed to do now was become the tracker he was hired to be. Truth be known, he had less patience for feysitting any of them, including his own friends, whom he had known and spent more time with in the past few years than he cared to admit.

He was the lone wolf; one that continued to remain living along the outskirts of the village the others lived in, despite their repeated efforts to get him to move closer to where the other riders lived. This made him extremely good at his job, for he spent a great deal of time learning the logistics of all the creatures living on this planet. He used that time wisely, watching each of the Fey clans and their particular habits, as the others had banded together into a group since the Dragon Wars had come to their conclusion.

Now he used that talent to its fullest potential, following any quantum particles floating about the air while he could still feel them. They had a shelf life of about ten microseconds before they simply dissolved, disappearing into the ether and never to be seen from again. If that happened it would prevent him from efficiently locating her Fey form within their fields, and he would be left using other abilities without this gift, taking longer to locate her before the desired time. Had Assha been near enough, he would have been able to bring them back momentarily with his majik, for Soren to find what he needed. But Assha was still with the remaining riders, trying to obscure Soren's departure from the Togernauts, leaving him to fend for himself.

He redirected the quantum energy into himself, thus preserving the particles' integrity, and held onto their particular molecular thread while he got his bearings, and moved to head Sibrey off. He had been trained by one of the masters of old Tameron, and smiled at the thought of his unique gift, with the arrogance of one that had never failed to deliver. She could run, but he would find her before nightfall; he didn't even have to think about it.

The particles she had left for him to trace made him almost high, while he concentrated on what lay ahead of him hearing the uproar of the ruse the Dragons had manifested just before he entered the tree-line. Their Dragons were louder than the resident green ones, and caused a ruckus that was fairly perfect for disguising his departure towards their quarry, who had made it as far as the beginning of the smaller treeline just inside the edge of the forest.

By the time he was away from the others in the quiet of the trees, he knew Sibrey was different than anything he had ever tracked before. It still gave him an edge, tracking her molecules from the forest floor rather than on the back of his Dragon. For that, he was grateful. If he had taken Tansar inside the treeline, the close quarters inside the confines of the woods would only be a distraction from his search. Then he would have to find a way around the top edges of the canopy, missing the smaller areas where she could fit her little body into. Soren knew his beast well; he tried not to consider the horrific fact that he was searching for a damn Shapeshifter, who could appear to be anything at all. It was best that his beast stay with the others, and find him when the time was needful, as he directed his retrieval from an area the Dragon could land safely in, when the little fox had been returned to the hen house with a leash around her damn neck.

Shapeshifters always made him nervous, and this one had abilities he could taste; ones that would inevitably try his damn patience to its extremes. He would undoubtedly be tired when he had her firmly within his grasp, leaving his Dragon to do most of the other work. He moved along the ground, shaking his head at the reason he had agreed to do this in the first place. Dragons had been born with an ability to search out their riders. He would be found no matter how deeply he became embedded within the trees. When the others left the village, his Dragon would follow the others, while Symin produced the imagery that would keep the Togernauts from realizing he was flying alone, riderless without his Aelven escort. The very image of the shadow of a rider astride his back, without the village realizing he had gone on foot after Sibrey alone, was crucial to their success in capturing the little runner. Symin had that gift; one that Soren would be able to utilize to the fullest extent, while he searched every rock, nook, and cranny along the edges of where Sibrey had shifted into, while Symin hid the figure of his frame from those itching for a fight at the bottom of the ravine.

He might have been able to make it to the edge of the trees without Symin, but the Togernauts were known to be dangerous, and had a lot more hands on swords than the twelve remaining warriors sitting on their Dragons had, waiting to fly at the first sign of a shift in power. It might have been a different story had they been at any other village; however, this one could undoubtedly kick their little Dragonlord asses when it came to hand to hand combat, if they weren't careful. Dyareius wouldn't be taking any chances.

The forest closed in behind him, majikally adapting itself to replace what he had trampled behind him, obscuring his footsteps to even the most adept tracker. Even if it was done with as little damage as possible, they still would have reset themselves; it was the nature of the beast. Everything on the Fey worlds had some form of sentient life in its molecules, no matter how little or miniscule it was. He had only travelled about half a mile, when he realized, nothing at all remained of her Shapeshifter signature; Sibrey had quite suddenly closed up shop and disappeared without a trace.

"Bloody hel. You're good, little kit, but it's only a matter of time, sweetheart, before you make a mistake and I find you," he growled out into the forest surroundings. He listened to the echo and frowned. Her particles of trace, along with any lingering scent, literally fell unfettered upon the ground, disappearing within whatever opening they could fit into and were swallowed whole. Soren took in a deep breath, within which nothing could be felt or tasted, along the insides of his tongue. He sniffed the wind; still nothing. Damn Shifters, where in the spacial infraction could she have hidden? He bit his lip in frustration, as he thoroughly turned over every branch and fern within the small area, then turned back to where she had first entered the forest to try and pick up her scent from there. Damn, this Shifter was smart; what had he missed?

Shapeshifters, when hunted, usually stayed put. But nothing moved or flashed away as he made his way back through the same area he had previously entered. Sometimes, during moments of desperation, they even let you touch them as they continued to remain hidden out of visual range. However, most of them when doing that, scattered their particles outwards when the object was touched, producing an energy reading that could be picked up faintly by those who had been trained for its arrival. He had sight for that; sight that made him much more special as a tracker for the Tuatha De`Danann.

He squatted down on his haunches, brushing the tiny fern fingerlings softly feeling for her essence, and closed his eyes breathing slowly. Still, nothing resembling that transference majik remained. The only thing to have been in the area, besides a rabbit, and likely not too long ago at that, was a rather big cat judging by the scent. But, no Shapeshifter. No, this one had simply vanished into thin air without a single trace particle for him to find, leaving him feeling rather annoyed at her achievement. He ran his fingers over the imprint of the cat that had passed by, but saw nothing, then moved off further into the forest sniffing any molecules that may have been hiding inside something else. Again, there was simply nothing there to smell, other than the normal range of flora and fauna that the forest surroundings naturally produced inside their little world of decay and rebirth. Her scent had virtually disappeared from the planet's inner world of rings.

Off in the distance, one of the forest cats screamed making him momentarily lose his concentration. It was close; he would have to move quickly if he wanted to catch her in time.

He hated backtracking; it was a necessary assurance, but a waste of valuable time for a tracker. They had only a limited amount of time given to them, when they had been given orders to retrieve the girl. He would have to re-evaluate his plan of action, knowing he had come up empty handed despite having such a brilliant head start.

Up ahead another print of the same feline came into view, and this time a single fine black hair was within the print of the animal's soft pads, and as he reached out and held it up to the light, the strangest thing began to happen. He saw her quantum particles within the shift, just as she first entered the woods. He then followed that mirrored image given to him and brought it up to his line of sight, and watched in fascination as he was shown her movements through the visual cortex of his gift. He was stunned by the level of accuracy she had achieved; if he was correct in his understanding, right in front of his eyes was one of the most extraordinary scenes he had ever encountered.

He watched her slowly blending in full shift, then landing within the cat who was seen waiting for her just inside the perimeter of the forest trees, without her having touched or set foot on a single part of the forest floor beyond her initial shift. She simply seemed to float right into the actual animal in her wispified pre-corporeal formation, drift into where he seemed to be waiting, and move off, disappearing from sight. He watched her giving the feline its headway without the big cat even reacting, and then as if by devine intervention, without even a single flinch or muscle tick, it headed off through the undergrowth. Both moved seamlessly as one down the very same pathway he had just searched, towards the depths of the Lypurnen Woods ahead, leaving nothing in the mud but one set of animal tracks. This was nothing really out of the ordinary for someone searching for any large animal. However, it was everything to a certain tracker out hunting a particular Shifter, who had now become part of the very animals this damn forest now belonged to; not to say anything about the much larger game that had only recently started to wake up, further complicating Soren's task.

These revelations were going to make it interesting; he liked a challenge. He was intrigued by these complications, with this new bit of information; she had evolved much further than they had hoped. To think, he now had an entire different species to hone his skills on. He grinned at the complexity of his hunt, and felt the arrival of the evening twilight on the edge of his eyelashes; it had been far too long since anything this interesting had given him reason to work at his skill. He wasn't worried that there was no visible trace of the Shapeshifter anymore; he had done a grid search just to make sure she had not tricked him into having this false sense of new found security, then carried onward watching his step in the pre-dusk light with a new found bloody lightness to his stride.

The feline's energy was all that was left of what she had morphed into. She had, quite literally become part of the actual living core of this breathing animal; merging within and finding a place to rest while hiding. It was amazing. Symin would be pissed that he had missed this. Odd things were more his speciality, and Sibrey was probably the only Shapeshifter in the entire kingdom capable of pulling this off. Soren would have to thank Dyareius for the challenge, even considering the extra mileage that he would have to travel in the actual hunt to capture such a prize. Unfortunately, he wouldn't find her before nightfall, as his arrogance had first lead him to believe. But the smirk on his face signalled his regained confidence, and he moved with renewed vigour, back the way he had come.

His arrogance was cut short as he got up and turned back to follow her feline trail, running smack into a tree, almost knocking himself out cold. "Damn it, what the bloody hel in tarnation?" he exclaimed. He fought his frustration at the bleeding cut on his head, unsure whether he was mad at himself, or just frustrated at the turn of events that had led to his own stupidity. Unfortunately, he didn't get a chance to wonder for long, as he applied pressure to the wound, spitting bark splinters out of his teeth. Just when he thought he had a handle on his new found sense of control, the tree snorted, woke up, and carried on rambling off into the forest as if nothing had blocked its pathway.

It shuffled away slowly, as Soren watched several large roots trailing along behind it, the size of an Aelf's thigh. He really needed to pay attention to what he was doing, especially in the middle of a forest known for its unusual events. His cut would take time to heal and, as he put up his hand to wipe away the blood beginning to trickle down his face, he wondered what the hel had just happened. He shook his head to clear any blood that had made its way into his hair before it had time to congeal, messing up his scent. The last thing he needed was the night-time creatures coming after him while he left them a wide open trail covered in drops of blood for them to track.

A moment ago nothing had been anywhere near the pathway that he had chosen to take. What the Kepet was a tree doing sleeping in the woods? He watched it walk away, shaking his head and nursing several small cuts to his forehead that had appeared underneath the blood he had wiped away. Imagine his surprise when he found his blood in the process of turning into red coloured dust the moment he had wiped it from his head, instead of forming the smear of blood that should have remained on his hand. He watched several of those particles of red dust drop from his lower thumb as he shook them free from where they had appeared. Lightly, they drifted towards the ground, blending into the forest soil making him wonder what this forest was doing to his mind. He found the powder slightly unsettling, but it wasn't until he reached for his dagger to get a sample that he realized the damn tree had taken his bloody knife. "Bloody Hel!" he said, beginning to understand the complexity of these woods. Now, he was pissed; not only did he have to deal with strange majik; he now had to deal with thievery.

He moved to go after the tree, and realized it was gone. Not just gone, but having left no trace of the actual pathway it had just carved out of the forest floor with its thick roots, smashing into things as it moved slowly along. He had been a little preoccupied with nursing the wound on his damn head, and hadn't even heard the noise of the forest picking up anything the tree had dragged along behind it. It was just another extension of the forest noises going on around him, and he hadn't even bothered to pick it up. When they had first been sent to retrieve the girl, he had fought back the need to speak and followed the decree set before him without judgement. It was unlike him to be so moody, but his mood had not improved of late; this was just another example of why he liked to work alone. The wound would heal, the pride would never. He was just glad the riders had not borne witness to the collision, or he wouldn't have been able to live it down for a long while — as far as his knife was concerned, he had better get it bloody back!

He started to move away from the route the tree had taken; any trace of her in that direction would have been destroyed and replaced by the forest sweepers, and any footprints, feline or not, would now be long gone. He would need to pay closer attention to what this forest's local residents had waiting for him; to think that yesterday had been just one of those ordinary days, where nothing ever happened.

Three days past, things had been put into motion with a flurry of activity that had challenged his outwardly normal rising. He had always awoken well before the set of Leberone or, if not their moon, the rising of what he liked to call the Mauntratic dawn. It was during these times that he used to revel in the darkness, using the time to think about life and what he had become. Then at certain periods of its darkside, there would be nothing to light the trail except the various planets in their own orbit, as they reigned supreme in the skies overhead during their rotation through their skies.

On those mornings he would stumble along the pathway, heading down to watch the phosphorescence play in the ponds, forgetting the bare essentials of leather footwear, creating a whole host of other problems with his feet. He would then spend the rest of the day regretting it, lying flat out floating on his back in some nearby hot springs, which would pretty much give him the perfect excuse for doing nothing further for the remainder of the day. However, most mornings he took himself for an early swim in the river; his cottage being the furthest away from the village had given him the privacy of taking his time alone, without the others interrupting him. He liked the darkness that still showed its tiny fingerlings as it stretched into the morning mist out towards the first awakenings of the new dawn; one that was still hours away overhead and off to the right of a recent hatching of Firefox Faery dens.

At times, if he was lucky enough to time it, he would wake in the wee hours of the midnight stars, when the fog still lay shoulder deep inside the lower dells of Quick's Bottom. It was a time that still allowed him his solitude, away from the village voices that would soon enough try to encourage him into whatever was coming into play for the coming day. Most days he ignored their pleas, while others he found himself swept up in something he had no business being involved in in the first place, and wishing he had stayed in the lake and drowned. He hated those times, and found himself getting up earlier and earlier just to avoid those that he knew would be coming to take him away on whatever quest they had decided he would enjoy.

He sat and watched as the primordial drippings of first light had awoken the skies that morning, beginning to initialize dawn's silent arrival. He liked this time of morning, long before anyone else from the village would open their sleepy eyes and yawn. Those were times of perfect peace; with a steaming mug of coffee in his hands, he would open the door of his cottage to watch the morning peek out quietly, with its crimson streaks spreading out across the waking sky. He loved his mornings, with all their peace and tranquillity, especially since he usually got into some kind of a fight by nightfall. He grinned with the thought, adding in the old perspective, that is if he was lucky enough to find one. If not he would start one, so he didn't have to wait until one began to formulate and brew.

But now, who was going to fight a blind Aelf that couldn't even see a bloody tree that was right in the middle of his path? Crap. Life as a Dragonlord without a Dragon to watch his back was nothing short of just plain sad. He was going to have to talk to Symin about this. Maybe they could take off to Naunas for a while; at least there he might still have a little fun. Maybe there he could at least make the trip worthwhile, and find a Sage to have a look at his damn sight, without the others laughing their heads off at the whole idea. There he could remain anonymous. Although that too was becoming harder and harder with each passing day.

THE BEGINNING

Part Two, Three Days Earlier

He had still been dripping wet, and had only begun to towel off, when his trek up the pathway was intercepted by his friend Symin. On certain days that was not unusual; sometimes Symin would get up and join him on his swim within the river's deeper pools. But, it was as if the Gods were absent this morning to wake his fool hide; Soren had been alone reveling in the quiet solitude, when he had come tearing down the path, out of breath, yelling his fool head off.

"The Aelfs of the Dragonlords have been summoned. Hurry up and put some clothes on you lazy sod, we're bringing the Dragons home!" he shouted. Soren winced, almost falling flat onto his ass, skinning his knee in the process after tripping over a tree root and coming within inches of Symin, grinning away.

"Are you flipping serious?" Soren snapped. "What in the hel is going on? Seriously, the Dragons?" He shook his head trying to clear the cobwebs that continued to hold court in his brain. "Our Dragons? Not something made up in that liquefied brain you've concocted." Soren replied, almost feeling his friend's sense of anticipation, mixed in amongst the small tendrils of excitement sitting at the base of his own stomach. Finally, something to do besides babysitting a village full of morons.

Symin nodded, smirking away; he had never been one to hide a damn thing; he had always worn his feelings on his sleeve, whether it was necessary or not. He was a creature of habit, and one that Soren could be damn sure would go out with a bang, as he vibrated off the face of the planet into the ether regions. That would never change till the day he crossed his life force into their dogmatic crusade. But, to actually bear witness to the calling of the Dragons back into this new game, whichever it was written to be, was another thing all together. The huge animals were only used in times of war, and as far as he knew, they hadn't been at war for nearly a thousand years on any of the Fey planets this side of the Hydrous Secular Nebula.

Symin tried to look nonchalant at Soren's question, but clearly it was killing him to find out what was going on before the others. He shook his head while thinking what he wanted to add, but there was nothing he could include. He was also in the dark as to the reason why they had been called to bring the large war-Leviathans back home to Tameron.

"I have no idea what's going on, and I hate not having the background information on this. Whatever it is, we've only got a few hours, and I haven't the foggiest idea where we are going with them, let alone where the Dracore reside now since the old war," Symin declared, grabbing Soren's arm when he looked slightly unimpressed, literally pulling him towards the dirt pathway that would take them towards his cottage. "Come on, I was sent to get you. The others are already packed and waiting at the Stones!" Soren looked at him for a moment, letting the information settle inside his brain.

"What, we are actually going somewhere?" he asked, looking smack into Symin's eyes, hoping to see what had lain hidden there for years. But Symin only grinned back at him, leaving his mind closed off to anyone that tried. "Seriously my friend, one day you're going to forget to wall up that doorway and I'm going to get in, before you slam it in my face." Soren growled.

"Fat chance, never going to happen," Symin grinned wider, watching Soren mentally try to break through his barriers. "Now come on, we're wasting daylight."

Both Aelves moved, albeit one a little more quickly than the other, simultaneously approaching the doorway of Soren's home at more or less the same time, as they went inside to get Soren ready. Leggings, a shirt, and a pair of boots were found lying across the nearest chair, and several books were knocked sideways and scattered about the table when Soren suddenly slammed his sword down on it.

"Seriously, you're not pulling my leg on this one? Because if I find out you and the others have some kind of elaborate scheme planned for the day, I'll be more than pissed," he said, reaching to put a foot into each boot after getting on the drier breeks he found draped over the back of one of his other chairs. Symin looked slightly put off.

"Honestly, Soren, you really have no trust in us. Seriously, whatever happened to camaraderie?" He looked somewhat taken aback by Soren's mistrust.

THE BEGINNING

"Camaraderie my ass. When was the last time you followed anything similar to that rule?" Soren yelled back at him. Symin simply grinned, as laughter rumbled out of the back of his throat.

"Just trust me on this one, you old fool. I've never steered you wrong, even if the wool momentarily grew slightly over what we as brothers, needed to get done for the day. Besides, you always have fun no matter what we do. However, if you recall, none of them involved herding Dragons, so pull yourself together and let's go." He threw his sword at Symin, and both ran through the doorway as Soren tried to pull on his woollen shirt, and retrieve the knife on his bed to put in his boot.

Swords passed between them, and the material of Soren's silk shirt lay lopsided over his eye, but he managed to pull it on just as they both began to run along the pathway that would take them to the Stones. It was a hodgepodge event, getting clothing and weaponry in their proper places, until Soren looked up and yelled at Symin to hold up. He skidded to a halt, just as Soren pointed to the lack of overhead trees, providing a firsthand view of the wrong trail heading he had chosen. The one Symin had led them to would have taken them into the backside cliff-area of the Capourian Mountain trails, instead of the right one that would take them directly to the Stones. Symin grinned awkwardly, and both had to retrace their footsteps to correct taking the wrong pathway in their haste.

"Seriously," said Soren, looking up and shaking his head at Symin, "one of these days I'm going to have to stop letting you lead. Every bloody time, this happens. For whatever reason that is ingrained inside your thick skull, you seem to have this warped sense of direction, and it never seems to fail that you take us sideways down the wrong path. How long have you lived in this village, you idiot, and still you can't remember the proper path that leads us the hel out of here?"

"Hey," yelled Symin back at him, "I was kinda busy getting your ass moving to begin with. So don't go and lay all the blame on me. If you didn't notice, you didn't say a word, and followed me without reminding my idiot ass that we were going the wrong way!"

"True, but that's not the point. Over there, you know the one without the damn stones underfoot, is the right path," Soren said, pointing to the path running vertical to their current position. "So come on; if you say the others are waiting, now it would seem I have a reason to tell them why we're bloody late."

All Symin could say was a simple, "Shut up and keep moving, or a few of your secrets are coming out into the damn wash, as well." To which Soren merely grunted several short swear words, as they both turned around to start again, with Soren remembering something else.

"And I don't want to hear the excuse about you living with the damn Elementals again, and that's why you're so dysfunctional, because, if I hear it one more time I'm going to strangle you!"

The Stones were a full mile from the village, each standing almost fifty feet high, almost five feet thick, and as long as a pair of outstretched arms. The energy that lived within them was powerful enough for those that lived here to feel them, even at that distance. Moving towards them at a speed greater than a leisurely stroll brought new meaning to the word stupid. No one in their right mind ever approached the stones without moving at a snail's pace. To go any faster would make them feel like every bone in their body was about to turn inside out, then fry itself into oblivion. It was even more dangerous to anyone that had use of their majikal abilities, like the Dragonlords. To run there, even for the ones who were veterans, was simply insane. The pain that came from their energy vortex would take hold of your nerve endings and twist them inside out until you begged to be released. And, if that wasn't bad enough, they would pick you up in the air, drag your body towards them like a magnet and then add whatever brain-cells you had left into their massive collection of stolen energy and leave you drained of all your life-force.

Because it wasn't in your best interest to actually do what they were in the process of doing, they had no choice but to slow their pace to a slight jog. By the time they had arrived, blue sparks were igniting and white rods of electrical magma were forming at the tips of the stones. The energy alone as they slowly made their way up to the others, was stronger than what would be regarded as safe.

"Slow down you two, or we're all going to get smoked," yelled the group of the other riders who were also on the path, waiting for them at a reasonable distance from the stones. But it was too late, and the electrically charged bolts started landing all around their legs and feet, as each began to duck away from the extra charges striking in close proximity to each of them.

Soren grabbed onto the back collar of Symin's shirt, and pulled him back. He lurched backwards after losing his forward momentum, and smacked the back of his head into the top of Soren's throat, just under his chin, as one of the more powerful bolts crashed down around their feet.

"What the bragna?" Symin yelled at him as Soren maintained his hold, and they both fell backwards from the force of the blast. They landed together in a heap out along the edge of the trail, with Symin landing on top. Soren shoved him off before Symin found his voice, shaking moss and dirt off his ass. "You always take all the fun out of this."

Soren gave him a stern look, as Symin threw a rock in his direction. He ducked, and it went on by overhead, creating a backlash, which amplified the stones' energy bursts into a much stronger stream, giving all those present the feeling that they were starting to sizzle and cook in the heat.

"Seriously one of these days, old boy, you are going to get us all fried. I'm not sure whether you have a death wish, or are just testing the waters; however, when the rest of us are around, do you think that maybe you could try and kill yourself without getting us all involved?" Soren shouted at him, while Dyareius yelled for both of them to quit fooling around.

Symin didn't respond verbally, instead he looked up at Soren, who was almost a head taller, and blew him a kiss. "Great," Soren rolled his eyes, "now I have a stalker. Would you just quit it, and get walking." They were not far, just coming into full view of the stones, when they heard the last of the riders behind them come into the clearing as well; breathless.

"What the hel happened?" each said in turn, as Soren pointed to Symin and growled. They looked from one to the other and shook their heads.

"Should have known Symin was involved," shouted Bynffore, over the drone of the stones.

Each of them began to move towards their assigned steps, carefully watching and wading through the electrical sidewinders that were still sending charges outwards into their midst.

"Just once, I'd like to be able to step up on this platform, without having to dodge the bloody strikes," Cassmarr said, to no one in particular, while Symin grinned at all of them.

"Seriously, you are all a bunch of babies. Come on fledglings, let's go and play with the mean old wolf." Symin laughed, as he walked right through the electrical charges like it was nothing special without any hesitation or a backwards glance to see if they followed him. The others merely shook their heads at him and shadowed closely. They moved quickly beside him, hoping against all odds that the density of all of them together would prevent anything from actually hitting them. It had proved to be a gamble, but was the only choice they had, without starting the next sequence of events into play that wouldn't tear their skin off their bloody hides.

The big pillar of black manganese centred in their midst would be the one that directed the other lesser stones towards the centrepiece in its volume of charge. Off to the right and away from where they were standing, was another larger section of stones not so thickly covered. This was the entranceway where the Dragons would find the doorway into this realm, returning the formal calling they would make to the Aelves' summoning. Should they not hear its initial calling, the doorway would have sent the locking quadrants a set of coordinates outwards to a juncture point, which they could find at another set time to open the doorway up on their own side of the Dragon home-world.

Dyareius looked to see if all had made it through the crossing, looking at each of them; they appeared to be present and accounted for. Each time this certain rite was performed, it was all he could do to not laugh outright at each of them. For standing inside this circle of highly charged particles, was a group of renegade Dragon-riders in various forms of unusual attire armed to the teeth and down to the bone, while all around their Tuatha heads waves of hair floated in the extreme electrified charges that filled the air, making them look almost comical in their appearance.

He silently snickered at the thought of how they looked, as he watched the highly charged atmospheres in the air swirl and flickered around all the riders at the same time, creating an electrical charge that would send the wave variance out towards the edges of the circle. It was truly a sight to see, and anyone looking in from the outside world would have surely left the area in fear for their lives, as the wild renegade warriors of the legendary black Dragons came madly to life. But, he had no time for silent observation; their arrival had changed the frequency of the rotation of the rings, as the initial colouring of the charge took on a new exposé of sound.

Markus, second in command of this troop of wildly charged travellers, was to Dyareius's left. He looked around the circle to make sure all were within their vibrational breech points, as he used his gift to look through the centre ring in-between the flux points, to see if they had touched those needed to reach their goal. All pressure points were fully on target, and he came back to the outside world, nodding to their commander. Dyareius looked towards the others as each of the Aelves greeted him with a grin, joined by drifting hair that floated without containment in the maelstrom. Each in turn looked from one to another and nodded, sealing the final connection and stepping lightly as they approached the building turbulence through the outer-rings.

This was their favourite part. Each time they approached the stones, their chances of getting killed were fairly certain; however, each time they made it through by the skin of their teeth, they beat those odds, and the nitrogen that coursed through their bodies made them crave it more. Once inside, all nervousness went away, and the high that came from being in the proximity of their powers superseded the danger they had faced getting there. Each of the riders could feel the energy streaming through their bodies, filling their veins with its majikal molecules, as they bathed in its substances and filled any missing bits they never knew they had lost since they had last entered the rings.

As soon as this was completed, they still had to actually move up the stone steps. They moved as one entity, stepping onto the stones together, so as to not single any one of them out alone and have their energy crucified by the sting it drew. They were directed through this by Assha. He was the one that orchestrated the majik; without him, they would most likely be dead before they took another step. He gathered their signatures into one push, and entered them inside one solid energy flow, creating a single entity that would trick the stones into believing they were both substance and Selmathen at the same time. He had the majik the others were missing. After all, these stones belonged to the home-world of the new race of Selmathen creatures, a race who had been born on the elusive planet of Anthros; the same planet that, when the storms had made one of them a castaway, it had been trapped for thousands of years deep inside the crystal caves that hosted their mother matrices.

No one but a being of Selmathen blood could use them; unless you belonged to the cloud realm. For, without the majik that Assha provided for them coursing through their veins, the stones themselves could tear the flesh of the average Fey and leave nothing but a bare skeleton in its place. This was a safeguard set into their molecular strands, straight from the matrices that released them to this world, at the time when they were transferred from their home-world. For without safeguards, anyone could have taken advantage of their powers. The stones were renowned for their abilities, and the crystals that lived on Anthros inside the planet's atmosphere, had access to many things that lived deep within their memory lines. These lines would come to be known by certain species as Lemurian lines, an ode to the reverence of that particular civilization; one that was rumoured to be among the greatest scholars of all time.

They moved up to the next level, within ten metres of the stones' outward ring of flow, passing the one ring that would seal them in, and grounded themselves into the stone with their boots. They came instantly into contact with their signatured crucibles; the very ones Assha had sealed deep inside the thirteen stone blocks put into place to generate the link which they would need to maintain the energy. Each of them had questions, all of which could wait until this was done, but none more than Soren. That secret was locked away deep inside of Assha. How was he able to use these stones without Selmathen blood in his veins? That question had haunted him for a lifetime, but the answer would only have confused him, and as far as the others were concerned, they didn't care to know as long as it continued to keep them safe.

Soren shook his long mane of hair as it swirled in the electrical current, trying his best to keep it from slapping him in the face. The answer would never be told in its entirety, he was sure of that. However, one day in the not too distant future he would stumble on part of its truth, and then he would have a long chat with his friend without the others being aware he had found out some of the reasons of the why. It hadn't been that long ago that he had been perfectly happy swimming in the river; until Symin had basically turned his morning around, and shoved him into what now presented itself to him. Why this was happening was anyone's guess, but for him, next time he got up early, he was planning to go for that swim on Naunas; at least then he would get some peace away from whatever insanity presented itself to them in the coming days. And maybe there, the truth would simply present itself to him without causing any grief in the revelation of its hidden word.

For now, each of them was committed to go forward; swords were removed from scabbards, and the flicker of silver steel threw reflections off their blades to join together with the morning light that would find the shadowed edges of where they would touch the stones to begin the ritual. To bring their Dragons back home to Tantaris's realm was going to take some work. They would first need to find the Dragons among the shiftpoints before they would be able to arrive within the centre of the stones. And to do that was going to take the whole damn day that was set before them. Soren closed his eyes and groaned, thinking of what would present itself to them, as the others rolled their eyes listening to Symin yelling loudly in the background. "Come out, come out, where ever you are!" Yes, the enigma of life would have to wait. This was going to be a long day. He now wished he had stayed in bed!

As soon as Symin quit horsing around, the first of the electrical ribbons surrounded and blanketed each of the Aelves as the stones erupted with newly charged power. They closed their eyes to prevent the light from blinding them during the initial burst of energy, as each Aelf became part of the ground and the air at the same moment. The second ribbon moved around them and found its place within the metal core they each contained within their own bodies. The third ribbon centred their flux, giving their voices the amplification they would need to attempt the signal that would send the message towards the Dragons. The fourth and final ribbon would go through the doorway in search of their sentries, as it all tied up the calling in a neat little tidy box of electrical fusion.

Their sentries had instantly appeared just outside the stones' rotational pull when first they had entered the outer-rings. They hovered lightly in the morning air, waiting to rejoin their host's energy signature the moment the Aelves returned from the middle of the atrium. Their awareness was centred on the individual symbiont host, and was put into play during the fourth addition, as the ribbons reached into the Aelves' awareness and aligned their molecules with those of the Fey. This being done, they protected the Dragon-riders while their bodies were directly linked to the Stones of Panthor's matrix. Once that happened, the riders were vulnerable to attack; that is, if anything was stupid enough to try from deep inside the tidal fluxing that ran in waves along the edges of the stones. Nevertheless, they guarded the Aelves' signatures until they were no longer needed to do so.

This was something the Elementals gave in exchange for coexisting in this world with the riders. Their energies mixed in with the Aelves the moment they moved between realms, and arrived on this plane of existence. It was what they were made for, and gave them sentience when first they had been called into this world of Sopdet's ruling order. It enabled them to move about, and in time would give them a place of ranking among the Elementals and their guardians. For without ranking inside the realm of the Elementals, they would have to fight for space alongside other entities that had adapted themselves before them.

The sentries were given access by the fourth ribbons, and their own signatures became mixed within the stone's matrix. This in turn would lead them into the Aelfen mind link, allowing the Aelves to find the rhythm they would need to sustain their atoms within its core. The ritual started with a single humming noise sent in by Dyareius's vocal cords, programed to resonate with the crystals hung about the centre stone's engravings. Then, each of the Dragonlords followed their own songs, and brought the stones on line with their own pitches, as the stones began to activate and become fully awake to their arrival.

A single point of violet light shot out of the stones' interior, and went straight through the ground, in front of each of the Aelves standing upon their raised platforms. It reached a pivot spring and sent the steps forward into the inner ring's violence, holding all the Aelfs in an individual safety net, set within the circle of protection that was given to them by their sentries. This gave them the resonating pitch they would need to reach the homeland of the Dragons, which could be found somewhere in the land of Symarr, off the southern tip of Water's Deep.

They began to sing as the stones sealed them in; the ritual began to ring out through the Stones of Panthor and into the meadows and trees surrounding them:

> *Aelfen kind stands here with you, ancestors old and those of new.*
> *Hold the gate in times of then, circle broken, then back again.*
> *Open the door that stands before, to the time of Old Dracore.*
> *Beating wings of power be, let us in and let us see.*
> *Honour bends and twists around, locking forward into ground.*
> *In times of old we asked of you, to join the heart and make it two.*
> *We give our service to your land, out to forward then back again.*
> *Join us now we ask of thee, we give our word to see you free.*
> *Swords are risen, our battle cry, outwards onwards into sky.*
> *Be it so that you shall fly, until the day from which we die.*
> *Come forth to form of which you dare, through the stones and into air.*
> *Follow through and follow me, as sky above I ask to see.*
> *Doorways open and set to fly, join us here from there to sky!*
> *Vermada seetay forquois, Vermada seetay formada,*
> *Vermada seetay forquois formada.*

The chant would be repeated throughout the morning, for the next few hours. If they were lucky, the Dragons would hear the call and make it sooner. If not, they would continue until they had said the spell nine times nine. Then, and only then, each warrior of the Stones would look down on the ground with swords at the ready, and drive them up to their hilts in the stone floor, as the molecules parted to let them through.

Then as the energy exploded within the circle, they would bow their heads not in prayer, but in protection against the receding sparks. The stones eventually would calm down and flicker back into the silence of the alien homeland, continuing the normal hum that resided within their own atoms as each warrior took his leave, silently moving as one towards the exterior of the stones' main artery without their weapons. Their swords would then be released once they left the area of the stones and found somewhere within their own homes upon their arrival, without them having to do the work of retrieving them from out of the solid rock.

No one had spoken during the silence that followed, all deep within the thoughts of his own multi-dimensional mind, trying to understand how best to deal with his own mortality. If the Dragons being summoned meant war, how in the hel were they going to get out of this one alive, when the last one almost killed the entire race? Soren remembered his thoughts on this, when they had moved off towards the Great Hall talking more among their own minds than the ones that reached through their individual hearts.

With that remembrance, begins Part three...

The day had set, and the moon loomed in the shallow part of the sky. This could only mean one thing...a full moon tonight; plenty of light for the hunt. Sibrey needed to move the cat deeper before sleep overtook her body completely; this way she would fall into a blissful kip, without having to watch the process of the night's hunt. It was her least favourite fragment of becoming part of the cat. Blissfully, the feline had taken care of the basics of its natural behaviour and had always thought of her needs first, alongside those strange idiosyncrasies that came with moving about on two legs, instead of his four. It had come without the asking, and with the assurances she would not have to watch what occurred during these nightly jaunts. For this, she had given him in return her complete and utter trust. Both had accepted the gift without even asking.

The cat stopped to listen to the night air, panting. He stilled the outward flow of Sibrey's still active molecules, as the evening shadows brought movement alongside the trail. He focused his attention on a small fox, finding its scent along the path they were heading down, and moved off in the other direction, choosing not to encroach on its hunting range. He growled briefly in his throat to send a warning, as the fox scurried into the underbrush, disappearing from sight. Both listened as it carried on down another trail, followed by another much younger, who had been out of their sight waiting for its mother to give it the all clear. The Panther turned away from the small footsteps receding in the background, doing its best to heed the quips of warning its mother had sounded, and the two were off for their own night of foraging. The Panther sent out another low growl, mostly as a warning to others that they might meet along the way, giving it clan protection, at least for the time being, while all trace of the fox and her kit disappeared into the darkness. All was as it should be...

Sibrey grew weary, while her feline companion watched the pathways that would lead him to his hunting grounds. They had merged as two, and now one belonged to the night vision of the Panther's body, letting Sibrey move alone without him deep inside the world of her Shapeshifter dreams.

She had relinquished her hold on the feline around five microns ago, as her sleep began and the cat started to relax. Sibrey's world would be fraught with enough dangers, without the added distraction of having her mind involved in the Panther's tactical skills that were needed to keep him fed. He moved about the night alone, secure in the fact that she would have no memory of the night's events. He needed to hunt, and for that he needed to kill. He would not do so with her mind active inside his body, so he waited patiently until he felt they were far enough away from the hunter, allowing her mind to relax enough to knock her out on his terms. His gift in her final waking moments was sending out protection for one that he normally would have hunted, just before she slid into the realm of the Goddesses' and their own world of dreams.

He moved methodically now, listening for signs of pursuit; when he heard nothing that could be construed as a threat, he moved to subdue the hunger pains that had been building inside his own body, since the previous day. He had not fed until he had deemed it to be safe. She had not been so, until now. The fox and her kit, were given a pass. That wouldn't happen again, if another of her species crossed his path later.

Sibrey safely locked inside, fell into a slumber; one that she would not wake from for many hours, if not days, depending on when the Panther deemed any future danger had also passed, and the availability of the game he needed to maintain his energy levels. He would move quickly to those feeding grounds that belonged to his pride, as the hunger grew into a raging firestorm inside his body, and the Shapeshifter moved restlessly in her sleep to match his mood.

The tracker had stopped his pursuit as he reached the outskirts of the territory of one of the more unusual creatures that lived in these woods. That he had decided to relinquish the chase had not gone unnoticed by the big cat. However, it could only be a momentary pause, and one that he would take with cautious gratitude, despite his suspicions as to the meaning behind it. The hunter had given him a fairly big head start in leaving them to their own devises. Instead, the Panther moved silently, almost stealth like, as he carried her deeper into his own domain listening for anything that would take flight and spoil the anticipated meal he craved.

Soren now began another hunt. He was a brilliant tracker, but his speciality was not in tracking animal kind. His teaching was that of Fey, and he had used this skill primarily to hunt down those affiliated with the old King. But it was his friend Symin who was much better at animals than he would ever be, and it was while thinking this that he began to talk out loud momentarily foregoing his rule of silence.

"This Shapeshifter had better be worth it." He hesitated. "Symin, can you hear me?" But the others had already shifted with the Dragons away from the village. He had watched them go as he entered the clearing; he knew he was on his own, and they couldn't hear him any longer. With a short shrug and an unaware sigh, he moved deeper within the majik of the Lypurnen Woods.

He needed to find another touchstone within these woods that would take him past the centre of his new arrival. There were several stone clusters he could use out near the north end of the ravine he was heading to. They had been dropped there many years ago, back when the riders had been deep in the middle of the Dragon wars. The entire continent of Water's Deep had several of these clusters around various areas that he could use, well hidden and out of sight from the other Fey that lived here. Unfortunately none of them were close enough for him to use now. So, he would have to hoof it a while longer to reach them. He knew there wasn't a hope in hel of him finding her before the allotted time he had been given was up, especially considering the new state of being that she had acquired. Now he would have to find the others and see what they could come up with collectively. In the meantime, he would follow the tracks he could see and if he caught her sooner than later his Dragon would have found him before he even had to go in search of the stones.

He couldn't remember when that rite had been taken away from them, but sometime during the old wars, the Dragonlord Aelves had forfeited that right and were unable to shift on their own merits. The black Dragons were their touchstone for that purpose, and they had also left him to his own devices. He caught the edges of a sneeze as he wandered too close, lost in his thoughts to a sneezing lichen bush; he moved deeper, finding nothing further that would lead him to believe she had gone this far west.

The evening sounds of the day animals preparing for sleep began, and as each animal prepared themselves to bed down, some still kept a vigil watching the goings on silently out of the corner of one eye, as sleep slowly took over the animal brain. The night-time creatures began to slither and shake themselves into wakefulness; moving downward from the canopy above, which had allowed them their much needed rest during the daylight hours of the Mauntra's heat. In another realm they could almost miss each other; here on Tantaris, some would definitely come head to head. Soren hoped none would have that meeting with him. He was not in the mood, nor was he confident who would win the battle if he wasn't able to find Sibrey before such an occurrence.

Meanwhile,

Off in the distance an owl hooted, calling out to his mate; she answered then joined him, as they both flew off into the darkened night sky. A shadow crossed in front of a troop of Firefox Faeries dancing about the forest floor. They scattered in all directions shrieking gleefully around the shadow creature, and disappeared into the night air sending a trail of Faery dust in their wake. He smiled at their antics. He was not accustomed to dangers from the outside world away from these woods, and wondered where they might be off to in such a hurry. They were one of the few creatures not afraid of him, and spent most of their time scurrying around picking up the remains of scattered thoughts; the very thoughts that had been left along the forest floor by whatever creature had passed this way during daylight hours. It was strange behaviour, and he never asked what they did with it all; he simply enjoyed their company as they gathered it up and left in a flurry of translucent wings. It was never enough time, and before the evening shadows took them away into their nightly excursions, he slowly stretched his lithe frame without a care in the world, as the moon brought forth his Human shadow into the midnight realm of the Panther Fey.

The sounds of Soren's breathing had not yet reached the same moon he looked out upon, and the pale creature breathed in deeply with a strange little chuckle that inhaled the night air deeply into his lungs. He scratched his long raven hair watching the Fireflies dart from one huge leaf to another, and wondered where they actually lived. They had always been here, and every time he had tried to follow them through the trees after a long night of hunting, they had quite suddenly just upped and disappeared into the sides of whatever was in the vicinity and he hadn't seen them again till the following night. Wherever they lived, he had finally resolved to let it lay, for Tamerk had said they were creatures of majik, and to follow them home would resort in losing that mystique.

He turned to move in the direction of the trees to relieve himself, and found himself almost along the very edge where Soren had been searching. It was pure coincidence that they came into contact with each other; had he gone in the other direction and followed the Fireflies like he normally would have done, the two of them might never have met. Then again, things met by design rarely let one know that they had been planned, or at least told in mixed company with another race from a different world.

He had not been paying attention to his surroundings, and when he turned to come back to the sanctuary of Tamerk's home, he found himself face to face with a rather startled Aelf. Both creatures, one of Fey and the other more of Human design, moved simultaneously in opposite directions looking as if they had both seen a ghost. Disturbed by the sighting it only made matters worse when both looked back at the apparent apparition, and realized nothing could be farther from the truth. For in truth, the creature that had looked to be spectral in appearance was very much alive, and looking back at him in just the same queer way. Furthermore, to complete the horror of the situation to its fullest telling, each in turn couldn't believe that what they were actually seeing was indeed what both had feared to be the truth.

For a moment Soren had thought he had been following the Shapeshifter, only to discover a more deadly enemy already here, amongst his own lands. To have the Human pop out of nowhere was unsettling; to breath the same airspace was infrucktuous. He spit the offending molecules out on the ground in a show of defiance, while the creature merely looked at him blinking several strides away, hoping against all odds that the Firefox Faeries had sprinkled something toxic in the air, and the Aelf was nothing more than a figment of his own imagination.

Soren wiped his mouth trying to remain calm. He hated the Humans, that was self evident; however, this was something Dyareius would want to have information on, if he didn't already have the evidence tucked away. If that was the case, he had done it to protect them all from an active cell that had already bloody arrived, and needed further investigation. Crap! Now he wondered if he had missed the memo, and the others were aware of it and hadn't told him. If so, had it been brought up while he had been so tied up in Symin's antics, that he hadn't heard the warnings? He wondered how they could have made it this far south without prior knowledge of the area, and at that, a damn Fey guide that could take them into the trees so far. Had they been deceived by one of their own? In that case, had this cell lived among the majikal woods inside of this sector of the Fey worlds for longer than they were led to believe?

He was slightly confused. His orders were from Dyareius, who had received them directly from King Llyemyllan. Were they wrong; as far as the timing anyway? Or had he just not listened? They had only gone into the vortex of the stones three days before, with the Dragons themselves only arriving earlier that day. Soren's focus of attention was instantly diverted away from the Shapeshifter; she would have to wait. He needed to get back to the hidden cache of traveller stones, so he could shift back to the others and let them know the Humans had already arrived and seemed to be thriving here in this realm, without the Tuatha being aware they were within Sopdet's boundaries.

However, that was not to be; it occurred to him as he had begun to take those rather large steps in another direction, that he needed to bring the Human male back with him, so they wouldn't have to go hunting through the trees for him again. He turned to retrieve the Human, but he simply wasn't where Soren had heard him start to move back into the underbrush. The Human had mysteriously disappeared from Soren's tracking sensors, and no matter which way he turned, the Human seemed to have vanished with no actual trace of him having been there at all. "Great, another creature that I can't find," he hissed. It occurred to him that maybe it was the Shapeshifter after-all, and that she had replaced the feline and turned herself into the one creature he loathed, just to get him to move away from where she had hidden herself. Smart little Shifter. Hum, he thought to himself, where does her little shape begin and the shift end?

He went over the ground, and searched for tracks; instead, he found the entrance to what looked like a well hidden cave. He smiled at the discovery, and moved towards the entrance way. A branch broke right near the entrance, and Soren quickly reached around and made contact with flesh and bone belonging to what appeared to be Fey and Human alike. Slightly confused by the sight, he was angry enough that he didn't judge the difference, as he scrambled to hold on to whatever he had grasped. It stayed this time remaining firmly caught in his grasp, pink and smelling of petrified Humanity. Soren didn't need to move quickly; he already had whatever it was by the throat, without even thinking whether he had the ability to hold onto it or not. He dragged it up against one of the huge trees that lined the area without too much effort, leaving his feet to dangle above the ground like a rag doll.

When he turned it around to face him, he saw it wasn't the Shapeshifter after all. The creature exploded with an annoying scent he remembered quite vividly from the Dragon wars. It was definitely Human, there could be no mistake. That made him more irritated. Soren wasn't sure whether he was just annoyed, or whether his dislike for Human kind had finally snapped when the Human pissed on the tree. But most of all, he wanted to know what a Human was doing on a Fey world, steps away from a colony of one certain Shapeshifter he was currently having a very difficult time locating without a care in the world, pissing on one of their damn trees!

He growled at the terrified creature, just to make clear his revulsion at finding a Human on this planet without any kind of backup. It would never have been that way, had they been on their planet. Just think of the Human's audacity at walking alone among the Fey, who would sooner crush his little hide than ask him what he was doing there. It took hackles for one to have that kind of courage, despite the fact that the scrawny little creature was no match for any of Soren's race, let alone one of the riders of the black Dracore. He either was very unlucky, or something else was going on that currently Soren couldn't feel.

Soren adjusted his hold on its neck, then lowered the Human's face inches from his own, squeezing his fingers tightly around his trachea. He snarled words that came fluently from his mouth in an old language that had not been spoken here on Tantaris in over a thousand years. He had remembered it well in the years since, and had gone over every nuance of its vocabulary, just to be sure he understood their meanings. It listened to Soren's words in its entirety, even if the pronunciations might have been slightly off. The Human stayed silent in response to his line of questions, but Soren knew he was not deaf by the way he cringed after each word, regardless that they may not have been perfect in their enunciation. But still, no spoken words came from his lips in response to the interrogation. However, what he did see made him grin cruelly.

The Human was literally terrified of Soren, even though his reflexes appeared capable of using the knife that had majikally appeared since Soren had first seen him. He held it in his right hand with the death grip of a corpse, as Soren eyes moved from one side of his body to the other sussing the chances of another hidden somewhere else. As soon as the Human saw that Soren had spotted the knife, he opened his fingers and dropped it without even trying to raise it towards him. "Smart little Human. But, I would much rather you had tried to use it. Then I would have had a reason to kill you outright," Soren reached out and shoved him harder against the tree for emphasis, adding crushing pressure to his back against the hardened surface, "instead of slowly strangling the life out of you. You see, death has no glory Human if you don't defend yourself, but then again, you Humans really have never known Fey glory, have you? Well," he drawled, "not on our terms anyway." He spat at the ground beneath his feet.

Still, the Human didn't speak to Soren, making matters worse. There was no way for him to break free, yet he continued to squirm, trying to find any weak spot in Soren's grasp. Soren only tightened his hold, making the Human gasp for air in a desperate attempt to claw his way through Soren's fingers. It was at that moment, Soren realized he was crushing the Human's windpipe, and as Soren watched the man starting to lose consciousness, he was disgusted with himself at how he was killing the creature. Aelves didn't use that kind of force, except in war. For now, one little Human didn't constitute a war. Still, with the others coming or already here but hiding from his sight, he needed to get answers not create a corpse that couldn't speak, and tell the tale that needed words.

He growled in disgust, then slowly released his prisoner's throat. The Human dropped like a stone; collapsing like he was nothing more than a pile of rags upon the ground, as the air around the glen seemed to feel lighter. Soren watched him crawl to the edge of the structured nest he called home, and with huge gasps of air, immediately reach for where Soren had restricted his windpipe trying to force air into the rather bruised and injured organ, now obviously choking. He wouldn't be going anywhere soon; Soren had made sure of that with the crushing blow. Even in the fast approaching darkness, the luminescence of the tree moulds lit up the pale face, and the dark welt that was rapidly spreading along his lower jawline. He didn't need the forest's natural illumination to see the dark fingermarks forming on the delicately thin skin that belonged to a real live and somewhat breathing, Human bloody hide.

Soren shivered, thinking about it. Nevertheless, he bent down within inches of the man's face to make his point, as the creature tried to back up against the tree to avoid Soren's fingers reattaching themselves to his windpipe again, lest he actually choke to death. Soren easily followed him, bringing him back and pinning him to the tree's bark. Soren placed the blade he had picked up against his neck, and again fired off a volley of questions. There was nothing like the sweet justice of holding another being's knife to their own throat, thought Soren, as several other newly thought of questions fired off with rapid succession. "Where are the others that accompanied you here?" Soren peered around, looking to make sure none of them were moving in behind him, still holding the end of the knife he had in his hands to the opaque throat.

The Human didn't answer him, which only infuriated him more, as the man suddenly became more animated and began to slump sideways. Soren moved slightly back looking a bit suspicious. "Seriously, you're going to play that card?" He raised one of his eyebrows to show his scepticism, as he went to apply pressure to the blade. "Well, I'll be damned, seems like you're having a wee bit of trouble maintaining that air supply you're so fond of. Hum, seems like we've come to an impasse in our little war of words, wouldn't you say? And when I say little, Human, I mean I speak and you say little." The male responded by only grunting in his direction, which Soren found funny, and broke out in amused laughter.

"Typical Human, always have to be dramatic," Soren continued with his tirade of insults, passing the time before he was able to just knock him out cold, as a final insult. But first, he had a series of questions that needed some answers. The Human shook his head, struggling to break away from the situation, taking on an almost blue coloured hue along that white neck, and continued to gasp for air.

Soren moved to readjust his hold on the Human, while he coughed his head off looking more confused, as saliva started to drip down his chin. "How did you get here?" Soren snarled, barely containing himself as he swore into the man's face, wiping the Human spittle off his fingers and onto the Human's own shirt. "Try not to drool, it's really not becoming of your species. But, then again, Humans don't live on this world. You can't exist here, the air's too thin for your kind. It has that lovely effect on all Humans, creating large volumes of saliva in your bronchial tubes, and then...." he paused, to emphasize the ridiculous point to his story, "you explode, and turn into little Human particles that get eaten by Trolls!" he shouted at him.

The Human looked like he was ready to vomit; instead he went into another coughing fit, that sent Soren from overdrive into the ridiculous. To prove his point, Soren used his other hand to turn the Human's chin from side to side. "Nope, not a single gill that would allow you that right. So, what are you, one of the half breeds that have been sent to spy on us?" He let go of his chin, and ripped open the Human's shirt. "See, not even a breathing apparatus attached to your skin. That is not possible, Human. For one that looks like he has been nesting and set up house, you should have something that allows you to maintain the oxygen you need for your Human lungs while you gather information about our kind. So, what are you then, part tetrapod crossed with some form of Pyaan?"

Still no answer from the terrified man, who tried to shove Soren's hand away, so he could cover up his bare skin again. Soren let him, releasing his hold momentarily; giving him a false sense of security, when he realized the Human wasn't buying his ridiculous banter. He hadn't known Humans were uncomfortable about bare skin; he could work with that. The Fey

Stolen Child

relished in their nudity, although for him it was more showmanship than exhibitionism. However, he did like the way the water felt on his skin, when he swam in the river each morning unadorned. But, he knew several clans that lived in the hills, who moved about their daily activity in nothing but what the forest provided for them. The Human seem to need covering more along the lines of some form of security. Lucky for him, he still had a shirt left, and Soren hadn't sliced it off him just to see if he had hidden more knives around back of him.

Crap, he hadn't thought to check his back. Soren reached out and rolled him over, while the Human snorted his displeasure at being manhandled. When Soren finished his search, the creature shrugged the shirt back into place, but didn't try to retie any of the front laces; instead he let them lay flat against his skin, alongside the sweat that had begun to appear. Soren began again; he knew his captive was agitated, and would provide a far better response, than if he were comfortable, waiting on something that was about to happen. But, this time the interrogation didn't last long, for no sooner had he started, they were joined by a host of Firefox Faeries that suddenly appeared out of nowhere and threatened Soren as he continued his line of questions, trying to dodge the little suckers.

These new creatures began to create all kinds of havoc. Soren waved his free hand and tried to squash a few of them under his boots. Surprisingly, it was too this action the Human showed a noticeable fondness for these creatures, as Soren continued to swat at their bombardment. However, every time he seemed to make contact with their little bodies, they zoomed right through his hands and went right out of the backside of whatever he had pinned them up against. The Human broke protocol and started to shed tiny droplets of salty tears on his face.

Soren knew the Human was angry, but the tears had caught him off-guard. He had been battling the Fox Faeries, when much to his surprise, the Human started to shake like a little Aelflet producing huge raindrop sized tears, that began to well up and slowly roll down his cheeks. Soren hated tears. But still, no audible sound came through the man's mouth in words Soren could understand. "Stop that bloody whimpering! Seriously, a grown-un like yourself, shedding tears for a creature that I wouldn't waste my spit on." Soren frowned; something didn't feel right. The air around their immediate vicinity smelled slightly off again. But this time it didn't give off the heavy feeling like before; this time it was brushed with a slight majikal fragrance, resembling some kind of weird sage, mixed in with freaken pipe tobacco.

He sniffed the air, looking for the source, and came up empty. Even the hair at the back of his neck could be felt to respond in kind. It was something he had not felt before, at least not for a very long time, he suddenly remembered. But the recollection was not within his reach, and he still couldn't place its strangeness. It was familiar, yet there was no memory of it having ever been something he had felt at one time. It was as if he knew it, but just couldn't put his fingers on what it was.

For now, his mind raced; he felt each follicle of thought take on a life of its own, floating in the air all loose and weird like, bringing to memory the resemblance of snakes on a Gorgon's head. They seemed to move about his brain as thoughts tend to do, but at times he swore he could hear strange hissing noises overhead, as each sliver of hair took on a life of its own. He swore he felt them actually move, and separate themselves from the others like vast fields of wheat. Then, some form of light majikal breeze blew along their ends, and drifted upwards to their edges. The Faeries suddenly up and left him. They could be heard chirping away with nary a care in the world, as he continued to fight whatever demon had him tightly in its grasp.

Cackling laughter in the background didn't give him a chance to see if indeed his head was full of snakes. Instead, Soren moved fluidly to face the new threat, bringing the Human along with him in one swift motion, despite the appearance of something growing on his head. He pulled him close to his chest, then turned the distraught Human away from him, using the front of him as a shield. He should have felt tears if there were any to feel, but in his haste he didn't notice that the man's face showed no signs of having had them just moments ago. Soren was too preoccupied to notice the difference, as he moved backwards to get a better grip on his hostage, and the knife he had managed to hold onto on the way around. He looked wildly in all directions, trying to place where the sound was coming from, just as a crumpled old Wood Sprite came into view sporting a gnarled face, with a body only about three feet high.

Soren started to laugh, shaking the nervousness that he had felt about the demon, as it came out of the shadows, looking like something that had lived within the mud of some long forgotten hole. He was the ugliest thing Soren had seen in a long while, resembling a piece of hardened discarded fruit that had been put out in the Mauntra too long to dry. He watched the old thing take a draw from a clay pipe he had resting in his hands, and smelled the warm tobacco wafting upwards into the night air, as it drifted in large rings of smoke that melted and played majikal pictures in the darkened environment. "What the fragmire?" Soren growled at the creature.

The creature stayed where it was and winked at him, while Soren swore an oath up one side of him and down the other. The Sprite didn't advance, instead chose to lean somewhat cross-legged watching Soren from his position, as the rant continued, smoking his pipe and listening to the words. Soren stopped swearing and looked at the odd creature, while tightening his hold on the Human. The Sprite continued to smile, cackling away in a language Soren couldn't quite make out the words to, revelling in his pipe's unique aroma, smiling at the pair of them. Soren growled at the Woodlyn creature, aware of what the majikal beings that lived in these kinds of woods were like, and the cackling continued to annoy him. He moved to protect himself from whatever this creature had in store for him. But nothing seemed to be imminent, and the creature with the dried-up face continued casually standing with his back up against the wood frame of a tiny door, at the entrance of what had looked like a cave before.

"Hum, seems like we have ourselves a situation. But I'm betting it's not the one you might think," he cackled at the words he had given him. He moved ever so slightly, coughing from the smoke he accidentally took in when he laughed at what he had thought was a witty comment. Behind him, Soren could see, as the light flickered from around back, the interior of a rather cozy home, and by the smells coming from inside, both the Human and the Wood Sprite had just finished some sort of meal together. Soren could smell the aroma of some sort of stew, with homemade bread still warm from the oven, wafting up into the outer edges of the hovel.

Before Soren could sneer at the old creature calling him a traitor, the Wood Sprite pointed his pipe at the Human, and, turning to look back at the Dragon-rider, he said to Soren, "he doesn't talk none, since the

Faeries took him as a small child." He was smiling and cackling away, with some private joke. "Matter of fact, you could say my tracker friend, he'll not be much good to you at all." The Sprite pointed to the Human slowly falling, apparently having being rendered unconscious, now laying limp against Soren's chest. Soren looked down in disgust, instantly releasing the man, who dropped to the ground at Soren's feet. He stepped away from him, moving sideways as if the Human was nothing more than fodder for some future meal. The Sprite seemed to be amused at his reaction, further prompting Soren's over-exaggerated hand movements as he brushed the Human molecules off his chest, taking them away from his side, then physically spitting the remainder of their odour out of his nostrils on the ground away from him.

"That is just wrong, harbouring a fugitive, and a stinky Human at that," he finally verbalized to the old man. The Sprite didn't respond to his opinion. Instead, he put out his pipe, then slowly walked away turning his back on Soren and went inside, calling to him in a nonchalant fashion.

"You'd best bring him in here," he sighed, pointing to a wooden cot from the inside doorway. Soren could see just inside the cottage entrance from where he stood, and noticed the sound of food still bubbling hot in an old cast-iron pot, steaming away over the fireplace. "and I'll grab ye a bit of something warm shall I, for your troubles?" Soren could hear the old Sprite moving about inside the tree banging a few pots around, and winging a plate from one side of the room to the top of something that sounded like wood. Soren didn't move; instead, he looked around thinking about what had just happened. The sounds continued inside and somewhere, something that sounded an awful lot like a wooden spoon, came screaming down one side of the table to the other and then rolled to a stop. And before Soren decided to make a run for it, it sat glaring away at him at just the right place the Sprite had decided he would sit.

He was just about to abandon the Human and disappear into the woods, when the moonlight landed on the Human's face, and Soren realized the Human had changed and now presented himself as only a boy! He swore an old Aelven oath, muttering away to himself; no matter what he thought of the Humans in general, he would never hurt a child, even if it was Human. He looked at the boy, and swore again. He groaned loudly and started to curse.

"Ahh, crap, I hate freaken Sprites, always messing with your mind." He turned, and lifted the Human up into his arms, cringing at the touch, and moved towards the entrance of the home. If he moved quickly, he still had time to eat and get the hel out of here before the darkness got too thick. He would after all be needing some kind of fuel in his gut before too long, and if this crazy old Sprite wanted him to eat, who was he to ignore what could fill his belly before he moved on. Then he was out of here and away from this stranger, who liked to play with alien creatures that had no business being here in the first place.

His movements quickly removed the limp child from the outside world of the trees, into the surprisingly spacious interior of the old Sprite's home. Soren uncerimoniously dumped him on the cot, while the old man smacked him over the head for the careless way he handled the boy, and shooed him away to the table as he looked the boy over. Still talking away to himself, the Sprite pointed to the far side of the table, where Soren spotted a freshly poured mug of hot coffee waiting for him. Then the Sprite reached for some form of fibrous cloth, and Soren watched him dip it into the contents of the inside rain barrel, and point a rickety old finger at his chest, while Soren reached for the mug.

"This, here," he pointed to the young lad again, "happens to be one of the finest Humans I've ever had the pleasure of meeting, be careful with him you fool!" He shook his head at Soren before poking his long gnarled fingers at the child, then glared back at Soren. "Matter of fact," he cackled, "the only Human I've ever really met; not like you, who have met thousands during the war." Smiling sadly, he turned to Soren, who seemed surprised he knew anything about his life. "Damn dark-Faeries took him away, actually stole him from his Human family, can you imagine that? That's when I come across him, and thanks to them, he could barely walk. Just about killed the poor child, they did. I took him home, after sending the damn things a fluttering down to whatever rock they crawled out of, before I yanked their own necks off and fed them back to them."

Soren snorted at the comment, until he realized the old man had stopped talking, and was looking at him with a queer stare. He took another sip of the hot beverage, before throwing up his hands in surrender, when it appeared the old man was going to start in on him.

"I didn't say anything, honest, just drinking this stuff you call coffee." The Sprite completely ignored Soren's sarcasm.

"Hum, didn't see you actually drinking the damn stuff, just a yacking your jaw off like you did out there." He pointed to the trees outside. "Hum, looks like you might be a tad smarter than you look. And call me Tamerk. I got a name dammit, everybody's got that right," he said slightly affronted, as Soren continued to sip the liquid he had placed on the table. Tamerk turned ignoring the Aelf, and returned to his tale of Fey meeting Human, and the wayward Faeries that stole the boy.

"Damn shame, but what was I to do with a Human child, you know? Take him back to the jump point and push him through back to his own world? Seriously he could have landed anywhere. Then I would have been in a heap of trouble and we would have had Humans swarming this old planet in droves. Did we need that? No, I think not. They'd have come after us, and someone would have had me strung up like some kind of chicken!" The Sprite shook his head. "So I raised him, did right I did. Turned out to be a pretty good hunter too, learnt fast. Not like some Fey that I know, that keep hunting in my woods. You know, now that I come to think of it, nothing pisses me off more than some creature coming into my woods and taking my animals without asking permission." He turned to Soren with an after-thought, "and if you want to find that Shapeshifter by morning son, you'd better drink up; long night ahead with plenty of hours left in the moon."

Soren drank the whole cup he was offered starting to feel a little stupid, as the old Sprite carried on through the drink, as it passed down his throat and into his stomach. He had only taken the last of the dregs, and turned to meet the Sprite during the statement about the Shapeshifter, when he dropped like a stone to the floor of the cottage, and was out cold like a fish.

The old Sprite got up and poked Soren with his foot, then burst out laughing. "Never could hold your drink, eh Aelf? When some stranger offers you coffee, don't drink the shit stupid! That'll teach you for hurting my boy. You Aelfs never listen; some tracker you turned out to be; you can't even hunt yourself out of a damn mole hill." Tamerk grabbed Soren by the foot and dragged him to the fireplace before letting him go. He sighed shaking his head snickering away at the sight. "That was too damn easy, must have lost my touch."

For his stature, he was a lot more than what he appeared. He began to wrap the Aelf using an old woven chain, and tied him to the fireplace ring that had been installed in the old stonework for whatever reason the old man had decided on when he had first built this place. He took away the sword Soren had in his hand and brought it over to the wooden table they had just finished their supper on. He found the knife Soren had placed in his boot that belonged to the boy. Tamerk lifted an old jar from the back of the warming plate above the stove, and placed it with the other one he had taken previously on the pathway when he had run into the Aelf earlier, then walked over to attend to the Human child's swollen throat, clucking away with a song about nothing in particular and everything in general.

He knew the boy was only bruised, or he would have hit the Aelf a little bit harder, and without the added benefit of coffee. It wasn't all that bad; he had seen the boy take down a full grown JoieGiun bear when it had charged him and tried to kill one of the young Taber owls he had raised from a fledgling. He knew it was mostly noise that the Aelf had first heard when he had tried to take him away; the boy had that certain way about him ever since he had come into contact with him, when he was a small waft.

Speech was something they had not had time to work on, having so many other things needing looking after to get him ready for when the Aelves returned for him. Tamerk moved towards the stone pantry and reach inside for the glass jar that held what he would need to put on the boys skin. Inside was the herb he used on the markings of this kind of bruising. Tormentilla Salve would take away the swelling, and help relieve the kind of mild pain he would undoubtedly have when he came to, in the next few hours. He wished he had more time to spend with the child, but having the tracker here hunting the Shapeshifter, only proved that that would have to wait for another day. The Dragons were on the move, and their riders were in tow. Things were progressing faster than he liked, and by the end of the day things were about to get even bumpier. He needed to keep moving if he wanted time to complete what needed to be done by morning.

He hadn't got to that level in the boy's teaching as of yet, but the boy would have lots of other teachers through the coming years that would supply him with the necessary information, now that the Aelves had arrived within his woods. For now, he would just give him this one last bit of healing, to get him into the right frame of mind for the trip ahead. Tamerk brought one last thing to the boy's mouth, to provide him with peaceful sleep. He had a small errand to run, before both of them returned back to the conscious world inside his small home.

Tamerk knew the child could look after himself if it came down to it, the boy was just not aware of it yet. He always knew time was limited with his young charge, and the coming of this tracker, he suspected, would be the very thing he needed to get the boy to learn more on his own with others of similar backgrounds to himself. Tamerk smiled with that thought. He turned and looked at the snoring Aelf. "Could have been a little taller, but I'll take what I'm given." He went out the door and closed it behind him. He spoke the words that instantly put up the wards to protect both inside from what was still hunting with sharpened teeth and razor-like claws on the outside.

He scratched his head, thinking. *Might have been better to just let the damn Panthers eat his hide. At least then we could have been done with it.* Cackling away he disappeared in a trail of majikal tailings, and the home came alive with ethereal life.

CHAPTER FOUR

Sibrey's Dream

Sibrey dreamed within the Panther, deep within the same forest, while the big cat made his first kill of the night. But Sibrey didn't hear it, nor did she have any emotions associated with the mechanics of where she was or what the cat had just taken down and killed. Safely asleep and away from outside surroundings, she fell deeply into the dreams of her youth, and away from the carnage of the Panther's world of night-time feeding.

Her pounding heart slammed deep in her chest, as panic once again inserted itself into her dreams. She could see herself running dangerously close to some jagged cliffs, as several smaller stones along the area she had just traversed slid out from under her running feet and crashed into the pounding surf far below her. The cliff side was sharp and ragged, and loose from years of unstable slides. The stones that had rolled and shifted from the most recent one made the pathway before her difficult, and she fell several times skinning knees and ankles alike.

The creature she was dreaming about was behind her, crashing through the underbrush on horseback. What it was, she couldn't see clearly, however it was not one of the Aelfs she was accustomed to seeing around her village. Nor was he of Shapeshifter blood. In fact, he seemed almost feral in nature, but then again, that could be a result of the perspective she had. She was, after all being chased through the meadows of her childhood, and taken on a journey, that had taken an entire lifetime to reach the sea. She could hear the horses panting, and almost feel their breath on her neck. Yet they were still not in range of her eyesight, as she looked back almost dreading what she would see this time. In the past, during the different seasons of the moon, she had witnessed several images of these strange creatures, who pursued her relentlessly through the landscape. Sometimes they were simple creatures that looked almost benign in nature, while other times they were pack wolves, choosing to track her from the ground instead of on their steeds of black frothing madness, who accompanied them somewhere in the background.

She wasn't afraid of the horses; they were just following orders from the lunatics that rode them. At times she almost pitied the animals, as they were pushed beyond their limits, and could be seen to almost collapse in their final push, as the dream completed itself and the threads of consciousness woke her up. She had stood on the otherside of that realm and watched the curtain of mist hover in place obscuring her view of them, until they too vanished into its watery substance. When next she turned around, everything was back as it should be, and she was sleeping somewhere in the trees.

She had spent many years delving into the reason of that thread, and wondered the moment she had made significant improvements in her majikal studies, if there had been a way she could manipulate its movement to wake her sooner than what was ordained. However, the more she studied its behaviour, the more devious it became. It had made her crazy in the beginning, but soon she realized that the dream was inconsequential, and the threat itself became the lesson.

The lead rider was not far behind her now; she could hear him crashing through the trees at the headland, on horseback. He was trying to prevent her from traversing the unstable cliff-side that crumbled all around her; she ran as though her life would come to an end beneath the enormous hooves of the stallion he sat upon.

This time the horses were gaining headway; two riders split off on the far side of the ravine, trying to find their own way to prevent her from disappearing amongst the hedgerows outside the forest edges. The horse and rider nearest her was still soaked to the skin, with not even a shadow of a break allowing them all to catch their breath — continuing the nights pursuit of her across the Sageheathers. The moon time had taken her through the torrential rains that had followed the previous day's tracking frozen footsteps across the heather; the very heather that lay buried deeply in the snows of its winter.

She had wondered briefly, why the nights' dreams were so vastly different in their climatic atmospheres, from one night to another. Then, as the years had passed, she realized it was her own mind that was creating the image of those differences. On nights when she was calm, there had been nothing but warm sunny days in those dreams. But, had she had a fight with one of her brothers, it reflected in the chilly winter months that they chased her through the colder landscape. Had the creatures from her dreams actually been real, she was sure they must have wondered what kind of creature she was in the outside world, to have so much turmoil in her life as to cause the climatic changes in their pursuit.

This night was different again. This time they had actually come very close to reaching her on horseback, positioning their horses between her and the sea that was just behind her running body. This time they had actually called her by name, and as she turned in response to the surprise, she had seen the hidden trail off to her right heading down to the ruins she had tried so hard to find, on previous years of searching. Still, she had no memory of knowing the riders, and any past memories of knowing who they were had quickly flown the coop, as it always had in the past the moment she had spied the trail she had been searching for. It was how the world of the dreams worked. Despite the exhaustion that was settling inside her to the very core of her bones, she was somehow able to stay ahead of them, and move into this newly found part of the dream, that felt no longer part of what she had created.

Again, the dream changed; she heard the conversation between the rider on the cliff side just behind her position, and the ones up on the ridge, as she made her way down. This time she heard the panic in their voices, as she moved towards the trailhead that would take her to the castle that had always appeared just out of reach; one which they had for years purposely prevented her from getting to. This time she had seen the colour of the black stone rampart of the once beautiful but long gone castle, which had lain in ruins about the edges of the rocks at her feet. It suddenly appeared out of the mist. And this time the dream changed, for the first time since it had arrived in her sleeping world.

Somewhere inside that mess of broken stone was the cavern she was looking for, but each time before she could reach it she would awaken, never able to reach its interior footholds, or the things that waited for her in what she presumed was her safe harbour. She had been told of this very harbour by some form of creature in another dreamscape, which ran perpendicular to another, on those odd nights her shippel brain couldn't seem to remember the proper opening-sequence to this one. It would have been odd for someone not accustomed to the crossing over of dreams from one day to another. However, it had happened on numerous occasions when she had been small, and unable to distinguish between reality and fantasy, and as the years had gone by she slowly grew more adept at translating their function.

She had tried to find refuge during last night's dream, but the riders had managed to track her during the storm and move between dreams, and she was now scrambling hel-bent for leather towards the castle's outer walls like a stray kitten, moving slightly ahead of the pack of wolfhounds who were ready for an appetizer before their main meal. She let the dream run its course, and then as if by majik, she saw the pinprick of light leading her towards what appeared to be another outcome.

Tonight she had made it further into the dream than she had ever been before, and this time when she let it take the lead she began to decipher the actual smells and sounds surrounding her in the dream's outside air. She smiled at the cleverness of her discovery, and had almost made it down the broken pathway within the rock wall itself, when all of a sudden she felt like she was falling. She screamed, thinking she was about to impale herself on the sharpened rocks that lay all around the base of the path, when she hit something soft. Instead of feeling the pain of actual rock pushing itself into her skin and splitting her brain in half, all around her streaks of daylight seemed to drift into her conscious mind, and she realized she was actually back in her Fey form again having fallen out of the very tree that the Panther was now preening himself in, high above her. She giggled with the arrival of that knowledge.

The Panther watched her land, disturbed only for a moment, growled at her for disturbing the morning air, then carried on preening a previously ungroomed section of his fur. It was then that she noticed as she picked several sheaths of grass out of her hair, and blew the few strands of loose stragglers that hung in her eyes skyward, that morning had arrived above her in all its coloured form. She whistled through her teeth, grinning at the transference the cat presented her with each time his fell away, bringing her around to her own two legged form.

The motions that were taken to return Sibrey to her own consciousness, were well thought out for an animal that would appear to not have much in the way of intelligence of the affairs of the current Fey worlds. How wrong the others were, in thinking that they were the superior race. For, walking among the trees that seemed to have actual substance was another kind of life; one that moved all, inclusive of anything that was in sight of their two-legged companions, who thought they were the only ones with true sentient thought. The Panther race refuted that opinion; for, the Panther's actions brought to mind that she didn't always have to think, to ask it. She knew, without thought, that she must have been free from any danger, or the Panther would never have booted her out so unceremoniously at such a precarious and important juncture in her dream. Mind you, she should be mad, but how was he to know what was going on inside her head? All that mattered was that his job of keeping her safe, had been achieved.

Just to prove the point of this exercise, the Panther decided it was time to move along. He got up and vaulted from the branch he was resting on, disappearing back into the dense growth of the trees that shielded Sibrey from capture, without a backwards glance. Her friend would not stray far, they never did, but he would return to check on things within his own pride first, and then once more track her signature in case she needed assistance from him again. She checked to make sure everything had returned to its proper position, then followed suit.

She looked up at the sky and watched the Mauntra's light filter its morning rays, which were flickering and touching her face through the sheltering foliage she now found herself within. It was not as thick as it had been the night before, when she had first found herself entrenched and fighting for her freedom. But, she knew that having this mode of transportation didn't always, okay ever, give her control over its directional mode of undertaking. Sometimes she could be miles away from where she had wanted to be, only to find that the Panther would backtrack itself into the same place as she had been in the beginning, making her start all over in complete frustration. But, at least she had the element of surprise on her side. To those that had expected her to be coming from another direction, she would always be shifting in the air around them, far from their actual line of sight, and already having found the means to arrive behind them as she proceeded to kick them in the ass.

That thought made her smile. So many times her brothers always had the upper hand, before she had moved into the forest with the Panther clan and her studies had changed her way of listening. They soon learned not to be so smug. But she had more important fish to fry this time, and if she wasn't careful that tracker was going to be on her before she had time to take advantage of the added benefit of where the Panther had dumped her off.

Before she left the area, she noticed the remains of a deer that was slung over the upper branches, and a drop of blood actually hit her in the face, making her blink. She brushed it away without thinking, smearing it across her forearm and began to take stock of her surroundings. Then quietly she brushed herself off, gave thanks to the Goddesses, and was off on her own before the sphere of light high above her had taken its rightful place in the morning sky.

CHAPTER FIVE

A meeting of Minds

Soren groaned and put a hand to his forehead. From the angle he was currently lying at, he couldn't tell whether he was inside or out of the hovel. He remembered suddenly, without any warning, keeling over after drinking the damn coffee the old man had given him and then, that was pretty much it. His vision as of yet, was still not fully functional. In fact, he felt as if he was still not altogether on this planet, as several things that he knew lived and moved in the spaces in-between seemed to drift in and out of his conscious mind. It took the better part of a minute before his mind finally verbalized enough of his awareness to his head, letting him make sense of his confinement. It was just starting to get bright out, but the lack of birds singing, or the lack of loud birds singing, brought him to the conclusion that he was still inside the old man's hovel.

He heard the chains long before he felt them, as he stretched his legs. Then, when his sight gave him enough vision to see them through his blurry orbs, they seemed to disappear somewhere up around his back, giving him just enough mobility to move from one position to another. But try as he might, as he fought in his somewhat lucid state, the awkward thrust of his limbs proved they were tied with more than just a steady hand.

Majik had that incredulous property of stunned arrival, each time he awoke from its wrath. The more he tried to remove his limbs from their incarceration, the more his chains fought every muscle flexion that rippled along his spine. He finally gave in to their apparent control over his body, as something began to shift in his confinement. However, it was just not enough to let him fight his way to a sitting position, and he gave up frustrated by its arrival. It would appear the old coot relished in his commitment to the Human, and for whatever reason had him; a bloody resident, hog tied down on the floor by the fire, like a common criminal.

He now felt the heat that was just starting to find its way onto the backside of his head, giving him that warmth that he had first assumed was the Mauntra beginning its morning assent through the outside trees. His head was still full of odd sensations, not unlike a solar storm crashing into the atmosphere of the planet, instead of something as benign as a simple fire crackling away in the background. When the sounds finally drifted into earshot, he heard the fire pop and sizzle, sending relief through his tense muscles. It occurred to him that the sound was nothing more than some kind of resin, that the flames had suddenly discovered in the kindling's interior core, and not some wormhole of an interdimensional shift-point that was sent in to destroy him, on the outside of voided space.

No, the star had nothing to do with where he was being held hostage inside the Sprite's hideout. He found he was rather excited to discover that fact. For, at least then he could eventually beat his way out of this newfound situation with his fists; whereas, before, he highly doubted he would arrive safely on the other side of some celestial event that was hel-bent on his kind's destruction; courtesy of the Human race the Sprite had decided to give refuge to.

He started to find that funny, then it occurred to him that he was still on the losing team, and this wasn't where he had intended the day to begin. No, that he decided, he would take as more of a lesson in coffee decorum. From this day forward he thought, when a Sprite offers you a wee touch of drink in their home.... don't drink the damn shit without visual backup! Mind you, the name home wasn't something he would use to describe this hovel. That was negated by its having anything to do with a creature that would stir up the entire planet, and send the resident Fey into hand to hand combat. This place had nothing whatsoever to do with an actual, ordinary residence. No, on the contrary, it was anything but a home; for, lying on the floor stuck, with your hands tied in chains up to the middle of your bloody oesophagus, was not what he would like to think of as someone living in an ordinary home.

So, from his vantage point, he watched the dust particles dance across the floor of his prison cell, or what he thought were dust particles, in his limited vision. They moved together then separated, and he realized they were actually something he was creating all on his own, and not some involuntary response to karmatic majik. He could feel his legs jerking across the old dusty floor, as he tried to find a better position in which to lie without hurting his back and neck. But, try as he might, the chains were interfering with his ability to move into a more comfortable position, and he only made it worse. He tried to find enough wind to clear the particles, and ended up blowing dust through his teeth where the damn particles surged upwards, momentarily blocking his vision. He blew them away from his nose after sucking them in by the mouthful, giving him the sensation that he had swallowed an entire rabbit, flipping fur and all.

When he tried to move to prevent them from repeating the process all over again, his upper body seemed partially paralysed by whatever herb the Sprite had crushed into his drink. All he succeeded in doing was thrashing his legs back and forth, which resulted in moving his body closer to the burning fire. Yeah, that was brilliant, now how long before his actual body decided to retrieve enough heat from the back of his head, and find what it needed to combust out along the bones of his spine? Brilliant wasn't the word he was looking for.

He heard the two of them moving around him, before the smell of cooked food assailed his nostrils, then their pretence of ignoring him simply pissed him off. He had fought long enough, trying to find a position to relieve the tension from the chains before he spoke with more violence than he had anticipated; it suited his needs just the same.

"I'm going to kill you, old man, when I find out what you bloody did to me!" he hollered at wherever the old Troll was. At this point in time he couldn't decipher if Tamerk was indeed a Sprite, or something more along the lines of the reef Trolls that lived out along the edge of Kartouche Island near Tameron.

He tried to move, only to discover the creature had him not just hog-tied as he had first thought, but actually chained to the fireplace. Soren's vision began to clear, and as he watched the two of them come slowly into view, it appeared the old coot was having none of this, and was getting breakfast ready for the young Human child who was sitting, staring intently at him from across the table. "Get me out of these, old man!" Soren roared, struggling with the irons, showing his immediate rage.

"Or you'll what, beat me to death? No, that's not it, is it?" he shouted loud enough for Soren to hear him plainly. Soren only growled. "Ok, our Human friend here then." the old man cackled away, not having any of it from the angry Aelf, who had suddenly woken up pissed off in their home. "No, I think not; you'll have some breakfast, then you'll hear me out, and then, depending on your answer, we'll talk some more." He smiled and did a small dance along the wood floor, all the while putting food on a plate and placing it on the table in front of an empty chair set out for Soren.

Tamerk went over, got a stick, reached into the hot stove, and lit his pipe then deposited the burning firestick back into the belly of the stove. He then walked over to the chair where the boy was also eating his morning meal, and drew his old body into a sitting position alongside him to eat his own breakfast. Once done eating, the two of them continued to talk to each other ignoring the Aelf completely, as the Sprite settled back in the rocking chair staring at the Aelf, while Soren roared in the background for almost another full twenty minutes.

The boy ate slowly, and kept watching Soren each time his head moved into a position that appeared to be crossing his line of sight, and then would avert his eyes, carry on with his meal without glancing back up, until Soren would give up and look away. That amused the old man. He chuckled and whistled some old verse that was in his head, moving about the interior room fiddling with various things. Soren continued to bellow and holler, trying his best to make a nuisance of himself, which only proceeded to make the child wince at his vulgarity. As for the Sprite, he ignored Soren's constant blustering, and finished up the morning chores. Soren finally stopped moving, and spoke with as much sarcasm as he could muster.

"What do you want, old man?" The old Sprite looked right at the tracker when he answered.

"You'll find you're Shapeshifter soon enough, but when you go and you face the Humans in your war, I want you to take this boy and give him back to them. He needs to be with his own kind, not some gnarly old...what was it you called me? Oh, yes, there it is; a Reef Troll." Soren winced, as one of the links on the chain suddenly hit one of the nerve endings along his left wrist and dug its heels in.

"Bloody hel, stop that you old fool! I haven't got a clue what you are, you just keep moving around my field of vision, changing your appearance. As for the boy, not a bloody chance old man, now let me go!" he yelled, almost foaming at the mouth. The Sprite turned and pointed his newly lit pipe in Soren's direction, ignoring what he said.

"You need to promise me you will take him home before I let you go. Or you can sit, chained up 'til the frogs come home, for all I care!"

The boy stopped eating and listened to what the old man was talking about. He had been agitated, watching the exchange between Aelf and Sprite, wearing the look of what appeared to be a caged animal that had given up after years of being trapped in his confinement — then just as suddenly, deciding it was nothing to do with him, released his attention to the fight. He resumed eating. Soren, completely caught off guard by the Sprite's request, spoke again.

"I don't do favours for Humans, and besides, why are you even bothering with the filthy creature, after what they did to us during the war? Where have you been living, under a damn rock?" he said, with as much venom as he could muster.

"Hum," the old man pointed with his pipe, to their surroundings, "yes, that would be it exactly, in case you don't remember where you are Aelf, I live in the rocks." Soren only growled at him.

"Why don't you just hit it over the head, and be done with it? That way we can both be on our way, and the damn Human can rot, when you roll it out of your house and down some ravine!" The Sprite hooted, and slapped his knee.

"Oh my, such language in front of a little child. Does your mother know you eat with that mouth?" Soren didn't react to the comment; instead he took a different approach.

"How in the hel can I do what you ask? He'll only get me hurt, and be in the bloody way. Besides, his stink will send the resident Fey ahead to warn others of my arrival and it will get us both killed." Soren went to turn away from the conversation, when it occurred to him that something else had been part of the statement the old man had first asked.

"Wait a minute, you talked about two things that you shouldn't have the privy of knowing anything about! How is it that you know about the Shapeshifter I was tracking , and also knowledge of this ones kin coming, old man?" Tamerk snorted and Soren could hear his thoughts beginning to form a statement about putting more than just coffee in his morning cup; Soren frowned and began again. "What else did you put in that coffee, you old toad? Damn it, now you're in my head. You really need to stop that. It's not right reading someone's thoughts when they haven't given you permission to do so." The old man didn't answer him, and they both just stared at each other, not moving or breathing for going on some time, then got up and poured himself another cup. He held up another for Soren, who took it upon himself to refuse, shaking his head. "Not bloody likely."

The old Sprite sat drinking his coffee, in the silence following Soren's question. "Suit yourself tracker, but it is awfully good if I don't say so myself." He got up, leaned down by the fireplace, and put in another piece of firewood, stoking the embers into life and watching the flame take to the new addition with more of a purple hue than the last time – Soren only groaned louder.

"Well, this old toad as you like to put it, knows many things my friend, one of which is that I know they are coming, and this," he pointed to the Human boy, "is one of the reasons they are." The old Sprite looked a little unhappy, but kept on talking, all the while stoking the fire and smoking the pipe that was almost finished its draw of burning tobacco.

Once done, he banged the pipe against the stone fireplace, as Soren sneered, hoping the old man would get within range of his teeth so he could bite him, despite his head reeling with questions, that he kept going over and over, within his mind. Tamerk sidestepped Soren's head, and walked over to the boy, gently taking the hand of the child still eating silently, watching the exchange. As soon as the boy finished with his spoon, the old man, with his weathered palms turned the child's hand over with as much love and affection as one that raises one of their own kinfolk. The boy looked up, surprised, but Tamerk nodded his head and the boy let him continue. He showed Soren what had been placed beneath the skin, holding it up for the Aelf to see.

Etched on the palm of that hand was a marking, a birthmark that had been placed, as if by some unseen artist at the time of his birthing. It was marked in green dye, circling around the Sanskrit word for joining, within three intertwining circles. Interlaced among the circles were the engraved markings of the word Dracore, carefully sculpted within the branches of a thorned leaf that held them all together tightly nestled inside.

Soren went pale, and cursed quietly under his breath. He had only seen that drawing once in his lifetime, and that had been when the King had given them a description of the female Shapeshifter. She had the same birthmark on her other hand, with another inscription engraved on her palm!

"Bloody hel," he whistled at the sight. "I'll be damned. This better not be a trick old man, cause from where I'm standing, it won't fare well for either one of you when I get my hands on you." The Sprite started to laugh.

"From where you're standing Aelf, even the mice are taller than you!" He pointed to the very creature slowly starting to stalk the Aelf's hands, chained behind his back.

Soren hollered at the creature and kicked his legs in its direction, which only caused a cloud of dust particles to accumulate, as the mouse moved like lightning towards his fingertips, and crawled upwards along his back to sit happily atop his shoulder. Soren yelled his head off trying to knock it off, while the creature, for some reason continued to annoy him, digging its paws into his shirt, and hanging on for dear life.

Tamerk tweaked his finger in the Aelf's direction, and the mouse disappeared, only to reappear on the table, where the Human was still finishing his meal. The boy grinned at the rodent, looked at Tamerk, and took his hand back talking silently with the creature like he was holding some form of insane conversation with the mouse, that no one else could hear.

'What is in the drinking water on this side of the continent?' whispered Soren to himself, as Tamerk smiled at the boy and the child grinned widely at Tamerk's gift. "Great, now I have a Sorcerer to deal with." Soren groaned, looking up at the two of them with disgust. "Life doesn't get any better than this," he said sarcastically to no one in particular. "All right, I'll play

nice, just get me the hel out these old man, and I'll be on my way." Tamerk shook his head.

"Not before you hear me out."

"Fine, just get me up. Then, if I don't like it, I get to leave without him, and you will allow me my peace." Tamerk grinned.

"Well now, my Aelven tracker, if I could just believe you. However, I will remind you that if you go back on your word, our little whiskered friend will not be the only mouse in the house." He pointed to his previous demonstration as Soren sighed.

"Fine, it's a deal, now what's for damn breakfast? It's the least you can do for me after kicking my ass from the Ocean of bloody Souls, to the Saltwater shores of Kartouche."

The old man released the shackles he had around the Aelf, without touching a single part of him. Soren moved to the table and reached for the food the old man put before him, leaving the coffee aside in case the old guy was still pissed at him for treating his Human pet like a ragdoll. He was hungry, and his stomach's need, outweighed the possible chances of getting food poisoning again from something the old man had spiked the food with. He sniffed it, as he brought the spoon to his nose, and smelled nothing but warm delicious food; as for the mug the old Sprite passed toward him, he declined shaking his head. Instead, he chose the whiskey that now found his hand. It wasn't until he had almost downed the entire glass, that he realized the old man had already gone ahead and poured it silently for him, knowing that coffee would no longer do the job, with the new bits of information rattling around in his brain. Damn, had he not learned his lesson? He needed his head examined; why had he gone and done that? For all he knew, he was about to end up ass over cast-iron stew-pot upside-down on the far side of the floor again. But, before that happened, he had to admit, Tamerk made a fine tankard of spirits. Tamerk looked through his newly lit pipe at the Aelf, and started to laugh. '*Yup, a very fine tankard indeed.*'

Back at the edge of the clearing, another of the Dragon-riders was about to enter the playing field. He arrived and landed close to the area where a particular plant came to grow and feed along the clearing's borders. As he flew in, he could see its foliage hovering high in the air, lapping up the morning Mauntra and hissing at the others trees that came within range of its very large and lethal leaves. It stood to be one of the biggest Caspian Beaver Claws that had grown this side of the Tuatha's encampment. It had reached its maturity several thousand years ago, digging itself into the bank; thereby giving it full breathing rights among the other plants in the vicinity of Tamerk's woods.

Symin was that rider, and he took both of the Dragons to that particular clearing, and after asking their approval to wait, he ducked into the small woodland and found the plant hovering above the trail waiting for him where he had been told to proceed along with extreme diligence.

Many of the plants and fauna that lived in Tamerk's woods had taken on somewhat of a personality. Tamerk had bred into them these unusual differences through long acting various climatic interferences and majikal polarizations within Leberone's world of shifts. Only a few creatures in existence in the Fey worlds had even heard of this particular species of Net fungus, let alone had any experience with its rather disgusting habit of snaring unsuspecting travellers and consuming their flesh. This one had been approached along the trail at a very bad time of the day, and had already come across a few horribly intoxicated Gnomes with nasty depositions. And was in the process of dealing with a rather large mess of bruises, courtesy of their drunken punches, alongside several broken and battered flowers seen wobbling alongside the wounded stem.

It could normally be found on a good day, to be rather obnoxious in its spoken language to any hapless travellers that happened to have the bad luck of choosing the pathway it had decided to grow over top of. But today, it was completely in a state of total inebriation, due to the vast amount of mead the Gnomes had consumed themselves the previous day, and having eaten every alcoholic bit of the Gnomes except for their shoes and the tips of their pointy hats, it was in no mood for sober company as it spit wooden slivers of those shoes out the backsides of its teeth.

When Symin had finally landed, various parts of the Net fungus branches from its stem to wispy air roots had been lying about the trail, seriously drunk and in a state of absolute disarray. As he got closer, it burped rather loudly as it thrashed around in this drunken state, sending mammals from out of their hiding places scurrying into the forest beyond.

THE BEGINNING

The directions the old Sorcerer had given him were not difficult to follow, but he now wondered whether this meeting was due to chance or something a bit more cynical from the mind of a madman and not what he had led them to believe.

As it would happen the previous day, all the Dragonlords had arrived back at the appointed area of the shift doorway, where the stones that they were supposed to use to transport themselves back to Tameron had always been located. The stones instead, had been strangely absent, and their trip back to Tameron would have to done the hard way — through good old fashioned Dragon wing power. This would add several hours of unnecessary travel time onto a very delicate time schedule, and leave the Dragonlords not much leeway in their arrival time back home.

All of a sudden to add to their confusion, a weathered old creature had appeared in their clearing from somewhere over the western rise, calling to them to wait. He had hobbled along almost hidden from view, making no sound that had been audible to any of them, until one of the Dragons had got wind of him, and sent up an uproar causing the Aelves to come armed to his location, where he had promptly disappeared from sight with a sudden rush of wind and a yelp. They were just in the midst of going over most of the ground work to find out just what they were dealing with, when once again he arrived within their midst with a small Elemental Sylph on his shoulders. By that time it had become mysteriously dark, and when he had reappeared this time he looked very different than first he had shown himself to them.

He was taller and appeared more intellectual than first observed. He spoke with a tone of authority and directed the conversation like that of a general speaking to his troops, while the Sylph fluttered in and out of flux beside him. He told them Soren was being held captive by a source that would not release him until the time when the stones would reappear the following morning. At which time one of their warriors with Soren's Dragon joining him would then be allowed to come for him, and take on a small passenger that would be travelling along with them. This was non-negotiable, whether Soren decided to cooperate or not; the warrior chosen would be expected to take on the passenger, regardless of how difficult the task was to be. In the event that Soren chose not to cooperate, he would be released unharmed – minus the ego, after they had gone on without him to return to the Dragonlords as he saw fit. The stones would then be returned for travel, and all would be as it once was. If, at any time, they came to search for Soren during the night, the Dragons would all be returned to their homeland and the connections severed for all time between them and the Aelven nation now living on this planet; however the passenger was going whether they liked it or not, and they had till morning to decide which one would go and get him.

Dyareius remained quiet, thinking this over, knowing full well the others had no idea just how dangerous this creature really was, as the Sorcerer looked from one warrior to the next, waiting for some word of their decision. The warriors had only taken this in for a moment, watching with interest to see what Dyareius would do with something that seemed to be nothing more than a threat to their intelligence. He stood there with his eyebrows raised, in that true Dyareius fashion; in the past he had been known to play with his food, before killing anything that could be put immediately out of its misery. But that was not today. Finally deciding what his approach might be, and deciding to test his accuracy, he slowly drew his sword and pointed it at the old man as the others in turn found ways to repeat the gesture.

The old man smiled a big toothy grin and watched the Aelves arrogance shift towards his own smaller frame; then he watched it flicker into life as it flowed and drifted towards him with confidence, still unaware of what he was, before he lifted up his staff. He smiled with the reaction it produced, immediately changing the iron of their swords into nothing more than plain wood, and their arrogance immediately shifted gears as they watched the swords they cherished most, turning from that beautiful sheen of pure Mercorian steel, into nothing more than simple dead twigs. To make matters worse as they looked from each other to the Sorcerer with abject horror, the swords slowly began to disintegrate and crumble into dust, blowing away into useless particles of what best could be described as nothing more than expensive sand. The Sorcerer then released the Sylph on his arm, and it circled the area taking the particles on the ground into the air; it flew away leaving nothing in their place to show they had existed.

Dyareius smiled, while the others began hollering behind him. The Aelves were used to tricks, and they had no fear as of yet for this creature so he let them vent their frustrations in the only way they could. Dyareius then stepped back letting it unfold watching him, as the old man continued shifting things around them. The others were able to sidestep most of the majik he created, but Dyareius didn't interfere while the majik continued all around them, and watched him pull the water molecules out of the peat bog between them and the Dragons behind them. The moment that illusion began to take shape, he quietly sat down waiting for the majik to run its course knowing there was nothing he could do until it exhausted itself.

The Dragons themselves had immediately chose not to participate, as they leapt into the sky the moment the old man had started using sorcery, and could be seen making their way onto the far side of the clearing well in advance of the old man sending out the first initial threads of his majikal might. Which in itself should have been the Aelves' first clue, but they had been so busy arguing about what to do about the stones' disappearance, that the general consensus of the warriors really hadn't paid attention to the Dragons' migration, away from where they normally would feed. Dyareius noticed, but chose to remain quiet knowing he would only hasten the outcome. Symin on the other hand, had done his best to remain hidden, but once the swords disappeared into other things naturally occurring within the environment, and Dyareius hadn't lifted a finger to direct them otherwise, he stepped out into the open to prevent another flurry of activity directed towards discovering his whereabouts.

The moment arrived, then was instantly served up like a platter full of steaming hot coals, within that time frame of Quist's actual eye contact with the old man; all thirteen Dragons in attendance disappeared as birds of prey, and momentarily could be seen soaring through the evening sky. They flew as falcons straight up amongst the clouds, until their bodies began to dissolve and float towards the ground changing into nothing more than ordinary leaves that flittered down and landed amongst the forest floor, all mixed together with what was already settling from Tamerk's majikal tirade.

The leaves from the trees themselves were now indistinguishable from those starting to fall from the sky, joining the occupying space of their predecessors. The Sorcerer, now identifying the one Aelf amongst the group of riders who had tried to hide himself away from his sight who could undo all his work, took the one rider who could help him in his deed, and centred his attention on him. The Aelves gathered themselves together, bringing Dyareius to the forefront of their little band of Dragonlords, snarling against the realization that they were suddenly without the very things that made them impervious to his volatile conjuring of majikal substances. But the Sorcerer dissolved the energy burst that was Dyareius's own signature, separating it from the others and taking it into the mist he had created, all the while cackling away at the wind as he too disappeared.

"Come morning, all shall be revealed, sleep well my Aelven brothers I have what I've come for." And he promptly took their leader Dyareius along for the ride, disengaging Symin's power right from under the Aelf's nose.

Symin felt it leave the moment the old man disappeared, as they all stood within the clearing looking at the mist floating above the ground, and then down at the leaves which held the molecules of the now fully dematerialized Dragons, resting within the ground. Nothing further needed repeating, as the intent had been fully understood by all present. All they could do for the moment was wait, and come up with a plan to execute come morning light if things didn't go as planned. They talked amongst themselves long into the night, and came up with various ideas, but it was to be Symin who would lay the groundwork for Soren's rescue. It was him, and him alone, that recognized just who the Sorcerer was, and come morning when the Dragons had been reinstated and the stones returned, he would be the one to go and retrieve Soren from whatever he had got himself involved in, and return their brother by whatever means necessary.

Sleep would be long in coming, as each of the eleven riders no longer had the luxury of taking any bit of that particular sensation into their tired bodies. But before they could resist that thought, the mist that still hovered around their encampment settled around them, knocking them out cold without their permission, resulting in a sleep that put no dreams inside their tired heads. Symin had known what that mist could do, and had taken himself to a position when they fell, to produce the smallest amount of damage to his body as possible. The others not so lucky, had literally dropped where they had walked, as he was unable to explain to them what was about to happen, for fear of exposing the truth of who he was; he could only wait as it slowly lowered itself to their current positions.

When it wore off, sometime in the early morning hours of the next day, Symin awoke first and turned to watch the daylight come, hearing the hum of stones exactly as if they had never been disturbed, followed by the sound of Dragon wings stretching and flapping along the bone ridges of their leathery backs. He quietly watched alone, as the majik dispersed in the morning rays that stretched along the ground behind him, with all the snorting Dragons grazing nearby sounding like all was as it should be had they never encountered the majikal spirit of the old Sorcerer. Everything else soon returned to normal, as each of the warriors in turn began to stir beside him, and the day started once again, without delay. It wouldn't be too long now, until all would be revealed anyway, but unfortunately now was not the time nor the place for that truth. One day soon the Sorcerer and himself were going to have to have a little discussion, and when that day arrived, the old man was going to be on the other side of the continental drift, as his majikal ride could literally be forced into retirement without him moving a single muscle to re-enact it.

To anyone else, the scene would have appeared like nothing out of the normal morning time routine. To the Aelves that saw the old Sorcerer, this was far from any normal routine; they quickly scrambled to get ready for what was about to transpire. The Dragons appeared happy and none the worse for wear, having just spent the evening and overnight hours lying about as a puddle of leaves. Even the jump jaw crickets sang happily in the morning air, quite oblivious to the goings on of the night before; Symin had checked. He made sure even before he left, that all is how it should be.

But Symin was a bit worried; not because of the situation Soren had got himself into, he knew that was not the issue here. Soren had been in worse circumstances; he had always made it through on previous missions, no matter how difficult they had become. It was the other reason that Symin knew why he was the one chosen to attend, which was really on his mind. He knew others of their group were just as good at what they did, it's just that Symin had a secret, and Dyareius knew that if Soren had truly screwed up, it was Symin alone that would make it through to get him out.

It was this that made him a little uneasy; he didn't want the others to get hurt, if he had to use his gift to pull Soren out. The others would find out who he was eventually, and that put him a little more on the cautious side of things. To show them who he was before his time, could prove disadvantageous to his situation on this planet, and send others to hunt for his own kind among those that lived nearby. His approach would need guidance, and the situation Soren had gotten himself into would require patience. Both of which could prove fatal, if not handled properly; he would use the majik of his kind only if he really had no other choice, and only if the damn Sorcerer returned it in its entirety.

The men started to break camp, preparing to go onto Tameron as soon as Symin returned, if he was able to get through the void without incident. Both Soren and himself should be able to meet them before the Mauntra met its Venus. Hopefully all would go according to plan, and he wouldn't need to activate the right that Dyareius gave to him without thinking.

Symin was antsy, and could hesitate no longer, as the rest of the Aelves began to make their way to where the Dragons had been grazing at the edge of the field. He prepared himself to retrieve both Dragons he would need for the trip. He quickly caught up to them, just as the group had suddenly stopped short of the field, with Assha holding them back. There, in the middle of the path, were the missing swords that the creature had stolen from them the night before; some were half laying, others half standing, but all of them were there in their entirety, woven into one of the most ornately intricate designs he had ever seen. Yes, this was going to be an interesting pursuit.

Symin had seen that pattern many times in his lifetime, but only once while he had been billeted here on this world, and never so ornately designed. They were patterned in the shape of two circles mixed amongst the local vines and flowers, those which had been picked and folded into the bits of moss, like someone was designing a piece of artwork out in the depths of the forest floor. Written in dirt alongside the artwork, was the Sanskrit word for "joining". The group went quiet, as Assha started to move around the strange site, cautioning the others not to move ahead as he looked closely at the way they had been set into the mainframe of the entire piece. He pointed to Symin sighing, as he looked towards the face that already knew what was coming.

"This is for you, Symin," Assha said to him, looking tired. Then, as an afterthought, one that perplexed even him, he turned away to retrieve his own sword, with the words drifting along the wind as he walked away. "You, my friend, will know the reason soon enough."

Symin bent down to pick out his sword from the foliage — the others had already left. He had stayed riveted to the spot longer than he wanted to, as each in turn slowly retrieved their weapons while he remained lost in thought. He watched them retrieve their weapons, even knew what to expect as they did so; however it felt like it was happening in slow motion, as the moment the swords were touched and lifted from the work of art, it dissolved into nothing more than generalized scrapings that one would find resting on the forest floor, after a storm. Assha felt his concern but left him to his peace, that peace would soon find more questions than answers as he moved to begin the process of extraditing Soren's from the tangled mess that had arrived and singlehandedly kicked their asses.

It wasn't until he was airborne that the true meaning was further revealed; for, down below where the other Dragons still continued to be unaffected by the evening festivities, was an enormous Sanskrited emerald rock formation, double circled and shining in the morning light with the Dragons grazing away without a care in the world, right smack in the middle of it. Off to the left, where they had spent the night in camp was the triple helix sign that gave them protection from whatever the Sorcerer hadn't wanted them to see. No wonder they couldn't see the stones, they were blinded by the placement of rocks forming the double helix; it wasn't majik at all, but good old fashioned witchcraft. The sly old fox! Symin smiled at the sight, and carried on to the place of meeting, as the others moved back to the camp, waiting for his return. 'Sorcery my ass,' he whispered and blinked out into his shift.

The Aelves on the ground had been watching the two Dragons slowly fade from their solid imagery that gave them life, and straight into transparent particles of air, when, through the stones' central compass points, Dyareius came walking back into their midst. He shielded his eyes from the intense light that came from the shift of Symin's transfer, and moved forward into the mixture of male voices speaking with one another all at once, in the confused morning light.

He explained to them how he had found himself alone shortly after the Sorcerer had taken away the Dragons from the skies, preventing him from communicating with them until morning. But, unlike the others, his assurances from Tamerk had been given with an oath that they would be returned with the Dragons, come daybreak. He had waited alone, throughout the night, beside the campfire that both parties had simultaneously occupied, at the very same space and time, but on very different planes of existence. The others had spent the night around the very same firepit, without seeing or being aware that he was within reach.

The evening hours had gone by a little more slowly without Dyareius assuring them the morning would be a creation of newer beginnings. It appeared that by separating the two from each other, Tamerk had taken away the means by which they would have finally come into the realization that they could theoretically have found a way to get past the mirage to locate Soren easily — Phaetum's twist would have given that to them. Had they done so, it would have prevented Tamerk from taking the time he needed to bring the Aelf back to his original condition. The specific condition that was neither conscious, nor loudly screaming at Tamerk to restore him to his upright position, after Tamerk knocked him out and had him chained to the firepit. Tamerk needed the time so he could talk some sense into Soren, and at this particular moment in time, he wasn't so sure he had actually accomplished that deed in its entirety.

Dyareius watched with the others, as Symin's molecules reversed his position and headed directly into the beginning of his shift. They would wait for word from him, whatever it was, and then they would have to formulate another plan of action. Somewhere, someone had more to do with what they had been told about the Shapeshifter, and until Soren and Symin returned with their passenger, they would just have to patiently wait to find out what they as a group would be doing about it. Dyareius turned to ready the riders for their arrival, and stayed in the clearing to check on his mount, while the day began to stir and the Dragons tweaked their ears to what had been said alongside the words they had heard that the others had not.

THE BEGINNING

Symin pushed through the threads of jump, landing near the location that the old Sorcerer had given him mental directions to, the very place where he would find Soren alive and probably very pissed off that they had not formulated a rescue sooner. He located the plant easily, as it tried unsuccessfully to swallow a phoenix that flew just a little too close to where its head was currently resting along the upper limbs of another tree. When the bird exploded into flames, causing the plant to suddenly become a little more sober, it still couldn't function enough to focus on the Dragons that suddenly arrived within its line of sight.

Symin could smell the Tameronian whiskey that had spilled along the remains of the Gnomes it had just ingested. The plant tried to feel its way towards where it thought the new arrivals had landed, only to have Soren's Dragon bite it on one of its tap-roots that had side swiped the Dragon, in a lame attempt at recovering his dessert.

As Symin slid off his Dragon, he reached around back of him and threw it a flagon of Kendoffalous ale about the size of his arm, which he had brought specifically for it, and carried on down the trail, leaving the Dragons to fend for themselves. It caught it and had it digested before he even left the main trail. That trail wound around several huge vines not part of the previous plant, each as deadly, had he not been anyone other than himself walking in these parts of the woods. He smelled the wood smoke long before he arrived within the thicket, and watched for anything further the old man had lying in wait.

He watched the smoke as it curled up and rose from something that resembled a chimney, intertwining with various parts of different bark that had been deliberately placed into the shape of an old tree stump. Symin moved to the side of it, knowing that it was anything but a simple tree. But took the steps anyway to view the structure from a different direction. The stink of majik was all around it, giving it the appearance of ritual creation, one that for those considered to be of lesser Fey intelligence, it would appear to be something it was not; point proven immediately without a single moment of hesitation, he watched it snarl and snap at passing bumblefied insects, just as he moved cautiously through the last of the trees. He concentrated on his position then moved to assess the ground before him, placing the sword he carried into the sling along his back, deciding it would be more than useless after yesterday's demonstration of events.

He checked the knife that he carried within his boot, adjusting it to be within reach, in case he had to cut Soren loose in a hurry. Coming through the shift, things had a way of moving about and not being where they had initially been put. Just to prove its point as he closed his hand along its hilt, he realized it had shifted again, and was resting slightly above the area where he had last put it. He closed his eyes and listened; something was close, but he couldn't find the signature of its host, and it moved on.

He opened his eyes to reveal the iris that had slid sideways, and watched the shadows that seemed to move everywhere at the same moment. Something shifted again as he stopped to smell the air, and once again moved away before he advanced inside the ring of trees. Even the wind felt different, like it was taking on a life of its own. The Elementals that lived within the trees around his home village where he had grown up, had that same influence on him. It was that little bit of alien mystique that made the hair follicles stand up on every pore on his body.

The wind picked up something that smelled familiar, but things had a way of travelling through the air from different areas; he needed to be extra vigilant with his assumptions. But, his nose picked it up again; this time it was coming from the area that resembled something almost comical, belonging to something with the signature markings of a Tetrine toad. What was a toad from Naunas doing here? He smiled, smelling the distinctive aroma of coffee, along with the luxurious scents of other morning odours that meals normally pair with. No, not a toad then; at least he didn't think the Tetrine variety were into that particular vice. But, coffee it was, and it was wafting from the interior of that home built for a member of the amphibian family.

Again he smiled, listening for something, but not a single sound passed through to the outside world to give him any indication that there was an Aelf still living and breathing on the inside. He would be going in blind. Whatever was waiting for him knew he was here. He rested against the backside of the nearest tree and caught his breath, closing his eyes, waiting for a sign, and feeling almost sick. The wind shifted ever so slightly, and then, just as he caught on to why he felt so uneasy, he heard it move.

THE BEGINNING

"Ah, Symin," the old man cackled, "so good of you to join us." Symin whirled towards the voice, knife moving into his hand, but he was too late! He had been shifted inside the hovel without even feeling it. The sensation of queasiness overtook his lithe body and dissolved him into majikal particles. He realized just a moment too late, what had happened, and dropped like a stone the moment he rematerialized, crumbling on the floor by the fireplace. The knife in his hand rolled onto the floor away from his reach, landing at the edge of Soren's boot.

"Yes, where were we?" The old man smiled at Soren, who watched him pick up the blade before Soren could reach for it himself, and place it on the stone hearth, still snickering away. "You damn Aelves seem to have a thing for sharp stuff." This time Soren laughed at the insanity of the comment, while watching his friend slowly get his bearings — opening one eye, then speaking to the voice that he could hear, but not really see.

"Soren, you all right?" Symin grumbled from the floor. Soren got up and patted his friend on the back.

"Shifting's a bitch when you're not a party to it, eh old friend?" he turned to Tamerk, laughing. "He really didn't feel it! You were right. I would have laid stones on that one. Come on, I'll help you up." Soren still laughing, moved to give Symin his hand.

"Nah, I think I'm going to stay here for a bit, get my bearings, you know find a wife, get married, raise a family, then freaken die," Symin groaned loudly leaving his face to rest along the wooden floor, while Soren stated to roar with laughter.

"OK my friend, I'll just be over here having some breakfast. Call me with the arrangements for being best man." As Soren walked back to the table, Symin could be heard rather loudly grumbling.

"Get that food away from me before I hurl all over your damn floor." At this, the Sprite merely laughed, as Symin continued on uninterrupted. "When I'm dead, old man, I'm coming for you."

"When you're dead," replied the Sprite, "I'll be waiting!"

"Yeah, about that," said Symin, rather sarcastically, "humour is really not your strong point, old man. Best stick to finding something that will better suit the ass kicking I'm about to bring your way." Tamerk merely grinned at the two riders.

"My, my, my, temper Symin. Really, I thought you were more methodical when it came to this kind of majik." Symin grimaced slightly, feeling the effects start to turn his head into a full raging flurry of blinding pain.

"Yeah, about that, the silent ones are much more dangerous than the mouthy, so I'd put a lid on it old man before I'm forced to do something you're going to regret. Soren, I now leave him to you, I feel I'm about to give you something to bitch about." Symin groaned, and promptly was taken by the sensation of being rather sick.

It took the better part of an hour for Symin to get up on his feet. As soon as he was able to do so, the effects of the shift fell away, dissolving at his feet instantly and without the side effects of his recent sickness. Soren reached over and passed Symin a mug of steaming coffee laced with the whiskey he had been drinking.

"You might need something more than just coffee, he has a tendency to put funny things in the other and this might counter the effect of what he tried to do to me last night." Soren looked at Tamerk before continuing, "don't worry, this one I brewed myself." Symin moved towards the table to sit, but just before he did, he caught sight of the boy, as Soren poured another dollop into the steaming mug.

"What the flipping hel is that doing here?" Symin yelled, almost losing the contents of the mug, as he stepped backwards, knocking his chair over. Soren at that moment in time, had tried to get out of his way, but only succeeded in tripping him; he then landed almost directly in front of Tamerk. Now remember, Tamerk had not been in his true form, and the one he currently was using was instantly interrupted by Symin's energy. The illusion he had been able to keep up for those present, momentarily sent him into another illusion that Soren had not previously seen, one that Symin had seen last night – the old Sorcerer. Tamerk sidestepped to the right, moving out of Symin's way, and right into the path of his true form taking the full brunt of Symin's wrath.

Tamerk froze time using a time Goddesses energy bits he had been stealing, trying to keep Symin from registering his true identity, as the being came out and lit up the room. Symin only caught a glimpse of it before he locked all of them in a somewhat diluted time dilation, until Tamerk was able to contain it. Revealing his true image for only a split second had not been enough time for the others to adjust their eyes to what he was. For Symin it was more than he needed; he had recognized exactly who he was, in an instant.

As soon as he was able to contain his signature and reattach it to the image of the Sprite, Tamerk unfroze what had been rendered still, and the room returned to its normal time frame. However, Symin began to grin at his deception, while he instantly reverted to the image that Soren and the boy had grown accustomed to.

"How did you find me, old man," he said, under his breath, just before everything returned to its proper time. Unfortunately, the question would go unfinished and unanswered by both of them, as the unexpected appearance of this highbred being Symin had seen, instead of the majikal Sorcerer from the woods, didn't even make him blink compared to the Human child sitting on the other side of the table, eating his breakfast in relative silence. "The Humans, they're bloody here?" He turned to Soren, choking on what he had been able to swallow of his coffee, before stepping away from the table and spitting it sideways, making a landing along the edge of the table top.

"No, it's just the one," Tamerk smiled, watching the coffee laced with whiskey make its way down onto the chair leg. "You want a pair of spectacles, with that coffee?" He got up and threw a rag at the Aelf, nodding towards the slowly spreading stain that ran along the floor. Symin growled at the old Sprite, then purposefully threw it back, choosing instead to smear the growing pool of dripping coffee into the wooden floor, eliminating it from the bottom of his boot.

"And you, old man, something tells me you're not a Sorcerer at all?" he said, with relative accuracy, just as the others seemed to be picking up the conversation from the far-side of the room after it had more or less returned to its normal energy readings.

Symin grinned at the motion of his foot leaving a wide stain along the floor, when suddenly it began to grow warmer. He looked down just in time to see Tamerk try to set his foot on fire. "You're trying my patience, old man, is that all you've got? Seems to me you're lacking something in the way of individuality, old boy." Tamerk snorted while Symin tried to put out the flames along the leather sides of his boot.

"Hum," said Soren in the background, now coming out of his apparent freeze. "Didn't expect a floor show with breakfast, but carry on you two, there's still enough whiskey in the flask for me to make a considerable dent in it, without the two of you getting your hands on it." Symin turned to his friend, watching his face to see what Soren had seen or heard.

Apparently all he had been concerned about was the whiskey, and hadn't the slightest idea why Symin was staring at him. "What, I can't drink while you two have a pissing match?" He looked from one of them to the other, watching something that seemed to be just on the edges of his memory. It quickly left his conscious thoughts, and he couldn't for the life of him remember what it might have been, and didn't have the energy to go chasing it.

Tamerk directed both of them back to the conversation at hand, looking Symin straight in the eye, and nodding at the bottle of whiskey Soren had latched onto.

"I'd say have at her, old boy, and as far as you are concerned," he looked to Symin, "I do believe, had I appeared as my own self, you would have come after Soren right then and there. Am I not correct in my assumption, Aelf Symin?" Symin shook his boot, extinguishing any chance of actual flame taking hold, glaring at him.

"Seems like you like to play with fire, old man. One day someone's going to call your bluff and you're going to get burned." Tamerk shifted positions slightly, giving everyone, other than Symin, protection from another shift variance he now threw at the air within the room. But this time Symin was ready for him, and grounded himself into the dirt at his boot heel's hidden inner core. He balanced himself and pulled the shift movement out of the air, sending Tamerk slightly sideways, in the full out action of his second assault.

This time Soren was paying attention to what was going on, and yelled at the both of them to quit it. This time, they had an audience, and he told both of them that their little demonstration of each other's testing of wills was starting to get in the way of someone in the room, who was not privy to their reasons for attack. He pointed at the boy, who had been watching the actions between the two of them with growing apprehension, which was beginning to have a greater effect than the two of them causing the imbalance.

Symin switched his train of thought, and followed another line of questioning. "Did it ever occur to you my friend, that you were also part of an elaborate hoax, and that the imprinting you have given the boy was meant for another?" Tamerk stopped in his tracks, turning towards Symin, and started to laugh.

"That may be true, but something tells me you are not being truthful when it comes to finding a way out of this predicament, without abiding by the arrangements we had agreed upon." Soren instantly stopped what he was doing, and looked back and forth between the two of them, now noticing the difference in the air that had shifted almost all the smoke from the firepit outwards. The smoke now encircled the outside doorway, forming into something that seemed to be impenetrable. Alarm bells started to go off in his head; he grabbed onto Symin's arm and yanked him free of what was about to happen next. Tiny tendrils of smoke wafted into the cottage's interior entranceway, forcing their way up the back of Symin's hair, and tried to get a strangle hold on his neck.

Symin quickly freed himself from Soren's grasp, and then caught the back of the smoke's trail, reversing its direction. He glanced back towards Tamerk, with the beginnings of an idea forming in his mind.

"You didn't do this, did you?" Symin queried. This time Tamerk intercepted and caught the back end of another ring of smoke being sent in Soren's direction; stopping its tracking mechanism, before it left the boy's hand.

"Nope, the boy has learned that one all on his own." Tamerk hollered scrambling to get things under control, just as the boy began to pull all the air out of the room.

"Crap!" shouted Soren, looking up just in time to see the boy's eyes had turned a burnt shade of yellow and the irises had gone from a simple Human Child to that of Fey within no more than a few trilla-seconds. It brought all of their attention around to watch, as the energy within the room started to build and reach its peak.

"That's not right," Symin yelled, just as Soren flew to the other side of the room, as something hit him full in the chest, knocking him with nothing more than a nod of his head.

"How in the hel does a child from earth have that kind of knowledge trapped inside his brain?" Soren wheezed, struggling to his feet, only to be knocked down again, as Tamerk moved in one full stride, with his pipe still held within his teeth, and caught the boy just before he crumbled to the floor, collapsing, and everything reset itself as it was.

"What in the Goddesses have you been teaching that child?" Symin directed his question towards Tamerk, who gently laid the boy down, bringing an ear to his chest to make sure he was still breathing.

"The question I have, is one that needs just a little bit more breath than I currently have," wheezed Soren, "but it would be more along the lines of, how in the hel did he do that?" Soren tried to scream at the Sprite.

"Beats me?" Tamerk said under his breath to both of them, looking somewhat concerned, as he continued to monitor the child.

"Human children don't have that kind of capacity," Symin yelled again, shaking his head. Tamerk ignored both of them until he had found Ryyaan's heart, pumping strong and firm, beating deep within his chest wall. All the same, it was now considerably lighter than its erratic behaviour of just a few seconds ago.

Tamerk called Soren over to give him a hand lifting the table, which had been knocked over in the cross hairs of him going down. Once that had been righted, he was able to bring the boy over to the small cot that was his across the other side of the room.

"I hate to bring this to your attention," Symin started to speak to anyone that would listen, "but this child is no Human, or at least not like one that I have ever met. So, a meeting of like minds needs to occur before we can begin to try and figure out what just happened. Or, I think Soren and I need to be going on alone, without the child as first agreed upon." Soren heard just the tail end of what Symin had just said, responding not very favourably in the process.

"What are you talking about? That child is coming nowhere near the Dragonlords, after what just happened here. He's bloody dangerous!" Tamerk looked at Symin, but it was to Soren he directed the next statement.

THE BEGINNING

"I told you it wasn't going to be easy."

"Yes, you did," said Soren, "and I told you that we as a group would need time to discuss this, but once again you forgot to mention that he had a bloody gift that would directly put all of us in danger." Now Symin had something to say, and jumped into the middle of it all.

"If you had just allowed me to come last night, all this could have been prevented, but no, you had to bloody wait until morning to get your point across. So, what now my friend; what was so bloody important that you couldn't let me come last night?"

Tamerk looked towards Soren, just as the boy had started to come out of his state of unconsciousness, and tried to inject a bit of humour into the telling of his reasoning, as he tended to his young charge.

"Your tracker friend," he moved his head in Soren's direction, "was a little tied up at the time, and had you arrived before he was awake, it would not have gone in my favour." Tamerk laughed with his crackling high pitched laughter, as the both Aelves stared in disbelief at the crazy old Sprite and nodded.

"You got that right," they said, in unison. Symin was not the only one that was not amused; Soren stood there looking ready to hit him all over again, but had not even got the chance before Symin carried on with his little rant.

"Not after you took the stones and made the Dragons disappear, we weren't," Symin responded, with dripping sarcasm. Soren turned to Symin, spilling whiskey along the edge of the table top, not even trying now to get it in his mug.

"He what? The Dragons are gone? Where are the Dragons, Tamerk?" He smashed the flagon down hard on the table, to make his point. "We need the bloody Dragons, you old fool!" Tamerk ducked as Soren threw his mug almost full of whiskey, before the information Symin had could pass his lips to pacify the situation. He watched his friend then drain the contents of the flagon straight from the bottle in a single gulp, then it too, was thrown straight at Tamerk's head — both missed the target. Soren compensated without a change in stride, reaching for Tamerk's neck instead.

"You Aelves really like to judge a fellow before letting him finish the reasons for his story." Tamerk's huffing continued on, while he tried to duck out of the way as Soren lunged for him and missed. "They're back, or didn't you notice when Symin arrived in the skies overhead? I put things right, as soon as it got light out, so your friend here could come and get you and bring another Dragon. Yours, by the way, not one that just happened to be flying by at the time. May the Goddesses give me patience; you Aelves really have a flair for the dramatics! How did any of you actually make it through the Dragon wars without a sense of humour? Does it not occur to any of you that something bigger is happening here?" Tamerk turned towards the Human boy. "Ignore them child, they know not of what they believe," he said as he ducked out of the way, coming dangerously close to one of Soren's fist.

The child, for some reason, had decided not to repeat the previous events; instead, he chose not to move at all, staring at the two of them from the cot, while Tamerk began to make preparations for the coming day. Both Aelves kept an eye on him in case something started to happen and he changed his mind, preferring to kill them off by other means. Symin spoke to Soren, trying to let his stomach catch up with his feelings of queasiness, making everything lurch about inside. That was the second time he had that feeling, like something wasn't as it should be. When they returned to where he left the others in the camp, he was going to have to have a private chat with Assha. Maybe he would have better eyes on all that Symin was feeling, with this strange flighty sensation that felt as if the ground was ready to swallow them all whole. He needed to respond to Soren's question about the Dragons, but it had to be there, without Tamerk messing with his mind. He moved over towards where Soren had started to get his things together; before he had time to start talking, Soren yelled over at Tamerk.

"Where'd you put my damn sword, old man, I'm not leaving here without it." He looked at Symin, who tried to pull him aside. "What? I want my sword, don't you?" Symin laughed at him as he continued to rant. "So, what's this about the Dragons? Go on then, spit it out." Symin knew until Soren had his sword right in front of him, everything that he said would be going in one ear and out the next. Tamerk pointed to the firepit, and Soren reached up above by the cast iron pots, and brought it down to rest alongside his arm, resuming his seat at the table, looking at Symin, who had poured him a mug of steaming coffee from the pot Tamerk had just

THE BEGINNING

made. "I'm not drinking that shit without whiskey taking up the majority of space, and while your being so generous give me back my damn knife!" He slid the whiskey back over to Symin, who traded mugs with him, and poured a large amount into his mug, replacing the one they had smashed.

"Ok now, smart ass, you want to hear this or not?" Symin yelled at him and settled in to tell him what he had seen from the air. "When we got back into the air and shifted, before the whole village decided to be stupid and take the Dragons on, and a little after you took off to hunt for the Shapeshifter, we had a small hiccup in the plan for getting back to Tameron." Soren drained his mug, wiping his chin with his hand and pushed the mug back over to Symin, seeing that he had already drunk his mug of the coffee, without any ill effects.

"I think coffee will be fine," Soren said, after Symin had started to fill his mug with more whiskey. "Looks like he didn't put anything in it to kill me this time, but I'm watching you old man." He started to smile, as Tamerk came and sat down, also filling his mug with the hot brew passing him the knife he took in the woods. "I knew you had it you old fart!" Tamerk smirked as he put it in his boot. "Damn tree, my ass!"

"If I'd wanted you dead Aelf, that would have been accomplished by now, trust me!" He saluted Soren, and Symin carried on talking, ignoring the both of them, as the story moved across his lips into the inside of the room.

"That is where you come into play." He looked towards Tamerk, continuing on with his thoughts. "Seems like someone didn't want us to go anywhere for a while, so he took the Dragons away, like I said. Then, this morning we woke up to them feeding alongside the camp, just where we had left them the day before. It's weird though, now that I come to think of it." Symin looked as he talked, in the direction of the old man, to see if he could see even a small tick or flinch of his facial muscles that would give him away, to prove he wasn't just feeling uneasy. "When I went to go through the stones, I found that the whole area that we were camping in was covered in this emerald moon design, that only could be seen from the air."

Tamerk had got up and walked towards the cot where the boy was still lying, staring at the two of them. Symin continued. "Just like what we were told the Shapeshifter's ha-nd..." he stumbled on his words as Tamerk picked up the boy's left hand, showing the exact same design on his palm. "It's the same?" Symin asked, as he squinted to see from the angle he was sitting at, across the room.

"Seems to be a good way to strike up an awesome conversation, knowing there is two of them, don't you think?" Tamerk said, without sarcasm.

Tamerk almost got hit again, but the mug that landed found only airspace as it bounced off the far side of the wall. The old man moved faster than anything both Symin and Soren had ever seen, as he went quickly out of throwing range, still talking away to the two of them. When both Aelves settled down again, Tamerk moved towards them, leaning along the edge of where they were still sitting, striking up a newly lit pipe. He hesitated in answering them, as he drew on the spicy tobacco and breathed in the smoky essence, while he thought it through. "I didn't make the insignia upon the ground; it's been there for centuries. When I found the boy, and discovered he had the same design on his hand, I thought it only fitting to take the time and stay near it. I just never got to the reason for it all." Symin looked a little sceptical, raising an eyebrow while Tamerk carried on with his tale. "Then you showed up, and well, you know the rest," he said quickly.

"The rest? Really, you're going with that explanation? Why is it you make things very hard to believe, with anything that comes out of your mouth? It's like, as you're talking you're making it up as it comes." Symin spoke aloud. "Every time I seem to think I know what's happening, something else comes along. I don't get any of this; it feels like nothing is as it's supposed to be." He shrugged and left the table to pace about the room, glaring at Tamerk each time he passed him at the table.

Tamerk ignored him, and stopped talking for almost a full minute. Then, as if he had been waiting for some kind of theatrical applause, said a whole lot more than what either Aelf had expected from his cracked and dried out lips.

"Your mind is as you believe," Tamerk said, "you," he turned to Soren, "ought to spend more time thinking with your own head, instead of throwing things. Your friend here is correct in the timing, as things that are not said are happening in real time, and he has a reason for his not being able to trust me." Symin started to say something, but Tamerk held up his hand.

"Please let me finish. It will come out in the moment that is to be chosen, and not before, as it is not my tale to tell at this time. The travelling that you three will do, will be fraught with dangers; listen to that voice of caution, and it will save your lives." Soren groaned, and the Sprite glared at him. "This child is far more important than any of you can know, protect him with your lives; it is possible that doing so will save us all. Remember my words, if you can do that then you will live a life with honour, please trust in that which I have said. But, for now we must say goodbye and prepare for your leaving."

As both Aelf and Sprite were talking amongst themselves, the young boy started to become exceedingly more nervous the closer they got to leaving. The old man went to him, and began talking with him in whispered tones. It had come to deciding between the two of them, who would take the boy. It quickly became apparent that the decision had been made already, when it was time to leave, as the child who had gotten to his feet had moved towards Symin alone, glaring at Soren in a rather odd way.

The four of them moved towards the clearing where the Dragons had been grazing. The Aelves could see how difficult the road before them was to become, when the child saw the Dragons for the first time. He literally froze stiff in his tracks.

"Well at least we still have that going for us, if all else fails," Soren said. "We'll just sic the Dragons on him, if something gets in his head once more, and he tries to kill our asses again." Tamerk ignored the Aelves talking nonsense; instead he gently knelt down before the child bringing the boy towards his knees, and told him to stay put. Then, without a whisper, he walked to the edge of the clearing where the great beasts were grazing, speaking in the old Tantarian Dialect of the old world — watching everything and nothing at the same time. The two Dragons stopped their grazing and slowly made their way over to Tamerk, listening with great intent with heads cocked to one side, and looking back and forth between the four of them.

The air around the glen started to change, starting with the wind picking up, and followed by the guardians of the four great airts appearing unexpectedly from out of the ether, out along the boundaries that Tamerk called to. Each popped their heads in out of the clouds, rushing downwards to join the molecules of the wind forming a tunnel cloud, with their long necks stretched downwards at an odd angle. As it continued to whirl and whipped itself into being, the guardians bodies shot out from the other side, and joined their heads to form a larger, more prominent cloud, that sparked and sizzled with the added flecking's. Tamerk continued to shout his majikal spell, listening for the final level of his ritual to be heard above the whistling fingers of wind, and stepped back away from where he had begun the majik, to allow the energy to find its mark without the interference of his own fragments that had been nearby.

The air around the feet of the Dragons began to change — like the image you see filtering around the edge of a hot stove, and slowly made its way up to cover the entire body of both Dragons standing there. It wavered in the morning air, drifting loosely along the ground until it reached the edges of their ears. Molecules began to shift, then change their forms, as they drifted in and out of their reality, and back around in a fluidic dance of falling snow and ice. Faces and bodies swam in and out, a wing twisted inward, and the sound of popping noises could be heard all around them, as mystical music filled the time of their arrival. The wind picked up with the branches making noises in the woodlands overhead, and the rustling of leaves tore through the open meadow, exposing the light of a new species that had previously been the forms of the two Dragons, only moments ago.

Soren could hear the rushing noise of a brook growing louder, and the molecules turned into a form of mist as the whirlwind picked up speed, passing right in front of their toes on its path into the woods. Moving with purpose through the mist, as it began to dissolve, two beautiful woodland Sprites stepped forward from out of the great beyond, and right onto the ground at their feet. The boy gasped at the sight, as the Sprites stretched out their arms, hugging Tamerk as he clapped his hands in glee; they approached the two beings standing waiting for them. On the other side of the glen, sheer bewilderment was the only thing currently sitting on both Symin and Soren's faces, as each could only stare at what had once been the black Dragons they had called their own.

The Sprites hugged Tamerk, in a bracing of hands, elbows, and tiny fingers, while the two Aelves just stood rooted in one place, with looks of shock and disbelief replacing the looks of bewilderment on their faces.

Tamerk turned his head and winked at the boy, who smiled broadly from Tamerk to the two Sprites, ushering the boy to quickly join him in the open meadow.

"Quickly child, I cannot hold it for long! Come and meet Tansar and Quist." The boy moved towards Tamerk, but held onto his hand, holding back like a shy child. "You see, not scary at all. They are Dryads of the earth clan Kyafth. Tansar, Quist, meet...oh dear," Tamerk turned to the child, "I'm so sorry, but we never named you."

Tansar turned to the child, reaching out for his cheek, and tussled his mop of long black hair. Putting his finger on his upper lip, he pointed to the boy.

"I think we shall call you Ryyaan." He turned to Quist, and slung an arm around him. "Sounds like a good earth child name, what do you think?" Quist just grinned.

"So, shall we pretend to be Dragons again, and take you for a ride, young Ryyaan?" And, as quickly as all that, the two Wood Sprites stepped back into the circle Tamerk had created, that lay waiting out along the edge, and waved heartily to the youngster and disappeared into the mist. Before the Aelves could pick their jaws up from the front of their open mouths, and wipe the stunned expressions from their faces, both Tansar and Quist began to revert back into the huge black Dragons that they had been, only moments ago. Symin whistled.

"That, my friend, is going to take a whole lot of talking, to explain to the rest of our group!" He turned to Soren, and punched him in the forearm. "I'll let you do it, shall I, because seriously, that's one warped bit of information that I can't for the life of me explain away."

Soren opened his mouth to actually speak this time, yet only a little squeak arrived in the attempt. He tried again, and this time the anger followed from deep inside him and started to fester.

"Tamerk," Soren pointed to the two Dragons. "What in the world was that?" His temper was beginning to find its place again. Tamerk started walking towards them, cautiously with regards to the placement of Soren's arm and fist this time, and quietly replied.

"That, my two friends, is what the black Dragons actually are, in their purest form." Symin coughed into his hand, grinning at Soren.

"It would seem things really aren't what they appear to be, after all." He looked at the Sprite as he added the next sentence. "Anything else, old man, that we should know, or are you just going to let that one slide and let us go into the bloody blue yonder, with more unanswered questions?" Tamerk ignored him and continued to smile from one of them to the other, with this stupid grin on his face.

"They're Wood Sprites?" Soren roared, flipping his knife from his hand into a fallen tree stump. There was a yelp and a small Nixie looked up and disappeared into the trees. Soren's eyes followed the sound for a second, and then pointed to the Dragons beginning to yell. "You're telling me we're riding bloody Wood Sprites?" Both Dragons began to flap their wings, slowly rising up from the ground, and landed again, snorting with indignant laughter, obviously annoyed by his words. One of them started to whip around, and his tail came crashing down, almost knocking Symin into a tree.

"Hey, come on," he yelled at the closest one, "I almost got toasted. I'm not the one offended, you bunch of overgrown dogs!" Symin snorted, just before Soren started up again.

"We fought a war with them, Tamerk. How in the hel do Wood Sprites become war Dragons? It's ludicrous." The old man started to cackle, but quietly snickered, and slowly began to talk.

"You have to understand Soren, it's not their fault." Soren was pacing back and forth, a hand in his hair and the other on his hip. His anger had always been short to fuse, but this was more than he could stand. First the Shapeshifter, then he got knocked out, chained up, dosed, and now this.

"How am I going to explain this? I'm a bloody tracker not an insane Slaugh! I'm supposed to be bringing back a Shapeshifter, not a herd of freaking Dryads!"

"You don't have to tell them they're Dryads." Tamerk looked indignant. "They've been known as the Dracore for a thousand centuries. They are still Dracore. Only their soul inside, where the Wood Sprites hide is Dryad, Soren. Your clan doesn't need to know what I have shown you, at least not yet." Smiling, he turned to Ryyaan and said, "If this boy had not been here, you would not have more than likely ever known. They are still very much Dragons, in every sense of the word; the very Dragons that you fought with, side by side in the last Dragon wars, for Goddess sake. Look at them, can you tell me that they are not?" He looked at both Soren and Symin at the same time, as if nothing was different or had changed.

"But I'll know, as well as Symin," Soren roared, pointing to his friend. "It is something that I fear to keep. It's dangerous, old man. You need to at least keep us up to date, when these things come up, and bloody change." Symin nodded once, and then raised his voice in the mix.

"We are risking our lives after all, and it's not just our war Tamerk, putting what you said into play. It has to be both ways, if we are going to get through whatever is in store for us, and you know damn well something's coming, right?" He looked at Tamerk, who only shrugged.

"Why should we not tell our clan? They have a right to know." Soren pointed to Symin, who nodded at Tamerk. Then he turned back and looked at Tamerk, straight in the face. He yelled loudly in response to the old Sprite's nonchalant attitude. "WE, have a right to know! At least give us that!" Symin was standing silently, watching everything unfold. He spoke quietly and directed himself to Tamerk again.

"Old man," Tamerk switched his focus to Symin. "What does the Shapeshifter have to do with this, and why does Ryyaan, who is Human, and not even from this world, bare the same birthmark as she?" Symin spoke softly, away from the boy.

Tamerk sat down, and quietly tried to shift the attention from himself to the boy. "There are things happening before their time. You," he pointed to Soren, "were not supposed to be here."

"What do I have to do with it?" Soren hollered.

"Plenty, but be quiet please. The time was not to be, and has been rather rushed I'm afraid, and, for whatever reason, has chosen to descend upon us. You were not supposed to find the boy yet; his destiny is not written, and he's not from our world, or at least not from the world as you know it. It's as if this space and time threw him through the stones too early, and he should have been older before he was exposed to you. He's too young yet. Even you, when first you saw him Soren, what did you see?" Tamerk placed his hand upon Soren's heart.

"I saw a man," he replied, trying to move away from Tamerk.

"Exactly," said Tamerk, "he's out of sync with the surroundings. He should not be part of this, yet here he is. It was to be the Shapeshifter who held the key, and yet," he pointed to Ryyaan, "we seem to have two." He shook his head, and patted Ryyaan on the cheek.

"And the Dragons?" Symin said. "How did Wood Sprites become a part of this?" Tamerk brought his attention back towards Symin.

"The Seelies did this." Tamerk pointed to the two black animals, finally settling themselves down, and returning to graze closer to where they were standing. "That is what happens when a pack of bloody wolves decides to exact revenge on a species." Soren instantly returned to the present conversation, faster than he had wanted.

"Oh hel no," Soren said, protesting louder. "We're dealing with bloody Sith?" Soren swore. "This just gets better and better!"

Tamerk all of a sudden went blank, cocking his head and listening to the foreground. Symin instantly pulled a knife out of his boot, looking around to see what Tamerk had heard, while Soren moved to retrieve his from the stump. Nothing seemed to be outwardly wrong within hearing distance. Tamerk reached inside his jacket and removed an old smoothly worn crystal, from an inside pouch. He wrapped a piece of rawhide around it, and placed it around Ryyaan's neck.

"Quist says you will need this, child, it's a touchstone and it allows you to speak to them." He touched Ryyaan's temples. "You know, in your head." The boy held it up in the light and smiled, flashing it about in the rays of the Mauntra.

Tamerk then rose up and stood, turning to Soren. "Tansar wants you to know about the Witch called Kashandarhh. I haven't the foggiest if she's still alive, but I'm told she lived in the village of Kilren."

"Who's Kashandarhh?" asked Symin, putting his knife away, and looking up.

"Her mother, Kamera, grew up in Llavalla, and moved along the fault lines towards the Damonian Woods, sometime back." Tamerk continued, before Soren cut him off again.

"But, that's Aelven territory! What's a Witch doing with the Kancie Clan?" Soren looked at Symin, as Tamerk continued on.

"Her mother, although born a high bred, escaped there and I'm told she has a rather interesting background; should you be interested to hear. It seems she has some very unusual hereditary traits, which Kashandarhh her daughter has also acquired, and it is to one of these that she no longer lives in their isolated village. I'm also told that it was during this time with the Kanoie clan that she had met Kashha's father out on one of her more distant forays into the woods, out along the shores of Dead-Monkey rocks and that story, is the other reason she was forced to leave the Wick. You see, Kashandarhh's father is one of the Nereids that live out around Vaukknea Island and his heritage is of the Selkie descendants, which feed out on the Undinecis reef, along the west-side of a moving landslip they call home. All of this is important, should you need to know the history of who this Witch is, and who she will align herself with, in times that are yet to come. Furthermore, it is imperative that you remember all of this, should you find her, even if it doesn't seem of importance, in its telling."

"It seems Kashandarhh has a very unusual talent for foretelling things that seem to be rather relevant in today's world. Many years ago, she foretold a story of the rise of a new kind of Dracore. Those that you ride upon today are a known fact of what she was talking about back then." Soren lifted one eyebrow in response to Tamerk's story, and groaned rather loudly, while Tamerk continued talking. "If you can't find her, she's got kin somewhere along that ridge. Tansar says they'll tell you about her whereabouts, if she still lives. She knows stories of the Sith, that may be relevant to your Shapeshifter."

"How do you know she'll talk to us?" Symin inquired, pointing to both himself and Soren. Tamerk pointed to the two Dragons.

"I think they give her a reason to."

"I bet they do." Soren said, rather sarcastically, under his breath. "They give me the willies, just thinking I'm riding one of your damn cousins.

Tamerk heard him, and chose to ignore his ignorance. After all, he was neither Dryad, nor Sprite. But, that was all in the way you looked at things, and this world was full of creatures that pretended to be something they were not. All of them now moved off together, towards the clearing, while the Aelves talked amongst themselves, keeping an eye out for any sign Ryyaan might suddenly decide that they were going to be a threat. Unfortunately, that was not the problem they were about to face. As the group was about half way into the clearing, moving towards the Dragons, all of a sudden the ground around them started exploding upward, like small land mines. They were quite suddenly bombarded by hundreds of small artillery rounds, which came out of nowhere, causing thousands of dust explosions about the size of a pebble, from every direction. Looking down towards their feet, they realized they were surrounded by a small, barely audible army of Nixies, who were charging the ground that they were standing on.

All hel broke loose, as Tamerk cackled away in the foreground, dancing from one explosion to the next. "Time to go." Symin grabbed Ryyaan in one single motion and threw him up around his shoulders, not even giving the boy a chance to complain, as both Aelves began to run towards the Dragons. Soren swore, and tried to sideswipe a few with his boot, and landed upon Tansar, his demented little Dracore flipping Changeling, he had ridden on for most of his life. There would be no further argument about who they were inside all that skin for now, but come later when all was said and done, there was going to be some changes with regards to their lack of important knowledge.

All they could hear of Tamerk, in the hysterics of the situation, were peals of laughter, as he disappeared in the wind, and they could no longer distinguish him from the cloud of dust gathering higher around their Dragons' legs.

"That's what you get for pissing off a Nixie! Better get a move on boys, looks like you got yourselves a war to fight. Oh, and careful with Tansar's left wing, looks like the little buggers just bit him." He cackled away. True to form, the Dragons were thrashing about like the ground was on fire. No sooner had both Aelves leaped to their backs, the five of them were airborne, with Quist taking a final swipe at the Nixies with his tail, and sending about 150 of the little buggers into the lake. Still floating in the air, as they rode, was the old man's voice, as they were just about ready to go towards their shift. "Take care, Ryyaan, it's been an honour, child." And then they were away, listening to the beat of the wings flying through the clouds, as the hum of stones and the flicker of blue light met them airborne, changing their molecules into nothing more than a whisper of molecules and aromatic dust.

CHAPTER SIX

The Leviathan of Leberone

Sibrey smelled the lake long before she laid eyes on it. It lay inside the peatbogs, filled with rich loam that had filled the deep crater on the edge of the upper far ridge. It had taken her almost a full hour to actually come into range of its spectacular view; when she did, she was amazed to see its lakeshore sparkling away, with purple amethyst and turquoise green waters, while she continued to hunt the horizon for any sign of pursuit. She put up her hand to shield her eyes from the Mauntra's brightness, spying the snow peaked mountains of the Symarr Dragon Ranges far off in the distance, still deeply entrenched in their year-round snowfields. They were always beautiful at any time of year, but next to the waters of this lake, they now seemed to pale in comparison.

Her world was deep in summer here, but parts of Tantaris had glacial ice fields and weather fluxes that she herself had never seen before. She could smell sulphur in the air, and, adjusting her vision like the second lid of a Red Dragon Salamander, she spotted the place where the amethyst water turned just a bit pinker, farther along the west shore of the lake. That was where, she needed to be.

She stretched tired leg muscles still trying to adjust to the return of her Fey form, as she held her hand up to her face, allowing the other side of the lake to focus itself to her unusual molecules. They quickly familiarized to her form, and she internalized her healing ability towards her sore muscles, commanding them to remain perfectly still while they paired with her Shapeshifter bones. They released a certain chemical endorphin into her bloodstream and quietened down the cramping that came from transformation, giving her relief from the agony of moving from one shape into another, as they had done in the past.

She was thankful for that, as she moved closer to inspect the sandstone cliffs on the far side of the lake, now heavily foliaged in what appeared to be the ferns called Damsel Ariattace. At least, she assumed they were Damsels, but anything could really have been flowing down into the lace pink jasper boulders from this distance. However, whatever they were, they seemed to judge her peering from the far side of the embankment, and promptly disappeared in the rising steam bank that rose high up into the morning air. She squinted, trying to peer further into where they had disappeared, but it was to no avail and she gave up trying, turning instead back towards the old deer trail.

The entire place around her smelled of hot springs, along with a hint of something sweeter that filled the air around her nostrils. There were several smaller rocks along the ridge where she was walking, remnants of a slide that showed the trail further up to be a little more unstable than she had first thought. She'd have to find another route down to the lake quickly, before it gave way under her weight and triggered another. She reached for the pouch that was slung along her hips, and slid rawhide strips she carried within to the soles of her soft leather boots, to help her find her footing among the sharpened stones.

Water always smoothed away the aches and bruises that were associated with transformation, and in the coming days who knows how long she'd be on the run before another body of water came again to into her line of sight. She needed to make it down to the water's edge. At least on this side of the lake, she had a better chance of making it across. It could be a long time before she had this chance again; those chances were made even slimmer if that Dragon tracker had been able to keep up with the scent of her shift.

As she made her way towards a smaller more undefined section of the ridge, she caught a part of her left shin on a Cammond Berry thorn, and a small drop of blood welled up from the skin that had been broken through the scratch. It dropped onto the trail side unnoticed, as she continued on her way, unaware of the transfer. Upon reaching the lake, the scratch had begun to heal out in the heat, and she shed her clothing and slipped into the warm waters, diving deep within its depths.

It felt like rich chocolate, soothing and luxurious, as she floated for maybe no more than an hour. But time has a way of moving slowly when you aren't paying attention, and she needed to keep moving before she became too relaxed in this environment that she became complacent in her flight. To be able to take the body into the zero gravity, of nothing more than sublime liquid, was more than wonderful, and water so fresh and pure nourished the skin in ways drinking the fluid never seemed to achieve. The Panther had drained her of those minerals, and she drank deeply as she paddled outwards away from the edges, and into the deepest depths of the delicious lake.

Small ripples of water moved ahead of her as she made her way slowly to the other side of the lake, where she had seen the hot springs from the Cliffside. All felt right with the world, at least for the time being, but that could all quickly change in a heartbeat, if she wasn't careful. She quickened her pace; she would need to remain vigilant, even if she knew she had a head start.

She looked backwards as she swam, to assure herself she was still moving in the right direction. At this level in the lake, she could easily be sent off track, and she could end up further west than she intended to aim for. Nothing seemed amiss, and she continued on, not noticing the small amount of electrical energy she was heading towards.

She figured she was at least a day ahead of him, and if she kept up the pace, she could make up valuable time lost in the swim she had wanted to relax her body with. Nothing could be seen from any of the vantage points she could see through, and she continued on her way, unheeded by what apparently was hovering about surface level in the middle of the lake. Had she seen it, she wouldn't have perceived it as dangerous, for it didn't have any reading that she could decipher. It was just there, waiting for her like some blind benign spirit, waiting to hitch a ride as she moved through it without noticing.

In another part of the woods, Soren and Symin gave the Dragons their headway, going through the shift. The electrical charges of light associated with the fluid motion of transfer, meant that their skin felt like it had become alive, and was breathing on its own. The Nixies below, now long gone, seemed to have done little damage to Tansar's wing. Just encase something had been missed, Symin turned Quist towards Tansar's bitten wing, and flew sideways along both sides of his body, to check that he had not torn any of the horned tips which allowed him to push himself into the middle of their next shift-point. Everything seemed to be in working order, and Tansar was not favouring it in any way, as far as Symin could see. He gave the thumbs up to Soren, and both Dragons and their riders carried on unimpeded.

Ryyaan soon became lost in his own world, and seemed to relax once they had begun their ascent, discovering the hidden world of his touchstone's gift. The conversation soon became lost on both Aelves, as the boy seemed somewhat transfixed with his new gift, talking in his head with his hands intensely animated, and moving at such a fast pace that both Aelves soon lost interest in the long detailed world of the touchstone's domain. All they cared about was that their passenger was relaxed, and his gift was safely bestowed in a faraway place, deep enough inside of him and far away from where they would feel its wrath. He was dangerous, they had no doubt, but for now his body language showed they were not in any danger as long as he was relaxed and conversing with the Dragons. They intended on keeping him that way.

Quist and Tansar had relieved the Aelves for the moment with their conversation, and true to Tamerk's word, were obviously helping along with that details, keeping Ryyaan engaged and enjoying the flight. The challenge would happen with the arrival of their group amidst the remainder of the Aelven guard that awaited the trio back in the meadow. Funny how that amused Symin. He would have thought that the Dragons would have been the bigger obstacle, on their final arrival. However, things had indeed changed.

They finally made their way through the shift, looking to the outsider like they'd been chucked out of a pin hole, and then tried to fly silently into the middle of the clearing, where they said they would meet the others. It was not to be...

Greetings came on abruptly from the other black Dragons, who had been grazing upon the ground waiting. They suddenly began to wildly flap their wings and roared loudly at their arrival, making it look something reminiscent of Piranhas feeding on a Bull Cathor. It appeared Quist had sent news ahead of the child, and every bloody Dragon who had been within earshot had competed for position, all talking at once, to the sheer delight of the boy Tamerk had called Ryyaan. Even the wild resident green Dragons had flown into the area. Soren watched them overhead, blinking several times in stunned disbelief at the sight that greeted him, as they jockeyed for position. For, right in the thick of the others, and straight out of the old mythological stories he had heard as an Aelfling, was something he had never seen before, as they made their final approach through the tops of the trees and into sight of the riders on the ground. It was upon seeing this, that both Soren and Symin began to understand the complexity of what they now were starting to discover, that the Dragons were not the only creatures that would present themselves in the presence of the boy.

Meanwhile, the day before this all began: The Aelves themselves had set up camp to await Soren and Symin's arrival, making themselves useful by sharpening swords and generally doing things to pass the time, until both returned with what they hoped would be the Shapeshifter. An entire day had passed since Symin had left, and they had all agreed he would be most adept of all of them at getting to the bottom of whatever Soren's search had produced.

Symin, being of sound mind and level headed, had always found a way around even their toughest adversaries. He also spoke the true old Tantarian dialect, that, though having been lost among the newer generations of Fey youth, was still widely spoken in a few remote Tantarian villages and used more among the older outlying tribes in the more isolated locations. It would come in handy if they happened across one of these reclusive villages along their path, or if Soren had fallen prey to one of the old sects.

Sometime during the early morning hours, as they waited for their return, Dyareius the Aelves highest ranking Lieutenant had been awoken by the night watch to come and take a look at the skies. The Byanadorian Moon was still high in the western sky and would not be setting until dawn, which was still about two and a half hours away, by the look of it. But it gave them enough light to actually see what they had woke him up to see.

Far above them, a most startling sight started to make itself known in the pre-dawn rays of the coming day. That most unusual sighting began to reflect off the moon's light, as the fluorescent backs of the resident wild green Dragons could be seen filling the morning sky, in rather enormous numbers.

This was more than unusual, as these creatures could rarely be seen flying about the skies in singular flights, let alone flying in the hundreds. Dyareius looked up now to see the morning sky filled with all kinds of them, filling the skies and flying about screaming their heads off.

"They started to arrive about ten minutes ago, sir," said Cassmarr, as he nervously rubbed the back of his neck, watching the spectacle before him. Dyareius could see them dipping and curling their bodies along the ridge of the tree-line, screeching away as they moved above in slow wide circles in a search pattern he had often seen in times of war.

Below them, the black Dragons who normally would be showing displeasure at the greens' arrival, were basically ignoring the oddity, and calmly watching the numbers grow skyward, as they lifted their heads to chew the long grasses they had been feeding on. "Markus," Dyareius said, "stay within the trees. I'm not sure what's happening yet; let me know if anything else changes? I'll go wake the others." With that he turned away and walked back to the fire they had lit last night. The Dragons of the Symarr never mixed with the locals; something was definitely up.

THE BEGINNING

The huge war Dragons had always been given a wide berth by the resident greens, since first they had been discovered, deep within the most southerly range of the Symarr Mountains. To have even one of the wild ones show itself within air space of the black Dracore, was unusual. To see twenty or thirty was unheard of; to see three to four hundred was a cause for alarm, proving without a shadow of a doubt that something was definitely up and heading this way.

Dyareius woke the few remaining Aelves who hadn't already stirred from the Dragons' arrival and each of them moved quickly, arming themselves in the pre-dawn light. Each in turn, continued to watch the skies in disbelief, as more and more of the wild ones began to fill the brightening sky, with the initial warning that had awoken the Aelves to their aerial displays. As daylight began to find its birth, it brought with it the rays of the Mauntra shining through the limbs of the furthest trees, as more and more of them continued to fill the skies. As the trees silently witnessed the spectacle from below, stretching outwards, warming their bark in anticipation of the Mauntra's heat, high above, a single White Dragon could just be made out, joining the ranks below, soaring in from far above.

"Sir, look!" one of his men pointed to its position. Dyareius was floored. The Great White Dragon race lived far out in space, and occasionally one could be seen soaring along the edges of one of their last remaining moons, called Leberone. This was a first for him, for he had never heard of them ever entering Tantaris's atmosphere below the outer-rings of Tantaris's orbit. Instead, they could be found living within the weightlessness of Tantaris's biggest moon, and only one of those belonging to the tribes had been spotted there in recent years. Dyareius didn't even fully understand whether they could actually live within this atmosphere, and shivered to think what was about to begin.

"Symin and Soren had better get here soon," he whispered to whoever would listen, as they all watched from below in awe, as it slowly made its way into the airspace of the large collection of flying Dragons.

There was something big just out on the horizon. Dyareius could feel the flicker of its arrival just before something else began to erupt among the Dragons. It was beginning to get heavily congested, and everything with wings had joined the fray; a soft low moan began within the Dracore's encampment, out on the fringes in their clearing. It came across like a single rhythmic hum, beating low without finding its voice within the flow of the others in its wake. It quickly rose in volume, with the shrieks and screams of the wild greens growing alongside it, when, suddenly the black Dragons burst upwards in full flight, joining their ranks in the skies, as if it was nothing out of the ordinary and they had done this every day.

They now found themselves arriving into the skies, finding their wingtips touching others of their kind who glided and pitched willingly alongside them, without a single incident or fight erupting amongst them. This new vocalization of excited short quips and low humming noises sounded musical in nature, almost as if the ground itself had joined in with a harmonized accompaniment of Dragon-bells. Then, with a single burst of light, showered in electrical blue sparks, two more black Dragons arrived with their riders alongside their backs, into the complete and utter insanity that lay before them.

This was what Dyareius had felt, as every single Dragon that could fly surrounded the pair of them in their airborne world. There had been a few skittish greens who had nervously landed just before the new-comers had arrived. They could be seen instantly taking off, in a flurry of feathers and scales, setting off further alarm to the waiting Aelves that watched from below. The alarm had not come because of the deed itself, but had actually scared the daylights out of the closest Fey still watching quietly from within the trees, closest to the greens taking flight. They could be heard screaming in startlement as they scampered down the living bark of several of the resident Tree Morrigans, who had shifted right into visual range of several of their own riders. They, in turn, yelped with the discovery of the Morrigans standing so close to their position, and all around the vicinity, Aelves came to their defence in a show of force. Further concerning the wild greens who had delved deeply within the crowded airspace that was already filled to capacity, they careened madly towards the already well defined structure of the onslaught of flying Dragons.

But, although this seemed to be the start of a disastrous undertaking, it proved to be the beginning of an already well-engineered play, and all became caught up in the flurry of excitement that sang and purred with pure joy all around them, as the dangerous manoeuvre only proved to be a well-orchestrated instructional map of choreographed flight. From below, Dyareius and his warriors could only watch with anticipation mixed with horror, as the new additions careened their way through the congested skies, screaming their heads off in sheer joy, while they themselves sought the cover of the trees in anticipation of several Dragons crashing headlong into their vicinity.

The Aelves below, completely at a loss for words, moved instantly and leaned against anything big enough to hold them, in case a collision sent one of the Dragons spiralling downwards in their direction. The Morrigans simply vanished into the greenery of the forest beyond, instantly blending into the background, having seen what they had been summoned to witness. The Aelves simply watched in fascination, but a few grabbed onto whatever they could use as a shield, while feathers, quills, and scales flew down from high above, haphazardly landing wherever they happened to fall. Things had started hitting the ground on all sides of their encampment the moment the first Fey had slithered down the bark of their trees, as they watched the aerial display that was being performed above them explode with new life. This was nothing unusual with any winged creature flying in the skies above. However, nothing had prepared them for the several thousand pieces of quills that seemed to come out of nowhere, looking like they had been instantly pulled out of the Dragons' bodies by some wicked Puck out for a stroll, who started throwing them wily nilly around the field.

The Aelves hadn't needed to worry, and soon their fear of something happening was replaced with renewed wonder, and the supposed Puck never materialized, much to their relief. It wasn't too long before they found themselves caught up in the spectacle above, flying around the exact glen they had camped in the previous night. It was exhilarating to watch and something that they didn't get a chance to see often, being themselves the riders of those beautiful beasts, and never a casual observer from the ground. Their own Dragons passed by overhead, creating some of the more dangerous aerial displays, as each of the Aelves below now watched from a very different vantage point. In truth, it was out of this world, and before long they witnessed numerous newly formed flying strategies that they had neither seen nor heard of before, and each seemed slightly amused by their own Dragon's ability to out-manoeuvre the others around it.

It wasn't that long before both Symin and Soren's Dragons could be seen coming in from the far left, after they had completed several circles around the others who had parted to let them through. It was evident that they would be landing shortly as, far above, Soren yelled for Symin to watch out for the wingtip of Dyareius's mount, as he came almost within touching distance, nearly knocking Symin and Ryyaan right out of the air. He looked at the Dragon as it made eye contact briefly, watching for signs of the Dryad within. He saw only happiness, and it passed on by without further incident. He didn't know what he had expected, but whatever it was he probably would have fallen out of the sky had it even tried to wink at him.

Dyareius's Dragon manoeuvred at the last moment, sliding into a spiral roll that was quickly mimicked by Soren's Dragon, Tansar; all three rotated the 360 degrees and moved out of the way. The greens followed the new trick and soon all could be seen repeating the tricky roll, as they dived about trying to stay away from each other's bodies in the crowded skies, high up above the Dracore's landbound riders.

Nonetheless, with all the insanity of their arrival, it was the large White Dragon above all others that had made both Soren and Symin gasp with the sight of its arrival. They had not seen it at first; instead, as they made their way around the others, trying their best to keep from colliding with each other in the confined air space, they had come across it quite suddenly by accident, within the middle of their upside-down roll.

Their first view was of an enormous white body taking up half of the area of sky they were about to fly into. As they came within a hair's breadth of its outer bone-tips, they quickly shifted themselves, still upside-down, onto the wingtips of their mounts, closing both eyes and holding on for dear life, begging the Goddesses for safe passage in case it ended badly. It wasn't needed, and both Dragons compensated immediately through sheer force of their own will, actually getting the momentum to shift enough to the left, before they were able to squeak by within a hair's breadth of the huge talons that raked by their heads and ear-tips, as they felt the warm breath of the great Leviathan glide on by. They moved along the breadth of its body, taking a full five microns before they were finally out of range of getting themselves split wide-open and killed along its feathery flanks.

The great wingspan of its body frame was so enormous that even the black Dragons with their excellent flying ability had a difficult time not getting caught in the downdraft, as it moved off slow and methodically from above. The hundreds of other winged escorts that had just arrived in the clearing now seemed to be folded into the great space underneath its wings, as they tried to get ahead of this true giant of the skies. Where they had come from was anyone's guess, for many of the new additions were not even from this galaxy, let alone from Sopdet's arena of space.

He came in for a final pass, trying to get his huge body frame into a landing glide without hurting the wild greens still fighting for survival, who also manoeuvred around him to get out of his way. The strange Dragons and flying creatures that arrived alongside him seemed to almost move in a ghost-like way, as several of the greens appeared to fly right through them, as if their ghost-like bodies were made out of nothing but thin air. But unlike the others, he was definitely coming down and landing, regardless of what the others had decided they would do. Whether they were going to let him accomplish that goal or not was entirely up to them, but he was coming whether they liked it or not; he came in for his final approach, and almost knocked every Aelf in the vicinity on their ass.

Tansar and Quist followed, with the remainder of the black Dragons soon following suit as the ground shook. The greens remained airborne, calling out to the Dragons below, showing great skill with their aerial displays and wild antics, before they also settled in amongst the blacks already grazing along the field grasses and fitting their little bodies into the tight fitting areas left between and under the larger Dragons' wings. The Aelves watched in fascination, as they all squabbled for position, as one or two would get airborne, and then quickly land again, still deeply entrenched within the discussion of their fears. All trying their best to get within reach of the newest arrivals who, although grounded, were still in what could best be described as a single spot in a mine field of live and very active fire-belching Dragons.

Had the Aelves been able to speak their language, they would have heard the strangely muted whispers of one that did not belong among the fold. Surely that would have wiped the grins off their faces much faster than actually first seeing the passenger Symin had with him now, before they had spotted him with one of their own.

"Bloody hel in Clanations!" Dyareius swore rather loudly at the sight he now saw. It would appear that he hadn't been the only one to notice what the others were now finding fault with. Some had lost their reasoning and remained quiet, looking to the others for their insight. Others were indignant and openly voicing their opinion. However, the whole damn lot of them quickly fell into rank behind Dyareius, as Symin helped the boy down, and swung both of them free from Quist's scaly back. Yes, they had arrived in all their glory, covered in buckets of loose armour plating and trickles of Dragonistic sweat, and true to form, the riders were doing exactly what Symin had predicted. Crap this is all we need, he thought. I knew it was too good to be true. This was going to take some explaining.

Before that could happen, Symin yelled for Soren to head them off, looking at the warriors as if they were from another tribe of clans, and not belonging to one of their own caste. He hung back where the other Dragons had been trying to land amidst the turmoil, trying to keep both himself and the boy from being stepped on and crushed by hundreds of Dragons trying to migrate towards the first act on a bard's stage; the very stage of the first order of calling the Dragon legions of Tantaris to its newest festival of sights. He hated the deception that would herd his own clan away from the Human child, oblivious to their race's hatred of Human kind. It wasn't easy, but it would be easier for him than for Soren. If he had left it up to Soren, the Human would have been drawn and quartered already, and his clan would undoubtedly have applauded him. This was going to split the riders in new directions, with outcomes that he himself could not predict with any great accuracy. But, whatever the outcome, he knew there was need, and if they gave him enough time, they might just give him the benefit of the doubt.

Tamerk had known what he was asking, and it had not been Soren he had waited for all those years, holding this child. It had been him, and with that little bit of information, Symin had wanted to knock him flat on his ass when he had first seen the old man. However, true to form, it would not be him that had to deal with the race of riders who now appeared to be hunting one of their own. For that, he would have to thank Tamerk for bringing it to the forefront. For that, he should kill the Sprite outright the next time he got the chance to put his identity in jeopardy. If it wasn't for Soren, whom he respected, Symin would have finished the deed already.

He hadn't got far, when a roar came out of the White Dragon that sent an energy blast of wind that knocked most of the Aelves, and any Fey creatures stupid enough to have ventured out on to the grounds, to their knees. The sound wave hit the Aelves at full speed, sending several of the wild Dragons nearby instantly airborne. Before Symin could get both Ryyaan and himself mobilized, the Great White placed his body between the advancing guard and the young boy at Symin's side.

Soren was watching everything happen in slow motion. He was still digesting what he was witnessing, when Symin grabbed his friend by the arm, moving both of them out of the way of the huge Dragon's agitated body. Symin literally picked Ryyaan up, securing his little body between the two of them, as Soren rolled to the left. Symin yelled for Soren to watch what was going on, as he placed the boy back on his two feet, away from the dangerous legs now stamping out a warning at the approaching Aelves.

He needn't have bothered; they were in no real danger. He should have known. However, Soren had distracted him enough to make him uneasy, and he had needed to get things under control, at least for Soren's sake.

"He's protecting the boy, look at Ryyaan," Symin shouted. Soren turned to see that Ryyaan had the touchstone out, and was mentally talking to the Dragon in very much the same way that Tamerk had spoken to the Dryads in the clearing.

Symin spoke to him, as both became locked out of the time-loop that others seemed to be in. He watched as both Dragon and young boy seemed to be in some sort of deep conversation. It seemed reminiscent of what he had looked like back in the cottage, when he was about to smash Soren's head in. Soren watched from a distance, and moved around the spectacle, out of the time-loop that everyone else seemed to be set within. He saw the warriors of his village in small glimpses, as the huge Dragon constantly looked between his conversation and the Aelves currently staying out of his range of field. Everything felt odd, as he swallowed air that no longer had any taste. His focus moved to the boy, who was talking without any words, holding his head up high, and smiling with eyes as clear as shimmering glass.

Calmness before the storm came in through the outer edge of his vision, as everything around him drifted in and out of sync, and the sounds of the outside world could no longer be heard. The wind moved in and around the image he was seeing, like it had a life of its own, as it moved around the circle of energy the boy had created around them. It moved in simple waves at first, like a curtain blowing in a tiny breeze, then it twisted and turned backwards, shooting in all directions as everything came back into full focus, with the volume returning to its original screech.

Soren dropped to his knees at the noise, as the reality of what had just happened made him all the more certain they needed to return this Human to the outreaches of space. The Dragons all around him became a little more vocal upon reading his thoughts; the wild Greens added into the mixture, brought in anything with wings towards them – advanced on their position, dive bombing the Aelves from above. They came in from the skies trying to defend in any way they could, while the White Dragon on the ground growled at the severity of what Soren had been thinking, sending the occasional hiss of fire directly at the Aelven guard still attempting to get around the huge creature. He had not hurt a single Aelf in his defence of the boy despite his obvious size and the sheer bulk of his own flanks as he twisted and turned, curling his lips to reveal huge teeth gnashing through his wide-open mouth.

Soren sidestepped around Symin, still watching the commotion going on around him, just as one of the tail feathers came crashing down alongside his arm. It jammed itself straight into the ground, with its girth glancing off of Soren's shirt and tearing the outer edges as it fell. Symin hauled him away from another that appeared in its place. It came flanking the first one, and jammed sideways into the grass, knocking his sword to the ground. Getting themselves clear, they watched the boy still communicating with the White Dragon, who occasionally stopped his assault to listen to the boy, who was talking to him with telepathy, without any of the words spilling out and filling the glen with their conversation.

"Tamerk did say he could talk to Quist with it. It must work with all of them." Symin pointed out. "Look there, even the greens have calmed down, and they're bloody wild." Soren glanced over, watching what Symin had pointed out to him, with complete fascination. The green Dragons had already started to land, keeping themselves further away from the area where their previous ground assault had occurred. Both Symin and Soren continued to watch as every Dragon that had been able to land had, and began settling down quietly, watching with either their heads laying down upon the ground and whining like big ole hounds, or cocked to one side, like a bunch of bloody Dragon pups.

"Good Lord, what's Tamerk done to us? If the Humans get their hands on him, we might as well give up right now! We don't stand a chance without the Dragons on our side," Soren said, pacing again, swatting at flies landing all around the area where the Dragons were settling in and disturbing the grass.

"I don't think that's why he let Ryyaan have it." Symin whispered rather loudly, when Soren started to move around a few of the Dragons currently in his way. They ignored him, continuing to listen to whatever the boy was saying to them in this new form of communication. "Remember, it was Quist who asked him to let Ryyaan have it." Symin continued, following Soren, as they both moved in the direction of the others. "I think this," Symin pointed to the Dragons all around them, thinking with absolute clarity, "is how we're going to beat them. It makes me wonder about all this, with everything that has happened since first we laid eyes on him? He hasn't acted like any Human we've ever seen." Symin continued, without looking to see if Soren was actually following him.

Soren was watching his footing, trying to stay out of the way of various tails swishing back and forth over the pathway they had been tip-toeing around.

"True," Soren looked towards where Symin was pointing, "but how do you explain what just happened?" Soren pointed outwards, all around them, shifting into a better position to greet Dyareius when he arrived. "There are bloody Dragons all over the place, that's not a coincidence, and that big white boy and his followers, they're not even from this bloody planet," Soren whispered to Symin.

"I don't get it either, but Dyareius is coming towards us, so let's go deal with whatever this is with them, instead of trying to figure it out alone. Besides, we're still going to have to explain why we don't have the Shapeshifter with us, and I for one, am not telling him about the damn

Dryads," Symin quickly added, before Soren had a chance to outwardly groan at the memory.

"Yeh, damn, I'd forgotten that little tidbit, thanks for reminding me." Soren said to Symin, as he growled back at his friend. "I was hoping to forget that, now it seems like it's spreading like a fungus trying to pick my brain apart. Shit, I was really hoping we didn't have to think about that yet," Symin growled his response back low, without too much thought.

"Then don't...just remember what they will do if you tell them in this frame of mind." He whispered to Soren, watching the big White Dragon beginning to allow the Aelven guard to proceed to meet him and Soren, shifting its enormous body enough to give them passage. Dyareius had begrudgingly asked his Aelves to leave their swords behind, while they went out to meet their clan brothers. Each of them was just as handy with a knife, which could still be found in various boot tops and tucked away in hidden areas of their breeks, as they advanced forwards into the enclave.

After the bellowing and hissing had calmed down to a dull roar and had somewhat settled, the White Dragon allowed them to move slowly towards where Symin and Soren where now standing. Symin breathed a momentary sigh of relief, not realizing he had been holding his breath, as he watched the warriors move around the huge tail. But that was before he realized that the boy had moved further away from the back of him.

His shadow had moved from the area he had previously been seen in by Symin, as he talked to the Dragons, now completely alone. He last spotted the lad just before the commotion had reached its peak, and was now horrified to see the young lad moving within reach of this humungous animal's side. Before anyone could move or yell out a warning, Ryyaan could be seen reaching out to touch the Great White's face, and a collective gasp could be heard across the entire meadow they were standing in, from those watching from the trees.

Soren watched the Aelven guard as they came around the flanks of the great beast to the rear. They had arrived just as Symin sprinted in the other direction, and all watched him go, before looking to Soren, who had remained rooted in his boots. Fear was something the Aelves very rarely showed, and this facial expression was all over their tracker's face as they came into view. Soren still hadn't moved; Dyareius turned and spotted the boy just as Ryyaan touched the huge Dragon's face, and immediately got caught up in the cry of alarm.

This instantly brought the entire population of green Dragons skyward, and the mayhem began all over again! As the Dragons began screeching, their wings began to take in the deep draughts of air and the fire began to reach the boiling point within their gullets; one lone Dragon could be seen heading directly into the fray. He appeared out of the midst of the greens, and didn't veer off like the others, as they corrected their manoeuvres within reach of the Aelves that had returned back towards the trees for their swords.

A single black Dragon could be seen flying below the others; it came in at an odd angle, reaching for both Symin and Ryyaan with one of its claws, and lifted them airborne into the morning air. He glided away, taking his cargo without harming them and carried them upwards, away from the immediate area into a steep vertical incline. He then proceeded to circle back, as all below became a mad house of hollering and shouts from several of the riders that had witnessed what he had done. He returned, not having gone far, and proceeded to move towards the Great White's vicinity and simply dropped them with a single release of his talons onto the back of the huge beast, as the Aelves gasped in angry fright. He then circled back, methodically dipped his wings, and landed beside the others in his group, while the Great White immediately became airborne soaring over the tops of the furthest trees, leaving a huge mass of falling feathers and sod that had come loose in the upheaval to fall all around the fleeing Aelves, as he gained his altitude, flying away from the glen.

Soren watched them disappear from sight, as the Dragon went into his shift, and the light took them away from their vantage point. He appeared calm, but inside he was anything but. In fact, deep inside he was seething mad. It was at that time, as his heart began to race and his body took on that sickly colour of deepened green, that he turned his head quietly without moving his body, and found the Dragon who had returned to the others, all the while ignoring him.

Soren could only stare at Quist, now quietly grazing along with the others of his kind, while the Dragonlords ran with Dyareius towards the Dracore, and mounted their backs to take after them and find the shift-point that still sizzled with molecules hanging in the air. But, try as they might, the great war Dragons refused to fly, and remained firmly grounded, leaving the Aelves to holler loudly at each other, as they desperately sought a way to get them airborne. But the Dragons ignored their pleas; instead, each of them continued to graze as if nothing had happened, uprooting the big strips of trampled grass that not more than a second ago had been covered in every Dragon from the entire vicinity.

Soren moved towards the big war Dragon that Symin had called his own, firmly planting his feet near the Dragon's lowered head as he ate the grass, and punched him square in the jaw. "How the hel does this happen?" Soren yelled. "Quist, what in the hel were you thinking?" He was so angry he didn't even see the greens moving away, as one by one they went from the sky above them, and followed behind the other who now was only a pinprick of light. They followed where he had disappeared into the distance, and were no longer visible to the landbound Dracore, as each blinked out following the White Dragon to whatever destination he was heading to, far away from the Aelves now fully grounded and out of his reach.

But Dyareius wasn't looking at the Dragons who followed the White Dragon's sudden departure. He, for some reason, was looking directly at Soren, and calmly spoke through the haze of the events that just took place.

"Who's Quist? Soren, look at me! Who's bloody Quist?"

CHAPTER SEVEN

Dreamscape of Ancient Tameron

Sibrey found the waters exhilarating in this new lake, and after spending only a few extra moments drifting in its warmth, she gathered herself together and swam to the shallows on the far side, where she had seen the pinker rocks. As she arrived in the shallower waters, her form instantly adjusted her skin to produce new layers, which majikally appeared and settled themselves to fit her form, revealing a turquois silken shift. She slid across several of the smaller boulders she had spied underneath the clear waters and, finding her footing there to be somewhat awkward, she was forced to pick her way through the minefield of stones, placing her feet precariously along their slippery edges as she continued to make her way towards shore.

Her mind on high alert, she felt the sensation of something else floating within the air. However, sensing it was nothing menacing that would put her in danger, she quickly dismissed its signature as nothing more than the result of simple nerves. The energy continued to flow from out of the water slightly about knee height, allowing warm sensations of beautiful abundance to fill her head with a natural glow which captivated her, as she carried herself further on shore. Whatever it was, the molecules surrounded her signature, producing an aftereffect that calmed her mind, thereby giving her the ability to relax despite the tracker still in pursuit behind her. Her body, enchanted with this warmth, pushed her forward to explore her new surroundings, while the invisible boundary opened downwards from out of the lake, to allow her passage into its domain. The moment that happened, she felt the threads of this new sensation explode within her veins, and the sensation grew warmly along the hairs of her body, sending a feeling of perfection upwards along her nerve endings. Sibrey greeted it with joy, and moved without further discovery of what it might be.

The motion did not go unnoticed from above, as an invisible doorway opened that Sibrey could not see, and let her in. Inexplicably, she neither felt nor heard it, as her body, conditioned to such phenomenon, only let her relax in its protection, as she drifted in unaware of her passage. Strong wards that had been set in place activated, allowing her to move through their protection rings without sending off warning bells that someone had breached their interior cells. Unaware of what had happened, she moved along the invisible barrier set before her, watching the scenery that she had visualized from the other side of the lake unfold before her eyes. It was breathtaking to behold, as she moved inside whatever had presented itself to her, and the beauty of the lakeshore ahead beckoned her warmly, giving no sense of impending doom.

As soon as she passed through the wards, without realizing their significance, they re-set themselves behind her, preventing anything else from entering the secluded lagoon, and the realm disappeared from Tantaris airspace. She continued on, as they quietly settled behind her locking the module that had allowed her in, keeping her out of harm's way, as the Goddess realm welcomed her inside a place that didn't exist inside the normal Fey surroundings on the planet's surface.

High above in the sky, the reflection from another Mauntra seemed to have made its way down to the lake's rocky bottom, giving her an excellent view of the stones beneath. Not able to tell the difference between the one she had come to know and this new one, she was unaffected by the shift. She stopped to admire the many varieties of smaller round rocks, which lay in the shadows of the larger boulders she needed to move around. They had an unusual phosphorescence that played along the surface of each of them, and shimmered in this new Mauntrated star's atmosphere, sending feelings of euphoria inside her skin, as she played lightly in the water, bathed in their cosmic glow.

The stones were polished and smooth, as she placed her face up to the edge of the water's surface and peered into the liquidine environment to watch the fish move in amongst them, immediately changing only her face into that of a creature that could sustain breathing through its newly formed gills. The stones stood to be a living memorial to the violence of volcanic activity from ages past, now making themselves known to the world of the air-breathers up-above, as if their fingers needed to speak to those that would listen. She listened briefly to their song, then reverted back to her old Shapeshifter form and stood upright to smell the morning air.

Nothing of the tracker was present, and, feeling safer across the water than she did on the other side, she stepped lightly trying not to disturb any of the sand under her toes, watching for the different fish that seemed to make these shallows their home, as they darted in and out between her legs and around several of the larger boulders in her path. Their brightly coloured scales reflected in the warm rays of the Mauntra's light, which lit up the shallow water in the reflecting pools as they swam with incredible agility, making their way around the small cove and back again. She watched them play, seemingly enjoying something beneath the surface other than her legs; they followed her footsteps while she made her way towards the sandy shore.

As she watched the little fish, she noticed the shift of colours that moved along their spines, as each of them passed several of the smaller stones along the bottom of the lake. Each time they passed by certain stones she noticed that each produced a different coloured hue, sending the patterns they created along the length of her calves, as she passed briefly by over-top. She watched the colours change from dark purple to light yellow while she smiled, putting her hand into their painted hue, letting her fingertips swirl the liquid around in circles as they continued to change to different shades.

Several bubbles exploded outwards moving skyward, as they burst in all shades of the rainbow, raining down along the sand. They filtered among the shore's crystallized quartz that lay along the upper-sand, as she made her way through the shallower water which sparkled in the reflection of the morning rays. They continued to twinkle in the light, as the new movement caused some of the fish to come to the surface, where she heard the distinctive sound of bells tinkling near-by, as several fish poked their faces out of the water and blinked at her in the outside air. The sound disappeared as her movement stopped, and it was only then that she realized she was creating it herself with the passage of her fingers, as she moved over each of their surfaces in the reflection of the light. The fish smiled at her with brilliant teeth, then dipped themselves backwards into the freshwater brine of the shoreline, and moved back into their own atmosphere, swimming in circles among the smaller stones looking for tiny shrimp to sink those teeth into.

The shallows created several sound effects from below, as each of the stones hummed different vibrations calling the sound upwards to the surface world. The surface waves sent the ripples with her passage, having been disturbed by that movement which splashed along the shoreline as she waded upwards onto the beach; they drifted away, then repeated the chorus all over again, as the fish darted in and out in grand chase after a school of wayward Toole shrimp.

Her senses picked up the heady sweet scent she had detected across the lake. It began to grow stronger, bearing the sweetness of the Jasmine blossoms that now lay all about her as she continued onwards up the sand. A fairly large Anforian Sugar Maple came into view where the Jasmine blossoms seemed to have integrated its branches as a host for the petals to flourish. They fell continuously from its branches, forming snowdrop like petals that floated all around the cove in the air currents, as they regenerated and continued the loop of their existence. They moved about dancing in the small breeze, landing and instantly bursting open on whatever came into contact with their molecules, producing the fragrant smell that permeated the entire cove. Immediately the surfaces that came into contact with the flower petals began to wake up and collect the fragrant pieces, and soon several new vines could be seen growing in different areas of the cove, where they had landed and immediately taken root, creating a lovely curtain of the fragrant blossoms.

She made her way around the gnarled roots of the tree which had pushed itself upwards into the warm soil near the far shore, giving the illusion of something quite stoic and unmoving. But the moment she came into contact with any of its bark, it instantly laced itself around her ankles and she had to physically tickle the tree to get it to release her. This tree was known for its healing properties and grew in climates that were fairly warm, giving large amounts of Euphoria Issadalfae to unsuspecting foot traffic that passed within its lovely reach in return for the Fey nutrients. The root system of the beautiful Maple had infused itself with large amounts of peat that seemed to dot the landscape when this planet's creation had opened a vent from somewhere down below, giving many of the species a foot-hold within this unusual cove.

She moved on before it found a way to entangle her again, and slid her fingertips through the long-hanging maidenhair ferns that grew along the Cliff-side. They moved gracefully aside, as they draped their beautiful long fronds of feathered leaves down the banks and dipped them towards the water's edge to drink as each moved up and down the beautiful pink boulders — each drenched in that mist that they collected from the fresh water at their feet, giving life to the living menagerie of birds that drifted in among their branches and made their nests to raise their young.

The place was simply alive with everything. Sibrey made her way through the maze of foliage up on the shore. She watched several species of salamanders, whose tongues were pierced with sparkling gems, as well as creatures she had never seen before that had brightly coloured skin which shone with several encrusted jewels embedded along their backs in the mist of the sanctuary's amazing life cycle. Each creature seemed to move in a continuous motion along the branches or leaves that housed the various foliage, which allowed them to survive in this virtual terrarium.

Sibrey smiled as some came out to visit, touching her fingers slightly as she passed, while others simply ducked backwards into their dens or warrens as she continued on her way. But nothing seemed as visual as the rare one now sitting before her, who simply stared back at her and croaked its tiny voice from behind the stone it had been basking on. The Tyne cliff frog seemed unafraid of her Fey form, and blasted its four huge air sacs from its little face as she passed by, producing foot long porcupine quills that hosted actual live yellow star-flowers at their stems. It was strangely comical and beautiful at the same time. They drifted in the air currents and captured one of the insects buzzing around, attracted by the motion. Its long tongue snapped the insect up and it continued on with this bizarre feeding ritual until it was full of the long toed insects flying within range, and simply went to sleep snoring away behind her.

Everything seemed so bizarre and alien within the grove that it really made you wonder if you could still be on the same planet as the lake you had just swam across. She forgot about the tracker searching for her signature, and made her way inland away from the water's edge to explore the exotic cove.

A feather floated down within reach and, as she picked it up, she noticed all the incredible parrots and songbirds that could be seen flying throughout the tree canopies high above. Nothing seemed to follow any particular genetic code that she could decipher from things she had seen before. There were many different shapes and sizes in the patterns she could see, and most seemed to be more of a blending of species, as each made their way around the newest entry that had arrived on their shoreline.

So much to take in, with so many incredible sights and sounds filling her sense, that she didn't happen to see the caverns at first off to her left, as they slowly came into view. Everything she touched and felt was alive with colour, forming a complete array of appealing scents and fragrances for her senses. Everything including the peat from the floor of the ground she was now walking on, to the flowers that grew to such incredible sizes, all smelled intoxicatingly beautiful to her senses, as she moved about the cove. Not once did she smell the sulphur that permeated the air from the lake behind.

She turned to her left, looking skyward into the crystalline reflection of the huge leaves of the tree which towered over the entire cove she was standing in. She slid her fingers along the ridges of one of the larger leaves and watched in utter amazement as the water droplets that had covered the leaf came to life. They seem to move as she touched the surface, running in reverse, backwards up the leaf of the tree as she held it in her hand. They circled around the leaf's inner veins and drifted in a circular pattern, going skyward towards the canopy far above.

She moved her attention over to the bark and examined its texture, which seemed to be both alive and breathing, as the rain water ran over its highly sensitive outer skin. Each of the trees within this magnificent grove had similar occurrences that were just as unique with their own physiology. The water droplets still puzzled her with their reversed polarlithic flow, but before she could investigate their unique physiology her eyes finally spotted the cave's outer walls. Her attention became so involved with this new visual sight that she instantly forgot all about the trees and their unique ability.

Finally, the enormous pink boulders of the cavern entrance that had stood beckoning her to go beyond, had caught her undivided attention, and she moved towards it to explore. What she saw before her, was different than any structure she had ever seen before. She stepped over several small stones that had fallen along the edge of the pathway that would lead her inside, when the sight that suddenly appeared in its entire splendour nearly took her breath away. She had to actually stop and use one of the bigger boulders to keep her upright, as she stumbled knocking a few that had lain on the pathway skidding outwards under her feet. "Oh Gam! Where in the fragmire am I?"

She literally had to stop herself from tumbling onto the floor and nearly spraining an ankle, as she moved towards the last bit of sand that had breached the entrance, before peering inside the cavern. She was immediately taken aback by what her brain was telling her she was seeing. Before her inside the cave's reflective interior, was an infusion of pure crystalline light. It seemed to be everywhere at once, and all around the interior of the cave. However, looking further inside, it appeared to be coming from a huge crystal geode which covered the length of every wall, towering far overhead towards a series of other caverns beyond.

She followed the line of the crystal matrix with her eyes, as it flowed inward, looping around the sides of the caves and joining each of them together within its energy of lighted fire. They glowed and reflected their light outwards in a fiery crossing of light pink and purple amethyst points, mixed in with a single strand of red amethyst she had never seen before. They then crossed several bridges of Amber resin, before coming into contact with the pure resin chamber, which had dripped along the heat vents from the hot springs underneath, producing this warm Ambertine glow along the Crystal-Lynianesian stones.

Sibrey was without speech, as she looked all around the entrance to the cave, imagining the Fire Elemental that must have at one time resided here. She had only moved from the outside for a moment, when all around her feet she started to feel the wetness of water, as she made her way inside the crystalline maze of underground caverns. Looking down she noticed a small stream of water that she had seen from the outside trees, making its way inside the chamber. It flowed along the bare stones, carving the central portion into a shallow well, as it wandered through the caverns along a forward decline, and drifted downwards out of view.

Her eyesight finally adjusted to the darkness of the floor, in comparison to the light from the geode, and she could visualize the small cracks and fissures that had been exposed to whatever lay beneath the central cave. Whatever was below the surface must have been fairly vast in comparison to the vents that pushed the heat upwards into the pressurized steam, which came in contact with the rocks she walked on. Tiny air bubbles came from beneath certain sections of the central portion of the floor, where the water flowed a bit deeper and much faster, as she made her way into its inter-sanctum.

The heated water continued to pick up speed and ran on a downward slope perpendicular through the centre of its core, bubbling up in different sections, with the occasional obstruction causing the water to fall in pools and swirl about the cavern, causing holes of super-ionized water. The water, now up to temperature, cascaded from pool to pool as it overflowed its banks into another cooler water source, called a feeder stream, that suddenly appeared out of the walls along various cracks and holes that had been split from the surface world up-above. The sound was majikal, sending several of the small waterfalls colliding into each other as they made their way to the edge of a huge wall and disappeared from sight.

Sibrey walked over to the wall and discovered that it was made out of wood. She placed her hands onto the texture of its rough exterior and felt a heart-beat. She took a quick step back, and stumbled on one of the crystal shards that had broken off of one of the ceiling stalactites. She reached down and picked it up before it could skid across the cave floor, looking at it pulsating in her hand. It felt warm to the touch, as it vibrated slightly in her hand; she turned it over, admiring the structure of each of the crystals housed inside. They seemed to be alive and changing colour, as she twisted her fingers around the shard's circumference, warming the bit of resin from the Anforian Maple she had just noticed had found the back of her hand. She must have come in contact with a bleeder on its bark as she moved around the roots, when she first arrived on the beach.

THE BEGINNING

The drug inside the resin began to calm her nerves, as she watched it dissolve and meld into her skin and then completely disappear, leaving her skin smooth and clean. The crystal shard began to pulsate, mimicking her own heart-beat, as she watched both her own heart and that of the shard's sentient life-force return to a normal rhythm — now completely in-sync with one another, before returning back towards the wall to explore the strange phenomenon. What could possibly be causing this strange occurrence, beating in complete syncopation with an actual heart-beat? With her right hand firmly grasped onto the crystal shard, she pressed her ear to the wood wall again, and closed her eyes to listen. What she heard astonished her even further, as she realized that the wall wasn't a wall at all, but a living tree with sentient life, standing deep within the depths of the cavern she had walked into.

The moment the shard touched the wood, the walls to the cavern rotated backwards away from the tree's bark, revealing the vastness of the tree's girth. The cave slowly withdrew from around it, completely exposing the darkness that surrounded it, leaving Sibrey standing on the precipice, listening for some monster to come crawling forward out of the deep. She shivered at the thought and stepped back slightly. It must have been vast, to have covered the entire wall at the far side of the cave with its outer bark, and not show the circumference of its rounded edges. She had first thought the hot springs where the brook was trickling through the geode, were feynominal, but she was truly Goddess-smacked at this new sight that stood before her, deep down within the actual cave system.

When nothing came over the lip of the ravine after her, she looked over the edge again with renewed interest, pushing several small stones with her foot into the blackness, to listen how far down the ravine went. Sibrey could not see the bottom if her life depended on it. It could very well have been thousands of feet deep, and, being rather caught up in other aspects of the cave, she decided to forgo taking her life into her own hands, and go and explore the other parts of the cavern's other chambers she had spotted on the same level she was currently on. She didn't hear the splash as the stones finally hit bottom, somewhere down below in the darkness; they began to crawl back upwards, instantly growing long sharp claws as they hook themselves along the tree's entrenched root system in the dark, and scurried back up to the cave floor they had originally lived out in the light of day.

She started to wander away from the ledge, long before they could be seen coming over the lip of the ravine, settling down once again along the edge to roost, as they continued to nourish themselves from the sulphur they were breathing in from the vents below. Still feeling rather claustrophobic beside the big tree, she wondered how something as big as this tree could find such an unlikely place to continue to grow. Just as she moved off she could hear the wall again closing behind her, sealing the room off from further access. She took the remaining shard that had found its way into her hand and placed it back near the area she had first spotted it, in case she could return to for it later; then she may have time in the future to explore what it had waiting for her to discover, in its complexity. She carried on, taking her photographic memory into the remainder of the caverns she did have time to explore now.

The caves all seemed to run fairly deep into the cliff-face, away from the lake's shoreline, where she had first waded ashore. Each one was an offshoot of the main corridor of trickling water, which now swirled and warmed her body, as she walked amongst the caves and caverns she found herself to be in.

The river that fed itself from the lake now became a stream, as she moved deeper inside the central part of the moving water. It moved about her calves, sending ripples along ahead of her to the edges that ran deep into other grottoes. The pools at the sides were deeper and warmer here, as she made her way into their depths. She could see that they led to several smaller caves that were hiding under stone bridges along the surface of the water, and she would need to duck her head underwater to reach them, if she wanted to explore.

She dove deeper into the warm water, moving through its clarity, as she swam under the nature stone arches, then surfaced up into the air exhaling spent lungs, like a mermaid emerging from the ocean depths, into a beautiful fully formed grotto in the cavern to her right. She took a breath of the sweet scented air that permeated the smaller cave, allowing the water to ripple around her arms as she swam to its edges. This new grotto was covered in several different flower and fern species, which had found their way inside the lava tubes from somewhere far above. They anchored themselves into the tiny fracture lines along the heated tubules, finding various cracks and crevices which allowed the plants enough light to survive below ground.

Water dripped slowly off the walls, and formed small waterfalls which ran in rivulets, creating a very majikal mist from the stream below. The cooler water drops coming into contact with the pool's hot water steam-vents, produced larger clouds of swirling mist inside the entire grotto, creating the perfect growing environment for the plants to survive within.

Sibrey smile with contentment, as she drifted along in the middle of the secluded pool, feeling at ease for the very first time in her life, and far removed from being chased through the valley of the Goddesses and back again. There had been many times she had dreamt of similar pools, but until now she never really thought they were anything more than just childhood dreams. She closed her eyes and let the water take her away, soothing the tired muscles that had transformed her into the creature she had learned to become.

The pools were incredible; some were only shallow basins, while others you could actually swim across, with an upward depth of twelve arm-lengths or more in the deeper sections. It was into one of those shallower pools of about three feet of water which she finally found refuge and sank in, letting the steam and water soak her tired muscles giving her mind a moment to forget that she was still been hunted in the outside world. She momentarily closed her eyes, and drifted off to sleep.

This is where she was, and why, when a giant **White Dragon** crossed over the skyline outside and disappeared from sight, she didn't see the spectacle she would soon hear about, in the weeks to come.

Far above on the surface, where she no longer ran in the shape of the black Panther, she could still hear the creature breathe as it made its way around the lake, tracking her scent. It would follow her wherever she went no matter how difficult it was for him to get to her. He was her protector, and after looking out for his own family he would have found his way to where she had left him last, and followed the trail. What she didn't know was that he had found the blood on the Cammond Berry bush she had cut herself on. He wasn't just returning as her protector, he was coming with a vengeance, thinking she had been hurt in his absence.

Twilight began to manifest within the cavern before she actually wanted to leave, and forced her to roused herself from dreams faster than she would have liked. She made her way outside the cavern of pools to find several tiny winged Firefox Faeries scattering about, with their phosphorescent tail rudders now beginning to light the darkness which was descending upon them. They seemed to be waiting for her, guiding her way through the twilight, to find the shelter she would need for the coming night. The big Anforian Maple Tree could still be seen, as she exited the pools; its silhouette seemed to take on a more sinister aspect in the dark. But knowing that shadows don't always present as what imagination suggests, she took hold of the base of the huge tree and found the footholds. She wouldn't use her Shapeshifter abilities again this night; she still feared it would be easily felt by the tracker the Dragonlords had sent after her.

She instead climbed the outer bark the old fashioned way, wishing she had thought to at least bring her outer cloak, to cover herself up from the cool night air. Her Shapeshifter molecules adjusted to the environment as she found grooves that seemed to be placed at just the right intervals for someone of her size and frame, and she moved upwards into the branches she could still see in the darkened sky. She thought nothing of the strange coincidence, and continued upwards without a thought as to why it was a perfect match.

Her climbing skills were legendary; even from a young age she had always been able to climb anything. It used to drive her family nuts, watching her make her way up these huge trees as her mother fretted, ringing hands and shouting for her to be careful far below on the ground. She spent many hours in the canopies of these giants, thinking and pondering, or just plain using it as an escape from her annoying brothers. She found out quickly that they had never liked to climb, and it had become somewhat of a sanctuary from torturous days of studies and chores, and their relentless searching and destroying her peace.

Climbing to great heights had never bothered her, or the solitary lifestyle she led when she climbed high within the branches, spending many hours within the upper canopies. The few friends that she had managed to acquire along the way had long since found mates and one by one vanished from her life, giving her a different peace than she had attained before. She loved her time alone, and would often use that time to reflect on the different things she hoped would transpire in the length of her lifetime. It never really occurred to her that people in the village, whom she hunted and lived alongside, would whisper behind her back, and that the young girls who had been her friends, would soon begin to giggle as she walked past, each sharing a private joke at her expense. Still, it mattered none; she knew her own mate was out there somewhere, and when the time was right, he would find her regardless of anything they had whispered about her being different, and not of their clan — but that had not yet come to be...

She finally reached the long limbs of the tree's lower branches, and moved higher up, searching for a wide enough branch that would keep her secure while she slept through the night. As she moved about in the darkness, she disturbed a few birds that had been roosting in their nighttime perches. They squawked at the disturbance and moved to another branch, just as she found a spot that would contain her body in sleep, with a bit of a concave recess near the tree trunk, and perfect for preventing her from crashing onto the forest floor far below.

She yawned and looked sleepily up at the remains of the Byanadorian Moon, which had two days ago stretched its neck over the horizon and began its ascent into the steel blue night sky high above. She settled herself into a foetal position and drifted off with thoughts of the mate whom she knew fondly from her dreams since birth. Maybe soon he would take her away from all this craziness, and help find her Shapeshifter family once again.

Another dream, one not as friendly, began within moments of her returning to exhausted sleep, even before she settled into the certain depths that would break open the very essence of its own arrival. It could not be prevented, it was just something that melded inside her chemistry and forced its way outwards when she went into deep-sleep.

She made it to the actual battlements of the crumbling castle walls this time. But the fallen rock still lay smashed all about her feet, as she tried to pick her way through the crumbling mess. She could almost feel its soul, as if some massive energy field had blown everything up, and it lay mortally wounded all before her. The horses above her now came into view, moving about the stones she had just moved through far above her. But they were riderless now, moving without purpose along the upper edge grazing on the tufts of grass that lay along the rim. She adjusted her field of vision to look below, where there was movement coming along the torn up hillside, and came into contact with the sound of skidding rock, which made her turn around to judge where the warriors now on foot, might arrive.

She felt them close, and this time they were closer than she would have liked. Damn, she was running out of time... and they were moving better through the broken rock at her feet, faster than she was picking her way through the rocks to the trail she now travelled on. She fled down the path that seemed to suddenly open up in front of her eyes, and didn't even question where it had come from only moments ago, when it had not even been viable. They followed, hot on her trail, shielding the Mauntra that threatened to blind their eyes, as they moved towards her with renewed energy.

In reality, Sibrey continued to stir restlessly in her sleep, but the branch secured her softly; she would not fall tonight. And far below on the forest floor, a single shadow moved within the garden. He was Arddhu, the Keeper of these trees, and Sibrey's watcher for the night. He would stay until the Panther made its way through the last of the treeline, and joined them in their nightly vigil. At least for now, she was safe; he lifted a hand and gathered the energy he needed from the plants around him, while the ancient grove of trees gently rocked her to sleep. He touched the ancient bark when he had enough, and sent the energy she required to move further into the dream world, unlocking the area she had not seen before. Then, with a final wave of his hands, he sent it slowly steadily upwards towards her sleeping form. He turned without worry, moving about the garden humming silently, stepping away to give her the rest she'd need before it all began to loop itself around once again, and start all over.

Sibrey's dream-state followed the fractured pieces of rock that once contained the battlement of some long since destroyed structure. It seemed somewhat familiar, but she couldn't place why and continued quickly through the rubble. She scanned everything as she stepped carefully around a corner wall, and found herself within what must have been the Grand Hall of some long forgotten ancestral fortress. The far wall still held the remnants of a stone fireplace, part of which could be seen crumbling along an open gash in the wall — some of it had already started to fall into the sea far below, and the rest of it would soon follow in the coming days. She sidestepped several small stones skidding along the floor that had been hit by her boots, and watched them disappear over that open crevasse and fall into the water crashing on the rocks beyond.

The Grand Hall she had moved towards, still had several intact ornately carved Tameronian Elk Hound benches along the far wall, while others sat split and torn among the ruins, spilling their beautifully carved features out onto the floor. She picked her way around wall sconces with strange runic script written on them, which had slipped from the fire mantel, now laying in pieces joining them. They were scattered between the benches that had been torn apart, joining the remnants of a smaller rock slide from somewhere above that had come through the wood floors of another level. All around her the castle's former glory was lying in ruin. She spotted old lengths of silken fibres once belonging to a tapestry, lying on top of several artifacts, strewn about like spider webs floating in the wind. One such piece shone like silver, lying entwined about the mantel pieces, and then appeared to take on a life of its own as it floated in the wind. She touched it as it started to move past her, feeling the softness of its texture. It fell limply into her hand at the moment of contact, and yet, when she tried to free it from her, as she moved away, it became stuck, clinging tightly to her fingers like sticky honey.

The sound of boot heels from the riders hunting her got closer, and made her heart pound faster, as the gravity of her situation ground home. The sound came from the outer battlements around the old turrets she had first encountered. Her wrist started to bruise as she tried harder to tear the threads still wrapping themselves around her hand and wrists. But she had become so entangled within the threads, no matter how hard she tried, she couldn't break free. She felt it start to move around her skin in a most startling manner, and, looking down, she realized it had turned into a living thing, wrapping itself around her wrist and forearm, virtually pinning her to the spot where she stood.

She was trapped, and nothing she had felt before in the dream had felt this terrifying. She struggled to break free from the threads growing tightly around her body and squeezing the life out of her, but the he more she fought to free herself, the tighter it wound itself around her wrist; like a cobra finding its prey and refusing to give up its meal. Her arm began to ache from the pressure, as she watched the three Aelven horsemen scramble through the Grand Hall's crumbling interior, and spill out onto the floor steps from where she had become imprisoned.

They skidded around the last of the barriers that stood in place between them, and just as they almost reached her, and were within arm's length of actually grabbing onto her shoulders, the thread lifted her up through the air with a single yank and moved her out of the way! It re-positioned itself above the three of them — seemingly displaying sentient thought, it started to change direction and literally pulled her through an opening she had not seen, on the other side of the fallen mantle.

She fell through the air, still dangling precariously from her arm above with accurate swiftness, while the thread forcibly dragged her down a flight of stone steps into a hidden room below the chamber above. She floated for several seconds in midair seemingly caught in the zero gravity of the fall, while the distinctive sound of levers and pulleys could be heard sliding into place above her, and closing off any possible retreat or arrival of the warriors above.

As soon as it completed its mission, the bewitched thread slowly lowered her to the ground then unwound the tendrils holding her tightly in its grasp, and released her. As soon as her skin was revealed, the last layer of thread fell to the chamber floor, now hanging limply along the stones at her side. She fell to her knees, trying to catch her breath. She skinned her shins moving along the rough surface, trying to get away from the creature that seemed to be both jailer and saviour at the same time. She was taking no chance of a recurrence of it coming once again to life, but her fears were quickly assuaged that the chances of that were slim to none. The moment

THE BEGINNING

her feet made actual contact with the stones and she was safely tucked away from the screaming warriors up above, it began to return to its former substance and now lay lifeless as a simple silver silken thread bunched up around the last knuckle of her hands.

She scraped it off her wrist and flung it to the ground, kicking it away, where it stayed lifeless and without movement. She twisted and turned her body, trying to find any lingering pieces that may have attached themselves in other places, but found she was fully clear. She was not hurt, nor was she bruised from the ordeal, but magic was all around her with the sweet smell of scented jasmine, laced with the savoury scent of Barbary sage. Now nothing inside this room was making any sense. This was not her dream!

Sibrey looked at her skin where she had torn it open trying to remove the thread, and found the cut had disappeared, along with the pain of it wrapping so tightly around her wrist. She rubbed the area where the blood had pooled along the fine hairs of her arm, and they too showed no trace of the damage. Whatever had just happened, she had no chance to delve into its nature, as she realized she was now in another room, entirely away from the ruins of the castle walls above; unlike the other, this one appeared to be still intact and full of unbroken walls and ornately carved arches.

The room was nothing like what it had appeared to be, from the vantage point dangling high above. She had felt caught like a fly stuck in honey, then reeled in the thread's grasp, like some form of bait on a hook. On closer inspection the room appeared to be within the former foundations of the older castle's root system, that always ran deeply inside the old battlements. She remembered something taught to her as a young Shippel about that and it quickly came through old faded memories that had to be dusted off and brought forward, into the central surface of her forward vision, for her to understand the memory that had been put to rest.

There had been stories that all of the original royal Fey castles were very much a part of the forest's actual lifecycle. Those that had survived the plantings of these old worlds were grown deep within some of the most haunted sections of the old groves of the Selmathen fringes. These elusive creatures had built vast stone castles along the outer-rings of their shift-point doorways, just outside the Standing Stones of a Lemarr-Line. They ran deeply alongside some of the lighter Fey-lines, which followed similar energy points, that allowed them to exist within the vortex of the Fey home-worlds.

Each of the larger fortresses had been given full immunity from the advancing armies of warring tribes, which had fought and died out long ago in times of the past solar wars. Sibrey had heard about these ruins, and their scarred battlements drenched in myth and legend, from her teachers who fed the stories of their inhabitants in their fire circle rituals. But what stood before her had never been included within any legend that she had heard before, and furthermore, what she was currently seeing was greatly different than what any of the elders of her clan, who had lived during that time, had spoken about.

It would not surprise her if her arrival into one of these former mythological creations was not by accident alone. And, as a last thought to her thinking self, if she was going to take advantage of her arrival into this underground world, she would need to find some warmer clothes. She tried to create something to wear, but the molecules seemed distant and stuck, as if there was something interfering with the majik. She tried again, and almost lost her ability to stand, as something seemed to take the floor out from under her feet and shifted her sideways. She stopped the incantation, and it reset itself; going still, without causing further damage. She would have to do this the hard way and scrounge around for something someone else had left behind.

With that locked deeply inside her little Shapeshifter core, she walked slowly through the corridor of underground rooms, looking for anything that would constitute something she could wrap around her for the moment. Up above, she could see the stalactites that had formed, still growing all around the ceiling, untouched by Fey hands as they changed the chemistry of the stone's genetic codex into some newly formed calcified mineral that Sibrey had never seen before. They dripped with water which smelled of salt, leaving deposits along the cave floor, in strange crystallized formations that felt rougher than the velvet they had suggested themselves to be.

Sibrey moved around the bigger ones, trying to get as far away from the thread that remained dormant along the floor behind her, and the warriors still thrashing about far above. On the other side of the room she could just make out what appeared to be wooden tables that were laden with tons of food, with platters of fresh fruit and sweetmeats. They seemed to have just arrived, as if some vast dinner party was about to get underway, and she had disturbed the festivities. She reached the table, where old copper candle holders found themselves amidst beautiful flowers covered in mosses, surrounded by a large variety of dried fruits and nuts. Some of them she recognized, others were oddly shaped and arranged in large bowls made out of carved wood. All were edible, and all seemed fresh, as if they had just been laid out specifically for her. But that was crazy!

She reached out to touch the food, and accidentally knocked over a chair. It made her jump and look around her to see if someone had heard her. Instead she found lying over the back of one of the benches, someone's cloak. It was covered in strange runic designs, all stitched into the fabric along seams that had been hand stitched with care. The fabric wasn't something she had ever felt before, and seemed to fit her form as if it was made only with her in mind. She wrapped it around her shoulders, covering herself with its material, and smelled its rich scent. At least she would be warm, if nothing else, she thought, then bent over and picked up a scone along with some of the fruit that caught her eye. She sniffed its aroma as she moved along, seeing if it was edible before biting into it with hungry eyes and an appetite to match.

Along the walls she spied bits of smoke wafting away from huge tallow candles which cascaded down the stone, dripping hot wax rivulets onto the alcove's floor. Everything was full of life, but nothing breathed with contact of what must live below, inside the old stone fortress. She stopped to listen; still nothing moved. Someone must live here, or why would this room be bathed in flickering candlelight? How was it possible to have a party with no guests in attendance? Her mind started to race. Where had all the Fey gone, or did she fall into some parallel universe, and in doing so killed off all the inhabitants of this foreign land the moment her body arrived? Ok, now that's just weird, she thought. She assumed she must still be asleep, caught up in one of her more fanciful dreams.

She pinched herself rather hard, then listened for any approaching footsteps that would give her a clue as to their whereabouts, but nothing moved within the space she was now standing, crunching away at a feast made for others, while her fingers broke the skin where she had attacked herself. She sucked the blood that pooled under her nails, tasting none. She twisted her head around towards the candle, only to see that the blood was no longer there. Odd, she swore she had broken the skin. She looked around and saw another doorway, and spied other rooms along the adjoining corridors. With her thumb still in her mouth, and a bunch of fresh grapes in the other hand, she went over to see what she could see from the archways. Each seemed to be filled with large boxes and chests that glittered with silver mirrors and jewels that covered the floor. She hesitated for a moment in mid-bite, panicking that maybe she had accidentally landed among thieves, and this was their private stash of gold that had been pirated away. She moved into another room, ignoring the wild fantasies of her youth, finding a literal treasure trove of almost everything imaginable that lay in boxes and drawers, all crammed into every space that could be filled. It fed her fear even more, as she wandered through, looking around at both things present and things about to materialize in front of her wondering eyes.

There were paintings of wood nymphs and forest creatures in every imaginable shape and form, lying stacked up against the walls ten to twenty frames deep, shining in the reflection of the candle light from another table. There were other rooms in similar disarray, all of which were loaded to the ceiling, with everything crammed into the interior spaces as well. Each one of the following rooms held hundreds of household items, from kitchen tables to linens, all folded and neatly packed away. They were opposite to the other rooms in the front, those which had their things strewn across the floor like someone had been in a hurry to put everything right. Sibrey could only stare at the chaos, slowly watching the floor as she stepped around and through the contents of an obviously vastly wealthy household. It was unlike anything she had seen before and yet everything before her felt vaguely familiar.

She dismissed the credibility of this thought, and came upon a desk as she stepped around other boxes that were heaped with books and parchments that looked like if she touched them they would crumble into tiny pieces of dust. However, upon closer inspection, they were well preserved and from what she could see of them in the dim light, far from falling apart. Some of them were neatly stacked, while others seemed to have been

THE BEGINNING

thrown from a distance, spilling onto the tops of others that were stacked nearby, as if someone had neglected to return them to their rightful places when they had finished reading them.

The light from an oil lamp could be seen flickering throughout the chamber, cascading down the walls and lending a lovely amber glow to the sides of the stone walls. The lamp itself was resting in a chain, hanging ornately overhead. It swayed briefly as she passed underneath, sending scores of dust particles to the floor. Its scent accosted her nasal passages as she sneezed, sending dust in every direction along the floor. It was upon finishing the sneeze that the lamp light from above glanced off a darkened area not part of the table's original structure. Something darker than the surrounding area could be seen just out of visual range. She peered into the dimness, watching the majik dissolve around it, after being disturbed from her reaction to the closed in environment bleeding from the room.

The book suddenly arrived in plain sight, inside this vortex of space, exploding the wards put in place that had protected it from prying outside eyes. Whatever was written inside, at one time, must have been able to cause some form of harm with the written word for it to have been so meticulously wound up in these kinds of wards. Only the ancient ones with the knowledge of Wulushian Majik, would have had the knowledge of these old protective ways. Disturbing the dust from the lamp as she sneezed had given the exact amount of light needed to see the thing that had been hidden from view. She moved towards the darkness and found what appeared to be an old leather-bound book placed off to the side away from everything else, at the far corner of the desk. When she reached for it, the majik that remained firmly ensconced in the leather molecules of the hide seemed not to have need of even the slightest push, as it began to shift downwards towards her fingertips, and relocate without hesitation, to the atoms of her own body. She watched the unusual process with excitement brimming in her veins, for, not only did it tickle as it absorbed into her bloodstream, but by the time she had blinked one breath of an eyelash, it had instantly melded with the molecules of her physiology, and seemed to settle into her genetic mainframe, releasing something into her body.

What it was, she had no clue; instead, she hesitated to put skin onto the texture of the books cover. For that fraction of a moment in time, whatever had entered her bloodstream had reset the molecules that had been inactive in her genetic codex, and rewired the chromosome that had been laying dormant, hiding deep inside her own body. She blinked long eyelashes and watched her body adjust to the new configuration, stretching her long finger bones in the light in front of her face, and watched the molecules dance around the effervescent light that seemed to permeate through the oil lamp's reflection.

Then time reset itself, and she, without thinking what had happened, continued on as if it hadn't. She touched the beautiful book, and fingered its leather exterior, brushing off the vast amount of dust particles that had clung to its leather from years of being below ground in the cave. It gave off a slight fragrance of sulphur, although nothing seemed to warrant that smell, which usually accompanied some form of ritualistic majik. There were inscriptions burned into its outside cover, and she bent her nose almost parallel to its deep set recesses to inspect the grooves and colouration of its unusual field. It looked surprisingly similar to one that she had seen in the days of her youth, having been done by hot irons in the old ways, before the time of the age of man. Most of them had been lost in the last Dragon Wars, and to see one now was simply not heard of, let alone to find one left alone without stronger wards put into place. She shivered, thinking of what lay before her, and mindful of its belonging to someone who must have had incredible power.

She felt sick. Majik always carried particles of what had created it in the first place. Everyone and anything that had touched this book would have left trace particles behind in their wake. She tasted amber dust now, and found her face flushed by its arrival. Some said they were only stories of the old ways. But others swore they still carried that Wulushian Majik from the ancient city of Lemuria, out where the home planets of the Fey used to be, before the doorway had been closed. What was it doing here? And how did this all become part of the old dream?

She had just realized that she no longer was waking up at the normal cut-off, and that the old dream had been suddenly shoved into another section much further along than she had reached in past nightmares. This part of the dream had become even more puzzling than the one of Aelven warriors chasing her into the ruins above. She had had that nightmare since she had been wee kidlet, and now she was uncertain she was even in the same space and time as the others far above her.

She stopped and took another look around. The cavern appeared to be different than when she had arrived. Slowly it occurred to her that it was. It was then, as if by design, she caught the slightest movement to her left. As soon as that happened and her awareness caught up to her line of sight, the things within the chamber began to move without shielding themselves from her eyesight and she caught them out of the corner of her eyes just as they started to unpack themselves in real earnest. Once she realized what was happening, something seemed to change within the room and the momentum immediately picked up her awareness and moved in rapid succession to finish what it had started.

She hit the floor the moment she became aware of that; listening for some kind of presence that had suddenly become aware of her mood within the room. She watched from a crouched position as it first started, with a transparent ribbon of light slowly making itself aware of her changing thought patterns, and then as the majik took hold with the slightest shifting of air currents that began to swirl around and appear hazy, she started to wish she had stayed upstairs in the room with the others. It twisted things around her like a curtain of energy, and then began changing the room into the Great Hall she had seen above her, back when time had deconstructed it and blown it apart. It moved quickly in the waves of energy of her mind, almost as if it was afraid she would falter, as the molecules inside her newly formed skin controlled its arch.

It gently tested her, and when she didn't freak out and react in a negative way, it seemed to be warming the inside of her mind, and beginning to place some form of memory inside, where the others rested from her youth. Instead of deleting the memories she did have, the storm of wind seemed to do nothing more than immediately knock her flat onto her back. Its very essence drained everything out from within the room, giving a dizzying rendition that made her close her eyes from the strange effect.

The wave of energy moved all around her in slow motion, and then it moved faster and faster. Dishes and linen started to move out of the crates, hovering in thin air around the various areas they had been piled, dancing around the molecules they were held in, then unpacking majikally all on their own. It attacked the furniture next, which moved into the air from their packing crates and positioned themselves around the dishes, which still hung between the heavier crates. They all became animated, taking on a life of their own, heaving themselves sideways then back again as they sped above her from one side to another, then changed direction, and hurled themselves single-handed into cupboards and onto shelves, majikally dusted and spit-polished clean.

She was expecting things to start smashing each other at the rate of speed they were moving, but they all landed right-side up and neatly stacked with nothing broken. She had rolled to the far side of the room by this point, and had dropped to the floor on her stomach to get out of the frantic movement that had increased with such incredible speed above her. She covered her head with her wrists and hands, just as another piece of heavy furniture picked up in speed, whizzing past her, and landed with incredible force. The moment that had happened, she could take no more. She covered her ears with her arms along the upper part of her body, and rested her head on the cold stone floor. It was then that she started to scream, rocking her body back and forth along the edge of reason, caring little for nothing else but coming out of this with her own sanity, by leaving the dream behind.

The air around her was blowing with hurricane strength, but nothing, had she cared enough to look, seemed to be breaking. Tears started to fall upon the floor from eyes that could no longer see, with the transplantation almost at its peak. She felt something change in her surroundings but, given the option, she stayed with her eyes squeezed tightly shut, afraid of what she might see that would send her somewhere even more volatile than where she was now.

It wasn't until her face pressed against something moving beneath her body, and she felt something other than the stone floor at her cheek, that she actually opened her eyes to see where she was. The room where the desk had previously been, was nowhere in sight. Nothing of the former rooms and corridors, where all the crates had been stacked, was anywhere in the vicinity either. As a matter of fact, she was in another separate section altogether than she had previously been in. Then, before she could get her bearings readjusted, she realized she had not moved from where she

THE BEGINNING

originally had laid, and all around her had been created out of what had presented itself to her, from the very boxes and crates that she had only moments ago squeezed tightly to fit past.

The room had literally re-created itself and was in the exact same location as the original room that she had previously been in. While she had laid in fear for her life, all around her had actually taken on a life of its own and became a fully functional castle room with a window and a doorway that lead to a fully made bed with quilts and pillows all fluffed up and ready for sleep. But before she could stand on her own two feet, a wooden floor could be heard planking towards her. She quickly pushed herself to a standing position to get out of the way. Sibrey backed up, watching as it pushed her towards the steps that she originally came down in the arms of the thread that seemed to have been possessed, and wedged her body between them and the last planks going in.

She couldn't move a muscle, becoming completely paralysed with the unknown, as the Panther she had always looked towards when things went bump in the night, was nowhere to be seen. Something bumped her gently, almost in a caress, and quietly picked her up, removing the staircase behind her that had jammed into her foot, and put the last plank into place. It then set her down from her perch within its gentle grasp, and everything went quiet. She froze in position, not daring to actually move a single muscle, in case it wasn't quite done with its creation, and the thread she had seen previously majikally appeared and took possession of her body once more. She opened one eye, but it was gone, and no trace of it having had been there was anywhere in this new room.

She heard her name being called from somewhere else, in another room, way off in the distance. She opened both eyes and peered around her. The sound took on a very familiar ring to it, as if she had heard it a thousand times before and it was nothing out of the ordinary.

"Sibrey, honey, where are you? We're going to be late, my darling, and you know how your father hates to be the last to arrive." She could hear footsteps advancing up the corridor. "Sibrey, did you hear me child?" The footsteps stopped in the outside corridor, and the voice seemed to be focusing itself in another direction outside, talking to someone else that had been down below. "Honey, have you found her yet, this isn't at all like her not to answer. Do you think she may be hiding in the Arboretum?"

The footsteps again started forward, and before Sibrey could move a very beautiful female walked into the room just as she dove under the bed. Sibrey was currently lying face down on the floor, covering her head and doing her best to stay hidden. However undeterred, the female smiled at her and said gently, "Ah, there you are child, whatever are you doing lying on the floor? Come, we're going to be late!" The ladey gestured at Sibrey to stand up and follow her, but Sibrey didn't move. None of this could possibly be happening; who was this female Aelf that knew her name, that she had never seen before in her entire life? It wasn't until she felt her touch actually land on her skin, making tangible contact and bringing her forward to a standing position that the reality of the situation began too settle in and the first time she really got a close-up look at her.

Staring at her, with the voice that had called her from wherever she had come from, in the outside corridor was a simply gorgeous female of old Aelven decent. She had to be the most stunning creature Sibrey had ever laid eyes on. But that's not what made her gasp, as she surveyed her new surroundings, it was what had appeared within the room she now stood within.

All around her, in the cavern that not thirty minutes ago had been her prison, was a place completely transformed into what best could be described as a beautiful home. It was not just any ordinary home that had suddenly transformed itself in front of her — it was her dream room, the place she had been dreaming about since she was a child! How does something like that even happen? Sibrey wondered. To have that occur was astronomical, even here in a Fey realm. So, to be living it as it unfolds in living colour, was unsettling; to feel the dream within a dream come to life right in front of your visual cortex....how was that even possible?

She took a good look around her, as she felt herself being pulled towards a window that looked out of a third storey building, with a full battlement below. As soon as she came within sight of what stood on the ground, she realized she was up on a level about three stories from the ground by a beautifully ornate window ledge, and not under any of the building stones she had been dragged through by the thread, as it pulled her below ground from somewhere where the ground had been all broken up and ravaged by some past catastrophe. This new vantage point that had been nothing more than dirt and crumbled rock not more than fifteen counts of the moon's rotation ago, had cobblestones on the pathway and horses; lots of horses, and not just any horses. These were Shadowland horses; huge blonde manes of fur with hooves the size of dinner plates. They belonged to the Caubertian Tribe, who bred some of the finest horses in all of Tantaris.

These horses were always accompanied by the Aelves of Tothray; the tribe of lost Aelves who had fled the Kanoie tribe of Witches out on the badlands of the vast plains of Sheymoar. The village was rumoured to lay somewhere deep in the most remote areas of the Cydclath Mountain range, just south of the Telpphaea Falls. But in ancient times they also had an old settlement that once was the most northern encampment of Fey on Tantaris. Tales told of ruins out along the west coast of the Sea of Contentious Souls, deep within the Islands of Mangoesa, and hidden from the world of the head Druid in Balor's court, called Carpathious. It was said through legend, that the horses were bred with the Selkie Waterhorses along the outer edges of the Undinecis reefs, in order to escape the approaching armies of the Fomorians. These were the horses of legend and myth, and each of them was exclusively bred to cross vast bodies of water without the need of any boats. In the Fomorians time they must have been horrifying to watch, as their armies, assured of a capture, could only watch in abject horror as the retreating army of Caubertian Aelves moved out to sea to evade being taken prisoner, aboard one of the many thousands that had been bred amidst their kind, in the watery stables where they roamed.

Who knows what they had thought, as their kind hadn't been seen in a very long time. As a matter of fact, now that I think of it, there are a lot of things that haven't been seen in a very long time that seem to be coming out of the pages of some long forgotten mythical world, transplanted inside this castle. For even now, the Caubertian Aelves live inland, amongst the mountains of the Cydclath range, and even though there are a few renegades that still might have made Mangoesa their home, the majority of the clan have found sanctuary far from the coast, and away from the dangers of the Sea Serpents that roam those waterways and cause extensive damage to the seafaring tribes that live there.

But to be fair to what she was seeing, nothing was as it appeared to be anyway. So, she watched the horses with her inner eyes, hoping to memorize their beautiful bodies in any way that she could, to keep the image safely tucked away when the dream woke her up, and she went back to her normal life. For what really is one more thing brought out of legend here in this pile of rocks, that only looks like a home, when the dream still carries on and she is fast asleep somewhere on the outside, deep inside her beloved Panther?

"Ah my Panther. Where are you now, my dearest friend?" Sibrey closed her eyes, hoping that when she opened them again all would be as it was, and she would at the very least find herself once more in the village of Sombreia, and not in the cavern below this newly opened part of her continuing dreamscape.

She was wrong, and was immediately brought out of her silent thoughts by the Aelven female still holding court within the room. She opened one eye to look at her, then the other followed suit; she silently swore, realizing she was still locked in the world of the dream.

"Sibrey, please do not dawdle, your father has brought the horses now, and everyone is waiting. Come on, my darling, keep your eyes open love, we must hurry." Sibrey swallowed her thoughts into their rightful place. Truth be known, whoever this female was she had never seen her before in her entire life. Yet here she was actually lifting her up, and carrying her down the hallway.

But something had changed once again, and as she felt the energy of the Aelfen female leave her skin, and her touch disappear from her arm as she started to leave; Sibrey realized she had another very small child in her arms, and was not actually touching her at all. Somewhere in the moments that led up to the female actually reaching for her arm, she had not actually made contact with Sibrey skin at all. What she had done was pull this ghost child out of Sibrey's body, while her own energy had remained firmly rooted in place. The child blinked, looking back at her and stared, and then just as she reached out her tiny hand to point in Sibrey's direction, drawing attention to this ghost of a shade that remained in place, it appeared as if some unseen hand made her disappear from the child's sight. For just then, she ignored Sibrey's face and yawned, rubbing her nose into her mother's shoulder, and placed her chin on her neck and started to dissolve in the mist that was forming at her feet. She slipped away from Sibrey's senses, as she watched them both disappear down the corridor in a drift of fog and wispy illusion, while the memory of actually being carried by the adult female stayed inside the room, and echoed its bones along Sibrey's skin. She felt oddly strange, and felt the illusion was just as real as the child being taken away by the Aelfen ladey down that corridor. She knew in her minds-eye everything that was happening, it was as if it had been her going down the hall and not someone else taking her place, as the ghost that was her was left behind in her own shippel memory; one that she had had all those years ago as a small snippet.

She needed to follow, but couldn't find the muscles that would allow her to move. Instead, she watched them materialize below from the window, as both descended the outside steps, and walked towards a solitary Aelven male that stood by the huge Waterhorses that were prancing nervously about the cobbles. "I've found her!" she heard the female say, but could not make out the last words, as she ducked into the covered carriage at the tip of the railing, and the horses began to immediately take to the air. At the last minute, as they left the cobbles, the male jumped up and joined them, gliding upwards like a dancer, slipping inside to join the others as they made their way off the castle grounds.

The horses, instantly taking great leaps into the air in a flap of wings and hooves, disappeared over the embankment and into the sea. When next she could see them; they came into view almost one-hundred yards past the shoreline, in full gallop, and were pounding the surface of the waves with their huge hooves, kicking up kelp that had broken off as they passed overhead.

So as the story goes, Sibrey had the distinctive impression at this moment, she may have fainted, as she felt her knees go out and everything started to go black. Off in the distance Sibrey could hear the horses screams as they pounded through the surface and rode away into the setting Mauntra. The very Mauntra that had started to settle into a distant moon. Then nothing more....

CHAPTER EIGHT

Dyareius and the Dragons

Dyareius moved closer to Soren, who had not heard him the first time he had asked the question, and watched his friend barely control his anger without howling with rage. Dyareius once again raised his voice to direct Soren's attention upwards to his face; still no response. However, this time he moved right into Soren's path, literally blocking the Aelf by bumping into his chest, still looking at Symin's Dragon. He watched Soren try and skirt around him, but again Dyareius moved into place; this time he yelled at his friend, who only momentarily made eye contact, still raging within his own mind.

"Soren, who's Quist?" Soren, still not quite able to talk without swearing at his commander, pointed to Symin's Dragon.

"That," he screamed, continuing to voice his hostility, "with extreme prejudice, I'll add, because I'm still...rather pissed!" Soren had turned momentarily to Quist and yelled his bloody head off. "AAAAAGGGGGGHHHHHH!" He turned back to Dyareius, dripping with sarcasm for a micro-second, and changed his mind hesitating for only a fraction of a second before moving back in the direction of the Dragon. He turned his head back in Quist's direction and glared at the beast daring him to make a move. He hesitated for only a fraction of a second, then as the Dragon continued to ignore him, he resumed screaming.

"And I said, I wouldn't do this!" he screamed at the Dragon, who continued to ignore him. "I could kill you with my bare hands, you thoughtless beast." Soren bent down to reach for something, before speaking to Dyareius. Hesitating only barely, he pointed at the Dragon screaming, "That, unfortunately, is bloody Quist!" Then quickly threw what he had been reaching for at the beast, who had turned and stamped his foot in defiance. Dyareius paused before answering, looking from one of them to the other.

"The Dragon?" He looked at Soren, with a puzzled expression, then had to quickly duck out of the way as the rock Soren had thrown seemed to take on a life of its own, and manoeuvred around, heading straight for the heads of the Aelves closest to Soren. Both Markus and himself had come dangerously close to having it implanted within their skulls, and decided to step back until Soren could be a little more rational. From past experience, dealing with him always got one of them hurt. Dyareius pulled the troops away from Soren, and then approached him again alone this time, as he continued to rage.

"Soren, are you going to answer my question?" he asked. Soren only glared at him before turning to yell at Symin's Dragon, who appeared to be snickering under his breath at the Aelf. This time Dyareius didn't wait for a response, instead he continued with his line of questioning, looking between both Soren and the Dragon, who had taken on an unusual appearance of actual humorous contemplation.

"You're able to speak with the Dracore? How is that possible?" Dyareius asked him, point blank. Soren turned to his Lieutenant, but still had trouble spitting out the words without flinging everything in sight at Symin's Dragon. He looked at Dyareius finally, after running out of things he could pick up and heave.

"Not just me," Soren said finally, to him, rather sarcastically. "All of us... unfortunately we can't actually always hear them, but the Human child we brought back, he could talk to them all; every single bloody one! But Quist took that from us, didn't he?" Quist roared at Soren, when a projectile hit him square in the head. Plumes of flame erupted and his tail flew around narrowly missing all three Aelves in the vicinity.

Quist had basically had enough of Soren's little fit. He turned on Soren, separating him from the other Aelves with such speed that Dyareius and Markus didn't have time to grab him. Quist bent down right in Soren's face, inches from his own, and growled, breathing hot Dragon breath on the Aelf's face. Soren wasn't hurt, only left with a few singed hair follicles. But every single scale that covered Quist's face was standing on edge; he slowly took his time and blinked, as Soren could see every vein that lined his inner eye lids and much of the atoms that separated their core.

Soren wasn't buying into the fear that the others had of them as he moved just that last inch towards Quist's face. They were on the verge of touching nose to nose, when Soren drew in a big breath, raised his fist, and punched Quist square in the nose once again. Quist just stood there, not even flinching.

"What in the hel were you thinking, you idiot?" Soren yelled again. Quist took in another breath, but this time the scales had moved just a little bit forward and pointed towards Soren, like they were ready to fly off and impale themselves into every exposed piece of flesh Quist could aim for.

It was at this time that Soren began to worry. He realized that Tansar had moved in to run interference with the advancing men, and right behind him the other Dragons were also heading towards the Aelves. With the commotion that had erupted the moment his fist left dead air space, he had been totally cut off and out of earshot from the others. Quist let out his breath and started to speak to the Aelf, inches from his own nose. He hissed loudly, then spoke clearly and concisely, forming his words in a manner that the Aelf wouldn't be able to misunderstand.

"Do that again Soren Aelf and I'll flatten you into the ground like a little ant," he hissed again, not as dramatically with the bloodfire as before, instead sending only wind upwards into Soren's eyes. "Symin and the boy will be safe, trust me on this one, you annoying little creature!" Soren couldn't respond, he just stood there with his mouth wide open, like a toad waiting on an insect sliding down a slippery leaf.

Quist took his front foot, extended up a clawed talon, and placed it under Soren's chin, speaking with as much sarcasm as a Dragon could muster, "and close your mouth, you look like a fish." Soren almost fell over; in fact, had Quist not been actually still touching him, he could very well have banged his head on Quists's scaly snout.

"You can talk without the touchstone? You little freak!" Soren was stunned.

"Of course, you're not the only thing living on this planet that has speech." Quist sat there cleaning his long nails, picking small stones out of his talons like it was nothing out of the ordinary. He spat out a smaller pebble, aiming directly at Soren's head, and continued while Soren ducked sideways avoiding the missile. "The touchstone is for Ryyaan, he's the one that can't speak, you fool," Quist spoke in hushed whispers so the other Aelves couldn't hear him, and looked a little annoyed with Soren for being so stupid.

"But, how?" Then Soren realized something. "Why did you never speak to us during the Dragon wars?" He was up in Quist's face, mostly because he didn't want the others to hear, but also he was looking for another reason to punch the Dragon in the face, as he looked between one eye and the other, for an obvious sore spot. He didn't find anything, while Quist continued to be fully aware of what he was looking for.

"We'll talk later about that," Quist said, "right now we're wasting valuable time arguing over something you have nothing to do with." Quist let out a huge hiss, and continued on with his train of thought. "Now, we need to get Dyareius and his men back to Tameron. Something has changed, and it doesn't feel the way it should. I'll go with them, while you hunt down Kashandarhh, but first you need to get everyone to calm down before you tell them what's going on, because right now I seriously doubt they're going to trust us to take them back, after that little bit of insanity you've exposed us to." Quist pointed with his head, in Dyareius's direction. "Now, go!" He shoved Soren in the back with his nose. "Remember, you started all this," Quist reminded him. "I had nothing to do with it, you little shit. So go and fix it, before you put us all in danger." When Soren merely stared at him, after he was pushed away, Quist whacked him lightly with his tail. "GO!"

Soren rolled his eyes and ran his left hand across his brow, trying to figure it all out, as he made his way around the Dragons. Tansar had managed to keep the Aelves away from their conversation, as Soren carried on through the grass to where the Aelves now stood. Dyareius spotted him coming towards them, and manoeuvred his body to meet him halfway.

"What is going on, I thought you said only the Human can talk with them?" he asked. Soren knew he had a lot of explaining to do, and very little time to do it in.

"Well, up 'til that bit of insanity, so did I." Soren shook his head explaining as quickly as he could about Tamerk, then the touchstone, and the bits he knew about Ryyaan. He also relayed what Quist had told him about Tameron and explained that en-route he could go into more details of the storyline, but it would be harder to understand, so it would probably be best if Quist explained it himself.

Soren watched the Dragons approaching as he was talking, and saw that now there was a bit more apprehensiveness in the group, towards them. But only Quist actually came to meet them; the others hung back until it was safe once again. The remainder wandered back to the field, beginning to move about grazing through the grasses, simply ignoring the little uproar that had just occurred. Once in a while they could be seen looking up, just to be sure things were still not going to turn ugly once again, as they waited patiently for Quist to signal them to come in.

Dyareius spoke first, turning to the massive beast that towered over him.

"Is Symin going to be alright?" he asked.

"Yes," Quist answered, as Dyareius looked incredulous at him, then back to his men. "There's something the Human needs to do, and Symin he trusts. Without Symin he will not be able to complete it."

"What is it that's so important you take one of my men without his consent?" Dyareius inquired.

"I cannot answer; only the Great Whites have that knowledge." Quist cocked his head sideways as he answered, looking at the Aelf from higher up than Dyareius liked him to be.

"Do you still intend to be honour bound with this new journey?" Dyareius continued on, not skipping a beat with him.

"As always, we swear by the blood oath of the Dragonlords." Quist bowed his head in acknowledgement to the Aelf, then rose and looked Dyareius in the eye. "But," said Quist, "the question is, **DO YOU, MY AELVEN BROTHER?**" he threw in with a toothy grin.

"We are not the ones who held back the truth," Dyareius put in, pointing a finger at the Dragon.

"All will be revealed in due time; not everything is as it seems," Quist was quick to reply in return. "Tact must be upheld in all things Fey. It has been told that it was a requirement, especially with the Aelven races we have been a part of. The black Dragons could not afford new enemies, within the Fey that live in this side of our realm. Quist went silent, waiting for Dyareius to speak.

"So, now, what is to be done that has not been said?" Dyareius looked at the creature with a question that needed answering, before they could continue, honour bound.

"Of which are we speaking, brother Aelf, Tameron or Dragon?" Dyareius could only reply to Quist, as simply as he could formulate the question.

"My homeland, I would think; must we fight as Dragonlords, or will the Humans be the war?"

Tansar had come up slowly behind Quist, and both Dragons seemed to be exchanging information of some sort between the two of them. Quist quickly nodded to his brethren, and continued the line of communication with the Aelf.

"The human child will be involved, but the humans aren't your cause. It will be a little more dangerous than that, I'm afraid." said Quist. "You see, the war that is coming will be within your own house." He blinked, sliding his face downwards towards Dyareius.

Dyareius was caught by surprise. The Aelven homeland had never been compromised. It was the one thing that they all could be assured would be their safety net; a place of unparalleled beauty that words had been always upheld, in all courts of its land holdings. Only one question of the many thousands Dyareius could think of at this moment could be said now.

"How?" Was the only word that Dyareius could find.

"That would be your Shapeshifter. Only she can tell that truth." Quist actually smiled.

But that brought only more questions to Dyareius' mind. They had been quested to return her to Tameron, and failed to retrieve her, as Soren had explained early to them.

"Quist, we need to find her before we can return." Soren spoke up. "We cannot return without her, we are bonded to do so." Quist turned to Soren, before replying.

"Ah, this is true, my young friend, but she has already arrived."

"What?" Soren and Dyareius said at the same time. "How is this possible, and why did you not tell us?" Soren spoke before Dyareius could respond to the Dragons. Tansar spoke to them in turn, Quist having relinquished his role, stepped behind, watching the others for signs of trouble.

"She sleeps beneath the city, within the old site of Tameron. She will dream, as she has for a millennial fraction of her lineal time on this world. But it is not time as you know it; it has special things attached and runs in a Majikal loop of interference. She will be there still, when we return."

Tansar moved away, starting to graze, ignoring the Aelves he had just spoken to. Dyareius was mortified.

"But we cannot go there! Quist, tell him, it is now filled with a substance that we can no longer breathe in." Soren was visibly upset. Quist once again took Soren into control, formulating the words that his brethren could not accept through their own understandings of Aelven physiology.

"She will awaken when the time is right, Soren. There is a watcher with her, that keeps her asleep. She will be awakened only when the time comes, by the ones who keep her safe."

Quist stood up to his full height. "It's time, Dyareius, gather your men," and he moved off to meet the other Dragons still out in the field, now moving out of range as if they had already agreed to go. Soren watched him go; it was going to be a long night ahead, once again. The Dragons lifted their heads and snorted at the approaching pair, as Quist had caught up with Tansar's movements. All eleven Dragons grazing suddenly stopped, and they started moving in unison towards the pair of them. Soren shook his head, time had suddenly just run out, and he hadn't even told them about the Witch.

CHAPTER NINE

Llyach Clan of Sylmoor

The ground had been rumbling for days and spoke using its own faulted medium. Even the animals that lived along the river had been showing awareness of its stress. A lone figure walked toward the water's edge. His village needed clean water, but no one could trust the wells within the village's limits now that the shaking was coming directly up from the mountain's very core.

It had been a long time since Tantaris had voiced her opinions on Fey matters and today seemed to be one of her noisier conversations within her line of comfort. He stood and watched the steam rise slowly from one of the closer vents, then continued on his way in search of an easier access point that would produce palatable drinking water for his village clan.

As he made his way through the trees to the water's edge, he noticed several of the smaller pools had ripples beginning to break through the normally flat surface. The surface waters usually ran smooth around the shoreline pebbles, but this morning it seemed more reflective, with new flashes of silver moving just within its edges. He stopped to watch, and discovered several pairs of eyes blinking and staring back at him. The creatures were Gwraqedd Annwn and given that they were mostly solitary creatures, he could only not even begin to imagine their fear if they were finding each other, instead of staying alone.

It was known that in times of trouble these small creatures would gather around their offspring, who could not leave these smaller pools, and transport them to safer waters that survived intact across the vast distances between the breeding ponds. As he watched, he came to see that the river he was moving towards already housed several of those tadpoles that had been transported previously, now resting in the shade by the water's edge, patiently waiting for the others who moved along the trail.

A large Sugar Maple, torn up by recent rains, had fallen within reach of the edge of the river, and its long branches dangled within the river's depths, providing the perfect shelter for these small life forms. The tadpoles in time would grow up to be the great solitary creatures he now saw scurrying about, gathering their young on their backs and scuttling from one pond to another as fast as their funny legs could carry them. In about another hundred or so years, these waters would ply with the likes of many different species and the Gwraqedd Annwn would grow strong enough to leave, to do it all over again.

He backed away and moved off slowly to allow them to continue, and headed further upstream into the deeper pools. He would not take the water from where their hatch points led them to the safer nest site. The water here was cooler anyways, and much clearer than the shallower pools he had left behind. There were several large, flattened stones that jutted out into the deeper section of the pools, and it was to here that he stepped, watching his feet in case something else had also arrived with the same idea in mind.

He could see straight to the bottom of the crystal clear waters, that the round river stone rested on down below. As he filled the water containers, he found these pools which had been formed when this planet was still a baby calmed the frayed nerves he had been experiencing for more than a week. The sound of the water moving over the smooth stones in the distant shallows always reminded him of the Faery bells he had heard about during his entire younger life.

The elders of the tribe had always told the smaller children that the Ferrishyn dwelt within the deeper pools, and would find the youngsters along whichever way they entered the river, to drag them into the depths and give them to their allies. These allied Nixies, who lived within the old underwater cities, could be found living in burrows of mud and fish scales, and loved to trade in anything shiny that they had found fallen or sitting near the river's edges.

Of course it was only a story told to the young to prevent them from wandering off and drowning in the fast moving water. But, for a while it would work; until the fantasy would become just that, and each would return to swim with the older broods, as they finally grew up and ignored these fanciful tales.

These waters in summer were usually full of those older children, long since divested of those childish fears, all laughing and diving amongst these very stones. But since the ground had begun its rumblings, even that activity had come to an end. The children would no longer leave their homes for fear of whatever was creating these difficult times.

He knelt down, filling up his buckets with fresh water to take to the village that he had just come from. He watched the current, making sure none of the tadpoles had been swept up by the swift moving water, to land within his buckets that now appeared to be somewhat full. He looked deep within the waters, as adults sometimes do, just in the faint glimmer of truth to the old tales, and laughed at the realization that the fear would probably always be within each and every one of them, long after they grew old and all knew better. But, as he turned to leave, a reflection in the water caught his eye and he turned his face skyward just in time to see the huge White Dragon fly overhead far above him.

Stephponias held his hand above his eyes to shade the rays that had momentarily blinded him, and blinked with the beginning threads of understanding what he was actually seeing. There was not a single Aelven family in his entire village, in the history of his clan, who would believe the sight he was witnessing, nor believe him had he tried to explain it upon his return. Several of the resident greens followed the Dragon along the treeline, gliding in and out of the waves of air that propelled its giant wing span forward, along with several other creatures he had no words for migrating alongside him. The vast amounts of air flow the Dragon was creating with those huge wingtips alone must have been phenomenal, and judging by the greens' reaction as they dived and yipped like small children playing in the under draft, the speeds were something out of this world.

He watched in awe and with a little trepidation, as its form began to block out the rays of the Mauntra the shadow now filtered through, throwing its reflection on the land below. He moved with the speed of one of the Taper deer that roamed through these woods, leaving behind the buckets of water that would only slow him down as he made his way back into town. His footsteps barely landed on the moss covered tree stumps that littered the pathway, which he had previously taken to reach the water's edge, with just the right amount of care to steer clear of the Gwraqedd Annwn, unaffected by the bizarre sight that had sent him careening towards them all over again.

He moved quickly, and had only just reached the outskirts of the village, when his ears could already pick up the shouts from the village residents, long before his actual arrival. With a silent whisper of thanks that he would not have to explain what he had just witnessed, he broke through the trees into the middle of those that had come outside to the centre of their village square to watch the spectacle overhead.

They were observing the giant wings slowly receding away to the east, as he skidded in to join them, just as the creature and his entourage began to leave the vicinity of their village trees. They slowly got smaller and smaller then disappeared from everyone's sight, leaving the residents staring at the empty sky the Dragon had momentarily occupied. A few wild greens still floated along the breeze, and then they too disappeared from sight, joining the White Dragon in his flight to the north.

Anyone who had been sceptical of the recent days could only stare at the vacant skies above. For things had just become a little more realistic to the denying few who still did not believe the stories, where a once mythical beast had just come to life, moving like the one black Dragon they had once seen so many years ago.

The silence settled for no more than a micro-second, then chaos erupted within the village square. But Stephponias could not stay, he had to find Coutinnea. She was still in Kilren visiting her kin, the very kin that were friends of Kamera, the Witch's mother. She of all people would know what should be done. He had almost begun his shift, when he noticed Lunesa's young son following him, as he rounded the other side of the town's granary. Lunesa was their clan leader's, wife. This young child was all he had time to speak to, seeing those around him begin to all run in different directions.

"Tell your father I'm going to find Kamera! Quickly child, I'll send word as soon as I can!" Steph shifted right in front of him, as the child ran, carrying the words he had no doubt would find Kaber's ears, before the shift had even been finished.

CHAPTER TEN

Travel to Kilren

Coutinnea had travelled the road that led to Kilren on foot for years. It was something she always did, preferring to walk the trails in relative quiet, listening to all that passed and lived within this environment as it calmed her body and matching sage-coloured senses.

She carried the herbs Kamera had requested in a leather bag that she kept slung over her shoulder, allowing her to keep her finely boned hand on her left side free and clear of any obstruction. There were many plants along the trail that she had harvested in the past, and having the cumbersome bag in any other position would often get in her way, as she balanced the cutting knife she held to reach for another specimen that Kamera had asked for in the past. This would be a gift in addition to the others she had placed in her order from the parchment Coutinnea still carried in her satchel; one that had been brought to her through another Sage's shift.

There were times she thought of the other Wildcrafters that walked these woods, each one choosing their own method of getting from one place to another, but something always seemed to make her just a bit queasy with the challenges of that method. She didn't like to use her shifting abilities, as many of her clanswomen did to visit others throughout the year. She had not the desire to visit people that regularly, in order to move quickly through the winter months when snow was piled higher than a person could physically walk through. Her home in the village of Sylmoor was adequate for all her needs, and should something come up she was more than happy to pass it along to another Sage if someone required it in a hurry, while the winter storms filled the passes with their snows and bitterly cold winds.

Coutinnea was taught by one of the old master Wildcrafters of another time. They had adapted their methods to pass along to others who might have the same fears she had, of passing through a door-way built in a faraway landscape of another race. The tendrils of fear of new-age travel would not change inside her mind anytime soon. Instead, she concentrated solely on the advancement of her own knowledge in the fields, simply harvesting what was her own.

It was very different for the younger crafters, who supplied the main cities with freshly picked herbs. She felt she had been taught the old ways for a reason, and having that lesson fully intact within her brain, she also thought her cargo would be compromised within the molecules of molecular travel.

Most of the wild crafters would argue that was out-dated, but it was the herbs that were picked by her hand that were requested more often than the others, so she maintained this level of belief, and used the time to enjoy the trip she had set herself up upon this day.

She stopped to smell the dampness which ran within the air of the darker sections of the trees. She sighed deeply and continued onward, walking within the woods that ran in somewhat of a north-east direction, away from her village. There was always her sanity that needed reaffirming, and the grounding it required to keep her in check. It would take many times along this trip, to breathe in deeply the essence of her medicine plants and their natural surroundings so as not to slide sideways in the world of complete chaos that had surrounded this planet during the last few months.

Things always came into play at the most inopportune moments, she knew. There may come a time when she needed to pay attention to what Stephponias had always warned her about in this form of travel. It was this thought that allowed her to move about the forest more freely than the others of her trade. And she had always been able to use the eyes of her hawk when needed, in times of uncertainty. She could still see him flying within the thermals, waiting for the time he could catch something that was starting to slither molecularly, within her line of sight. As if he read her mind, he immediately sent off a screech from high above where she was walking.

Her mate Stephponias, was more often busy with his own duties in the village; so she used this time to collect new herbs along her way that were not available near her own slip of picking grounds. It had been many months since last she had travelled to Kamara's home, and never in that length of time had Kamera ordered such a vast supply of specialty herbs. But with the Nasadh season approaching and Cian's son Lugh of the Tuatha De`Danann recently coming into power, she thought maybe Kamera was taking no chances that his army may be out and near the area she was living within.

Kamera was well known within the Tuatha De`Danann's ranks. It was to her they often found themselves coming in the middle of the night when an injury had occurred; opting instead for her healing hands, than those of their own resident healer. Furthermore, if times of injuries were on the rise in this new usurping of command, Coutinnea thought Kamera would need the extra stock inside her pantry just to keep a fresh supply at hand. Kamera did love her warriors, and treated each of them as if they were her own kin, so it only made sense that they would go to her. Especially as she doled out large portions of homemade whiskey once they received the help they needed.

Mind you, those that showed up primarily for the drink would soon find themselves ass over tea-kettle on the front cobbles of her home, as she scolded them for wasting her time, picking them up with her majikal mind and turfing them into the nearest lake. Whereby, anyone choosing to go that route would soon find themselves black-listed from her healing abilities, while the others would laugh their heads off that they had even tried.

Coutinnea's village, Sylmoor, was also in good standing with the Tuatha. They were part of a huge alliance with the tribes that belonged within its hunting realm. But she was not as well-known as the Witch in her healing poultices, and still a virtual unknown as far as the face that now travelled within these woods, away from the elder who was simply known as the Witch's mother. She knew Kamera had introduced her name many times to the Tuatha's own Sages, but until they had a face attached to the name she could still very well be mistaken for one of the Fomorians that lived just north-west of here.

She needed to remain alert in these woods while she made her way to Kilren, as their small skirmishes could often be heard in the dead of night along any of the different pathways that led away from her village. As it was, the young leader called Lugh was still a young man as of yet, and his killing of Balor was no different than how Balor had come into power himself, in the first place.

Those of the elder Fey who lived within this world had experienced several different leaders, who had come into power during various skirmishes along the Tuatha De˙Danann's borderlands. Accordingly, no one really knew how long the current transition period was going to take, as it went through the growing pains associated with another change in command. Lugh may have taken the command by killing his grandfather, but the young God in training still had to earn it from the race of Fomorians themselves, and they were still staging little coups along the trail heads where they had been running for going onto a good six full moons, and could at any time pop up in any of the smaller villages along the fringes.

As a result, patrols along the continental ridges were not an oddity, and she had also recently been informed by Steph that the black Dragons of the Dragonlords had been seen about again, which gave her more reason to pause. When the war had begun all those years ago, she had an opportunity to see one of those in the early years, as it had arrived hurt and sick within her own village walls. She did not want to repeat that again; having such a creature flying freely within the skies above any village was enough for one lifetime. They had not been heard or seen from again, since the end of the Dragon wars. If they had been recalled, Steph was right to worry.

She moved a little more quickly along the trail, watching from time to time the sky where Ganmole her hawk still continued to fly high, soaring in and out like some form of aviator from the great beyond. Steph had insisted, if she was going to use this form of transportation, she was to bring Ganmole. Ganmole had been with her since he first graduated from the animal training conservatory. He had been hatched there in one of the huge incubators, alongside others of his clutch, and trained from a young chick in the art of animal tracking majiks that was taught to all the animals within the school.

He had been with her for many years and was highly trained in Aelfen majiks to keep the Sages safe within her village. These animals had certain gifts in the tracking of dark majiks, which others of their kind could not see. And Ganmole was top of his class in other majiks the others had not been trained in, because of an inner ear condition that did not allow him to communicate properly with other members of his species. Somewhere in his training, he had picked up the means necessary to spot anything not right, that would harm his caretakers, long before they would pick it up with their own senses.

All the birds in their aviaries had certain skills, and were assigned to their particular Fey groups when they were deemed ready to take on one of the village Aelves as their guardians. But Ganmole was different; he wouldn't work with the other Sages. It was because of this that he was allowed to choose the one that was suited to his needs, and not the other way around as most of the connections had been decided in the past. To go against the rules, was unheard of in any of the Fey colonies. But Ganmole decided it was to be her and her alone, even though his kind was deemed to be Witch Fey; so, as the others looked on in horror, it was a solitary Sage that wouldn't shift that was given solitary rights to him as her companion, instead of the hierarchy of Witches that normally would have received his unusual gift.

She had to laugh at that day, when the Mauntra shone brightly overhead, and he landed on her shoulder as she made her way to the outskirts of the village, unaware of what had just transpired. Nothing could have surprised her more, for she had not put in for any of the familiars that were to be graduated that day. But, what was to be was to be, and nothing, come hel or high water, could separate him from her again, even though they tried with everything they could throw at him. So, today he followed her without asking, and all she had to do was open the cage and out he came to fly high above the tree-tops, where she currently discovered the herb that almost got missed as she walked along the pathway at her feet, wistfully remembering his first arrival.

So it was that on this day, as she gave that control to Ganmole overhead, she spotted the lovely specimen of Alraun plant that had been such an elusive specimen for those that had been searching for it. She had just reached over to take a bit of its leathery leaf, as was given in her agreement from the land holders of this particular section of the trailhead, when something unexpected happened not too far overhead.

You see, Steph had been having terrible nightmares, and the Alraun that she had dried in jars was beginning to lose its potency. This would not only replenish what she had dried almost two years ago, but would be more powerful with the Byanadorian Moon that had just passed through on its way to Leberone's darker side.

It was because of this activity, she did not hear at first Ganmole's alarm call, and feel the evil as it passed overhead of her small Aelfen body and then continued slowly on its way. The vaporous formation was already out of her sight when she finally did hear Ganmole's call of alarm, and her own senses at that time perceived it to be nothing more than a non-threatening life formation.

She rose up, halfway through giving thanks to the plant for the contribution of its offering, and quickened her pace through the trees that had begun to find them-selves much more mature than previously past. Whatever had set him off, had to be something she could not feel. And if that was all she got as a warning before she felt whatever had arrived on scene, she was currently in the wrong part of the trail for any help from Kilren.

She started to gather whatever she had hastened to collect — still loose within her arms, and placed them solidly within the satchel, so that they would remain intact and safe. She could ill afford to lose what she had gathered in her haste to get to Kilren now, so she secured the lot and returned to the trail she had momentarily stepped away from. Then, moving off slowly, she listened for her hawk, still perceiving it to be nothing more than forest jitters, and continued on down the trail. But this time she didn't stop to dilly dally along the way, fearing instead that maybe something might have been following her along the ground, more to do with the animal persuasion than anything else.

Ganmole followed the mist from a great distance above, watching it move about the air as if it was methodically searching for something. His senses were on high alert, and for some reason Coutinnea hadn't observed his original call. But, as it moved away, he circled behind it once, following its pathways to see what he had felt inside its thickening mist, then continued on another thermal, returning to Coutinnea and their mission to reach Kilren by nightfall.

The mysterious substance moved away and continued down the Valley and out of sight, disturbing a flock of ravens in its path. Their flight had taken them directly into the mass, and each that had touched the blackened mist instantly fell out of the sky and died without so much as a single sound. Whatever it was, continued on searching the skies as it manoeuvred away from the flock of falling birds without stopping to see what it had done.

Coutinnea made it to the outskirts of Kilren just before nightfall. She moved gently through the wards, waving her identity to the watchers that guarded the village of Kamera's home, making no haste as the Mauntra set and closed over the horizon. Ganmole glided in and landed in the doorway of her great aunt's backyard aviary, and entered without any further sightings of the thing that made the sky full of darkened death. He was greeted by the others that made this place their home, and accompanied by the screeching of a great horned Gwadrafed, he slipped into place alongside the others, and started to preen himself of the dark mass's energy molecules that had gotten underside of one of his wings. Large lumps of dead feathers could be seen falling about the floor, disappearing from sight the moment they landed. But nothing could be seen attached to any of his other feathers, after the wards literally vaporized anything that might have remained intact.

Coutinnea, tired from her journey, was met by her great aunt at the doorway to the family's northern home. Tomorrow she would meet with Kamera, the mother of the great Witch of the Tuatha De'Danann, but tonight she would spend her time with the one family member who had always treated her with respect. It appeared she had arrived just in time for the family's healing ceremony, rejoicing in the ending times of the

Byanadorian Moon. It was just about to get underway, when she came into view.

"Come child, it is time. I've saved you a spot near the firelight so you can find your rest while the others talk." Her aunt moved to help her within the warm interior wall of her home's outside planetarium. Outside, the moon was covered by an unusual shadow, as it started its nighttime journey into that darkened section of the night sky.

The next morning began with a lovely light streaming in through the windows and covering each pane of glass with its reflecting warmth. Coutinnea had been sitting with her great aunt drinking coffee for more than an hour, just chatting and enjoying the Mauntra-light of the morning sky when Kamera came walking up the pathway, and found them lost in each other's company.

"Your journey was enjoyable?" she asked, kissing Coutinnea on the forehead.

"Actually, it was just nice to have some time away from Sylmoor." Coutinnea smiled back at the older female Aelf, whose skin shone like porcelain in the garden they were sitting in. "Steph gets so busy with his work that at times he doesn't always get the time to go picking with me down the old pathways of the wildcrafter gardens. With the cooler season just around the corner, there has been so much to do getting things ready for the coming winter months, that it is a treat to be ask to come for a visit. Thank-you for that. And now with all the rumblings going on with the mountains to the south, we have also been unable to use the wells within the village to get fresh water. So each morning he is gone before daybreak, to fetch the water from one of the deeper pools which run alongside the cliff at the base of Sydclath Peaks."

Kamera patted her head, pouring the herbs she had received from Coutinnea's pouch into one of her own, without missing a beat of the conversation. "Whew," she sighed, "I just needed to get away." Coutinnea laughed, thinking of her aunt dancing among the stars last night, during the height of the moon ceremony. Kamera raised a quizzing eyebrow at Coutinnea's aunt, who shook her head in response.

"Don't ask." She said, while Coutinnea carried on laughing at the image and then changed direction to the current conversation that had been at hand before the laughter started.

"I was saying, I needed the change of landscape, away from the smell of one of the larger sulphur tubes near our village that had cracked wide open in the last shaking we had since the earth started its rumblings."

"Have the cracks reached the north section of the rift yet?" her Aunt asked, while she took a sip from her mug. Her Aunt looked a bit worried and turned to Kamera, who in turn silently shook her head, steering the conversation away from the dangers of the splitting of the southern ridge, away from the other sections of Sydclath Mountain Range. The last thing this girl needed was to realize how close they were to coming apart during the middle of a perfectly good cup of coffee. Coutinnea didn't see the warning Kamera had given her Aunt, and carried on talking as if nothing was said.

"So, I must thank you Kamera, for asking me to come. There are days that I really just need to find some peace and solitude, without having to play housekeeper day in and day out to a husband that seems to care more for a mountain than the everyday up keep of his home." Kamera smiled and patted her arm as she reached across the table for the extra mug placed by the coffee pot.

"Coutinnea, I wouldn't have asked for these herbs from any other Sage, yours are by far superior, down to the molecule."

"Thank you, Kamera." Coutinnea smiled. "How is your daughter, is she well?"

"Ah, my darling thanks for reminding me, I have something for her." Kamera patted her pockets and retrieved a small raw green stone from within. "Please, as a favour for me," she held the stone to her chest, "could you find my Kashha and give this to her?" Coutinnea put down her mug and smiled at her.

"Kamera, it would be an honour, but I don't understand? Why not give it to her yourself?"

"Ah well, these old bones tend not to let me travel much anymore, and I know how much you've always wanted to meet her, so," she patted Coutinnea on the head and smiled, "now you can. Besides, she spends far too much time alone up there. For me, it would do her good to have a bit of company that has more to talk about than her dear old mother." Coutinnea looked quizzically at Kamera, not understanding how one so fit could actually think she was too old to travel.

Kamera watched Coutinnea's face start to question her thoughts. "Truly Innea, it would be much easier for you to travel these trails than me." Kamera winked at her aunt, while she regained Coutinnea's nod in an animated response. "Thank you." Kamera took her own hand and patted Coutinnea's face.

"Well done, now tell me how the Llyach's are doing inside a village full of rumbling fools. We've heard the rumours of your earth shakings, so tell us more on what we can do to help." Suddenly Kamera sat straight up and listened intently, then turned back to Coutinnea, looking straight at the Llyach Aelf. "Well, we seem to have a problem in the aviary my dear. It would appear the Gwadrafed has just changed the colour of your Ganmole's tail feathers."

"What?" Coutinnea started to stand, spilling her cup of coffee along the table where it was sitting. She was just starting to get ready to flee to where her beloved Ganmole was perched, when Kamera started to laugh, looking at Coutinnea's aunt.

"Really, truly she is very easy to tease. Who would have thought that one so wise in the way of herbs could be so easy to bring down, along the edges of another's homeland Faery stories?" Coutinnea frowned, then suddenly stopped moving. Kamera started to giggle.

"Come now, I'm only teasing, my dear! Sit down." she patted Coutinnea's head, letting her settle herself back down. "I think this calls for just a little bit of something special in our coffee this morning. Don't you think child?" Laughter carried down the lane as all three females could be heard chatting away long into the morning Mauntra light, as the level of amber coloured liquid grew smaller and smaller inside the beautifully decorated flute.

The black mist moved towards the mountain settlement that contained the mines. One of Kanoie's famous ore mines resided there, and emeralds had been located at the new section they had just opened. The Trolls in charge hadn't noticed that they seemed to be pulling primarily emeralds out of the ground in most of the western mines, in greater numbers than any-time in the past; they were simple miners, that were only to happy to just make a living with whatever popped up on the surface cracks of the old fire tubes.

The creature sensing this, followed the energy trail to each of the new digging sites, soaking up emerald dust as each of the precious stones reached with their little heads and breathed the surface air. It licked the stone's essence, letting it flow outwards into each molecule of its being, and carried on into the shade to rest. The creature stayed there momentarily, gaining new strength. Then, without a backwards glance, it left the mine to search for more of the same, unaware that on the outer edges it had turned the colour of blackened coal, as the miners continued to sort and threw them alongside others that were the real coal specimens.

This time the creature retained some memory of staying hidden, and was more diligent about the area's wildlife it had found scattered about the search grid. It couldn't keep leaving traces of its arrival for the De`Danann to find, or they would keep away the very thing it was looking for, behind the wards they seemed to be so fond of. It would need to watch out for whatever energy they tried to hide. Soon enough, one of them would accidentally slip it into his very own field of energy, and he could return back to where he had originally come from without them even noticing.

The latter morning found Coutinnea with directions in hand and a small green stone tucked away in a satchel. Tucked along with it were a few other provisions that Kamera thought her daughter would like, but not particularly need. She headed northwest with enough daylight to bring her to the Damonian Woods where Kashha lived, and back again before nightfall. She was both excited and a little apprehensive with the knowledge she would be coming face to face with this well-known Fey she had known by legend and story alone.

She didn't think it was the fact that Kashandarhh was a Witch that made her feel so nervous, she had met Witches before, but it was that Kashha was used by the Tuatha De`Danann exclusively for her unusual talents that made her anxious. None of the Sages had ever met Kashandarhh in any of their dealings, and she was known by reputation as one you didn't cross. The Kashandarhh Witch was very much a legend, even among the Witch folk. She had after all been to Leberone and travelled within this side of their galaxy at will.

Coutinnea had never met anyone that had ever done that, so to be able to see her in person was a little nerve wracking, and she wondered if Kamera had really picked the right person to address this new friendship. But meeting Kasha was something she always wanted to do, even when the others had laughed at the idea of one so timid actually being chosen to accomplish that goal.

Coutinnea had spent most of her life among the small towns and villages that the Llyach clan had done its trading with on Tantaris. Mostly for her, it had been the places that had been within one or two day's walking distance of the villages that she would visit, not really being able to take the time to visit family or friends much further away than that. Steph had been the one to deliver her herbs to further townships, given his love of the actual shifting energy, but she herself was basically a little boring.

She didn't have the interest, as other people did, to see things or spend time away from her home, so she would spend her days within her own village. The herbs she required were plentiful and abundant, and it was a rare occurrence that something that was asked for wasn't to be found within that stretch of land that she cultivated. She was not an overly educated person, but she wasn't in any way stupid, as some of the village children would be caught at various times in the past saying, and singing the nursery rhymes of her youth.

'*Tinnea Innea, she is a Hyena, and cares not a whit for the day. With spiders inside her and people beside her, she never comes out to play!*'

The song had stuck and the lyric had fit, and now she found herself humming it as she walked towards something that she had no business being part of, in a world meant for others who would always turn their backs as she walked on by, ignoring the girl who would one day get to meet the famous Witch. She liked that sentiment and it suddenly ever so slowly made her grin with contentment to think what they would say, when word of this day spread like wildfire through the village she lived in.

She was happy within her own little world and didn't pay much attention to things that were outside the limits of her understanding. People had been good to her within her Fey circle and always treated her medicines with respect. But it was with Steph that current events had been discussed, and if it was something she needed to know only then was it decided by him to inform her of it.

So, today's little journey was indeed something so far out of her comfort zone, that it was laughable, that she was even considering it. But the chance to meet Kashandarhh was far too much of an opportunity to miss. Had she known that Steph was on his way, she would have gladly waited in Kanoie for his arrival. But that was not to be, and as she moved along the beginnings of the trail, she decided to keep Ganmole within the Kilren aviary. She somehow felt it would be disrespectful to arrive at Kashha's home with a hawk on her arm, as if she didn't feel Kasha could be trusted.

This mistake both saved her, and almost cost her that life.

Her movement away from the village wards had not gone unnoticed. The very thing that had screened her the first time awoke, and detected her presence once again. It called forth the mist to return to its position and positioned itself towards her. But, as before, sensing her innocent nature and the non-magical essence she exuded from having no molecules of shift transfer in her blood, it then turned and continued on its way without further detection from anyone within the area.

That was the mistake of its life. For, deep within the satchel she carried to Kashandarhh, was the very thing the mist had been looking for since it had arrived. The real reason Kamera had not wanted to carry it on her person had nothing to do with the fact that she was too old to travel. The real reason Kamera had let her carry it was the very thing she had hated most about herself all these years...her own innocent nature, one that belonged to a world, that wouldn't shift.

CHAPTER ELEVEN

The Caretakers of the Scared Grove

Sibrey woke up, to the best of her knowledge. However, to those looking from the outside in, she was fast asleep, still high within the safety of the huge tree. Sometime during her rest, one of the Fey Goddesses that worked alongside Arddhu, had slipped a whisper thin silken covering, made by one of the Drymiais that lived in the area, over top of her bare skin to keep the chill out.

Arddhu and Triduana had lived together in this beautiful sanctuary, and co-parented this huge majikal menagerie for more than half of their lives. He was the one that ruled the inside trees of their secluded cove, and she lived, more often than not, within the sacred hot springs that Sibrey now had made her own.

To have the Shapeshifter child among these treasured spaces was an honour not often given to the Goddesses of the Fey world. To have The Sibrey, the one child that would change the very planet, who they had fought long and hard to protect, was an omen of things to come. You see, it takes a lot for even one of the spirit people to become uneasy when things float along with that reek of evil, because in the world of the Fey, many things can be mistaken for that tumultuous feeling, including nothing more than one of the younger species outside at play. But, it takes a lot of false alarms before something sets them off that they themselves cannot begin to fix, and causes them to send the sky people in to take another look.

Triduana thought for a moment how long it had been before her and Arddhu were called in to investigate the anomaly that had suddenly come crashing into their skies. She couldn't recall whether it had taken very long before they had been informed of its existence, but Fey time and Goddess time were not the same creature. In fact, they didn't even register on the same time lines. For the world of the sky people ran straight through the Magellen star system, that moved perpendicular to that of the known Fey race that Sopdet had adopted as her pet project, for the last one hundred million years.

Sopdet had taken note immediately when it had arrived back within this solar system, and had reached out the only way she knew how, by getting both of the hidden sky people to close ranks and bring the child into their own realm — the very place that Sibrey crossed about mid-way through the lake, brought her into that realm. Had she already acquired her full powers, the cove that settled itself into the nest site that she now rested within, could have been blown apart with just a single flick of her little Shifter wrist.

Triduana shivered at the thought. It was a good thing Sibrey had her main powers taken away at her birth as she slid into this Fey world. If not, the damage she could have done to her current Fey family, let alone the doorway to their realm, would have been catastrophic during these times of dreaming. They probably caught her just as the transformation had entered the final stages, away from a feline that currently had arrived at the sanctuary last night around the time Sibrey had finally fallen into a deep slumber.

They released the wards, and let him enter along the shore-line before he had alerted the creature that hunted them both. She watched as he curled around her slender body, after he made his way once again back into the very branch that Sibrey had made herself at home. Sometime during the night he had gone towards the perimeter of their wards, and challenged the gateway as he paced its energy field, looking for anything that could find its way through fissures and Fey-lines not previously checked by Arddhu or herself. Damn smart cat. He had stood their screaming his fool head off, when something that he saw in his feline eyes had gone unnoticed by their sentries. They rectified it immediately, and only then did he return to the branch to take up his stance in Sibrey's protection, and once again return to be the big black Panther.

Once in a lifetime of a planet's conception, does an event like this arise. It is unusual to have a familiar, which changes the dynamics of a child's essence into another not easily detected by the outside world on any of the planes of existence. However, this feline was not what he appeared to be, and would in time show his true self. Triduana slowly cringed with another thought, which took precedence over the other. Even more unusual, it took a Fey child to do the work which normally was done by the gentry from the very skies that she had lived within, since their birth.

Oracles within their own realm foretold of this day, and even the Tuatha De˙Danann's Witch Kashandarhh had been warning the High Council of its impending arrival. But as it happens, you cannot do much until that thing that had been given birth, strays within sight once again and comes to the very shores you are sworn to protect.

Triduana would have liked everyone to have been able to prevent its existence from coming into the pathway of this galaxy. But no one could have foretold the entrance point at that time of its nether launching, or whether something could arrive within their own worlds to shut it down once and for all, once it actually arrived.

Others had tried and failed. So, Sopdet had sent searchers out on the Great White Dragons from Leberone to patrol the skies of space, but not even they had been able to trace its re-entry. So the grove had its best and highest paid body guards, to do what they knew could be done to keep her hidden from its presence. But, they also knew it was only a matter of time if the guard failed, before something got through and killed them all. Hopefully they were able to way-lay the inevitable, letting Sibrey make it through the void in time with the changing that was so close at hand. If it had anything to do with the big cat at her feet, she was positive that it was going to try come hel or high water to get her there in one piece, when the time came to do so.

Arddhu materialized beside her to take her place, giving her the rest that she would need before the others would arrive to take over. He patted her arm, and sent her to the chambers she kept below ground in the hot springs of her home. All that knew the secret of where Sibrey now rested, had completed the training of its controlled environment and would soon construct the dreams to change formation. Triduana nursed another wound, as she stretched aching muscles from a sore shoulder, that had taken a hit from the cat when it had tangled with the wards below. She was not as young as she used to be. The hot springs beckoned her body with a new determination, sending her downwards into her own solitary cavern, one much deeper within the cave system that Sibrey had not been allowed to see.

She smiled at the thought that Sibrey would now not be detected. They had set up the security corridor for events such as this. Her signature energy was no longer on Tantaris's realm, or any other planet that rested within this part of space. Triduana felt peace, if only for a few moments, thinking of the child that slept between in the immortal domain of worlds that only dead things had seen, as they slipped towards their own realm somewhere about four floors down.

Sibrey, for the time being, would not know that. So they did the next best thing, and gave her the one thing she had always had that allowed her to feel like nothing had changed. And so it was to be, as the childhood dream that she had always dreamt about continued, until she figured it out and woke herself up, and they would have to figure out another way to keep her safe, until the birth of the new beginning that was already on the horizon.

CHAPTER TWELVE

The Realm of the Cloud People

When one awakens from a faint, it's not usually a pretty sight. Most times, there is someone who is able to pick you up and dust you off; that is if you are lucky enough. Most of us do not have that luxury, and we find ourselves strewn about like a deck of Tarot cards thrown up into the wind when we come back into the realm of the living. As we wake up and try to regain some composure; it appears our limbs now all belong to someone else, seemingly numb from lack of use along nerve endings that had gone into overdrive, as we lay in some form of awkward position, just to humour those that have found us contorted into this bizarre heap of outlandish poses, with the not so pretty bruises beginning to formulate into that all too familiar shade of bloody, blackened coal.

Breathe...See I told you that you would eventually get one of these long sentences in this story!

As you know, blue doesn't come till later, and it's that ghastly rather ugly shade of coal, that wells up like someone coloured you in amongst the box of paints, while you lost the consciousness of your freaken mind.

Sibrey awoke to an array of drapery panels which had been pulled down from the walls as her limbs gave out beneath her, and in one final instinct of trying to remain inert, she mistook the cloth for the wooden structure of the newly transplanted window frame. Then to add insult to injury, the cloth from the curtains yanked the heavy iron rods that held them onto the wall downwards, and it must have hit her in the face as she lost consciousness and rolled to the floor.

It was into this weakened state, from much running and hiding from the Aelven men on horseback and little to no food that she found herself unable to free herself. She immediately came into full awareness kicking and screaming with frustration. It was again brought to her attention, seeing the image now facing her in the mirror. But this was not the child riding the waves among some breed of uniquely amphibious form of transportation, full of pounding hooves that sent spray in all directions as they moved about the sea. No, it was herself in her Shapeshifter paradox formulation, staring back at her own face in a full length oval free-standing mirror dipped precariously on its side, threatening to further unbalance the current situation and start the proceedings all over again.

It too had been disturbed, when she pulled everything on top of it, and lay hazardously on edge, tilting slowly towards the floor, as if it hadn't decided whether it wanted to dance with the others, or merely cause and all out riot. She had no memory of flipping it downward into the exact position she now lay in prostrate upon the floor. But somewhere in the back of her head, it was part of the dream she had clinging to the fringes of her imagination, when someone else had called her name and she had lost the use of her bloody mind!

She must have been out for more than a normal knock on the head. The face that met her staring back with swollen eyes, now resembled something you would ultimately scrape off of the bottom of your boot after walking through a forest covered in Cauper dog doo! You know those tiny slimy things that look like creatures that have no purpose but to make your life a living hel, as you find it smeared across your pathway in the middle of the night. Yes, that would be shit, crap, and poop or if you wanted something kinder, we should go with manure. But for the moment, it felt like shit.

She needed something in her stomach so she could hurl something across the room, which would throw itself up and self-destruct, roll backwards up the wall, and hit her in the face. But that was not to be. As her head turned into what best could be chucked at you in a prison loaded with torture devices, she became aware of a new sound, lighter and undetected until now; just on the verge of its arrival.

THE BEGINNING

It was humming, you know, like a song without words. And it was getting closer to the very room she now lay trapped in, under a medieval piece of wall implement, which could very well have had it out for her had it not had something else on its mind. She kept thinking all would be fine, no sense in panicking as whatever was coming was going to pluck another young child off the floor from underneath where she lay and all would be as it was — an empty room stacked to the rafters with boxes and old wooden trunks left behind by Goddess knows who and one damn mirror that represented the day she was knocked off by a piece of reflective glass!

But that did not transpire as planned, and a voice came through the doorway, and looked down at her kindly and spoke without any kind of amusement to what she must have really looked like to one so high above her.

"So here you are, child. What happ... oh dear no, not again! Sibrey, child, what have you gotten into now? How in Sopdet did this happen sweetheart....are you okay?" The voice came from a rather petite looking woman, with long ashen coloured hair pulled back from her face, wearing the clothes of an angel. *'Great, now I've bloody died!'* Sibrey thought.

The woman quickly moved to her side, and with a bit of effort was able to free her from the rod that had nearly killed her. "Oh dear, you are not alright, look at that eye." The older lady bent over her with a body looking as if it would break in two the moment she tried to lift anything. But to Sibrey's surprise, her arms moved easily and then with one eye open (that's all she had left to see out of, and at that, only half way at best) she was able to free her and get her away from what she had been trapped beneath.

She threw it to the other side of the room without a second thought, as Sibrey looked at her with an eye that couldn't believe what she had just seen. The older women ignored her stare and helped Sibrey make her way slowly to a sitting position — okay, not dead, only partway dead then. The lady started to talk away to Sibrey, then remembering something, changed direction and called to another to give her a hand. "This will never do, ARDDHU, come quickly!" she said, then continued clucking away like an old mother hen. "Where has Nina gotten off to? She's supposed to protect you child, while the dream state still runs."

Footsteps came running down the hall, as she continued fretting away. The voice in the room kept prattling away, but none of it was making any sense to Sibrey in what she assumed was her death state of crossing over, into wherever that might be.

"Even the sage stick has gone out, and look the energy is bouncing all over these walls almost ready to detonate!"

"I'm so sorry!" Nina said as she came crashing into the room all hel-bent for Taperskin. "I went to greet Horae when she arrived; time must have gone by faster than we thought." Arddhu finally joining them, started to laugh.

"Really, you're going with that analogy? With Horae being a time Goddess and all, I would have thought you would have come up with something more original." Triduana's voice stepped in and began to separate the two from taking it any further.

"OK, never mind you two, let's just try and get her untangled and back to bed and defuse the situation, at hand." Triduana waved the two of them apart, before something else decided to find its way into the room and she would have to send them both into other parts of the castle.

Sibrey started to feel four sets of hands shift her, as she somewhat drunkenly dangled off the ground while they moved her out of *'Oh dear, I think I'm going to be sick'*, that faze and into another room. From there, she felt a soft bed fold underneath her, and before she could actually throw up, a bowl arrived by her head from some unseen hand.

"Look at the state of her, we're going to have to call up Hexe to heal these bruises and put this child right."

"Arddhu, do you think Hexe should bring one of her herbal bags, when she comes? This child seems to be a bit accident prone in this state, and we can't just keep calling her up to heal every little wound, when the next round happens." She looked suspiciously at Nina.

"Well," Arddhu replied, "for all I know, she may be on the dark-side of Leberone and not hear us because of the void of courses that are all out of whack at the moment." Sibrey heard what sounded like pleading.

"OK, Nina darling, Arddhu and I will give it a try; you stay with Horae and put things right again."

That was all Sibrey heard, as she promptly threw up what little she had in her stomach. In slow motion she blacked out, but this time a soft pillow hit her in the face, that had suddenly appeared out of thin air and landed halfway up from where the bed currently lay about two feet from the floor. It moved slowly with her body attached to her cheek, as she fell silently onto the feather mattress and drifted lightly back down to the bedframe where she curled up in a ball and rolled over.

"I'm surprised she lasted that long, most Fey pass out with only one Goddess in the room." Nina smiled half-heartedly. "How can one so strong be so fragile?" Arddhu left the room as Nina and Horae gathered their charge and put her a little straighter on the bed.

"She's Fey," he said, "not Neanderthal." Then, shaking his head, he disappeared around the corner to attend to his gardens. "Hexe can deal better with the both of you, I have work to do, and please let's refrain from killing the child any further. It will never do to report we've lost her to the pain of falling out of a bed, to the Fey council elders. I mean really, Deities, act your age and get things together, and while your at it you might want to straighten this place up; it looks like a frat party exploded on scene!"

By the time Triduana arrived back with Hexe, Nina and Horae had thrown up the re-set on the dreamscape, and re-lit the sage at Sibrey's bedside cauldron. Hexe immediately moved towards the Shapeshifter, to remove the bruises and administer enough elixir to allow the dream state to continue unheeded. She then began to remove the wounds Sibrey had sustained in the fall, first moving to her face, followed by the bruises that had done the most damage to her inner-body functions, and then to her spirit as it drifted into calm sleep. She spoke softly with words of healing, giving them the extra renditions they required to the various salves that she administered to Sibrey's injuries. From the outside, she may have looked like someone bent over in complete concentration, administering the various herbs and concoctions in no particular order. But the science of healing was anything but. Each of the salves had to be placed with the correct timing after the one that had arrived on Sibrey's skin previously. They had to be placed with precisely the exact amount of pressure as the last one that touched her skin. Any variance to its touch could bring a violent reaction to the forefront of each abrasion, as they had occurred

Stolen Child

within transition of both worlds that lay sitting on-top of one another, inside a realm she had never been injured in before.

"How does this happen, Nina, in a world so far removed from this kind of injury?" Hexe had looked at the young Goddess with stern reproach, shaking her head at the child before her. Horae moved over and helped Triduana straighten up the draperies and wall fixtures that had come crashing down on-top of Sibrey's face, as Hexe completed the final obstacle of removing her hands from the now faintly noticeable yellowing scar that still continued to refuse to leave on its own. She turned to Horae and smiled, calling her over as Sibrey slumbered without being in pain. "Now, I think we can begin again."

Hexe got up and signalled for Nina to attend her side, while Horae, now busy with her hands, began to reset the time clock within the chamber's energy flux.

"Let's all get out of here before we cause any more damage, shall we?" She gathered their invisible forces together, and ushered all of them out of the room. Hexe looked at Nina, who had a single tear sliding down her cheek.

"Come on," she put her hand out to Nina and moved her towards the door. Nina whispered, barely audible to the room.

"I shouldn't have gone to meet Horae. I forgot how powerful her time balance is." Hexe smoothed the tears back down to their original position and smiled at the young being.

"We all make mistakes," Hexe patted her hand, "even us immortals. Now, go get some rest." She steered Nina in the direction of the hallway as she turned her attention back to the situation at hand. "Horae and I will watch over the re-set, then you will be well rested to guard her dreams once again, unheeded." Nina nodded sleepily and was off down the corridor before the tell-tale tick, tick, tick could be heard, as everything was again as it was before the incident. Both Goddesses looked at each other and sighed. "This is going to be a long bloody week, let's hope the Leberonion's have better luck with the other one."

"So... what are you thinking, game of Slither Taro, or shall we play Humans and whales?" The Goddesses could be heard laughing and humming down the hallway towards their private quarters, to wait and watch this one take its first set of steps without her damaging any more of her planet bound wings.

THE DREAM BEGAN ONCE AGAIN...

Sibrey again walked to the window. This time she watched the ladey move towards an equally stunning man, carrying the beautiful child that had been removed from beneath her as she lay on the ground in the previous version of her dream. The male was dressed in elegant riding gear, belonging to another era, with long black knee-high boots that met his black ankle length silken coat. It shone in the Mauntra's light, the rays bouncing off the carriage that figuratively came alive with a life of its own, alongside the pounding surf just behind. The man's hair was jet black, and with the wind from the sea changing its direction in a confused manner, Sibrey could see he held his hair in place about half way down on either side of his face, braided and twisted with silver rings.

Sibrey couldn't deny he wasn't Aelven in his features, and he definitely had an unusual way about him that she had not seen in other clans of this day and age. Both woman and child also carried that trait, as Sibrey looked on watching from the window high above the area that they were currently talking. But she could see something was different from any normal Aelf of this day and age, and it shone through into her Shapeshifter vision, causing her to gasp with the realization of what it was.

This male carried himself like a King from one of those long-dead ancestors she read about in Tamerk's books. She didn't know why it surprised her, given all the contents of this new castle, filled to the abutments with things only someone of royal ancestry should have in their possession. Besides, who lives in a castle with servants that move with ease as if they themselves belong to part of his own inner family? Those of which, were among the creatures surrounding him beside the Water-Horses laughing and talking as the three loaded themselves up into the elaborately decorated carriage. And that was another thing....who had Water-Horses tame enough to hitch to a carriage that you're just about to place your family inside, and cross over vast areas of what looked to be raging seas? Most Fey would have been crushed to death, or at least lost more than staff as the horses challenged everything that came within range of their enormous hooves. But strangely enough, nothing was further from those ideas than what she was witnessing; in fact, all seemed at peace with the normal occurrences of what was transpiring.

Sibrey noticed not one of the servants standing around them was the least bit afraid of the huge horses, as each one dipped and reared its front feet high up in the air then back again, stomping the ground restlessly, wanting to feel the wind beneath their blond manes swirling madly in the air. The manes seemed to take on an existence of their own, coming to life in a form of dance that moved and swept along their long lean backs. But as she looked further into what she had seen, she suddenly realized there wasn't a breath of wind anywhere around the group of them. The sea might have been raging, but the area they were standing in seemed to be protected by the outside walls of the stonework along the bottom edge of the castle. The manes were just moving about all on their own, in some sort of time dilation that was not only noteworthy, but strangely odd and thrilling to watch. The air itself must have been charged with some form of particle, because each horse that came into contact with the ground sent out little green sparks of light that encircled its entire body from one flank to the other. Sibrey watched the light burst wide-open as the horses ignited the ground where they made contact with their feet and lower shanks. The sound was deafening, drifting upwards to where she was standing at the ledge, and lit the entire lower courtyard with a green eerie glow.

The horses snorted in greeting as the Aelven male moved towards them, combing their manes with his hands and trying to get them to settle down, as the actual atoms banged together like a heart-beat floating on the snarling wind. But that only made some of them rear up with excitement as they snorted and screamed at ear-splitting decibels, stomping harder upon the ground as his hands found their fibre with his fingers. They left deep marks within the embankment, sending thunderclaps of energy through the whole group of living ghosts, which were sent scurrying in every direction away from the immediate area outside the castle walls.

"You need to hurry, it's almost time!" he yelled as he began to pace about the stone walkway just out of reach of the huge horses and their glowing eyes. Sibrey watched with renewed interest, but turned around inside, when

THE BEGINNING

the voice that answered suddenly seemed to echo inside the room she was actually in. It then faded from her range of hearing and the spectral spirit picked up again outside near the entranceway by the horses, as it drifted in the wind and found its twin.

"I've found her Llyemyllan; she was playing with the touchstone again, and creating a bit of a stir with the Panthers, naughty child. One day," she removed the beautiful green crystal pendant from Sibrey's neck, passing it outwards to the man, "those animals are going to bite you." She took her mouth and blew kisses all over the giggling child's face. The Aelven male moved to meet them both, reaching for the little child's body to take her high up, swinging her into the air. She screamed with delight, and he kissed her forehead with incredible love towards the one that belonged only to them. He made contact with his wife's hand and took the pendant from her. Llyemyllan held the pendant up to the light, squinting with one eye.

"It could also save her life, Llathieria, but I'll keep it safe for now." He put it around his neck in the leather pouch. Llathieria ignored his response, and continued on making sure her point got across in full technicolour even if he didn't want to hear it.

"She won't be just talking to them, Llyemyllan, she'll be riding them next, you wait and see, and then who's going to pick up the pieces when she's strewn across the courtyard?" He smiled, knowing that he couldn't win this fight.

"And that, my beautiful wife," Llyemyllan patted his wife on the behind, "I will attend to when it happens. Now won't you please get into the carriage? I'm sure Balorfynn won't be impressed when his favourite great niece isn't on time to witness the coronation." She looked back and grimaced at his well-defined mouth.

"Yes well, as soon as that crown is put onto his head and I get a chance to congratulate him on his succession, I'm going to take that crown off and whack him over the head with it for giving Sibrey such a dangerous gift." She quickly sat down inside the carriage with Llyemyllan, who immediately shifted one eyebrow up.

"Can't we just get through one of these family gatherings without just offing each other?" Then he laughed, realizing his own family was just as bad. "OK Vallmyallyn, you can let the boys know we're ready." And off they went, with Vallmyallyn leading the horses over the cliff and lightly splashing them down like a feather on a pond. His kind always controlled these beasts as though the horses were an extension of their own bodies, taking the lead horse and giving it its own head-way to direct the remainder that ran behind him about fifty feet from the shore.

The last time Sibrey saw the amazing Selkie, he was directing the grand horses across the waters of Kilchurn Loch; he was only about 200 yards from shore when he turned around briefly and looked directly at Sibrey. He quietly saluted her silhouette, still standing at the window opening and closing her mouth like the ghost of a Ferrishyn Kidlet. She instantly ducked away from the opening, only returning eyes and brow slowly upwards after they were well on their way as she felt his laughter fill the night air.

Sibrey watched her alternative family moving forward on the loch until they were just specs on the horizon. She was still reeling from what the Selkie had done. How had he seen her, when the others so obviously had not? It made her feel slightly unnerved, as she pinched her own skin to see if she actually was real or spectral in all of this. She slid down the wall panting, with the memory of what she had just witnessed; leaving her somewhat breathless in its arrival. Then, just as suddenly, knowing she could do nothing about it, she moved off to explore this obviously ancient castle, of this rather spectacular home; still feeling the wisps, of the ghosts that had recently crossed her path. She continue to look gingerly behind her, just in case someone else had other ideas, and when nothing showed its teeth, she moved with anticipation of what awaited her beyond. Had she really belonged to this place and been that child who moved about the air like she had within her own feline? And was this glorious looking family, of which she had no knowledge or memory of, just part of another dream, or one that moved deeper within another one that had yet to show itself? Too many questions and not enough answers that made any sense. She needed to keep moving before this too disappeared and packed itself away in boxes that would sit down below in the cavern she had first entered, waiting patiently for another that had called herself by her own name.

She soon found out the Aelven servants who had stayed behind could not see her in whatever form she had remained in. It gave her the ability to move about freely, looking through chests of brilliantly coloured cloths', and bolts of material that one could use to cover the entire estate and back again. Each room she entered held new and interesting things: from a nursery that had obviously at one time belonged to the younger version of herself, to a fully stocked kitchen, where she chomped on several meat tarts and grabbed a lemon shortbread twist while the cook was off checking on the pantry down the hall. However, before she could fully load up her pockets with others for later, a serving girl came across her at the last moment. Her eyes widened, as Sibrey lifted another twist right off of the tray she had reached for, and the young girl blinked with the knowledge she had ethereal company alongside the warm baking tray. She instantly shrieked.

"Damn ghosts, can we not for an hour have the company of the living inside these walls? Now shoo, the tarts are not for you; go eat in the other room where the groomsmen are playing with the dogs." At that, she swatted the area where she thought the ghost might be, and promptly left Sibrey standing in the kitchen holding the sweet and laughing her head off, as the serving female took the tray and disappeared through the open doors, moving out of sight and down the hall.

Crumbs still fell from her mouth as she gulped down the stolen food, while peals of laughter ran out from her mouth at the craziness of what had just happened. She had never been accused of being a ghost before, in all her Shapeshifter roles; this was a first. She wondered if it was even possible to accomplish that transmogrification when she did return back to her own time. After all, she could by all standards become almost anything, even a rock, so why should as simple a thing as a ghost hinder her shifting? With that still in her mind, concocting how it was to be done, she continued on exploring the castle. She slowly drifted through most of the rooms and had just made her way into a glassed in room off the garden, when opening the single small side door, she discovered there were two double main ones off to her left. Going through them, she discovered a well-lit cozy room, filled to capacity with walls of books absolutely everywhere. She'd never seen a library before, and quickly decided that this was a room she could spend a great deal of time in.

Moving inside, she drifted in the leathery smell that permeated the inside surroundings of hand-made bindings, and that earthy smell that came from old dusty books long filled with yellowed parchments lovingly bound with webben wax. She loved this room, she thought quietly to herself, and flopped down into one of the overstuffed sitting chairs that faced the huge windows, finally at peace. It smelled of leather and oil lamps and it, she decided, was divine enough to spend the rest of her life inside, if she took a mind to do it.

She finished her other tarts, licking her fingers and smiling to think what the people would do if she had been a ghost in her Panther form, moving without form through the hallway and into the kitchen for another tart. She laughed a moment in her contentment, and then began to think a little more on the situation at hand. If she could get in, how long would it take for the three riders in the chamber above her to also make it through? She straightened up from her slouch, forgetting the last of the crumbs that remained on her coat. She decided to not take any more chances, and bolted for the door, dropping the crumbs that had landed in her lap, along the library floor. The moment she felt the wood touch her skin along the bottom of her foot from the old wooden door jam, the illusion began to morph again. A curtain of energy distorted the image as it floated shut behind her, causing the rooms that had led into the library to dissolve into a completely different vision she had not been prepared to see again.

All about her was being pulled apart, changing into another underground corridor, with flagstone tiles replacing the beautiful wooden floors she had just walked on not more than ten minutes ago. She yelled at it to stop, hoping that was all it would take to return once more to the calm security of the castle's former trappings. But it didn't hear her, and it continued hel-bent for Coir Kats, destroying the image she had only just grown to love.

This time the ceiling that appeared as it began to come to a slow crawl, was arched in carved solid stonework of another age. Tallow candles high up on the walls in iron scrolled sconces burned and smoked as she moved slowly away from what had been that beautiful library. The room opened up into a scene from an old medieval castle that smelled of earth and dust. She was back in her old dream; she could feel it from deep inside her bones where the marrow ran its thickest, and this time the corridor was not only unhappy, it was hot, and she vaguely smelled the snippets of sulphur dusting in the background beginning to form.

CHAPTER THIRTEEN

Symin and the Hidden Army of Leberone

Symin did remember running towards Ryyaan as the young boy became dangerously close to the enormous white Leviathan. He remembered the size of the strange beautiful creature, and how it took up half of the clearing they all were standing in. And he remembered looking at the Aelves standing in that clearing, as they had stood there helpless, miniscule in size almost like mice, compared to the Dragon who continued to communicate fluently with the Human child. He remembered seeing the commotion; he even remembered the wild green Dragons showing solidarity with the Great White. But the last thing he remembered was his own Dragon plucking Ryyaan and himself off the grounds of Tantaris's bare earth, and releasing them as he fought to maintain any semblance of order, onto the back of that huge animal. Then everything went black, as the traitorous Quist flew away leaving him and the Human alone.

He was glad of that. He knew what he was capable of doing, if an opportunity had presented itself. What he didn't see, while he was being unceremoniously dumped from Quist's claws, was the beautiful structure of the soft leathery skin that hit his face and body when he made contact with that huge Dragon's back. He didn't see the beautiful designs that made up its body, as each of the scales moved as if it was alive and shimmering in the rays of the Mauntra. He didn't see the child land beside him, and crawl forward to speak to the Dragon, moving just behind its ears as he had lain along the middle of its wings, completely oblivious to the contact. He didn't hear the commotion that resulted from his abduction from the warriors of the Dragon clan, nor did he see Soren punch Quist square in the face, as he now had to explain to Dyareius about why the Dragons could speak. At least he had been spared that bit of insanity, although it would have given him great satisfaction to have watched Quist getting punched in the face, before he was able to free himself and kill the little snake.

So with all that going on, he had to think on what had actually happened to him the moment that he came within a certain radius of the Dragon's body. He felt a little nauseated, that he remembered as he moved about the air like a windmill paddle floating in a storm. And he did feel like he was about to throw up the closer he got to the huge Dragon's vicinity, so he could only imagine that the thing that knocked him sideways was some kind of etherized molecule designed to knock him out cold.

Someone else knew exactly who he was, and had taken precautions to protect the child, and had to have the exact dosage to do it so quickly, before he was able to initiate the energy transference that would have killed the entire herd the moment it came into its being. Smart, he thought. It could have been dangerous to all of them. He needed to find out who else knew his secret. It was far too soon to have someone spoil the fun now.

He was only just starting to get his senses moving, from whatever place they had left him to begin to find his conscious state in, when the noises about him that he had been aware of while he had thought this out, had begun to get a little bit sharper. They were voices, but in an odd dialect he had never heard before on Tantaris, and he at first dismissed them as simple background interference. The colours still swirled tightly around his head, as he felt hands reaching and moving him from something warm and hard, to something cool and soft. He, in his transition state of not being completely conscious, could only lay helpless at the mercy of whatever was moving him about. One thing that was crystal clear in his mind — that made him somewhat grin, was that this time he was going to let Soren do some damage, or at least beat the shit out of him to the point of unconsciousness! Bloody Dragons; he would have laid bets Soren would have already tried. But, he knew, that would never come to pass. Dragons were far too tough for even their little band of highly trained soldiers.

He felt his body being carried as they moved him from one place to another, in a room of sorts, indoors away from the wind. "Great, that will suit fine, put him here, and move him more into the centre where the lights aren't so sharp."

Symin heard them talk as they moved things about the room to accommodate whatever had been within the environment before. Someone had carried him separately from Ryyaan, he could tell by the echo that ran about the room and the energy readings of strange beings amid something else. The boy had not yet arrived to join in the little soiree that was about to take place. As a matter of fact, at this time, Symin couldn't even pick up his own energy readings, let alone the young boy's with all the drugs he had inside his body. But he did feel the bench as he was slid along its length and placed on it dragged, drugged, and right side-up.

He smelled the wood from the bench, lingering thickly in the air. Its distinctive resin permeated deeply within the grains, giving off the beautiful odour that was only associated with the Mathura Tree from Kalieas. His arm fell limply to the floor; small pieces of sand particles skidded under his finger nails as they hit the surface. Good, not too tall, he thought. Now if only he could get some feeling back in his legs and arms, he could make a run for it.

"Funny creature, you can't even feel your face." He heard the voice talking in his head, coming from somewhere within the area, but he still couldn't place where it was. "Yes, I know you can hear me, but can you find me? That, my friend, is the answer you will need to search for, before your eyes can give you that sight you crave so much." Symin growled low in his throat.

He could not as of yet get his eyes to focus, but his ears heard the scrape as they moved him more into the centre of, judging by the echo, a fairly large interior room. He wondered where they had put Ryyaan; as he was being moved about, he had not heard them discuss the boy. After he dealt with whomever had taken both of them, he needed to get to the boy and escape from whatever hel-hole they had abducted him to. That is unless he was part of this, and whoever was responsible had purposely abducted him, only to get to the boy.

Muffled footsteps moved something across the floor; he followed them as he was lying prone. Someone raised his head up again, and placed it back down on something much softer, like someone's... lap?

"Hold him still, while this clears his eyesight; he still needs to adjust to the atmospheric interference." Symin heard a male voice speaking in that strange Aelven dialect. He felt drops being placed into his eyes as he tried to move his head away, but whoever held him was stronger than he was at the moment. That would soon change, and when it did, they would feel his energy sliding underneath their hearts as he crushed the life right out of the muscle that surrounded them.

"Good, he's starting to come out of it." Symin listened to the dialect. It sounded a bit familiar, but everything was all so fuzzy, he wouldn't be a bit surprised to find he was with the Humans. After all, they were told the Humans were on their way, he laughed at the thought. Tamerk had asked him to return the boy to his kin, knowing fair well those creatures were reported to have died out after the Great Dragon wars had ended. When they had first been summoned, he had decided, telling the others about that little bit of information would only cause further complications. And it wouldn't be relevant to the reason of the summoning's, until he could figure out why they told them it was. Then it dawned on him, if it was true, and he was with Humans, then some must have survived those days after the war. Not only was he in big trouble now, so was the entire Aelven race!

Maybe the White Dragon was already in their grasp. That would be the end of the Fey worlds as a whole, for nothing on Tantaris could deal with an animal of that size. Even the black war Dragons wouldn't be a match for these animals. And when he said animals, he meant where there was one, there had to be others this close to the Tantaris home-world. Mind you, he still didn't know how long he had been knocked out, and the black Dragons were a quarter of their size, and judging by the last thing he remembered, with Quist's actions still racing about in his head; probably already on their side.

"Helfire, as soon as I get my feet under me, you're are all going down, then we shall see who is going to live another day."

The voice spoke again.

"Settle down Symin, we're not going to harm you," it said rather calmly, as it echoed from one side of the room to the other. "You can relax, we're not your Humans; just let the medicine work and do its job." He had begun to really resist, and had almost made it off the bench, when simultaneously he felt two or three more pairs of hands on him, as he heard his name spoken with frustration. "Hold him steady, and watch along that tattoo on his left side. He has a graft there where a knife blade has been embedded just under the skin."

How did they know that about him? He hadn't told anyone about the implant.

"Easy for you to say, with me being blind and all." Symin tried to form the words. In his head it sounded pretty good, but each of the eleven words that came outside his head and into the air made him sound like a very drunk Bowery dancer out on a bender that wouldn't end well.

"We've got about three more minutes sire, you probably should let the Commander know he's coming out of it," the voice nearest him added. "Syann-Clan's known for hitting first, and even though he's not one of them, he's been around them long enough to adapt to their way of thinking. So, as soon as his eyes clear up, everyone get the hel out of his way!"

They were wrong about the timing; it took only two seconds. Eyes that only a moment ago were pure white, slid in a final full blink downwards, releasing the lens protector all Feytonians are born with, and Symin was off the table hitting the floor with his vision clear and completely restored. He growled and rolled, taking the last one to let him go in the chest with his knee. The warrior crumpled, groaning loudly as someone from behind him grabbed his booted foot by the heel, and yanked him free of Symin's second blow. It hit the empty air, where moments before that head attached to the body he had just dropped had been pulled away. Another, not so lucky, finally made contact with Symin's fist and he could hear the howl of pain, just after the unmistakable cracking of ribs and then the rush of more feet coming towards him.

Before he could turn and shift his body sideways to avoid the crush, he went down in a pile of warriors pinning his arms and stopping his fingers from taking on the majikal thrust he was about to exude out of his body, theoretically producing enough toxins to fill the room and push them into the nearest wormhole that would open as he collapsed the atmosphere inside the room. Instead, it took some doing, but they succeeded in completely immobilizing him, restraining him to the ground within the time it would take a Human to breathe only once. No, definitely not Humans! Symin was completely unable to move in any direction, yet still he was able to find enough space to cause some damage to the one directly facing him who had touched one of the tear ducts along the farside of his face, as he released the smallest amount of toxin that he could release without moving his arms. He yelped as the others moved him out of the way, and dumped Kalieas stardust that they had moved into position on the burn, just in case he tried this manoeuvre. The warrior spread it thickly on his hands before the wound had time to fester, then possibly burn right through his tendons and down into the bone. This was what Symin had felt as he had lain immobile when first he had arrived. Not only did they know him by name, they also knew what he was capable of doing, and the one thing they could use in case he did.

"Let him up," a voice could be heard above the yelling and screaming, as Symin continued to holler as loudly as he could. One by one the warriors removed themselves from the pile until only two were left, and Symin was able to free one hand to punch one of them right square in the face. Reaching upwards with his free hand, he dragged that individual towards him and bit him in the jaw, before anyone else could attack. The others reassembled, and dragged Symin to a standing position, placing a warrior on either side of him to keep him from hurting anyone else in the room. They did not let him go, even after Symin had stopped struggling. Then ever so slowly, one by one of them disappeared from his side as they backed away, leaving him in the centre of two rings; one for the warriors and the other he spied had the unmistakable aura of his true race's protection grid — drawn specifically in the correct configuration to guard them from him.

Time seemed to stand still, with heaving lungs expelling air, as the Aelf, who had been leaning against the far wall, took his time to walk forward towards Symin in a slow causal gait, smirking away. Symin really hadn't paid much attention to him; he was still growling at the others who had pinned him to the floor, until he got within about five feet of where Symin was standing. Then, as this taller and more defined Aelf came into his sight with his lopsided grin fully intact, the others moved aside to let him through. Blinded by rage, Symin had thought of crushing the new-comer like a bear.

That thought disappeared immediately, with the arrival of the other into his full line of sight. Symin swore rather loudly at the Aelf he thought was a stranger, spitting at the ground as his eyes revealed someone that should not have been standing within this crowd of thugs.

"So, you do know me," the warrior grinned, standing in front of Symin, laughing at the Dragonlord. "You are a hard thing to pin down, my old friend," the Aelf said, rather humorously to Symin, as the former still tried to wipe away the gunk from his eyes that had resulted from the liquid they had used to clear his vision.

"Well, it would have been easier for you had you sent the bloody invite direct you old fool, instead of taking me hostage and flying me through hel and back." The warrior looked at Symin as he continued to berate him. "Or have you finally turned tail and run, joining the other Formorian bastards that run like thieves in the night?" Symin hissed again, fairly pissed at the much taller Fey warrior. The other taller Aelf only laughed harder, and pointed to his friend Balenas.

"I told you he had a way of making one feel slightly annoyed." Balenas only shook his head in disgust, nursing a very well defined bite mark along his jaw. As it turned out, Symin was in the most northern hemispherical sectors of the Tuatha De`Danann's outpost, and the grinning Aelf he was currently having this discussion with, was no junior officer in that command. No such luck. Symin shook his head; what new war had he gotten himself into? For there, standing not two feet away from him, was none other than Lugh himself... the high commanding warrior of the Tuatha De`Danann's bloody army!

Symin was annoyed, looking at the warrior. "Ah," Lugh replied, smiling, "so now your voice finds its place. Balenas and I," Lugh pointed to one of his warriors, "had a bet on how many of our Aelves would find your head cracking their skulls, before they could get you back on the ground." Symin snorted a small laugh. Lugh grinned, holding a single eyebrow up and turned to his Lieutenant. "I think I owe you a flask of Tantarian ale, my

THE BEGINNING

friend. The Syann-Clan's proclivities are stronger than I thought. This is good news, no?" Balenas looked at both of them, and growled with disgust.

"For you, maybe, but not so much for the veins in my neck, or the bruise starting to form along my bloody jaw!" Balenas howled. He looked at Symin. "You, my friend, will undoubtedly have a dialogue with me on a more level ground at a future date, mark my words."

Symin growled and showed teeth directly at the Aelf as he left the reunion and went back to the main building to get his injuries dealt with, along with the others that had gotten tangled in with his release; added in and not looking too pleased, the one Aelf with a severely burned hand.

"Looking forward to it, and at that time don't expect your head to remain attached to your bloody soul." Both stopped for a moment and simply growled at each other, before Lugh returned the conversation back at hand, and put his arm around Symin's shoulders, stepping through the circle, erasing it with his feet. Turning, they walked away in the other direction, and the molecules of the circle dispersed into the ether, allowing a strange sort of creature to gather it to him and vanish quickly into the mist.

Symin heard it go, and grinned. "I didn't know the Sigg had migrated this far west?" Lugh only smiled, pinching his shoulders and directing him forward — the Sigg were the least of his worries..

"Come, we have much to discuss." Symin went slowly, keeping his head clear and his eyes wide open to the things surrounding him, as they moved through the room that he had been carried in when they had first arrived. But it was Lugh, who actually kept his old friend completely involved in the conversations at hand, so as not to have him turn around and see how the Human was doing. If he had turned, he would have seen the bench he thought the boy had been lying on, was completely empty and without any trace of him having ever been there.

CHAPTER FOURTEEN

Ryyaan, the White Dragon, and the Tuatha De`Danann

Meanwhile, back on Tantaris before this had transpired, the moment the White Dragon was spotted in the skies above, in his gut he kind of knew it had been there for him. You don't fly all the way from another planet just to say hello to the new kid. As soon as Ryyaan came out of shift, he tried to mentally move in its direction to seek the voice he had heard so strongly in the skies above, long before the others had spotted his descent from the outer reaches of space. His touchstone had gone into overdrive the moment they had come out of shift, and as his fingers closed over its surface to stay its instability, he felt the warmth of its voice, deep and intoxicating.

He sank back against the Dragon's skin and sighed, thinking of Tamerk and the things he had left behind. He would miss the old Sprite, but to actually feel the wind on his face and see the ground so far below; it was nothing like he had pictured it would be. The Dragon continued to speak to him, and Ryyaan watched the things he pointed out along the way, as the woods he had called home drifted away behind them. Quist had assured Ryyaan one day he too would see the places in the stories the Dragon would tell him, as they moved further and further away from Tamerk's woods, and the home Ryyaan had come to like.

The wind started to pick up as they flew dangerously close to the edges of one of the mountain ranges that ran along the middle of the continent's interior canyon walls. Ryyaan's close proximity to the huge Dragon had never been a reason for him to be afraid, and he snuggled in towards one of its ears to shield himself from the prevailing wind that seemed to have suddenly shown its teeth. He shivered briefly and then caught himself shimmying into a heated section the Dragon had provided for him, absorbing its molecules, as they came from within to keep him from freezing in the cold mountain-air.

He briefly looked back at Symin, to see if he was still breathing, and saw the telltale signs of his rising chest as it moved ever so slightly in the wind. He turned to face the direction they were flying, as the Dragon continued to speak of things that Ryyaan had dreamed about for so many years, deep in the forest of another land in a time that was not his own. He started to yawn, and felt the beginning sensations of sleep drift across his vision, as the final jump was in the embryotic stages of its beginning wisps.

Now would be the time to sleep, if he was going to prepare himself for the long journey ahead. But something inside his brain couldn't justify missing a single thing, as all around him flew by in vivid colours of intense fascination. The Dragon made the decision for him, and just as the thought arrived within the electrical currents of Ryyaan's mind, it sent out small rudimentary waves that gave off a rocking sensation, which triggered the sense of peacefulness associated with heavy lids, and good old fashion sleep — the boy slumped sideways into a shallow slumber. Small tendrils of scales awakened by the activity, slid along the Dragon's head, transforming themselves into a hollow that allowed the boy to find a refuge and stay safe, deep within the shift that would take them north-bound into more familiar territory.

Ryyaan began to dream, and that dream returned him to the clearing just as he began to approach the White Dragon on the ground, with Aelven warriors coming at him from all directions, and the skies about to explode with Dragon shrieks.

He had not heard their fear, as the others on the ground ran to protect him as he had moved in somewhat of a trance, closer to the White Dragon's vicinity. Ryyaan had been brought up to believe he was special, in anything that was to be set before him that he could see and hear. The moment he had arrived in the clearing; the big Dragon had called to him to come forward, as he communicated with it and the others that found their wings along the edges of the touchstone's power.

Tamerk had given him many things throughout his young life, and this was one of the most unique. But even he was a little stunned at the Dragons that had been called to attend his arrival into this new world of the skies, as Quist had calmed his frayed nerves and given him what was required to understand the situation. Whatever happened now, he knew without a shadow of a doubt, that this would be the last time he was going to see this planet that had raised him as the Human they thought him to be. Tamerk had seen to that with the one gift Ryyaan now held tightly in his hands. Having the touchstone in his possession had basically given him a way off the planet with one of the only creatures that could take him home. How Tamerk had managed this without any interference from the Aelves was anyone's guess. Ryyaan would basically have to wing it, both literally and metaphorically now; but then again, he kind of thought it was past due anyways.

Things seemed to be moving in slow motion from the moment his feet touched the soil. All he could hear, away from the concerned faces with no voice, was the constant drum of wings and the thumping of tails hitting the grass that filled the meadow they had just landed in. He watched things in his peripheral vision, but concentrated on what lay ahead of him, stepping between toes and talons that seemed to move like the top of the waves along the ocean of some confused Dragonistic sea.

The Dragon moved along the movements of shift, rocking the air-waves like a skiff riding the currents of electrons, as Ryyaan tossed himself about in his sleep to intercept the warriors of Symin's clan. He didn't wake up as the wind began to fiercely whip itself into a fury staying tightly curled up along Sigrith's upper back, as frost formed along the outer bone-tips of his body and the depression kept Ryyaan out of the weather safe and warm.

Ryyaan stayed deeply rooted within his dream and, taking a brief look back at the advancing warriors that belonged to Soren and Symin's clan, he was only too happy to see the soil disappearing beneath him, as the dream continued. Now, looking back through eyes that had no sight, deep within the realm of the dream world he was currently visualizing, he had to admit he was more afraid of the advancing Aelfs themselves, than anything that the actual Dragons would have done to him, had he any choice in the matter at hand.

He had always had an affinity for creatures of the skies, more than anything that skidded about landbound on their bellies, and the Aelves of the black Dragons had already proved to him how very volatile a creature they could be. Dreams always had a way of making things appear quite different than what had actually happened, and with him being far too busy conversing with the space Leviathan, he had missed certain aspects of the struggle that had ensued around him.

There had been much vocalizing, and a few clashes of metal with talons and teeth, none of which had done much damage to either side, along the barriers that prevented the Aelves from reaching either him or the lords of their clan. Ryyaan had to concentrate on the images put before him, as the dream seemed to bleed the images from one scene into another. Strange, he had not thought that he had been in danger. As Soren's clan rounded the sides of the Leviathan's great mass, they arrived with swords looking like they were about to fight to the death, for...what? Was it for him? Or... no, of course not? The dream cleared its course, as Symin came into view, moving as if he was made of nothing but air, to reach his side as the others had come to his aid, in the horror of what was about to happen.

Ryyaan snickered in his sleep, and it came out in shallow snorts along the Dragon's outer skin. It sent a ripple of shivers that worked its way down the Dragon's spine, and he shook the feeling outwards into the air as they continued high above, in flight. The dream began to change its structure with that intrusion, but carried on none the less towards a more direct conclusion; one that Ryyaan had never voiced before within his mind.

<blockquote>The dream began in earnest now, revealing things to him he had never felt before...</blockquote>

The implements they called swords made him laugh. Especially since, based on what he had been shown by Tamerk in all the years he had been living with the Sprite, these shiny pieces of metal were nothing more than little sharp sticks. The things that could prove to be the undoing of the Fey races didn't come in brightly shiny metal, but they had a sting that could cause damage to muscle and tissue that would take time to repair. The Aelves had called them swords, but Tamerk had called them a nuisance, and something to protect their little bodies in times of strife. Ryyaan smiled at the image of what Tamerk's knowledge of majik could do to their frail Aelven skin. And he had taught Ryyaan many things throughout those short years that he had come to live with him.

Ryyaan frowned; it occurred to him that although he had been led to believe that Tamerk was a Sprite; there were so many creatures that Tamerk had become during the space of time he had known the creature, that even Ryyaan didn't actually know what he was. He yawned again and settled back against the Dragon's skin. Tamerk had warned him not to delve too deeply into those questions. And Ryyaan would have to agree with that, in every sense, as the dangerous one that they all needed to be aware of was none other than Tamerk himself! He wondered if the Fey of this world had figured that out yet.

Tamerk had said it wasn't time yet for what this was all about, but Ryyaan knew that Symin was the one that would bring things inside his own mind, back into the world of the Dragons and beyond. He needed to concentrate more on that, and not on some distant tracker who had knocked him over the head with his unruly demeanour, in woodlands that no longer had any bearing on what Ryyaan was currently doing.

Soren, on the other hand, had another path; one that would take him to other areas, away from where Symin and himself were headed, which he was thankful for. For, had he spent another minute alone with the Aelf, Ryyaan was sure he would have torn him apart, had Tamerk only given him the opportunity. And whatever this Shapeshifter was, she had better have a good head start, for if she had any clue as to what was on her tail, she would run as far away as she could fly, and keep on moving through the damn trees.

That made Ryyaan smile. Ryyaan had hated that Aelf from the moment he had laid hands on him, and didn't trust Soren as far as he could throw him. To lose his prize Shapeshifter would undoubtedly cause him great suffering of the mind, and if Ryyaan had played any part of that, it was truly what one would call... karmatic justification.

THE BEGINNING

In his world, the animals themselves had always given Ryyaan their absolute trust, and not the Fey species of this world, that Soren represented. Between the two Aelves he had met, it was Symin who was more animal like than he presently was letting on. Ryyaan applied this reasoning to considering things that seemed to have more thought or cleverness behind their eyes, rather than appearing intelligent behind a lens of deceit. But deceit wasn't the reason Symin was hiding his true identity, as far as Ryyaan could tell. He may not have trusted the Aelf as a whole yet, but there would come a time when he would have to trust him with his life. And if this Shapeshifter valued hers, whatever animal she had become, he hoped it would take her far deeper into the woods, where this so called Dragon tracker had not the slightest chance of catching her....from the back side of never!

He twisted again on the Dragon's back, and settled back into the dream in another position. He remembered Symin had smelled different; it was Tamerk who had said one of the Dragonlords would be not as he seemed. The moment Ryyaan had laid eyes on Symin inside Tamerk's home, he knew which one he was. It was the real reason he had challenged his ability during the middle of Tamerk's discussion with the Aelf, and not one that appeared to be done out of malice. He had needed to see what it was that Symin was not showing to the others. He wasn't sure he thought much about it, but somewhere down the line if he got into trouble, it would be Symin that he would be able to turn to for help.

Soren on the other hand, just annoyed him. He turned again briefly in his sleep, throwing his arm outwards to land along the frozen bone-tips, where it immediately melted the ice it came in contact with. Sigrith shifted a second time, moving towards the last juncture shift-point, then began to travel true North.

Ryyaan had been brought up in a world with things that went bump in the night, and had grown accustomed to those everyday survival instincts that come with the territory, within the forest realm of Tamerk's woods. Those Fey shadows rarely gave one a second chance. When he had first yelled for Quist, during the middle of what appeared to be an erupting fight, he was more than happy to get out of the way of what he thought was happening. He knew there was no way, at that moment in time, that Symin could get there quicker, but he had been wrong. He had never seen an Aelf in motion before, and Symin moved faster than he would have thought possible. But his surprise was within the grasp of a childhood world of dreams, when Quist picked the both of them up single-clawed and dumped them on the Great White Dragon's back.

But it hadn't given him the fright that the others would have imagined, given that he was a youth that didn't belong to this world. So, this frightened or even scared child, whom they believed to be Human, came through the wind and out the other side as he watched it all unfold from the vantage point that had been thrust on him.

He travelled within his mind again into the world of the touchstone, talking to Quist like he was once again back in the clearing, and planning on having it occur once more in all its technicolour glory. All the while, he watched the terror of those below at what had just happened, evidenced by their continuous shouting.

Ryyaan had watched Symin throw a fit and try to move out of Quist's talons, as he had twisted and turned trying to break free. When he realized he was not going to be taken towards where first he thought they were heading, Symin had screamed his head off and had almost broken free. But it was much to Quist's relief, and Ryyaan's for that matter, that he took another second to secure the talon that had gotten caught in Symin's right-side and readjusted his hold on the Aelf before he had completely lost control of his squirming body.

It was a good thing Quist was able to maintain his unsecured hold on the Aelf, because the fall itself could very easily have done some serious damage to his rider, never mind what Symin was capable of doing to him, with the other hand dangling behind him, if he had to let him go during the mid-air transfer. If Symin moved more than what Quist had calculated for, and broke free, he was sure the damage to his body would not be anything compared to what Symin would do with his mind, when he landed and sent the energy blast skyward towards both him and Quist, flying unaided without their rider. Even considering the fact that Aelfs were excellent at landing on their feet, Ryyaan had been nervous when Quist had grabbed a hold of him, picking him up by his sword arm, leaving the other free and clear. It was only a matter of time, not having his talon secured over that second hand, before the Aelf known as Symin would suddenly become something else entirely.

Ryyaan had remained firmly ensconced in the other side of Quist's right talon, knowing fair well where they were about to be released. But the screaming from below as well as from the vocal cords of his prisoner-in-arms, had continued.

Quist had told Ryyaan that Symin was dangerous, during their flight into the clearing when they had first left Tamerk's home. He also told him Symin would never hurt him, no matter the cost to his own species. But Quist was also nervous about not having consulted Symin for his approval of what was about to take place. They just didn't have the time, with Soren so close, and Tansar wasn't taking any chances that Soren would freak out in the middle of the flight, with having to manoeuvre themselves around so many Dragons that had arrived en-mass for the event. Quist had told Ryyaan that this could very well cost the Dragonlords something that they could ill afford, if Symin decided to get it in his head to leave the area.

Quist heard Symin whisper to Ryyaan that if he had been able to free himself, he would return with him at a later date to complete what had been asked of him by Tamerk, back in the mountains of the Symarr range. Quist hoped he could keep that promise, should Symin find a way to get himself to the ground before the White Dragon intercepted, and freed both himself and the boy from what the Aelf truly was.

Ryyaan also watched his new travelling companion lose consciousness as soon as he came into contact with the energy wards the big Dragon had around his body, to protect him from the gravity of this planet. Ryyaan had moved freely downward and landed, very much awake; listening as Quist had told him as he flew, that the blue mist would keep Symin asleep during the long journey that lay in front of them.

Once they were on board the White Dragon's wings, the huge creature began to converse faster with Ryyaan through the touchstones unique blend of understanding. He reassured him once again, in exactly the same manner as Quist, that he would not be hurt by it, and that only Symin could breathe it in. He explained that it was designed to stop the manifestation of Symin's special powers, of which needed to be silenced in sleep while they moved towards where Tamerk had instructed the Dragon to take them — away from those below.

Ryyaan listened while the Dragon talked about other things, as he watched them rise away from the clearing, once he had arrived aboard and felt the beginning shiver of the shift. They joined the flight amongst the wild greens that suddenly joined in on the fray and a few geese that got caught up in the excitement of the insanity. Then the White Dragon took them past the clearing, quickly manoeuvring them safely out of range of any danger that lurched nearby, and materialized only briefly for Ryyaan to catch his breath. They did that periodically throughout the entire flight, giving Ryyaan a few breaks to enjoy the freedom of the wind, until they reached the outskirts of the village of the city of the mound, and the Dragon groaned loudly to wake him up as he tapped his energy cells into wakefulness.

CHAPTER FIFTEEN

Aggulf Elkcum Mound

The stronghold of the Tuatha De`Danann army, was actually within the Aggulf Elkcum mound, not up on the surface as some Fey were led to believe. It was not far from the city of a once smaller hamlet that had called itself Fomor during the time of the ancients, where the latest skirmishes of a once very angry King could still find itself erupting. Many of the villagers had alliances with the common thieves of the extinguished former kingdom. When the mood took them, fights could erupt during a perfectly splendid day, resulting in battles that seemed to be created solely for the unnatural purpose of the village's complete and utter disruption.

Sigrith changed course with no more than a slight flick of a feather, as they moved closer to another kind of city that would be very different than anything Ryyaan had previously seen, while Sigrith continued the tale with his recent tellings, blending the rich history of the area they were heading towards.

Now, it is reported that it was around the time of Balor's great grandfather's reign, in another age and another area of the Tuatha De`Danann's current ruling quantum that this particular garrison was once again deployed into being. Ryyaan listened as they moved closer to the colossal stone rings, which came into his vision from beneath a few of Sigrith's feathers that had come loose during the flight and now whacked him soundly in the jaw. He ducked as they came around for a second time, but this time as they passed his head he moved them with his mind and they dislodged from the Dragon, falling to the earth never to be seen again, as they flew along the edges of the Morphana River.

Sigrith yelped and swivelled one eye in Ryyaan's direction, as Ryyaan pretended to look the other way as though he wasn't part of the actual deed.

"You do know you are a guest during this flight...right? And that another trick like that could very well land you in the drink," Sigrith growled at the youngster. Ryyaan simply shrugged his shoulders and kissed his fingers, laying his hand flat along Sigrith's head in apology, and asked that Sigrith carry on with his story like nothing ever happened.

Sigrith shook the scales along the area Ryyaan was sitting in, in mock indignation, and carried on with the tale of a past life melded into the present Faery-tale of the Aelven race. He continued to explain how the fortress came into being, and Ryyaan watched as they moved towards the entrance of something that appeared to be nothing more than normal flora and fauna of the area. When they had moved past the last set of trees he realized he had been wrong, as the enchantment was released to admit them into the protected zone, and what had been hidden had majikally appeared.

Now standing in plain view, tall and majestic and all alone among the greenery, was a gigantic tree smack dab in the middle of a thundering set of falls, alongside several huge black stones. The fortress built inside it, was mostly underground, and had been re-opened to the warrior class of Aelves shortly after the Fomorians had begun to pick an unusual amount of fights within the smaller villages. It was because of a skirmish that happened long ago, that started in more or less the same way as the one that started with the Tuatha's commanding regime of the time that the story now takes a turn.

Cian, Lugh's father, found himself to be directly beneath the White Dragon when it appeared to soar back in their direction, on the return visit to their skies. The alarm calls below ground had gone out the moment Sigrith sonar came into view. Cian scanned the horizon as he reflected on what this meant, while they all waited for him to arrive, and he moved to meet another visitor who had not been part of the trio from the skies. He could only guess if Sigrith had been successful in his adventure to retrieve the boy, and would not know as fast as the others who would meet the Dragon, as another creature only now coming into his village needed his attention in much the same manner, and didn't have as much patience as the White Dragon moving off to the mound.

True, Tamerk had no patience at all, but that was beside the point and he currently had no control over that anyway. He would know soon enough if the child had come, but either way showing any kind of concern would only cause the molecules of another who was still searching for him to locate him faster, while the Dragon continued on to the underground complex with his precious cargo. Cian hurried to make his appointed meeting time with the Sprite, as each warrior had immediately gone into full readiness the moment Sigrith had been spotted from the look-out. He continued on his way back to Fomor, away from the mound they were heading towards, as his sons warriors would be scrambling in any way they could to prepare the chamber for their newest arrival from the skies — giving him the ability to rest while sustaining himself within the gravity of this planet's heavy atmosphere.

The Great White Dragon's race had been a familiar sight on the other worlds that maintained their population of Fey without the added heavy grade of Tantaris's gravity. But this particular world had the means to kill this beautiful beast if precautions were not put into place properly. Having Sigrith here in Tantaris's substantial atmosphere for any length of time, was not going to be any easy feat for all involved. The most of which had been working day and night to accomplish what was needed; or die in the trying. Cian hoped it wouldn't come to that.

Sigrith could feel that inner-core start to come to a breaking point; he would have only a limited amount of time before his organs began to fail, so it was paramount to limit the amount of energy he needed to speak to the boy, as they were still a fair distance away. He spoke slowly, giving Ryyaan the opportunity to ingest the information quickly through other means, and asked him to place the touchstone along the central scale directly between Sigrith's own ears along the topside of the bone-ridge. In doing so, it would reveal the information he had to tell the child, without having to use any more energy than what was needed to keep him awake until they reached the safety of the inner mound.

The touchstone started to relay information directly to the boy's mind telepathically. The link would remain open inside Sigrith's mind until the story was completed or the link was lost, regardless of the stoicism of Sigrith's outside speaking voice. Ryyaan listened for the story to continue, as Sigrith picked up where they had left off and came within view of other interesting sights as they continued along the way.

Sigrith's story carried on while they sailed high above, and given the gravity of the situation at stake, all would be needed to keep the child informed, of what the planet's politics and general history was all about. When they arrived in two days hence, he would need that information inside his brain, while he healed in the ritual majiks that would bring the creature that was hidden inside him out into the open; the very blending that was long overdue, and Tamerk hadn't the time to induce before Soren had arrived on scene.

So, THE STORY TAKES OVER FROM HERE:

"Once that former war had begun, and the Fomorian race of generals had been left dead or dying, an odd mixture of other Fey had gotten in the way of the feuding families, which lived within the fields of its ruling clans.

To be honest in the telling, as the chaos of the Human war intruded upon the soil of this planet there were some Fey families that had been killed by their own factions, giving a false sense of security to those that were left to fend for themselves. Thus the insanity gave off the fear that the Human race and their worlds had more power than they had before, within this sector of the current Fey worlds.

THE BEGINNING

The White Dragons and their kin had lived in another part of space, some distance from this current collection of Fey worlds. They had been used by an older race of Fey that had travelled here to help in the recapture of this planet soon after the Humans had tried unsuccessfully to destroy their way of life. However, the Humans had come for another reason entirely than that of simple warfare. No, that had been entirely exaggerated and the tale had taken on a life of its own, from deep within the renegade tribe that had started it in the first place. You see, they, had come to retrieve those taken of their own kind, and given the results set before the tribes they had every reason to arrive as they did.

What transpired had nothing to do with the Fey as a whole, but was directed at one Fomorian King who had gotten too big for his britches, whose pride wouldn't let him concede that what he had done was horribly wrong, and he left it to fester in amongst the decaying rot of another races inability to understand his treachery. It was directly in response to one of Balor's grand schemes of stealing Humans from their homelands to create a diversion so they would come and start a war. That, in turn, would cause enough of an uprising inside this side of the galaxy of Fey, encompassing enough creatures on this world and those closely associated with its doorways, to be able to hide the real reason he wanted the Tuatha De˙Danann to be occupied elsewhere instead of focusing on what he had cooking on the pot in the background.

During that time of chaos and upheaval, some of the townspeople of Fomor had taken liberties against their dying relatives' weakened state of affairs, and had begun to ransack the villages around the old mound, when the Tuatha arrived in force to step in and settle the disputed landholdings. While the Humans came and retrieved those they could formulate a rescue for, unaware of the why's and wherefores of Fey politics. It quickly got out of hand, as the Formorian King created such a ruckus that those who lived around the area took it for something entirely different, and the Humans became engaged in a clan war one hundred times what should have been met with quiet reverence, from outside of the village of Fomor — meant for the exchange of prisoners and nothing more.

The Tuatha had already arrived to settle the Fomorian resistance, but Balor was having none of it, and refused to hand over his captives. Things got quickly out of hand; the Tuatha that had been sent to resolve the disputes were outnumbered ten to one, and it forced them to call in reinforcements. Already Balor had fled the scene and retreated to his stronghold on Toraigh Island, and the war raged on with him living in peace, away from the thick of the fighting he had started in the first place. In turn the Humans were systematically knocked off, one ship at a time, and the others that did find their way out of Sopdet's space were never heard from again. Word had come much later, through other channels, that most of their ships had never made it past the last shift-point doorway out near the northern rings of Goetutonias, but no one has heard or seen any trace of the Humans having landed or taken up refuge on any of the planets since, so who knows where they went?

The Tuatha, already entrenched in the battle, reopened the old abandoned mine shaft where the mound was said to have been hidden. The mound was discovered, still very much intact down below, after many thousands of years during which it had lain hidden from this current holding of Fey inhabitants.

To this day, the mound is still relevant in every sense of the word, and is occupied as a living and breathing entity of the Aelven nation of planets. It houses no less than ten thousand military Aelves and their Fey counterparts, who keep it alive and living as an outpost along the edges of its sister planet Naunas. Both planets share the same singularity of its shift-point doorways equally, forming the thread that locks this part of space away from those who have tried to destroy it in the past...."

Ryyaan moved, stretching his lower body and listening to all that Sigrith had to say, until he became too tired to maintain the stone's signal. Somewhere between when the Fomorians had killed off their relatives and the Tuatha had reclaimed the mound, he had drifted off to sleep again and was lightly snoring away, oblivious to the discomfort of his newest friend.

Sigrith smiled through his pain; he had felt the young whelp start to lose the storyline as he had gone into sensory overload at the overwhelming amount of information that was revealed to him. He had already seen the giant Stone Monoliths long before they flew across the valley floor, and had fallen asleep as they moved high overhead the continental drift. He continued to stretch his arms and yawn loudly, as they flew several hundred feet up and around the area they were set to land in. Sigrith quickly triggered the endorphins to wake Ryyaan up fully, and injected his little body with something else to keep him fully awake should he fall once more into his previous pattern, as they flew closer towards the stronghold's clearing.

Ryyaan yawned, trying to wipe the sleep out of his eyes, as Sigrith flew closer to the tops of the stones' huge escarpments coming up to his right-side, as he circled the gigantic pieces of rock set deep in the ground of the centre clearing. Ryyaan raised his neck over the Dragon's side, now fully rested from whatever the Dragon had given him, and saw that they were considerably lower in altitude than they had been just before he had fallen asleep. He saw that the Stone Monoliths they were heading towards were based along the ridgeline of the Zarconian Falls, which split the plateau basically in half. They seemed to be following thin cracks along the upper-ridge that had first appeared through the mist covered ground, some miles back. The slabs of black rock could be seen coming out of the surface soil, and were deeply entrenched around the main rings of a massive former slide of soft shale. It must have been one hel of an earthquake he thought, to have taken those huge boulders out of the bowels of the subterranean chambers that they lived within, as the planet began to form in the helical period of its genesis planting.

The stones had some kind of shiny exterior surface, which reflected brightly in the Mauntra rays, almost blinding Ryyaan as the Dragon flew around a huge central tree before he could see the actual courtyard in the clearing. The tree seemed to float in the middle of the abutment of rock, and its branches hung high in the air shading the edge of the river as it went over the edge of the very unusual cliffs.

As the Dragon flew between the branches and leaves, Ryyaan could see the trunk of the tree going downwards into the bowels of the earth and following the falls beneath the Tuatha-mound. Ryyaan had to shield his eyes with his hand, from the reflection off the slabs of rock, and the brightness from the Mauntra's spiralling light, as both converged together and formed some kind of conductive particles, all bursting into colours that ran along the rim of the falls. They were very beautiful, and like nothing he had seen before; they formed in an arch and bled their colours into one another, moving away towards the far side of the ridge. From there they turned into mist as they thundered over the edge into whatever lay in wait below.

Sigrith didn't land right away; instead he took another pass along the fields that circled the outer edges, which seemed to take them almost to the outskirts of the Fomorian village, a full mile away. Ryyaan watched the Fey inhabitants scramble on the ground as they sailed up above in the air, causing a dark shadow in their midst, which imprinted itself along the ground, as they circled back towards the mound that Sigrith said they would soon be landing in.

The Dragon continued on with his story to Ryyaan about the creation of the giant stones, called Monoliths. He said they were not stones at all, but made from crystals that had formed beneath another planet's core. He told Ryyaan he couldn't remember a time when they hadn't been here, as they had arrived long ago in another age, and in the time of an alien race of Fey he had yet to find.

"The slabs were made from some form of blackened crystallized quartz, which had once lain deep inside one of the lava tubes, beside a very active radiating Pulse Worm. Or so the story that I'm telling you is said to be." The Dragon grinned at Ryyaan, and retracted his talons as he lowered his claws into their landing position, as he carried on talking about the area they were currently about to step foot in.

"That old worm had created some pretty big fracture lines along the shift-point doorways of another world that sat just inside the perimeter of where the village now stands firm. It was through these hollows that the old worm moved between worlds and had been able to live alongside some of the more active volcanoes that still exist inside this area of the planet's underground tunnel systems. As time progressed, the black slabs near the surface of the worm's nesting ground spewed forward on a day pretty much like any other day of the waking, and caused much speculation for the people of Fomor for going on 25,000 years or so. But most agreed, had it not been found at all, travel to Leberone or Kalieas, may not ever have happened in the first place. That being said, travel to any other of Sopdet's planets further out in other sectors along the rim, would also not have been viable to anyone that lived within the borders of Tantarisian space along this juncture point, and that in itself would have been difficult for those living on this side of the great divide."

Sigrith stopped his tale. How they had arrived there was anyone's guess, but Sigrith was betting on the arrival of something that had yet to appear in the skies above for going on a million years. A final padded toe hit the dirt, and Sigrith settled onto the surface world of the current Tantarian home-planet of Fey. He breathed heavily now, leaving Ryyaan to watch other things below them from his back, as they landed in a treed courtyard specifically designed to fit the Great White's bulk and frame. He watched as several runners made their way towards their vicinity, as Sigrith explained things quietly to the boy.

"We shall not be here long my child. It is only for us to rest while we prepare to continue on with our flight skyward. It would appear that I can no longer maintain our pace, without some help from the Tuatha in order to carry on our journey. It will be at least another seven hours before the planets can provide us that little extra push and line up again anyway, so we might as well take advantage of the destination we have arrived at, before we head out again. The Tuatha have secured a chamber below that will allow me to with-stand the gravity of this world during the time that we have to wait; for which I am forever grateful. So, let us make the best of things and sleep a bit before the journey takes us further away from any safe harbour." Ryyaan touch the touchstone briefly, in acknowledgement, and continued to watch the flurry of activity that surrounded both of them from below.

All about the outside of the mound seemed to be actively guarded and full of different kinds of creatures within the Elemental spectrum of the Fey worlds. Ryyaan had a firsthand look into the outside workings of one of the most notorious mounds of an alien species, that belonged to another world, that currently struggled to keep Sigrith alive. He still couldn't understand the truth of the matter, but it intrigued him with its rarity, that a species that hated Human life in general had gone to such extremes to keep him alive as he travelled along with the huge Dragon and one of the notorious Dragonlords of a by-gone race of Fey that had proven to be more outwardly kind to him than he first thought they would be.

He wondered if somewhere out there in the open sky, there was a chance that his family could still be alive after all this time. He often thought of them on rainy nights back in Tamerk's woods, but he had never felt the time was right to get the old Sprite to talk about them. He guessed that time too, had passed him by, and everything around him just verified that it would more than likely be close to never, before he had that opportunity again. He frowned; he would have liked to have had the occasion one day.

He sighed and settled back to watch the things of interest that the Dragon pointed out to him, all the while staring with wide-eyed fascination for the first time in his young life, at something other than the old man that lived in the woods and the creatures that inhabited those dark places. He had to admit that this was by far the most interesting day of his life. Looking back in a few short hours that would prove to be a lie. What was about to happen in the short amount of time he had left, would more than make up for all the time he had spent away from his Human family in trilasecks. He continued to hear Sigrith talking, and turned to listen to what he had to say, while things inside his brain kept telling him something was not as it appeared to be. Something moved between the shadows of what should not have ever been a part of this and anything actually real.

Sigrith continued on with his Dragonistic speech about various things within view, and how they had been created to enhance certain parts of the shielding that the mound required to survive on this side of the massive falls. He explained how various things were needed to build a pattern of weightlessness to regulate the shield's energy output, to protect the mound from constant radiation from inside the planet's volcanic core. The worm that had created it, still moved about from time to time, and radiation was found from tubes that were recently discovered where it had travelled from another realm, and still hosted high emissions in those molecules that remained intact, despite their best efforts to eradicate them.

But Ryyaan was lost in other activities; constant radiation was the furthest thing from his little mind, and Sigrith's words became nothing more than sounds blending into the vast foreground that lay wide-open before him, on this planet of Faery tales gone wild. As the underground world of the Aelven military continued to take on new and interesting formulations every few milliseconds, he watched in fascination as each new one

THE BEGINNING

presented itself before him, unlike anything he had seen before with the previous one left behind.

As they continued along the river's path they were walking towards, an energy shield different than the earlier one was activated alongside of them, sending tiny sea creatures moving towards the edges of a clear glass barrier that had shifted into position as they stepped into the dirt near the rivers edge. Their movement along the trail just before they reached the trees, brought them from upstream to attach themselves to the surface edges as soon as the White Dragon advanced a certain distance down the trail-head.

Ryyaan watched in fascination as the creatures moved towards something that resembled shimmering clear walls near the water's edge, preventing them from coming any further towards them. As they moved within range, Ryyaan could see that it was an invisible barrier holding them back that prevented them from going over the thundering falls he could hear all around them in the background. They swam up to stare at the boy and Dragon as they passed along the pathway, and rose up and down in the air following their movements along the trail, as the Dragon lumbered along ignoring their small movements.

At one point they even moved overhead and passed to the other side of the smallest section of the path, as the water ran underneath a crack in the earth. The water that housed them was part of the river system that moved at the edge of the falls, which suddenly came into view and gave Ryyaan the smile that still was planted firmly on his face as he advanced down the path. It was unbelievable to watch; Ryyaan twisted around several times, following their movements as they made their way in the water at the path's edge, seemingly putting them in danger of going over the falls. Then, just at the last minute something pulled them back, and they began the process all over again — from the tips of Sigrith's nose to the length of his long tail. Ryyaan moved dangerously from one side of the Dragon's head to the other, and almost fell over the side as he watched in fascination at the little creature's hysterical antics.

He peered closer to the barrier, these creatures were swimming along near the outer rim of Sigrith's ear tuffs. He scrambled closer to the side nearest the water's edge, and reached out to touch the water where they flicked their tiny gills in and out of their necks. The moment his hand reached the energy field and passed through to the marine environment that filtered the water from the existing eco-system, the creatures swarmed his hand, along the fingers, scouring the surface of Ryyaan's skin like tiny suction tubes.

"Careful, young child, they have been known to bite," Sigrith laughed, producing a ripple down his scales that almost unseated the boy. Ryyaan pulled his hands back into his sides and hid them in his shirt.

The creatures flitted towards the barrier enmass, visibly annoyed at the loss of contact with Ryyaan, as Sigrith continued along the way and out of reach. The creatures tried to follow them as best as they could, moving up and down the energy surface along the barrier, creating a wave of motion that send shock waves away from their bodies and turned the water bright blue. Ryyaan looked like the little child from the trees, as he pressed his body snugly into the Dragon's skin, trying to prevent himself from further contact with the water, looking once again as he brought his hand forward into the light to see if he had received any puncture wounds under the nails of his fingers.

It was at this time that his hand began to turn from its normal colour to a brighter shade of pink. The creatures, totally fascinated by him, tried to entice him once again to place his hand back into the marine environment they resided in. But he was having none of that, in case they really did bite him back, as Sigrith had mentioned. Instead, he observed his hand turn from the brilliant pink of a few moments ago, to shades of blue green bruising that cracked his skin from the middle of his fingers to the nail beds. He watched in horror as it then began to morph into little tiny eyes and sharp little fangs, out where his fingertips used to be along his nails. His eyes didn't register what he was seeing at first, but just as he tried to hide them from Sigrith, under his shirt, they bit him in the arm.

He screamed as Sigrith slowly carried on as though nothing were out of the ordinary. "I told you they bite, but no, don't listen to the Dragon!" Ryyaan was horrified, as he pulled them out, away from his arm, and watched as they morphed back into regular fingers. He shook his hand, trying to find any lasting effects of the illusion they had sent to him. Finding none, he instead shrunk further into the middle of Sigrith's head and back again into the indentation that protected him from the outside world. He pulled the injured arm closer to his chest, placing the one that had morphed into sea creatures to one side, away from his body, just in case his fingers changed back into the creatures that had stared at him through the water.

The turtle-like things stayed with both of them, on the other side of the water barrier, until the end of the pathway; then, with a blast of bubbles emitting from their gills, they scattered back to where they had originally swam in from, allowing Ryyaan to see them from their tiny tail-fins as they disappeared into the distance and over the falls. He shivered in his own skin, wondering what would have happened had he actually dove into the water, as he had almost thought that he would have liked to do, when they had moved along his skin and he had felt them tickle his fingers. He really needed to pay attention to what Sigrith was talking about. Had the Dragon told him this was going to happen, and he had missed that part of the conversation? He couldn't remember. Tamerk would have laughed his head off at this, and surely the creatures would have thought twice had he been in attendance to the events of the past several minutes.

"Don't be so sure, my young warrior. Tamerk was young once himself, and has several bite marks on his body that are far worse than what you are currently nursing," Sigrith said to him, through the touchstone. Ryyaan put the fingertips up to his mouth and tried to suck away whatever had been living under the nail beds, and spat them out. Sigrith merely laughed at the behaviour and carried on walking without skipping a beat, as if nothing had even happened to the boy. *'Planet-dwellers never learn,'* he whispered to himself, amazed at Ryyaan's progress smirking away, all the while continuing his lumbering stroll towards the mound.

The Dragon continued on with his explanations and told Ryyaan that all who passed into the mound from off planet, had to go through the very same procedures (minus the events that had just occurred), in order to be allowed below ground. These unique creatures were employed by the Tuatha De`Danann in many cultures, on the different worlds he had visited, to read individual energy signatures and cross reference them with their species' genetic coding. This was done through alien facial lobes, which squirted blue inky filaments from lungs that were placed on either side of their heads, as they filtered the water in the river systems where the travellers passed them by. Each of these creatures had been selected from the Sea of Urious on the Planet Speclutec, and had a membrane that could pick up anything that was considered dangerous to the inhabitants that lived here, or anywhere else the Tuatha warriors might call home.

Sigrith explained that each traveller's vibrations that entered the area, would be picked up by the anomaly of the clear energy enclosure, sending the little amphibious turtle fish to come and scan their signatures to pick up anything within the range which could be construed as unusual and in need of attention. Then, should something come up in their unique telepathic scans, they would instantly change their squeaky little voice patterns, emitting silent screams inside their marine environment. That in turn would send off shock waves to those below monitoring their activity, and the Aelves would take action accordingly, to each level of dangerous activity that these strange Sirens from the sea had detected.

The Dragon continued walking along the dirt pathway, stopping briefly to catch his breath in the alien environment. His ears twitched, listening for anything that would cause him to take to the air again. He watched the skies above for any activity that could be construed as dangerous to him or his delicate cargo. He shuffled much slower now than he had when they first arrived on the ground; this environment was defiantly harder for him to breathe in than the air that lived in and around the planet's outer-rings. He would have to move faster if he was going to be able to get the boy below ground before something happened and they had to come and get him while he was still on the surface and unable to move.

Finally the pathway came to a division, and Sigrith moved in the direction of a shallower depression that lay along the middle of sandier ground. He shuffled his enormous bulk towards the centre of the clearing, engulfing the depression with his entire frame and stopped. He lifted his head and smelled the air, letting his ears twist around in several directions, listening for anything that should not be part of the silence of the glen. Immediately upon balancing all his weight on the spot, he heard that distinctive click and stopped fidgeting as the thing began to slightly shake from his weight. It centered, then groaned into life, as he pulled his tail around his legs so it would not get caught in anything as they descended below.

THE BEGINNING

Ryyaan watched as the ground seemed to split open from under his feet, and the vibration around the ground started to lurch into motion, sending the shifting sand away to the side of the depression. At first Ryyaan got his bearings all mixed up; as it appeared to him they were moving sideways towards the trees. But his initial belief was proved wrong. As soon as he settled his body into the correct position he thought it would move towards, they suddenly moved in another direction, sending him lurching and sliding down Sigrith's lower neck.

He grabbed on for dear life, and watched Symin take a short tumble from the area he was currently nestled within. The Aelf remained unconscious, and something invisible to the naked eye seemed to grab him and place him back where he had previously been. Other things began to happen around the same time. Ryyaan watched in fascinated concern as all three became part of the bigger picture, and obviously were not in control of what was about to take them inside the central portion of the Tuatha De' Danann's mound.

Any pebbles that had been lying in the vicinity, which had rolled towards the concaved center, immediately started to vibrate and bounce sideways away from the depression, as if a magnet had drawn them away from the edge by force. Ryyaan watched as they moved and shifted all around the general area, alongside several small bushes and a few precariously perched trees that happened to be close enough to the sands. The larger branches swayed from side to side as their bark seemed to come apart in tiny pieces along the roots, falling into the mixture of peat that made up the surface layer of the soil. The soil immediately reclaimed the partials, as the bark smoothed itself out and grew replacements for what had been torn from its edges.

As they moved in a downward motion, the sound of metal cogs and wheels could now be heard scraping and groaning to life, and they slowly began to drown out the thundering falls from below. Sigrith moved from one foot to another trying to maintain his balance, revealing a metal open grate that was slowly lowering from the middle of the depression. Several small stones could be seen falling through the grate, caught in the metal screen as they descended into the depths of the mound. Ryyaan peered over the edge of Sigrith's back and looked below as they moved deeper into the bowels of the earth. Several huge carved metal wheels started to appear from below as the inner cogs and wheels revolving slowly were revealed from out of the darkness. They moved further down the walls into a narrow shaft, followed by huge ropes the size of Sigrith's legs. Each had long metal spokes that turned in opposite directions, taking them further and further away from the surface world above.

They started to move faster through a solid shaft of volcanic rock that had been carved out of the bedrock by something that was cylindrically shaped, and connected everything together in the tube to what lay waiting for them far below. The shaft ran into the ground about 150 feet, and looking back high above them, Ryyaan noticed another similar grate closing off the upper covering they had first moved through, thereby shutting off the light from above. It clicked shut with a distinctive metallic noise, sending them into total darkness for a fraction of a second, making him increasingly more nervous as they continued to move further down the shaft that would allow them to arrive in the underground mound.

Small glowing lights started to fill the tube they travelled in with warm reflective light. Ryyaan heard the final click as the lever above them moved into position and closed the shaft completely off from the world of the air spirits, as beautiful volcanic Glowerites came awake inside the volcanic rock and lit the way inside the tube. They descended into the world of the Earth Fey. These Earth Elementals, feeling the vibration of the grate being lowered into the mound, had become exposed to the motion through tiny cracks that formed from the constant movement of Tantaris's molten core. They lived their entire lives deep within the fracture lines of the radiating Pulse-worm's casings and any motion related to the creatures of the world of the Air Elementals piqued their curiosity. They moved towards the fissures carved in the rock to watch the famous Dragon of the skies descend into their world.

Ryyaan could see tiny faces peering through the light that reflected along their outer shells, and as they moved along the tube they were in, they seemed to scuttle from one side to the other as each fissure became exposed to the trio descending further through their environment. As the lift carried them deeper, the creatures moved around, gradually turning off their lighted bodies again with each new level they came to, leaving small glittering tailings behind them as they scurried to the lower fissures to catch another glimpse of the child who had no voice.

Obviously, word had travelled about their guest to almost all the Fey colonies. Being here deep within the shadow of the mound and far from the trees of Tamerk's woods offered no exception, as several pairs of eyes tracked their movements through the entire tunnel system and into the mound's main interior chambers.

Sigrith's body was in the final stages of gravity sickness. He had been able to hide it fairly well from the child, until it had taken hold of the outer edges of his wings, and started to traverse inside his larger frame as they had flown the last remaining miles above the Tuatha's stronghold. If he didn't get help soon, it would start to degenerate his vital organs, and there would come a crossroad where he would not recover from the effects of this planet's heavily gravitized atmosphere — the sickness seizing his alien frame and killing his unique physiology. He visibly struggled to keep standing on his huge legs, as they travelled down through the main ceiling of the arch into what appeared to be an inner courtyard of enormous circumference. Ryyaan snatched the touchstone off the back of his head, in case it got lost in the shuffle, and quickly wrapped it inside his shirt. Sigrith began to collapse, unable to contain the tremors — the spasms causing great alarm to Ryyaan and whoever came within sight of him.

Alarm bells were sounded as an army of warriors rushed to the Dragon's side the moment he came through inside the mound, to guide him forward. Ryyaan was lifted up and slid away from the great body before the boy knew what was happening, while the Tuatha took charge of the Dragon and physically guided him towards the specially designed chamber that would be his home for the next few hours. His legs began to violently tremble with each passing quadra-second that he moved within the underground structure that had been hollowed out of the very centre of the bedrock itself. But the Aelves had been prepared for such emergencies as this, and the moment he had begun to struggle in outward pain, they quickly transported him towards his own chamber in a mass Aelven mind shift that they had designed specifically for this eventuality. This required a fair number of warriors, who banded together and mentally, shifted him into the chamber he could no longer get to under his own power, leaving Ryyaan basically alone on the outside looking in.

They had no more than arrived, when Sigrith collapsed in the inner rooms and was surrounded in Fey Elementals who quickly shifted him into the space gravity container that he needed to fill his failing lungs in, in order to keep him alive. They had come prepared and, having the Leviathan inside their mound, they spared no expense in looking after his every need. Ryyaan was immediately approached and softly spoken to, just outside the entranceway they had descended from — he was to be moved to a more comfortable atmosphere where he could rest, for the remaining hours it would take to revitalize Sigrith, so they could reduce the atmosphere further to the zero gravity realm of the Dragon's home-world. But the moment the young child was approached, he immediately sent up an energy field to prevent himself from being taken away from the huge animal, not understanding the severity of what was happening.

Sigrith spoke quietly at first to Ryyaan, through the touchstone's unique gift and then nodded with his halfway slitted eyes, as he tried to get the child to understand his situation.

"Calm yourself child, they are only here to assist us," he wheezed, trying to reason with the child. "Not take you from me permanently. I need rest before we can continue north and to do that, I require their unconditional help in keeping me alive and you safe, my friend." Then, Sigrith spoke with all the energy he could gather, to all that were within earshot.

"He is not to be hurt; care for him until my strength returns." This was done with a final discharge of his last remaining energy reserves just to make his point to his young charge, whose body language had suddenly grown quite quiet. Ryyaan looking worried nodded in acknowledgment and released the field so the Aelves could reach him and remove Symin and himself to the safety of the outside energy-rings.

The moment he was away from the danger zone an enormous hiss could be heard from the remaining air within the chamber. Ryyaan placed his hands against the blue rings of energy keeping Sigrith safely contained inside and whispered silently into the touchstone to his Dragon, who had entered the beginning stages of the Dragonistic healing-rite.

The Dragon whispered gently back to him.

"I am called Kithtar by all that have me as their friend; all others call me Sigrith. Remember that, when the hours are still and you're unsure of where you stand with me. Now please, friend, let me sleep. I will be fine; I am in good hands. Go now, child of heart," he said, with one eye barely able to find Ryyaan in the fog. When he realized Ryyaan had not moved he reiterated, "you need to go quickly, so I can heal. Let the Tuatha help me, and I will be there when we are ready to fly again." He was now incapable of physically responding in any other way to anyone, as his body spasmed and fell into an unconscious state; one that his species alone could withstand and come full circle out the other end without any repercussions; if they had gotten to him in time. For that, time would tell.

Nothing now could interrupt the final stages of gravity sickness, which he had acquired when he had put his life in danger to come to this world to retrieve the child. Sigrith had known this would happen the moment he had volunteered for the mission to come planet-bound. It would only be disrupted after the healing ceremony was completed in its entirety, or Ryyaan found the means to get them both back home to his original plane of existence, should something happen before he had been made well again. He sincerely hoped the latter would not happen; if Ryyaan reached maturity away from the teachers he needed to cross over into his new home, this planet might be in danger from those that still sought him out, and had lived through the last war.

What Sigrith had whispered to Ryyaan away from the others, gave him hope. The knowledge brought a smile to Ryyaan's face as he listened to the deep breathing of the great creature that had made him his own, and stepped away from the energy field fully engaged. At least it felt like Sigrith Kithtar was his Dragon, from the very moment of their arrival, and as soon as they descended from the surface world above it became even more apparent by how protective he was of anyone seeming to come at them, without having a purpose to his care. After all, the Dragon had come all this way to get him, from places unknown and so far away, so he had started to think of him in that very manner. Then, without looking back, he felt the time was okay to move and joined the others who waited silently behind him to escort him to his own chambers, to wait out Sigrith's unique way of healing.

Cian had sent one of the younger Aelves, around the same size as Ryyaan, to escort the Human child towards the main chamber where the others had been waiting to retrieve him. They had prepared food and drink for his stay, and were busy working on different things that needed to be done during the daily routine as they waited for word on his withdrawal from Sigrith's chamber.

The young Aelf who went by the name of Nymphatious, was, as far as looks were concerned, about the same age as Ryyaan. Cian had gone to a lot of trouble to select one of the warriors' sons that would meet the criteria of what was needed, the moment Sigrith arrived back in their skies to retrieve the boy. There had been much speculation as to how the child would actually arrive, and whether Tamerk had felt the child was ready to continue on with his training at a far different level than the one he currently had him on. With all sense of purpose, Tamerk could very well have declined the offer and had sent the Shapeshifter in his place. Either way, one of the young ones was arriving today, and if it had been the female, his wife Eithne would have selected someone else in Nym's place.

Both youngsters walked the stone corridor back towards the area where Eithne had been waiting to bring the child to let him eat and get some sleep before the journey that was set before him. It would be a long couple of days for the child, and every moment counted if he was going to be in top condition to return home to the world where he first was captured, all those long years ago, as a small infant.

The boys moved quickly until the main chamber opened itself up to Ryyaan's eyes, then he stopped in his tracks at the sight that stood before him. It was breathtaking in appearance, as far as things go in the alien city of the Aelves with some exceptional large carvings of stone statuary off to the left, up against the far walls. But to a child such as Ryyaan, with the imagination of Nymphatious egging him on, it was a very cool cave that could be used for play in so many different ways than its current use. There was no comparison to the woods where he grew up in Tamerk's care, but things inside this environment were far from ordinary, and he was about to embark on something even more spectacular in the coming hours, that would fill his brain to its very capacity.

THE BEGINNING

Ryyaan watched with eyes wide open, observing the bustling life of Elemental beings and Fey alike, working side by side with swords and daggers and many kinds of machinery he had never seen before. To the eyes of a simple Human child, it was as if his imagination had come instantly to life from within the pages of a story book, as the Aelven petroglyphs seem to dance along the walls, and each that had been only sketched a moment ago, instantly began to move in rapid succession like a picture book carved with the history of the Aelven races. They seemed to run faster the deeper he moved away from the Dragon's medical chamber, causing him to laugh as each of them continued to change with every step the two youngsters made.

Each of them had been there for as long as the planet had Fey life on it, and no one in the mound seemed to be watching them move about, except for him. Ryyaan looked to Nym to see if he was seeing the same thing that he was, and was instantly disappointed as the Aelven boy merely continued on his way. They seemed to move for his eyes only, and no one else within the huge cavern seemed to notice their animations; or, if they did they were so used to it that it didn't generate the interest it had in him.

They had started as soon as the boys had entered the main chamber, and had drawn Ryyaan's attention while they moved and danced in varying degrees of being created and drawn. They danced with the shadows of the cavern and became animated with reality of a life long ago lived, as the original Elemental carvers sat and chiseled those creations right on the cavern walls when this chamber was first created, several of those hundred million years ago. Ryyaan's eyes, now wide open in disbelief, could only marvel at the sight before him, as dust that flew from the artist's hands floated in the air and through all the sights and sounds that ran in Elemental Feytonian glory. Just as he began to get used to seeing them working away at their carvings, they smiled at his face and disappeared into thin air, leaving him alone with what they had created those many years ago, still viable and full of colour to his naked eye.

If at any time he had been impressed with the other-world above, he was even more awestruck by the inner-world below that belonged to the Tuatha De˙Danann. Following Nymphatious through the various chambers, as he led Ryyaan away from the movement of the sculptures, everything seemed to come alive. He watched with eyes that suddenly seemed to come into focus after having been blind for so long. He felt like something was different in his own vision, and was now having a difficult time adjusting to the flourish of underground activity and lighting that surrounded him on every side.

How had Sigrith been able to stand all the noise? Ryyaan marvelled at the Dragon that had come down the mechanical stairs amidst all this activity, without so much as a sideways skittering or stomping of feet and into the underground world that held a vast number of voices, all coming from different races of beings, mixed together and talking at the same time. It must have been awful for a creature who spent his entire life in the confines of fluid space, away from such beings as those that moved about the inside of Tantaris's caverns.

Nym had been speaking to him, and had actually stopped to point out the touchstone around Ryyaan's neck before Ryyaan realized he had not heard him. Nym asked his question again, pointing again to the stone as Ryyaan tried to find the means to speak to him aloud.

"Can you not use the words that are within your throat, without the stone that hangs around your neck?" Nym asked, looking over his shoulder as he waited for Ryyaan to respond. When he didn't, Nym simply shrugged and carried on talking. The two moved deeper and deeper into the centre structure, to meet Eithne in the central portion of the huge falls.

Sigrith had explained, while they were still above ground, that the village of Fomor may be on the surface, but the city of the Tuatha De`Danann was mostly hidden underground, deep within the security of the upper shieldings and their metal rings that lay hidden, deep within the huge Stone Monolith up above. The protection of the warriors of this race was paramount, and they wouldn't be waking Symin up until they arrived in Leberone tomorrow. Ryyaan stopped again, and took Nym by surprise when he touched his arm and pointed to the sand on the ground. He reached for a stick and drew a picture of the three of them when they had arrived, and pointed to Symin's stick figure, trying to ask where he was. Nym shook his head, and told his new friend that he hadn't seen another Aelf with them when he had been allowed to come and escort him to Eithne. Ryyaan became visibly upset, as they continued on their way, and Nym hadn't the means to understand its reason.

They didn't have very far to go. The ledge came into view, and a beautiful Aelfen female could be seen standing at the bottom of the base. She immediately turned to face them and shouted from below, shielding her eyes from the bright lights that covered the area Ryyaan and Nym were standing on.

"Finally, thank the Goddesses. I was starting to get worried they wouldn't be able to get you out of the chamber through the energy field you had created. Something tells me your Dragon had a lot to do with how we were able to move you to a safer location before things really got out of hand." Nym waved at her, introducing her to Ryyaan as the mother of the leader of their military family.

"She is called Eithne, and her husband is Cian. They live down the west side of the falls. That is where you are to stay until your Dragon is ready to continue on with his journey." Two adult males joined her at the base of the ridge they were standing on. She gestured for the Aelven males to go up and help guide him down. Nym stepped aside as they took the cliff with a single leap, and landed on the edge of where both him and Ryyaan were waiting. It may not have been a long way down for the Aelves, but to Ryyaan, who was still looking for another way down, it was extremely steep. Nym laughed at his dawning horror, as he realized they meant to bring him down the same way they had come up. He started to back away from the edge as they moved towards him, and if Nym had not been there to see it for himself he would not have believed his eyes. Both Aelves went flying sideways, landing about 300 feet away from where he was standing, hit by an intense shielding the boy had sent towards them.

Ryyaan had moved the Aelves with just a simple flick of his wrist, and sent them crashing into the falls. Both Aelves, now covered up to their necks in water shook their heads as Eithne dismissed them and they left the area visibly upset. Ryyaan turned to look at Nym, who immediately put his hands up and backed away from him, just in case he was still in the mood to do more damage. Nym watched in fascination as Ryyaan waved goodbye to him and thanked him with a hand on his heart, before disappearing over the edge unaided, to land beside Eithne just like he was born into it.

If there had been a time in his life that Ryyaan would have liked to see what their faces had been like, while he took a dive over the embankment head-first, this would have been it. Nym merely laughed aloud, and cheered as Ryyaan literally dove over the edge and landed on his feet, followed by Nym himself.

Eithne, however, was not impressed. She gasped out loud, watching the whole thing unfold before her eyes, and was absolutely stunned he hadn't killed himself from the fall. But she didn't skip a beat, and took her hand away from her heart where she had clenched it against her chest, extending it out towards his own.

She smiled with all the ethereal charm the females of this race could produce, and welcomed him to their military stronghold with a kiss to his wrist, apologizing for the awkwardness of all that had transpired since last he had seen The Tamerk. He smiled at her, and felt uncommonly comfortable around her from the moment she touched him. The word Tamerk made him smile and he found that although it was still quite alien to him, it no longer worried him to hear the name of his friend from the woods being spoken in the context of their existence down within the underground city of this new clan of Fey.

Nym caught up quickly diving with flare, not to be undone by his Human predecessor, and she walked with both of them slowly, allowing Ryyaan to get his bearings after riding on top of Sigrith for so many miles. Nym finally waved goodbye, as they arrived at the outskirts of a rather stunning home that sat on a vista a little way up from the ramp they had just come down. He promised to see Ryyaan once he got his bearings and was rested for the upcoming trip, and was off down the side of the pathway they had just come up. Eithne had made supper a while ago and had left it to keep warm over the hearth fire, not knowing when the actual time of his arrival would be. She gestured for him to come inside to eat, and rest his body.

Ryyaan stopped to watch the new friend he left behind make his way down the steep walkway, leaping from boulder to boulder, then travelling out of sight. He hesitated as Eithne led him towards the open archway of her home, insisting with his body language his desire to first peer inside the entrance, before even thinking about going over the threshold. Ryyaan looked over his shoulder to see the Aelves still making their way in and out the area in which Sigrith was being cared for. At least this vantage point on the bluff where Eithne lived, still gave him eyes on the chamber they had shifted Sigrith into, after he had collapsed in the open air of the main vault. It was higher up on the other side of the cliff face, but the ridge was still clear enough away from the falls that he could make out the chamber's distinctive entrance. He turned back to go inside the tiny entrance of Eithne's hovel, only after the mist from the falls had taken on a more opaque shade around the edges, and was slowly rising to obscure his view.

The home was in stark contrast to the sounds and voices that filled the barracks down below, and Ryyaan had just turned to go inside, when something else caught his eye. The mist parted and he could briefly see a company of warriors carrying a familiar shape, until the mist closed around them and they disappeared into its vaporous tendrils. For a split second he had been able to watch Symin finally being brought to another building to his right and below where he was currently standing. He had remained rooted in place, staring at the place he had last seen Symin dissolve into the mist, when Eithne came to the edge, joining him by placing a warm hand on his back. He turned to look at her briefly, then turned back to the rising mist, pointing to where he had seen Symin being carried.

She smiled at him, placing her arm around his shoulders to bring him into the warmth of her body, as she lowered her head sideways to the top of his curly black hair and kissed him on the head. She explained briefly that he was being taken to the infirmary for the soldiers that lived and worked within these walls.

"Don't fret, my dearest child, he will be treated with the utmost respect. His clan is under our protection; he will not be harmed." She laughed, then patted his head with loving care. "It will just be easier on everyone to only have to put him out the once, don't you think?"

Taking a finger, she gently placed it under his chin to bring his attention to her face as she winked. Ryyaan grinned at the image that came into his head, of Symin taking on the entire underground complex. He started to nod at Eithne, and her smile changed to laughter for the young lad as she tousled his hair. She could only imagine the things Tamerk had exposed his young mind to while the child had been in his care. She turned both of them around and started walking towards her home, guiding him inside away from the goings on of the inside workings of the mound, as the fleeting familiarity of something lost seemed to cross the pathway of her mind. The grief was profound; then it lost the link and was gone without attaching itself to the memory. She shook the energy left behind off her skin, and it crawled away replaced by the young boy at her side.

Eithne tried to ignore it, aware that ghosts occasionally roost inside ones mind when another energy crosses the pathways; it quickly shed its skin as they walked through a variety of chambers towards the old bakery room where the cooking fire still held its hottest flame. "Symin must mean a great deal to you child. I'm sure there will be plenty of time to visit later. Besides, I'm sure the two of you have already had a taste of each other enough for one day, especially back in the woods when he first came to....?" She waited to pick the images up he held tightly in his mind. "Ah, there it is, when he first came to your home." She had worded it in a non-invasive manner, nodding to the child when he had given it to her without a struggle. Ryyaan only shrugged, as boys often do, ignoring the question she had asked him about, once his very hungry stomach sensed food was within reach.

She reached for him with her hands, taking his in her own, and brought him along inside her kitchen. "Come, let's have some supper, you must be starving. Tamerk is not known for his cooking skills!" She winked at Ryyaan, whose small squeaky grunt still rang out, echoing through the hall, touching Eithne to the very bone. They both ducked through another doorway and went inside the deliciously warm inner sanctum of Eithne's home, leaving the question about Symin to wither and disappear within the air, as she moved them both towards the hearth.

She began the story that would accompany his meal, keeping him occupied for the limited time she had of her visit with the child, that reminded her of another, so long ago. The ghost of him arrived, then he too was gone, following the other that had visited her on the stoop. She wondered if ever there might be a time that it would find its rest, for to tear her apart for the remainder of her lifetime was surely something unbearable to even think of. She moved to break its hold and finding the words more comforting than an empty space in her heart, she spoke of her love for her homeland.

THE BEGINNING

Before long the ghosts slipped away into the stratosphere and the pain in her chest moved along to its proper place....

She drew in a deep breath and watched someone else's child consume her attention. At least she had that. If it had been her child lost and living on an alien world, she hoped someone else would treat them as kindly. She let that breath out, and began...

"The city of the Tuatha was actually built within the walls of one of the biggest meteor craters ever made on the Tantaris world. It was an ancient site that bled with the tears of the Fire Elementals that lived inside the rocks. Had the meteor actually hit the modern world of the Fey today, it would have been an extinction level event. But luckily that didn't happen in the story that I'm about to tell you, or both of us dear child would not be here." She smiled at him scoffing his food, in true boyish fashion as he devoured ever morsel she had put on his plate. "My oh my, didn't Tamerk feed you child?" He grunted and she laughed carrying on with the story, unable to contain her mirth while he didn't skip a beat, reaching for the remainder of the pot.

"The actual event happened a long time ago Ryyaan, when Tantaris was only newly formed, and the Fey had not as of yet made it their home." He smiled between bites, then wolfed down the hunk of bread he had suddenly realized he had been holding in his left hand. She grinned at his appetite, then carried on the tale watching the little one devour his meal.

"It had ripped into the atmosphere of gasses and molten lava, and tore holes in the very rock it became stuck within, starting a chain reaction on the genesis level of creational interference. Do you understand that word Ryyaan, or does the rambling of an old female occupy only empty space?" He grunted his understanding, munching bread covered in soft cheese, and she carried on with her story, unsure of where he was actually putting it all.

"This is what you see before you today, in the creation of this beautiful world that we all live beneath, far from the world of the upper Fey. It had all started in another part of the grand Galaxy that was within the Spiral Nebula of Sopdet's constellations. One of the lesser planets in a smaller star system had gone super nova, propelling a huge chunk of its inner staticular rock into deep space. Throughout its travels it had been transformed into various pieces of stardust, forming a bizarre network of meteors and asteroids that floated away from the blast grid, marking their turf as they moved about the drift site between Fey worlds.

Then something miraculous happened. A single shard of that molecule level galaxy that was part of the meteor bits and pieces that had hit Tantaris, formed huge lava tubes of molten rock that shot upwards out of the planet's rocky core. Over centuries of forming and transforming, it cooled and disappeared, leaving huge fissures that extended below the surface world for miles and miles on end. Over time the surface areas fell through, revealing these natural formations which the area's trees and animal life had made into their various nest sites and dens. They restructured them vastly, giving birth to a new creation of living entities that would survive the harsher climates and cooling temperatures of the vast climatic exchange of the outer-layer rift-points.

The Selmathen clans emerged, and flew from their various interstellar moons into these incredible caverns of lush and tropical spaces, making them sustainable for the current Aelven races that lived on other planets' surface worlds, far above and beyond this immediate galaxy. But it was the Tuatha De' Danann that claimed these caverns as their birthright, and produced this wonderful fortified city that you have seen today."

When Ryyaan had first arrived, it had been hard to drink it all in. Some of the trees were as tall as 800 feet, standing deep within the soil of these huge caverns, extending their limbs well upon the surface world above, shading and protecting the sheltered existence of what lay beneath in the world of the mound. There were many different species of plants he had never seen in Tamerk's woods. One of them was called the Trumpet Ivy, and it covered some of the huge trunks of these enormous trees that lined the inner-mound. Their main vines could grow up to an astounding size, giving off some of the most aromatic of fragrances which grew in any of the territories that belonged to any living sentient creature of the known worlds.

Joining them in the underground cavern was the river from above. These waters, came from a massive river system that flowed in from the Telpphaea Falls high up in the Cydclath Mountain range, and made their way down vast chasms as they cut their way through the middle of the continent to arrive at the head waters of the mound's own Zarconian Falls.

Ryyaan had first seen them from the back of the Dragon, as they came over the edge of the rim high above, smashing their way through the volcanic gorge that rested in the middle of the Panthorian Fault line. The water hosted a pair of twin falls which crashed down from the surface world above, coming in contact with a single massive rock ledge, that sat on the edge of the rim along the inner walls of the mound. Singularly, it would have been stunning; having both together coming over the edge was awesome. To see the pink quartz rock behind the falls as they crashed overtop, giving off an almost effervescent cloudy texture, as it began its descent along the ravines rocks to the bottom far below, were nothing short of spectacular.

The water flowed over the rim in higher capacities in the stormy winter months, and could be deafening at times, along the main chasm of the initial pool it created down the back side of the falls. Many side shoots of smaller waterfalls, with their own individual pools, could be seen on either side of the trees roots that had come straight out of the bedrock lying close to the fresh water streams. Each found whatever means necessary to survive in this underground climate, which now hosted several different kinds of flora trying to grow along the lengthening bark. The effect was startling in its creativity, in contrast with the baby blue Allushian mosses that were lying amongst the boulders out amongst the deeper pools at the base of the falls. Both were stunning alone, but together, breathtaking, even for one small boy visiting an alien planet that did not belong.

The boulders must have come from some huge volcanic blast, which must have sent them raining down in all directions, as they also littered the above ground spillway that the water had cut through to reach this ridge. The ones that had made it over the edge into the main cavern, were now strewn about like someone just spit them out from above, and could be seen lying all over the bottom pit of the fall's larger pools. Occasionally, in the summer months, on stiller days when the falls weren't running as fast, one could see the reflection of them, their shapes identifiable by large dark shadows lurking about like some alien species squatting in their underwater world. The others above and in the shallows seemed to stay covered in a perpetual mist from the spray of the falls, allowing for different mosses to attach themselves to their exterior surfaces.

Along the side of the falls, and all around the circular entrance up above, huge Tree-Ferns and a particularly odd strain of Bougainvillea littered the walls alongside Turquoise Jasmine, and Buttercup Katerpillar Odessa. They hung like ropes, dangling for several metres among the falls' rocky face, and dripped water droplets along the outer edges, as flowers that had a life expectancy of almost one hundred years could be seen peering out from their inner core. Most of the flowers within the Fey worlds had unusually long life forces, but those living within the cave environment boasted even more longevity, along with everything else that had been laced with the majikal waters of the mound's energy-rings.

Those rings had other challenges that existed in their production of mass energy. The force of the water alone gave the Aelves more than enough generated power to light an entire underground city, as well as stocking the reservoirs with an endless supply of fresh drinkable water to last long past the planet's life span. Should anything actually happen that caused the creatures to die for some unheard of reason, the generated power alone would surpass essentially anything, until life again would find its way back to inhabit this planet.

Even had someone decided to poison the river from above, in their insanity, the great roots of the most central tree, alongside the Aelven run recycling plant below ground, would keep the substances from ever reaching the toxic levels that would kill those below, giving the entire cavern its reserved rights at sustainability far past when the surface world above had died and withered into dust.

They also had huge fissures in a few of the lower caverns below the main Aelven city, that still existed today. Their open steam-vents ran into the main river that continued through the entire complex, heating the slower moving waters that made up the deeper pools that were used as hot springs. On any given day the pools could be found to contain various members of the warrior compliment, enjoying the communal bathing these particular pools created. Behind and below ground, the Aelves had made various clay water-pipes that ran perpendicular to the walls, to move the heated water towards their homes and work places. This central heating system was present in most villages that lived along the fault lines of any steam-vents that had made their way to the surface of the planet. The Fey always utilized the elements of their world to the best of their ability; anything that was found on this planet from lava to sand, could be found to have come from something that existed on this particular spot, deep down inside the planet's molten core.

Most civilizations away from the Human worlds maintained their waterways in the most pristine of conditions that were Elementally possible. The twin falls of the Aggulf Elkcum mound were unusual, as what was visually seen in the caverns of the mound was far from the actuality of the underground aquifer. The water did create enormous amounts of valuable real estate for the non-Aelven species of Fey. But, seeing as how a greater portion of its river system could be found far below the Tuatha's actual mound, it belonged to everyone that belonged to the clans that found their protection within their hereditary classes. The river was found to disappear into that shadowed world, as it made its way twisting down, deeper and deeper, into large cracks and smaller falls, to other areas far below the underground cities. And it was these areas that were vastly charted by the Seer clans of another race, which held the maps to a larger contingency of their land rights.

The peace between these clans had lain within these caverns for a very long time, if not for centuries, and the Tuatha were not about to let anything change that reality. It was only the formation of their elite separate army of warriors that lived away from the other clans of Aelves up above in the night skies, which formed the basis for the Tuatha De`Danann today.

Ryyaan had listened with great interest as he finished the meal that Eithne had prepared for him, and watched her with fascination as she told him the story of how the village of Fomor above ground came to be the city of the Tuatha below.

She would begin with the tale of the King of Fomor she said. "For that," she held her hand out to Ryyaan who had finished eating his meal and politely returned his dishes to the sideboard, "we need to go outside into the hanging gardens." The two walked hand in hand, out the back of the home that they had first entered, and followed the trail that the actual rock had carved out by its fissures millions of years ago.

The home itself had no doors or windows. Being below ground, the need for those fixtures was not great in the world of the Fey, and so everything except for sleeping screens was left open to the beautiful gardens. They themselves now became part of the individual homes, and their interior living walls.

Ryyaan watched everything through Eithne's eyes like a dramaturge, floating behind one that was both spirit guide, and author, while orchestrating and engaging some sort of vast theatre event being played out before him. The trail she led them through was part of the naturalized horizontal venting of rock, which had been carved out by the waterfall in centuries past. She led them through another lush cavern of slippery rocks, where the twin falls came over the ceiling and into one of the deeper pools, which branched off into a series of little inclined rapids that came into another smaller and discreet grotto that had small waterfalls of about two arm length's high. It was to these that she gestured for both of them to finally sit.

The water trickled the breadth of the cavern, and was much quieter here, compared to the actual part of the falls that came down through the ceiling. It was here that she would be able to tell the story to the boy without any interruptions from various Elementals flittering in and out asking questions as to how the child was doing, but still have enough visual interferences to keep him from being bored.

They settled alongside the brook, nestled among thick blue carpets of different kinds of mosses. Ryyaan went over to the pools and dropped a few pebbles into the slow moving water, watching several small fish dart in and out exploring what had descended from above into their environment. His attention was directed primarily at the brook, as he lay prone along the water's edge, dangling fingers amongst the ripples, watching for any of them unlucky enough to get within reach. It was soon beginning to be quite clear to Eithne, that he would be more interested in fishing than the actual reason they had come to sit. She allowed him his alone time to revel in all that was before him, and picked up a journal she had been writing in earlier, and had left by the rocks when the word came through that the White Dragon had arrived with its passenger on board.

She found these times of quiet reflection to prompt some of the best writing she would ever put to paper anytime else within her lifetime. It didn't take long before Ryyaan was sound asleep; compliments of the moss he was lying on, and since he probably had very little since the Mauntra had first risen, it was a good idea to allow him that time. She nodded to herself and looked on, smiling. The added majikal influence she had sent his way to make him sleep, was a necessity; if he didn't sleep well, then Sigrith wouldn't heal quickly, and both of them wouldn't be on their way to their final destination anytime soon. At least now he was safe and well looked after; for tomorrow would be a long and difficult journey. They would have plenty of time to answer any questions from the boy who talked with his mind, during the flight to Leberone; one that she wished had substance enough to allow her time to follow, instead of hearing the tale through the ears of another. Hum, she contemplated, change was a good thing sometimes; she would work on that.

CHAPTER SIXTEEN

The Village of the old Fomorian King

Meanwhile, above ground in Fomor, Tamerk slid in on his shift and was escorted to Cian to bring him word of the events of the past few weeks. Since Balor's recent departure from the Fey worlds, and Lugh, Cian's only living son, taking over the duties of the Tuatha's military campaigns, it had been left to Cian to take care of the above ground village of Fomor, since the recently departed King was no longer alive. The residents of this tiny village that had hosted another King, had just become used to this new style of non-invasive ruling with the landholders that worked the lands and lived inside its walls. Cian was well respected, and treated those that had built their homes along the borderlands of the Tuatha mound with the highest regard; unlike one previous King, who had gone out of his way to piss off every land owner and working citizen within a hundred mile radius. Unfortunately Cian, being as busy as he was, never seemed to find enough time to chat lately for anyone that came to visit, except the old man.

Not much went on in Tantaris's world of planets without the Tuatha being informed in one way or another; each day brought new information, and things that would be requiring immediate attention were dealt with in the utmost of care in regards to whatever had been done. They were after all, the ruling class of military might that all Fey within this realm called upon at one time or another. Each day things that had happened across the wide breath of their ruling area of space, needed to be recorded and attended to with the various factions of Fey involved that held interest

THE BEGINNING

in Sopdet's ruling — all of which Cian was now in charge of, despite his objections to the role. He often felt a little left out of the various skirmishes and forays they used to ride into. He never imagined that in his life-time he would have to settle his mind down and do the work of one of the scribes behind a bloody desk, and not one of the warriors of his clan, leading the skirmishers into some honour-bound battle. He had to admit he hated this kind of work. Unfortunately someone had to do it, and since no one else had his expertise, he had been selected to take over that role for the interim.

But Cian always enjoyed Tamerk's company. When the old man arrived in the village only moments after the White Dragon had landed within their skies, Cian was only too glad to put aside his paperwork, pour two Sanitarian brandies, and spend time away from what he should have been finishing up.

Cian's study, within the old stone building, was pretty typical of most estate offices in any of the smaller villages within his reach. It held a couple of overstuffed chairs, overlooking the one main feature of all workspaces; a lovely warm fireplace. There was also the usual stack of paperwork, that Cian would get to in due time, still piled high on the desk beside him. And an equal stack of paperwork that needed to be filed in the appropriate file, which Cian had not quite figured the whereabouts of as of yet, piled on the floor.

This had always been Balor, his father-in-law's domain (the old nasty coot), but with his recent and untimely death at the hands of his son, and subsequent departure into the great beyond, Cian should have gotten in here weeks if not months ago, while the old man's crooked Fomorian bookkeeper had still been employed. Maybe then some of the Fomorian gold would still be in the coffers, and not headed for parts unknown.

But that particular Fey nasty had taken a huge sum of Formorian gold, and headed for the hills shortly after Balor's reported death, only to be discovered dead as a door-nail himself, with no trace of the money in his mangled old hands.

Cian smiled with the knowledge of how Lugh had taken off after him, and had come back all pissed off and tired from wasting time on the old bookkeeper, after spending the whole day riding his mount hard on his tail. All that had been found was the animal he had rode out on and, having seen the horse the bookkeeper had always had well groomed and looked after within the stables, it was also something of a surprise to see that he had neglected to ride his own horse during his escape. The old nag that he had absconded with turned out to be a Shapeshifter moving through these parts, who had not taken well to the old thief's backside, and by the looks of his face when Lugh had finally caught up with him, he was also not amused. The jury was still out whether it was him who had done the damage and had kept the coins for himself, for when Lugh had come back to question him, the Shapeshifter had disappeared into the woods. Bad timing and bad luck on either accounts, or so some would like to think.

Well at least they had his prize stallion; the profit alone from having him bred in these parts was more than enough to compensate for anything the old coot had stolen from the village coffers; he had been untouched and still found to be eating hay in the barn. However, to have found the thief and brought back the bulk of the Fomorian gold would certainly have done Lugh a world of good in the eyes of the Fomor Aelves. That gold Balor had squirrelled away from the sharecroppers who worked these lands for so many years still remained at large, and Cian was having a hard time finding where it had all come from.

Each one of the villagers could have given a King's ransom and still not come up with the tidy sum that was reported to have been stolen. They each had paid their share in blood, and many had landed on the wrong side of Balor's thugs when they had not been able to make a profit with whatever scheme he had ordered them into. Having the gold returned would have gone a long way to gaining the villagers' respect, without the Tuatha having to prove themselves in other ways. But Cian was still optimistic, and he hoped with this new project that Tamerk and himself had embarked upon, that time would be coming to fruition, and the people of Fomor would come around, thanks to the influx of several hundred coins of Aelven gold in the hands of their elders.

Now it was up to him to sort the more pressing affairs from the ones that could wait for more than a bit of time. It was not such a daunting task; more to the effect of a tedious one. He would have liked to be out in the community, trying to get to know the new villagers and their individual problems firsthand. It was more pleasing to him, despite the few old guards and their still existing Formorian guardsmen mentality, which still existed in the odd inhabitant living within the compound. But until then, things needed to settle down before he could hire someone else to help him with the figures and sums, which had been left in such a state of disrepair that it was laughable to say the least.

Even then, it would take some time to complete entirely, and the old guard that still lived within these walls, were slowly disappearing thanks to someone who has yet to come forth and lay claim to the deed. Nonetheless, Balor was never one to tidy the account books up in the first place; instead he gave full access to his bookkeeper so he could hide the sums of money they had swindled, and spent the stuff they stole from those that they had taken offence to. Having that kind of control is never good when it comes to accounts. That should have been under the control of the village elders, and not some stranger from another place who was notably crooked in doing their books. But Balor had hired him and that was that, and anyone having a problem with it soon disappeared.

Balor was always trying to start a war with anyone, even people within his own village at times, so it was no surprise for him to have begun one with the Tuatha when they had arrived on scene to help in the dispute. Nothing he did in Fomor had any rhyme or reason. He had been well hated by all, so it made perfect sense why the bookkeeper he had hired cared very little for the finances of the Fomorian people, and more for the gold he could put into his own pocket. So for the grace of the villagers, one tends to tread carefully when something even though is inherently wrong proves to be better for all; the missing soldiers might have met with foul play, but Cian hadn't the time to delve further into their disappearance nor find the culprit that was at its source.

He had no time for speculation and until something crossed his path that was directly involved in something that did; he intended to let it rest. Instead, he had been working non-stop since their take-over with more important things, so his mind needed the rest that would come long after they got things settled. Tamerk coming today was perfect; his wife Eithne was busy with the Human child below ground, leaving him to have a longer visit, mixing both business and the pleasure of doing anything that didn't rely solely on having him record its financial future down on paper.

Tamerk had always been an oddity to the Aelven folk; despite his short stature and ancient looking face, though, it was his eyes that always made Cian flinch. He could be talking with you at one moment and the next it was nothing like you had ever felt before, as he took you into his world — literally; then everything that you knew and felt around you would suddenly change scenery and dissolve into something else not previously there. No longer would you be sitting in a comfortable chair, inside a study that's been in your family for thousands of years. Instead, you would be transported into the place he was talking about, so there was never any concern that his meaning got lost in translation. It was a very uniquely Wood Spriteish thing to do.

One needed nerves of steel to enjoy the old Sprite whenever he came to the village — especially in the hope of accomplishing something during that visit.

Cian could remember a long time ago when, as a young Aelven lad, long years before he had met his wife, he had come across a Sprite within the confines of an old hut he and his childhood friends had come across deep in the woods. It had taken his father three days to convince the old man to give the boys another chance, and let them go free. On the inside of the hut they had thought they were on an elaborate hunting expedition, and hadn't even been aware that they had stumbled into the old man's woodshed!

He knew better now, and gave Tamerk the respect those creatures deserved, even though others of his clan had gone to great lengths to keep away from the old man. Even Eithne's father Balor was uneasy about dealing with them, and used to call Cian's father Gabriel to help in the talks, so he could always be assured he would make it back in one piece. Somehow that should have been a warning to his clan and their homelands, when it came to trusting the former King, but alas time does have a way of causing people to forget even the basics when it comes to things that all should remember in foresight.

Balor had not been kind to his only daughter Eithne while she had grown up along the edges of his insane mind. But then again, had they not had to rescue her from the tower he had locked her in to prevent her siring any sons, Cian would never have met her all those years ago. It had been predicted by one of the Druids of Balor's kingdom, that one of her own offspring would kill him in battle, and take over the kingdom before he reached the ripe old age of forty. Why, they thought sons could be the culprits, when a perfectly innocent looking daughter could have done the deed far faster and much more deadly, was anyone's guess: Especially in this day and age when everyone, or everything, was basically born with a weapon in their hands.

It would surely have been kinder had someone actually killed the old coot long before his son finally got the chance, but then again Cian had only wished it had been him to do the deed; at least then things may have been easier for everyone involved. But for Eithne's sake, he had let events run their course, and Lugh had put him on the run for many years, before revealing himself to him as Cian's last remaining living son.

Cian had to admit he had learned many things from him, even though he had not liked the principality of how he had learned those lessons. In retrospect, Gabriel had been right, in that it had made him a better ambassador to Fomor. Anything he could do with this title was far better for the people, than everything Balor had done for them in all his years as reigning sovereign. Even considering the old mentality of the last few who had stayed behind, that now surely wished they had not, in the end. He laughed, as Tamerk looked at him with a raised eyebrow and moved towards the chair he offered. Some things never change.

So he had a good rapport with Tamerk, at least he was pretty certain that this was the truth, in his thinking today. He would hope that after all the two of them had been through together, with respect to his younger children, even Tamerk would be able to give him that bit of credit, long over-due by others of his kind. His ancient knowledge of things within the forests of the western regional provinces was always complete in its entirety. The Tuatha needed to employ certain credible sources to be able to bring strength to their fight to keep all of Tantaris safe, not just their neck of the woods — the Dragon wars had taught them that much.

For a thousand years that had been their way, and Tantaris had had peace. Sure, they had occasional squabbles among certain villages, that necessitated making an appearance, but that was Fey business, not Human. It was the Human appearance that had fuelled the war back then, and he couldn't think of any particular Fey that would allow that to happen again. It wasn't that he didn't think one of the Fey would betray them again, it was that the Tuatha had already set things in motion to prevent it, which brought things full circle to why Tamerk was really there.

"Good morning, old man," Cian greeted Tamerk with the usual token of Sanitarian brandy. "This should be more to your liking than the previous one." Tamerk smiled his odd grin and took a sip then raised its contents to the Mauntra-rays at the window sill, watching the clarity swirl around within the glass. It took on a certain sheen, and popped loudly inside the middle of the following swirl, bringing a grin to the old Sprite's face.

"Indeed, told you we needed to use sugar maple barrels, not ash," Tamerk said. Cian laughed, heartily, before replying.

"What were we thinking?" Tamerk grinned at him.

"Obviously you weren't!"

Cian had always liked Tamerk; his knowledge of spirits far surpassed anything the Aelven community as a whole could dream of producing. When Cian had begun the endeavour of corking a new brandy, he thought of surprising the old Sprite with a glass of it when next they had met. But when the time came and it was time to uncork it, Cian had been disappointed with its unusual flavour, and try as he may he just couldn't get it right. The moment Tamerk had appeared for their monthly Taro game, and tasted the ingredients as it slid across his tongue, the two year endeavour had been thrown out of the window and given a decent burial. With Tamerk's suggestions and truth behind his words, the new batch was far superior to anything Cian had ever tasted. That was five years ago, and this batch he had been curing just for him.

"Now give it another ten years and you will have yourself an award winning product." The little creature ducked, as Cian threw a book at him. "And you should have a doctor look at that arm, you throw like a girl!" They both downed their respective glasses and took the bottle to the armchairs and dragged them to the outside veranda. "Ah, now that's better. Beats the hel out of looking at a dead fire." Tamerk settled into the back of the comfortable chair. "So, how's Ryyaan doing downstairs?"

"I think he's got a crush on Eithne," Cian responded.

"Smart boy; don't we all."

"Careful old man, that's my wife you're talking about!" Tamerk only grinned.

THE BEGINNING

"Every Aelfen male within the surface of this realm, that's met her, has a crush on your wife, in case you didn't know. Just because I'm an old man, doesn't mean I'm blind."

"That could be arranged," jabbed Cian, taking a swing at the old Sprite. He missed, as Tamerk ducked and flipped over the chair, letting it land further down along the verandah.

"You, and whose particular army?" Tamerk looked at Cian as he picked it up and dragged it back, balancing his glass and the chair in between sips, and they both burst out laughing, spitting brandy all over the ground as it came straight out of their nostrils and shot across the chairs looking for a way past Tamerk's protection grid. They were after all, sitting right above the biggest military fortress in all of Tantaris.

"Okay, you win." Tamerk bowed in defeat. "Now, let's get down to the business at hand," he continued.

They sat for several minutes, savouring their brandy and not talking. By then Cian's main housekeeper had arrived with two bowls of Gajoe Bear stew and a loaf of homemade peppercorn bread, preventing anything further from being discussed.

"That's lovely Jazmyyn; you can put it on the sideboard over by the sill, I'll serve us from there." Cian dismissed her. He knew how uncomfortable his staff could be with the old Sprite, even one as gifted as her. She lifted an unarguable eye brow at his completing her job, and did it herself. Cian grinned at her veracity, *'no one told Jazmyyn what to do.'* If they did, they'd find themselves on the losing end of some kind of demeaning chore. Even being in the old Sprite's energy field wasn't enough to make her relinquish her job. Once done, she bowed her head to the old Sprite, then moved quickly towards the stone steps of the veranda, looking over her shoulder before disappearing within the lush foliage as it enclosed everything in behind her.

Cian had to give her credit for making it something almost comical. Jazmyyn had been a member of his staff for as long as he could remember, and if he was a betting Aelf, he would say that she also worked a wee bit for his father in the old days, before she came to help him in his collection of former staff. Jazmyyn was married to a member of the Caubertian clan from Tothray. Her mate was a tough old conk, but his skills as a mechanic had earned him an opportunity to work with the Tuatha below ground in the city of the mound, soon after its start-up in the early years. Sercovious was her mate's name, and he was one of their top Aelfs in the maintenance of the main lift. That lift was their hidden entrance into the world below ground, and it was the very one that lowered most things from topside to the main causeway below ground that were in need of secrecy, or at least, to be kept away from prying eyes.

Sercovious was one of the original seven metal-rats of the Caubertian clan's smithies, and probably the best one out of the lot. They were lucky to have him, and it was his blueprint and knowledge that had designed the lift in the first place. It was this design that incorporated the knowledge of his calling; to be able to bring the huge Dragons from Leberone from time to time, into the depths of the mound from the surface world of the skies. And it was a feat unmatched by any other clan of the Dragon's vast range of flight, while moving through Sopdet's constellation of worlds.

Jazmyyn held her own court upstairs in the main kitchens, and that woman could out cook anyone in all of the known worlds; even counting several of the Faery realms, if one was a betting fool. Her authority in that domain knew no boundaries; even the young field workers skirted around her as they brought produce in from the various barns and outbuildings that were needed to feed the people of the village of Fomor. She wasn't one to ever shirk her responsibilities for anything or anyone, so it didn't surprise him when his normal staff member hadn't appeared himself. Jazmyyn probably had him peeling Janjjaw plants or something demeaning that only she could make him do, after he refused to bring the meal that Tamerk and Cian were now enjoying.

"I think she's warming up to me, what do you think?" Tamerk winked at Cian. Cian took another bite of the bread, to keep from laughing, but that only proved to make him choke faster. He was going to have to thank Jazmyyn personally, after Tamerk was gone. However, before that happened they had work to do, and that would even have to wait; the food needed to become part of the interior walls of their stomachs in order for them to accomplish anything, for without it neither would be in any shape to finish their conference, with the brandy starting to affect their behaviour as it entered their bloodstreams. Cian knew if food was not introduced quickly, there was no telling where they'd end up in Tamerk's world, and for now, with everything happening as it was below ground with the boy, he'd like to see that through before taking any more trips through another galaxy where Tamerk use to live, because he was simply bored.

When all was said and done, they tried to peel themselves off the chairs that had decided to try and fit themselves to their warm bodies by wrapping themselves around their legs and backsides — as live chairs tend to do when you sit for a while. The real and the living always blend into the world of everything that becomes part of its land. So, after Tamerk actually cut himself out of his seat with the knife he had found besides his bowl, and after the chair tried to fight back and Tamerk had decked it, it was Cian that had asked how things were going in the outside world, which brought the conversation back to why Tamerk had come in the first place.

With his charge safely tucked away below ground, Tamerk regaled Cian with the whispers of something that had arrived with fetid breath, which had the tell-tail marking of something very familiar, that could be seen drifting among the outskirts of villages all over the entire planet of Tantaris Major.

He continued talking, after a moment of profound pause, then he took in a long breath, followed by another sip of the brandy that still lay within the flask that had been set out on the table before him. "There had been several villagers out among the trails, near certain areas of their hunting grounds, who had found a series of dead and dying wildlife with no apparent reason for the situation they found themselves to be in." That got Cian's attention faster than having been slapped. Tamerk watched him start the beginning threads of studious thought, as he rose to pace the veranda floor, pausing only to pour more brandy into his glass and gulp it down. He continued on with his line of thought. "Whatever the reason for their deaths, it seems to be a systematically patterned search of the Ley Lines of Kalmaskis, and all within a few hours journey of each of all the single shift-point doorways that join them to us," Tamerk explained.

If Cian's attention had drifted elsewhere, it was suddenly focused entirely on Tamerk.

"Have any of the villages near those points been compromised?" Cian stood up, knocking the flask of brandy to the side of the table; he needed to know the answer to that question now. If they had been compromised, he only had a short veil of opportunity to get word to his son. And that window of opportunity was growing increasingly shorter by the minute, below ground, where a certain Leviathan was starting to find his footing.

He would have to send a message along with the White Dragon for Lugh, if there were any that even had the slightest hint of its blackened scratchings. Tamerk shook his head squinting upwards, as he placed a hand over his eyes at the Mauntra's light that now shone directly into his face.

"None so far, but the village wards that have been put in place have been strong enough to protect them in circumstances that warranted it in the past. So it would only be justified to expect that this would be no different, being as closely guarded and monitored in each of the smaller towns on the outskirts of those ley lines, as they are." He begun again, but stopped short looking around, watching the waves of energy that moved about the trees. "That is, as far as I've heard." Tamerk spoke quietly, making sure that they were not heard.

Cian didn't need to know that they were being watched, he already felt the energy cross paths with them as soon as Tamerk stopped and pointed.

"All it takes is one; the villagers need to be diligent," Cian returned, louder than normal. "I think there is a time to panic and then a time to run. This might just be that moment to get going, and leave the village of Fomor to be devoured by the wolves as they make their way into town." He said the last part with a grin on his face, as both Tamerk and Cian heard someone gasp, then start to move away at a greatly accelerated rate of speed. Both of them looked at each other and started to laugh.

"Did you really need to give one of the old guards of Balor's reign a reason to gossip himself into beginning a war? At least you could have told them it was something other than wolves; I kind of like the creatures. At least you always know when they're going to come for your throat, not unlike the old guard, who suddenly without provocation just stick an arsenal of knives in your back!" Tamerk downed the last of the whiskey, and then continued on as if they had never been interrupted.

"No need, he won't be going anywhere soon, and when he does wake up, he won't be visiting any of his companions for a very long time." Tamerk grinned as Cian shook his head laughing.

"What'd you do this time?"

"Oh, you can say he might have a wee bit of trouble feeling his face for the foreseeable future," he smirked. Cian simply shook his head, deciding not to even ask.

"So have you any ideas on what is causing these deaths? If something makes it through the wards of one town, and it's a sentient being, the wards will fail just as easily in the other villages." Cian changed direction, got up and paced around the patio watching, just in case the last intruder had company. But, all seemed to be quiet.

The old Sprite thought this through, drumming his fingers on the wall as he watched Cian pace. "Then we need to caution Lugh on his military outings in those specific areas that have been searched, and find other pathways that it is reaching, my friend." He continued on as he thought more on the subject. "It seems to be very odd, that it all began the moment the Dragonlords were called into service." He was just as stunned by Cian's reaction, as he was to missing the clue he had not been given earlier.

"The Dracore are back?" Cian shouted above his brandy glass, not caring who heard him shout from the terrace they were sitting on. Tamerk carried on quickly, looking visibly shaken.

"The Dragon-riders were told that their clan leader was instructed by Lugh, Cian."

"That's not possible, he's not even here," Cian answered him, shocked. Tamerk carried on quickly.

"Quist and the others were waiting for Soren and Symin after the boy was first spotted in the woods. They thought Lugh had ordered it, and were sent to pick up Sibrey as well." Cian threw a fit at that bit of news.

"What, the girl has been taken too?" Cian fairly screamed.

"No, she was able to shift away, and has been driven towards the forest of the Panthers. She has since been secured, but that was not before she had been out of the Shapeshifter's village wards for almost a full day."

Cian was livid and moved towards the inside walls of the place that would suddenly become frantic with activity, as he called several guards into action. Tamerk used this time to walk the distance towards the Aggulf Elkcum Mound to check that all was well with the boy below deck, and moved down the pathway towards one of the strongest garrisons that had been built on this planet. All the while, Cian could be heard yelling his head off at everyone within range that cared to listen.

The Santarian brandy was left abandoned on the table. It would not stay long, as the moment the old house keeper returned to clear away the dishes from their meal, it was taken as payment for having to suffer in silence, with the one that no other dared to come into contact with.

Tamerk continued on the trail, moving out of hearing range of Cian's shouting. He could very easily have shifted into the mound's inner sanctum without too much trouble on any given day, but today, with the amount of brandy he had ingested it was anyone's guess where he would actually wind up. He could very well have found himself in the middle of a dark star's orbital gaseous outer-rings, for all he knew. It would do him good to get out and actually walk for a change. The Dragon wasn't due to leave for another few hours, and by then he would have had a nice chance to sober up, and maybe find out a few things that were bothering him about the black Dragons that he had assumed had been called into service by the head of the Tuatha De´Danann's military.

Well now, he thought to himself, that changes all things now doesn't it? He hoped the mound, and all its massive protection wards that moved in and out among the rings, was still able to keep watch over a small child that could possibly kill every living thing on this world if the creature got through their wards. Notwithstanding another creature even more deadly than Ryyaan's little gifts, that still found itself to be out cold, among them. They would find him to be a wee bit annoyed when he wakes up, after been taken against his will by his own Dragon.

He really hoped they had kept Symin sedated, and no one in their right mind had thought to revive the Aelf in all his glorified idiocy. That one was far more dangerous than the young child, and should anyone have reason to believe that he would be indebted to them by waking the Aelf up before his time, they would be in for the shock of their lifetime when the creature that came forward took the entire complex out the moment he awoke, especially without the proper safeguards put into damn place. Truly, this place was beginning to fall apart at the seams. What was Sopdet, thinking?

He hadn't gone too far down the path, when he was hit from behind and fell flat on his face!

CHAPTER SEVENTEEN

Unexpected Departure

Below ground in the Dragon's chamber, their unusual guest was beginning to show signs of gravity stress. His huge girth, not bred to withstand the gravity of Tantaris's placement with the Mauntra's gravitational pull, had accompanied and settled within the Great Dragon, the moment he had entered the planet's atmosphere.

These large space Leviathans had not been bred to withstand the small planet's attempt to capture solid form. Thus, planet bound fey were always affected by gravity. The very gravity that had begun to create weight on his lovely hearts, which sustained the existence of all things that made up this carbon life-force. The very life force that spent its entire breathing life in the vastness of deep-space.

Sigrith's physiology was unusual. And he was able to pump his blood to all parts of his body, with the help of six of them being planted and grown inside his large frame. But even one failure would be catastrophic, within his limited structured environment, thus posing a very real and deadly risk to the creature that now started to fuss quite loudly below ground.

As it stands, both Elemental creatures and Aelfs alike were doing their best to get enough minerals into the blood-stream of their enormous patient, but it was becoming very apparent that it was only a matter of time before that too was not going to be enough. The Tuatha had superior medicines, which were far more advanced than any of the races that lived within this system of worlds. And even with the newest devices designed to pump in the oxygen free atmosphere that he required to stay alive on this planet's gravitational field, it wouldn't be long before it wouldn't be enough to sustain his brain cells, and he would have to leave, or they would have to shift him once again into the confines of space. Unfortunately, those helping him move into this fluid reduction of airless spacial existence, would undoubtedly not survive the transference. So with that in mind, they needed to keep him on the fringes of stability, and then as soon as the planets shifted into the right position, he could then move on his own steam back into his specific spacial-induction zone.

Sigrith started to thrash about as a sudden pressure drop in vacuum began to destabilize the chamber from the edges of the outside pressure tube. The Dragon's huge body structure would not be able to withstand the gravity of Tantaris for much longer, and it was that failure to fly skyward and reach the non-gravitational space that would crush the very veins within his lovely white body and send shock waves through both of the worlds above and below Tantaris's Fey realms.

That was simply not an option anyone would want to explain to Lugh, as he was still up on Tantaris's closest moon, called Leberone, and anyone involved with its death (should that come to pass), would not be safe in any of the other worlds that he would run to hide within. So, word had been sent up that his departure must come within the hour, or their guest would tear the bloody place apart.

Daylight had just been born, with the first rays of light spreading with the Mauntra's rising as it greeted the morning sky, when something changed from that sudden pressure drop of an hour ago, within the mound. Ryyaan had awoken while it was still dark, and clung sleepily to Eithne's shoulders. As he was being carried to the landing grate outside, and coming into contact with Sigrith's energy pulse; suddenly the touchstone activated without any warning. However, this time another section not previously part of the mechanics that Ryyaan had earlier used suddenly came on line. It both startled and caught everyone within range off guard, as it hummed and pulsated, sending creatures big and small running in all directions to find shelter.

This time no chances were being taken with regards to the Great Dragon's timing, and this small crystal could very easily have been used, in the same way any of the activation crystals had been before. To have the activation in the hands of a child was disturbing. To have the timing blown apart by a Human child was unheard of, and they moved to make sure this was not going to happen any time so close to Sigrith's departure. They had gone to great lengths to reduce the energy output that would be sent along the grate's mechanical levers, to propel the extra energy forward and up. But this new device was something they had no knowledge of, and it could be used to expand the chamber and blow the atmosphere sky high if things were not monitored and kept in place.

Each of the Fey creatures present had been informed the Dragon would jump within this very hour, but nothing prepared them for what would happen in the next few minutes.

Symin's unconscious but well cared for form had just been carried to the platform, and could already be seen onboard Sigrith's back, along with supplies for the outpost that Lugh had given orders to bring along. But a new development had arisen in the riders' number count, and as evidenced by Cian's repeated objections, Eithne's decision to go along with the child had not been Cian's choice. She should not have been there, and everything Cian had done to prevent it had been ignored and dismissed as overprotective.

His wife was not one to argue with, at the best of times, and someone needed to bring news of Ryyaan to the Aelven encampment on Leberone, to show Lugh what had transpired down here on Tantaris when the boy had shown up unexpectedly. It would be better not to press the issue with Eithne, as she carried her charge and walked upwards towards the grate, cradling the young boy as if he was her own. Sigrith was unusually nervous and pranced on the spot like he had an overabundance of energy in his system, and hadn't been to this planet at all. Eithne approached one of clan's men and dared him to intervene, before heading for the platform that was the focal point of everyone's attention. She passed her young charge over to him and leapt up on Sigrith's back as though she had every right to do so. The young warrior literally climbed the Dragon's side, with Ryyaan slung over his shoulders, and passed the sleepy child over to his commander's own mother.

Cian had no choice but to let his wife join the group, knowing full well he would have gone himself, after learning what Tamerk had come to tell him, but Eithne had pulled rank and had bonded with the Human boy, which was something Cian had not as of yet had the chance to do. The child was powerful, and no one that did not have a rapport with him could get near, so even though he thought about replacing her, there wasn't a single Aelf or Fey in the compliment left below ground that would have gone voluntarily anyway. So she established herself in place, and snuggled the Human child into place in her seated position and settled in for the hour long wait, while Cian fussed and fumed out on the outside of the mound, to send her off.

With the ruling commander off world, Cian was needed here to bring the highest ranking warriors of the Tuatha De`Danann into the War Room and that gave him reason to find his place away from the action he so desperately wanted to be a part of that was currently going on right in front of him. He watched from a distance on the ridge, overlooking the comings and goings of the final stages before departure. To have been down amidst the foray of departure would have given him ideas on how to waylay her plans, and sure as hel the closer it got the more he would have fretted about her leaving. This way he could be assured he wouldn't do something stupid at the last minute to jeopardize the departure, and it was here he stood with a few select officers.

Everyone began to get ready to move inside the room that would be their home until decisions were made in time for Lugh's arrival back on planetary ground, in about a fortnight. A young soldier moved towards Eithne when instructed to pass the last remaining supplies she would be taking aboard, and began the motions of lifting them onto the back of the Great White, when something suddenly grabbed them from his hands and threw them in one fluid motion towards the Dragon's back, where they landed ass over teakettle into place. It then proceeded to push the Aelf backwards towards the cavern wall, until something suddenly decided it wasn't fast enough, chose to bodily move him across the farside of the room. He landed none to gently as he slid down the wall along the backside of a huge boulder, where he was seen slumped over and slightly unconscious from the intense energy field it produced. Before anyone could move to retrieve the poor sod, a buildup of energy suddenly went nuclear, and the Aelfs closest to the event were pulled into a protective shielding that suddenly came on line over the entire area, protecting all of them from the blast that came without warning, catching everyone off guard as things began to take on another unexpected manifestation.

The shift was for the most part something most of the Aelfs below ground were definitely not expecting. Not only did it happen the moment Eithne got settled, but it happened so fast that it gave substance to an explosion of blue atoms that at one moment had simply been there, then quite suddenly were displaced by others of equal status and far deadlier. Not easily done with an object as large as Sigrith. They were suddenly no longer in the place that had been occupied by the Great White Dragon and his riders. Instead, everything just disappeared, and what was left behind came crashing down in a sudden movement of displaced air and volatile atoms which brought the voided empty space collapsing in on itself, creating a horrifically loud explosion of a displaced internalized refraction.

In simple terms: it just blew up. They all collided together in one big mess, with rocks from part of the grate's main structure crashing inward among its own metal frame work, and landing far below in a mangled mess of twisted steel and iron plating. It was horrifying to be in the middle of the disaster, and anyone or anything caught in the middle of it should have been crushed, resulting in insurmountable bedlam to those that witnessed its execution up close and bloody personal.

Nobody had any idea how much damage could be sustained from anything of that nature in any of the scenarios they had run through in the past. They hadn't actually prepared themselves for something this catastrophic happening, anytime they had run through the systems checks when they had first built the doorway into their mechanical yield. But to be true, nothing that big had ever shifted above ground without the protection of the Standing Stones up on the surface helping to atomize its degenerational pull, let alone inside an underground cavern deep within the very stone mound that was built to protect such energy fluxes from ever happening in the bloody first place.

Even if they could have got Sigrith on the surface, within the protection of the stone circle above, the damage would still have been extensive. The shock wave that was generated within the touchstone's added field of flux, was felt along every ley line within the northern hemisphere on the entire planet. It moved incredibly fast, like a wave of pyroclastic flow, which travelled within seconds to every village within a hundred mile radius that had lain directly in its pathway.

They first felt its reaches within the village of Fomor, as it slid in sideways with one of the smaller tendrils of its energy pulses, before finally changing course and finding another exit point and continuing on south through the Panthorian fault-line. But the main damage wasn't done with the surge that hit Fomor, and it carried on to other villages. Nothing the inhabitants could have done could have changed its direction, until the molecules of the main blast ran their course and sprinted out of steam. What was left was a miniscule blow compared to other villages that that were in a more direct path, as it came crashing head-on into their wards and dropped them like a deck of Taro.

Fomor was indeed lucky that their township was not on that fault line. Instead, the village ran primarily along the shore of the Sea of Contentious Souls, where it squatted and hung high above the rocky shore that swept the salt from a nice little ravine, protected on all sides from the volatile fracture points of the Shivonian ley line.

However, that does not mean it did not take damage. The wards took the main brunt of the shock wave. The moment they lay on the ground, the energy the shockwave had been producing as it circled around the wards and raced through the electrical field, tore a hole in the western side of the majikal barrier, as it came at the town in the one place that had never had been attacked before.

It jumped the barrier rings as if it had sentient life and knew that this was the weak area of the town's protection field, and the town absorbed a shock wave that slid through the ragged shoreline, coming up from the sea. That was all the energy required, as it crashed head-on into the shoreline along the sandy rocks and liquefied the soil the town was built upon. That created a mudslide that tore through the edge of town, and flattened two brand new barns that were in the final stages of completion. It woke every single Aelven family within two villages bordering on this side of the

Zarconian Falls, before the surge finished its wrath, shattering every piece of glass this side of the Cydclath Mountain range.

And then, all went quiet. At least for a full breath of a hound as it breathed in and shot outwards in an advanced exhalation of breath, and then it began once more in eager enthusiasm, and the planet began to scream. But this time it was much stronger, growing in velocity as it gained momentum, reaching the outskirts of the southern previously untouched villages that were beyond its former fledgling's reach, as if something was thinking about what had just happened, and laughed at its previous attempt and decided that it hadn't quite proved its point. And this time it was mad!

The second wave of energy gained momentum from where it had left off, and rumbled into life with a screech, breaking straight through to the far-side of the Telpphaea Falls. There it followed the path of one of the most destructive fault lines that had made its home here on the planet, and straight down the shoot between the middle of both central mountain ranges, tearing a path of destruction in its wake. The fault line had been carved out along the inner-core back in the helical period, and ran all the way from the continental ridgelines in the central part of the land-mass and smack into a particular village known for its protection rites. This village of hidden secrets was known as Tothray, and the second wave of destructive force smacked head on into its protected outer layer and left it momentarily blind.

But, that was as far as the pyroclastic wall of energy made it, as it smoked and smoldered alongside the edge of this field and stopped just short of cutting the continent in half and sending it sliding into the sea. Tothray is known for its unusual ability to harness the volatile windstorms and severe weather phenomena that run the area like a gauntlet during the fall-winter storm seasons. One of their more unusual residents came from the storm Nebula of Centarraura, and his specialty was creating energy wards that were specific for the area's environment. When the surge blasted down the pipe, straight through the middle of both mountain ranges, the genetically altered weather ward that had been set up to keep the village safe, killed its forward motion and held it momentarily frozen in place as it began to vaporize the dangerous particles of Sigrith's unexpected shift. The shadow of vast energy hung there like a cloud of electrical currents, flickering in and out of visual sight, then fell to the ground like rain in a fall storm, dissipating into the outlying jagged rocks, and leaving the village virtually untouched as the energy died a slow death, fractured by the alien shielding.

For a fraction of time the village came into view to the outside world, the secondary wards he had designed took over and shifted the blanket of invisibility back into place, and locked it tightly against itself. A few hunters high up on another ridge watched the electrical storm as it slammed into their village with a dull thud. They felt the electricity move down along their arms and legs as the hair became magnetic and seemed to point itself in the village's direction, sending everything into slow motion for a fraction of a Quadra-second, before absorbing it back into the barrier set in place. They watched as the barrier took on a dark pallor, and winked back off line after resetting the village back into its invisibility mode, virtually obstructing anyone on the outside from re-entering the village for the time being. It left the entrance wards black and completely dismantled, as it sat there on the edges of their town smoking away in the distance, completely useless.

Aelves on this side of the blast zone were sent scrambling in all directions. Back in Fomor, Sercovious having actually been away from the mound and not in it when it blew up, didn't realize how close to the town the shockwave had actually hit, until he was able to get out on the veranda of the main castle holdings, and visually see what had been caught in the wave of the unusual blast that levelled everything around their village wards. Trees in all directions that the blast had travelled from were all lying flat along the pathway that led to the mound, resting along the ground. Each was strangely bent at odd angles, hanging precariously off centre, while the continuous pulse-wave front began to settle in place and restructure the trees' physiology back into their original formations. He watched the majik of these Earthen Elementals fold itself into position and shake the bent and broken limbs off from their damaged husks, regenerating themselves into place as if nothing had happened to them, before he was able to carry on to see what else needed attention down at the mound.

The village itself seemed to be more or less intact, from his vantage point. But the further he moved in amongst the cottages below, as he passed through to reach the stone steps to get out to the east-side of the battlements walls, the more he realized just how lucky they had been.

Further up, Aelfs started to swarm outside of their particular hovels moving towards the centre edge of town, dodging pieces of the metal grating from the mound that could be seen sticking into the trunks of some of the bigger trees around the perimeter walls of the village's main central courtyard. Those trees could be seen struggling to free themselves from the impalement as he passed them by, forcing him to sidestep through the edge of the woods to reach the area of land where he could move closer to the trail head before him.

But for some reason only other minor things were reported destroyed, and absolutely no broken bones from the villagers, much to Jazmyyn's total amazement as she joined the others in the street, ducking out of the way as one of those rods came whizzing past just as the tree it had been impaled in had freed itself. Many of their friends and co-workers still held sleepy young ones and mostly everyone in the village, except for a few that had surface cuts on their outer limbs and were now hobbling about, were fine.

Unfortunately brain-nerves were certainly going to take a lot longer to repair. Several little ones, affected by their parents' emotions, began to take up the cause of wailing in distress simultaneously, and tiny babies still not quite sure whether they were going to go into inconsolable tears with the occasional hiccup to mask their fright, as they continued to hold on for dear life, quickly followed suit. Their mothers, still very much afraid of what had happened themselves and terrified their husbands had died down below in the mound, tried to calm reddened soaking faces, still stretching flailing arms and hands that held on to their shoulders. Jazmyyn took all of this in, occasionally seeing one of the braver toddlers holding it together as he tried to peer into the mixture to see if he too could find a reason not to cry, when the wind suddenly shifted and blackened smoke could be seen coming from the direction of the mound, as the mothers gasped at the realization of what lay ahead.

Mind you that was as much of the upper surface that Sercovious could see, as he patted several terrified faces and heads that had come into his protection alongside the other males who had arrived on scene. His concerned quickly turned to fear, and he could not even fathom what might have happened to the inside of the mound. But then again, they had not received word of what had occurred to that particular structure, one still greatly entrenched in all the chaos of what appeared to be a direct hit in all this mayhem.

The village males immediately began to organize, and Fomorians and Tuatha warriors alike scrambled towards the caverns up the road, putting aside differences that only a moment ago could have turned into an all-out brawl. All along the drift site of destruction, branches and trees were littered along the foot path like matchsticks flung up in the winter storms, uprooted and caught hanging in other trees as the massive energy wave had made its way along the lines of ley that lay just beyond their village.

They found Tamerk on the way there, slightly askew, as a large welt could be seen coming from the backside of his head, compliments of a Firebrand who had simply been in the wrong place at the wrong time. It lay dead on the ground, finding itself a victim of Tamerk's unusual physiology, and its death not actually related to the explosion at all. He moved slowly forward and joined the others, who were already in the hundreds moving towards what they presumed would be nothing more than a bloody massacre down below.

As soon as they had arrived within about 500 feet of the pathway to the Tuatha's main entrance, they could see that the huge standing stones hovering over the falls were not damaged, while rocks from below were protruding upwards followed by the remains of the metal grate, which hung precariously over the hole almost ripped in half. The visual effect was not only overwhelming as to what could lay beneath the twisted wreck, but showed them what could be seen above the edges of the underground mound in all its destructive clarity. Nothing seemed to be left of the outer edges of the rings, and what could only be imagined inside was nothing short of complete and utter devastation.

Every kind of twisted piece of metal fragment which could protrude from the entranceway from below could be seen within the upper components of the outer rim of the mound's rocky core. Sercovious and the others that had just come on scene were stunned to see a good number of the warriors themselves already making their way to the surface from below, and were stunned that anyone had made it out alive. The Fomorian Aelves that had joined the rescue mission had already gone in to assist as

Sercovious surveyed the damage, calling to one of them closest to him over the sound of the falls.

"What the hel happened?" he yelled above the smoking timbers, at one of the Aelfs standing near where the fighters had begun to construct a makeshift pulley system to bring the trapped Aelves up from below. He was covered in cuts and bruises all mixed in with mud from the spray of the huge falls, and under all the mud he looked like he had just been dragged through the centre of a tar pit.

The Aelf yelled back at him as he went to grab a line that snaked loose from the rigging being fitted into place, and found the brunt of the edge as it hit him square in the jaw and knocked him sideways almost over the edge. He regained his balance just at the last second, and another warrior coming in from below caught hold of his belt buckle and hauled him back up.

"The Dragon shifted inside the cavern," he yelled back, just before it hit another Metalsmith, knocking him out cold, and he went flying into the boulders caught at the edge. Sercovious was stunned, and helped him grab the line as it tried to once again take aim for the side of his face and slip over the edge of the hole torn open from the explosion.

"That's not possible," he yelled back. The Aelf grimaced with the wound now drawing blood, and turned to face him for only a moment before he got up and gestured grandly towards Sercovious.

"Oh, it's more than possible," replied the soldier, "as soon as the young Human got settled, the Dragon just bloody popped out!" The Aelf was talking with his hands and brought them together with a big banging noise to make his point.

How in the hel does something like this happen?' Sercovious looked bewildered at the Aelf. Finding himself slightly frowning, he looked back and yelled at the soldier who was doing his best to help another secure the lines from below.

"Did Cian's mate go with them, or is she still down there?" he pointed to the collapsed cavern roof.

"Ask him," he pointed to one of the Aelven males they had just pulled up, who was resting on the ground and trying to get back into the action to help. "He was standing closer than any of us." The soldier he had pointed to was covered in blood, but was conscious and trying desperately to get past the others that were holding him down. As far as Sercovious could see, he was only bearing surface cuts and, judging by the way he was moving, not even harbouring a broken bone in his body.

"Let him up and stop fussing with him!" yelled Cian, as he also made it up over the mountain of rock within reach of the top edge.

"Did my wife make it out, Gelmeg?" he yelled at the man. The male could see that Cian was coming his way.

"Yes sir, everyone made it out."

"How many are hurt? Should we send to the Witches for help?"

"No sir, it's just the main cavern. Every one of us is accounted for. There are three more like me with surface cuts, mostly from fallen rock, and nary a broken bone betwixt us." By then the other soldier that he originally had spoken to, spoke again.

"It was the boy sir he held the shockwave back from all of us, I seen him do it with his hands, and somehow he helped the cavern absorb the brunt of it!" Cian just stood there and mysteriously smiled. "Seriously, if you don't mind me saying sir, I've never seen anything come close to what that little boy did, and as far as I can say, that child isn't part of any Human race that I've ever seen; at least no Human that I've ever heard of. That one's got Fey blood in his veins he has, because just when the shit hit the fan, his eyes went all weird and then bam! He absorbed the whole damn transduction as they went into their shift."

Cian looked alarmed, and couldn't fathom how he could explain what he secretly knew inside of him to this warrior, without blowing the whole situation wide-open. All he could do was try and backtrack.

"I think you've hit your head harder than you think old boy, and lucky for us whatever you did see, happened. You might want to go and give the others a hand in getting some of the others up from below. And if you don't mind, I'd like it very much if you don't let the others know what you just told me. Someone from Fomor might just think we are trying to pull the wool over their eyes on some top secret mission that we didn't want them to know about, and you know how much they want to start a bloody war." He winked at the Aelf and quickly carried on in the other direction, giving no chance for the Aelf to second guess his intentions to his command. When next he looked back over his shoulder at the Aelf, he was in the middle of removing some of the pulley system that had been trapped along the mechanical cogs and deep in the middle of nothing more than helping the others get to the surface. He hoped he stayed that way.

He was stunned at what the Aelf had told him. This was Tamerk's doing, he'd bet his life on it. Not only did he protect the boy growing up, he had bloody trained him. The old goat had held back that piece of information from him. "Well I'll be," he said under his breath, "I'll be."

Tamerk's secret had always been held within the ruling members of the royal lineage of the Tuatha. Each facet of that pedigree was passed on within that family circle and to be honest, no one outside those members knew who he really was: And at that, it was still somewhat of a crapshoot. Anyone that had contact with the Tamerk persona, and got to know the small Fey, would see him as nothing more than an ordinary Wood Sprite. He might have walked like a Wood Sprite, and did most Wood Spriteish things, but he was anything but, he could feel it in his bones. His home deep within the Lypurnen Woods had a massive cathedral grove that he protected like all oaks of this species of Wood Sprite did. He had even taken on certain features of the great Wood Sprites of the last millennium over the years, growing the facial hair that from time to time was combed and braided with oak leaves and feathers from the different birds that lived within the area. From times of now, and moments of then, he would often wear rare Porcupineous Tortoise shell hats that would keep the rain off his neck and made the Sprites of that area quite envious of his vast collection of different Drymiais paraphernalia. This proud Wood Sprite pranced about in the Ferrishyn fairs, riding often on a shaggy grey speckled horse he had either borrowed, won, or stolen in a game of Aelven poker. All who met him knew something was different. But that was as far as the comparisons would go towards the old man that they called a Sprite, and all that the Tuatha De`Danann would admit to. But Cian knew better than to trust what he was actually seeing in front of his face when it came to the Sprite, and word had gotten out to those in need, to leave it be.

You see, Tamerk was not what he appeared to be; he wasn't even a product of Tantaris or anything that was close to this side of the Faden Corpeous movement of stars. To be frank, he wasn't even from this galaxy. His kind had many looks, some exotic, while others very similar to this species of Sprites if he took a fancy to it, but he was anything but the strange benign creature that lived within the woods at the outskirts of the forest, by the Shapeshifter village of Sombreia. In fact, he lived there for only one reason, and that reason was still at large somewhere out in the damn sky.

He was going to have to have a talk with the Aelf he had just sent on his way to help the others manhandle the machinery; maybe just maybe he could get Lugh to move him to Leberone, at least there…there would be no rumour of what this child was.

Anyway, getting back to Tamerk and his kind. He was something that ran along the rivers of your unconscious thoughts, and if you were smart in those incandescent meetings, you needed to stay away from pissing him off, and never ever cross the thin boundaries of his friendship-veil. If you do, your life will be worthless, and the precious gems that one gives another to retrieve such readings in the game of Taro would be meaningless, that is, in regards to how you value your life and the sanity that your brain is held in check from.

But others of the ruling class needed him, and were not so quick to give him up, along with his unique ways that lay just on the verge of what we would call insanity born of reasonable knowledge. You see, Tamerk's knowledge of anything within the forests of the western Provinces was pretty much endless and unique. His being the image of a Wood Sprite gave him the ability to blend in, and the edge to be able to blend in without being seen by the ordinary Fey was crucial in his line of work. Some of us in the Fey realms needed to be a little more discreet in our methods of searching the creatures of other worlds that are not our own. Tamerk did that for us, and he always paid us handsomely with his friendship towards our family lineages. Cian would have to thank the old goat for protecting the city of the mound. His father's father would require that, and if Cian had learned anything at all in this life-line, it was basically not to mess with the ancestors, no matter who they were in this timeline of dead and gone.

So Tamerk came and went among the newly formed and the newly dead. His anonymity had given him free range to have both children within the same range of mountains, and that had been a brainchild of his from the plan's inception. The Goddess realm having given him the proper headway to keep them hidden for as long as he had was probably the only reason both children had made it past infancy.

THE BEGINNING

The female shippel had been taken to the Shapeshifter clan to be fostered, to allow her the edge that she would need when the time came to reveal who she really was to the rest of the Fey nation. It was believed, and spoken of in hushed tones on dark winters days, that they had been disposed of by Balor at their time of birthing, and that the Mother had been inconsolable when it had happened. That had not been the case. They hadn't died; the mother, yes. She had cried for months, but with time she had conceded the tragedy and her world, though dead to her, had carried on and tried to rebuild its bones from the ground up.

The male child had been quite another story, and had proved to be a little more difficult than they had hoped, due to his unique physiology. His power was something that needed time to control, so after spending a time with the Sea God Manannan, he was first taken to the home-world of a Human populated planet, on the opposite-side of the Fey galaxy. It had proved to be terribly timed; the Dragon wars having already started, were the outcome of this badly timed catastrophe, and were a lesson that needed to not ever be repeated.

So, in doing this transfer, the boy was supposed to learn the functionality of that alien race, and prevent any future mistakes that could prove to be fatal in the future of the Fey races' lifecycle. The last one almost cost our race their anonymity. To be seen as real and living among the stars they visited, the Humans had come seeking something else that had never been within their grasp from the start. The truth was just a little more on the edge of reason, and had to be hidden at all cost, for the survivability of the children's energy signatures, if they had any chance of making it out alive at all through this side of the reason they were born here in the first place.

There was only a handful of Fey that knew that the Humans died out shortly after the Dragon wars ended, and that was give or take a hundred years less than the rumour that was constructed to begin with. The Human race has one of the smaller lifecycles of organic matter, which was allowed to surface and continue on as long as they weren't causing any grievances with the Fey colonies to the west. Their numbers had grown exponentially over the last span of about 5500 years, but their lifelines were short as they grew hostile more frequently through the latter years of their supposed existence, and they died with fairly easy occurrences in their small and sheltered lifelines. But tales of their survival were greatly exaggerated, and scattered tales of Humanity throughout the galaxy within their Milky Way realm were more than enough to feed the rumours of the species surviving their actual demise, which became a perfect ruse for the boy's actual whereabouts and concocted heritage.

So, when the tale that a stolen Human child had been spotted in the Damonian Woods near Tamerk's tree had surfaced, it wasn't that much of a stretch to add in the story of it having being taken by the Shea and brought to this world, where it was located among the Fey. True Tamerk genius, for, had the actual child been Human in reality, it pretty much goes without saying the territorial turf war over said Human would have undoubtedly created such a stir in the Fey worlds, that even they would have done their best to keep out of his way. Not only would it keep the boy safe, as no Fey would approach him to see the truth of it, but it gave Tamerk the perfect alibi to have the child in his company.

Tamerk had always been known to do whatever he liked, even at the cost of others' safety and he was not one to be trifled with, on any occasion. Another good reason for the deed; Fey tended to stay away from his woods at all cost to their own lives, even on a perfect day. Perfect in its entirety, is all the Sky People would say on the matter to his face, behind his back he was quite sure a few jabs at his personality, had taken a hit from Hexe.

On Tantaris he was simply known as Tamerk, and only four members of the ruling family knew his true identity. But there was a fifth entity that knew much more, and remember the Aelven nation is not only run by the military might of the power of the Tuatha. There are many other branches this army is controlled by, and one day, not too far off in the distant timeline, the cracks that started to thin and fray would bust wide open, and the Tamerk of then would give the Fey of now a run for their bloody money.

So Cian kept the secret, hoping to hel that when all was said and done, Eithne would get Ryyaan to safety with the help of one now very reluctant Aelfan male who had no affiliation with the current Fey clans up on this tiny planetary world. And as soon as he could have a chat with Lugh, another Aelf was going to find he had suddenly been promoted, and the other problem of seeing the boy for who he really was, would also too.... drift away.

CHAPTER EIGHTEEN

The Witch called Kashandarhh

The land around the Damonian Woods hadn't felt right for almost a full turn of Tantaris's moon. Leberone shone brightly up above, showing signs of distress along her drifting pathways, holding some form of conversation with something yet to be discovered. Kashandarhh had watched the skies, fearing the sight she had been given at birth was becoming more of a reality than she cared to admit. She had spent many years within these very woods, and as of late she could feel it within her bones that something was wrong, while it flittered quietly on the edges of her protected mind.

It had begun with just small things at first. She started to see a flutter of shades moving just out of sight, but enough for her to see the small barely visible red outline that should not have been there amongst the planets main organism's auras. These, as all things living were protected within her woods. If she hadn't brought it in, or allowed it to come on its own, it simply wasn't within her walls. Things that produced those red outlines around their edges only happened with the dead on this world, and most things living that had a carbon-based life breath at one time or another, only showed that colour when danger was present and had passed them by.

She'd lived long enough to know that something was up, even had that not been present in the things that still breathed large with life. Kashandarhh had been watching the wildlife since she was a small wailing, and she could feel something new was doing its best to find its way in through her wards into her lands, then doing everything it knew not to set her off as it squatted somewhere out there just beyond the ridge. She knew every nuance of each and every one of the creatures that made these lands their home, each producing their own individual molecular pattern, which she knew from the smallest to the very biggest cat, and every single one of them was causing prickles along her Witchy spines. She was not happy, and becoming increasingly annoyed that something was even attempting the annexation.

There were nesting habits, feeding habits, hunting habits, and survival modes; the last beginning about three days ago, just past the waning of the Gibbous Disseminating phase of this moon. The moon had begun that passage into the skies around mid-evening, with enough light remaining from the full Wort Moon of a few days ago to notice the bats swarming and moving about in an unusual pattern of flight. But when one of her barn owls wouldn't go out and hunt for his meal, and instead remained indoors for the full three days, deciding it would rather starve, it got her attention and she went out to search for the creature's energy movement and confront it about trespassing near her realm.

She had also noticed lately, the weather patterns were bringing unusually cool temperatures on normally hot Lunesa afternoons. Even since the Solstice of Balefires Eve, the weather had been strangely cool, with huge thunderstorms that lit up the night skies for weeks on end when they should have moved on and left the area for a more mountainous terrain.

Something had scared off the horses in the southern pasture and by the time she had tracked them all down and rounded them up, she had missed a crucial harvest of Sticky Wort. The only other place the plant grew was near Tothray, along the edge of the far reaches of Lypurnen Woods; a place she had not the time to travel to, even with her abilities. She'd have to have a seeker run it for her.

Next time Kamera sent her one, as she always did, she would ask something for herself. Mind you, that's if she got the opportunity to see them. Usually, she found the medicines or herbs stashed; with her mother's latest ideas of what she thought Kashandarhh needed sitting on a log by the trail head; the seeker of choice, being too afraid to dare coming within sight of her. She had heard them whisper, from time to time, that they had gone far enough, and were much too close to Caorunn Range.

Funny how they all thought it was only the Caorunn tree that Witches used as a casting wand. Truth be known, it was that very reaction that brought her out here in the first place. For centuries, on the Human world, her kind had been systematically hunted and destroyed. It never made any sense how the natural order of things could get that far out of line that the villagers would resort to killing each other. Here in the Fey world there was fear, but that was only with regard to things they saw, not things imagined. Back on the Human planet, she had thought it was only a matter of time before her kind would find their own footing, the uprisings of religious doctrine would eventually quiet down in the end to stop the senseless killings that took more of their own kind than hers. But, she supposed Human kind was a little more unforgiving; she at least on Tantaris could live with the occasional thoughts that they put forward when coming in range of her senses, and brush them off with a sense of humour. Although, it was still warped by their fragmented ideas of Aelfan quantum physics, that need not apply for the purpose of the Witch-hunt of the female species. It was just as purposeful that there were equally as many male Witches in the Fey world as female, but in some areas of the home-worlds of Human kind, this was still a female predominant placement.

On this day, as she felt the shiver run down her spine like someone was actively hunting on her turf, she lifted her nose and smelled the wind. Even the air itself had the scent of displaced atoms banging about. That was never a good thing, and something had definitely changed in the air molecules in the last few hours out along her southern most wards.

The day had been one of those deliciously warm summer days that had the scent of warm leaves and earth mingled in with the wonderful smell of peat. The grass that had not been eaten by the horses still smelled sweet, even though it was a bit dry. After all, it was the growing months of the warmest part of the hottest time of the year.

She had been sharpening axes outside in the partly shaded area by the woodshed, when she shifted her focus to the air currents that rippled no more than three feet off the ground. They came to her in waves, like the pulse of a heartbeat, starting slowly at first then drifting as they moved in quick circles up and out, then for a split second seem to disappeared altogether. They returned only after she pulled their energy back, and followed their path as they made their way down the lane-way and up over the top of her woodshed.

The hair on her face began to prickle, as she quietly moved to put down the axe on the floor of the forest edge, and felt for her knife in the tree round where she had been working on splitting the wood. She went into a crouch and put her non-throwing hand flat on the earth to feel the direction it was moving in. She cocked her head a bit to the left, closed her eyes, and listened. Something else was moving about, unrelated to the original scent and movements of the initial energy shift. This one was female and Aelven. She could smell the scent, strong and clear as the movements of air became further and further displaced, and for some reason it was walking slowly and methodically with intent, towards her own cottage.

The other entity that had filtered in and out, and caught her initial attention, was just out on the fringes of the other. She tried, but couldn't quite place its origins, even though it seemed vaguely familiar, but then suddenly and without warning it moved up and off, continuing its hunt elsewhere. She would return for it later, but the Aelf was heading in her direction, and further along the pathway than any of the others that had made it into her woods, and that in itself needed attention.

Kashha then moved, mentally in search of the animal that accompanies one that isn't shifting, to see what their intent may be, and came up empty. That was unusual; all forest Aelfs had eyes about, why was this one alone? No one travelled anywhere, especially in the woods of a Witch, without eyes. This Aelf was either very stupid or extremely naïve; she bet on both.

She turned her attention to follow, not forgetting that other movement further off now, gliding with no particular direction, in the trees to the north. That one was just out of range, and would require her further attention soon enough, but this new seeker intrigued her. What had Kamera sent her way this time? In retrospect, she would have made another decision had she really thought about it, but for now, in this time frame, the seeker was by far more interesting, having made it this far without having run into Kashandarhh's friends. Leaving the other signature behind would be something she would later regret with much frustration, even more so with the knowledge of following an annoyance that happened to be in the same spot that the other had arrived in on the wind, at the very same time.

Kashha didn't waste any time, and disappeared into the trees with a silence only a Witch can truly attain. Even the Shapeshifters had difficulties mastering its consistency, while the Elemental wards she employed, wasted no time setting the locks tightly behind her; she blended inside the drift, leaving nothing to mark her passing. She followed the energy signature as it drifted along, making its colourful imprint down by the trailhead along which this Aelf was coming at her, and moved in behind. She watched the female for a bit, as she made her way slowly up the path towards the very tree that was one of her more unusual friends. Alerted to the healer's arrival it had taken up its position, and remained perfectly still. Kashha moved her hands to shift the air around her, to slow down the Aelf's forward pace, and then slowly drew in a deep breath to draw in the essence of the Aelfen female who moved away from her, as she flittered along beside her down the path in slow motion, completely unaware of what had just happened.

Kashha closed her eyes, waiting. She smelled the female's scent before she was even within range of the tree. Kashha moved towards the creature landing amongst its lower branches, to shield herself from the female's approach. She would have better luck at going undetected in the tree, than by leaving molecules to trace her arrival, deciding to watch from up above as the Aelfen female came into view. She chose this form of hunting instead of shielding herself from the female visually. It gave a much broader view of what was coming through the air, as well as what was moving along the forest floor behind her.

Kashha checked a second time to see if the air contained eyes belonging to the young female, and still nothing was present. Kashha had not felt the apprehension in the footsteps of the traveller until she smelled something that seemed to flit just on the edges of her body. Something had touched her as she moved towards Kashha's woods, but whatever it was still eluded her memory of its presences, and she shook it off as the female got closer and reversed the motion into the present tense.

The female's apprehension was not from uncertainty, but more along the lines of excitement, mixed in with a challenge that had been set, deep inside her mind from distant times. It seemed the young Aelf had been torn apart by teasing, as a child; she didn't outwardly show anger, as Kashha would have expected to see sitting on the edges of her sanity. But this, was something new to her and the Aelf had forced it to the surface.

But something else caught Kashha by surprise; this one had no fear, unlike the others, nor did it lay hidden, as some seekers liked to hide in the depths of their insecurities. That was also something newly hatched; no one came here, other than her mother, who didn't have some kind of fear. This tiny creature now had her attention, if at any time she didn't before.

She smelled the herbs before she was even out of the old trees which ran along Kashha's woods, near the old stream bed. So…a Sage woman coming from the direction of Kilren. Hum, she sighed. Kashha watched her move, stopping every now and then to look at the woodland bounty. She was past the Kilren boundary almost a full trylavector, and into Kashha's turf now. She wondered whether the woman would try to pick along her path.

It was not polite to pick without asking. Kashha smiled without thinking, tilting her head and moving a hand slightly above the bark of the tree, to get a better view. But as she watched the woman move down the trail head away from her, the Aelf continued without harvesting a single leaf. The Aelf was only admiring what was around her feet, as she moved along from the spot Kashha had been sitting in the tree. *'Good Girl might have to scare this one only slightly,'* Kashha thought; she didn't think that Kilren had any Sages left that didn't know Kashha's rules and territory.

This female was definitely different; Kashha knew the Kilren Sages, and this Aelfen female was not of their clan. She watched her walk past and away up the trail, before Kashha moved ahead of her silently, like the huntress she was. This time, as the young Sage moved past her, Kashha smelled something else; something familiar, someone from Kilren. Ah, there it is…mother dearest, you did send her. She smiled, whispering to the trees. 'Gotch yah.'

So, Kamera has a new pet; Kashha smiled with the knowledge that her mother had had contact with this new one. Kamera would never have sent the Sage without some form of offering or warning, she knew how much Kashha hated any sort of company. She'd give this one credence; she must be either really stupid or damned good. Her mother, bless her little heart, collected both.

THE BEGINNING

Kashha found another tree just coming into view, and swung herself up into some lower branches that were the size of a Centaur's thigh, as it moved on by. It adjusted to her added weight, and carried on with her leg over one of its main branches, to get a better grip. She loved this method of travel, and having made previous arrangements with the transient flora that moved about her woods, there was no better way to travel if one chose to remain bound to the soil instead of the airways.

She watched the female move once more off the trail, and instructed the tree to remain stationary until she had passed. Coutinnea followed the small stream bed that brought her to the base of the very edge of the tree Kashha sat in.

Kashha watched her, drifting slowly in and out of the trail herbs, tasting the occasional leaves for any trace of the herbal remedies they possessed. Then, as if by design, the Sage moved to the base of the trunk Kashha was actually sitting in, and put her hands on both sides of its breadth, closing her eyes in what appeared to be a surrender of her own thoughts, to those of the trees. Kashha held her breath, but it hadn't been necessary. The moment her eyes closed, she let a short outward gasp, blinking in total disbelief, moving away as though she was stung, shaking her hands and wiggling her fingers like they had gone numb. The tree had moved, Goddess bless his soul, opening its large oval eyes to stare back at her within inches of her own face. She hadn't needed to scare her; the tree did it for her.

The Aelfen female shrieked in awkward surprise, stumbling backwards until she tripped and fell on the wandering roots that trailed all around its base. All the while, Kashha couldn't keep herself from laughing out loud, watching the hysterics down below, at what had just happened. What the Sage hadn't known was that Kashha had been sitting in the arms of a very tall migrating Tree Morrigan. Kashha snickered to the tree, and patted it along the trunk she had placed her arms around, materializing from thin air as she slid down her friend's body. "Next time bring your eyes, Aelf, your bird would have told you we were here."

The Aelfen female was completely caught off guard; not only was Kashandarhh standing before her where previously nothing had been, save a very large unusual tree, but she had been sitting abreast a creature Coutinnea had never actually noticed. To not have known that, and laid hands upon the creature thinking it was nothing more than a tree, was unthinkable in her line of work. This creature was a living breathing Fey; one that albeit she had never seen before, but it was a creature none the less, and had special rights within the woods of this particular Witch. Coutinnea was starting to wonder whether this little walk of hers was actually a smart thing to do. What was she thinking coming into the woods of this very notorious Witch, who was known for hating everyone equally, including her own flesh and blood?

Coutinnea remembered she had glimpsed the unusual tree as it came into view from the pathway she had been moving along. She had come to feel its energy and see if there may be something medicinal to use for future harvesting and if the tree was even a candidate or would let her, after she had received a blessing from the Witch of course. It was, after all, her land, and that made it proper to ask the one that owned what was sitting along a common pathway. She was horrified to think that she had done serious damage to her reputation as a healer, and any future meetings with Kashandarhh would be in major jeopardy all because of a mistake that she should have known not to make.

Each plant or tree that she used in her herbal remedies had small offerings from the larger varieties; this one could have given her something amazing with its sheer size, and possibly directed her to others of similar properties. To realize she had placed hands upon another Fey creature that she had never even been aware of before, shook her to the core. This very big and very unusual creature, that looked more like an actual tree than a moving sentient being, was just as alive as she was, although not in the shape she had been prepared to meet in the deep dark woods of Kashandarhh's forest. But, then again, she should have thought about it for a moment, this was after all one of the most enchanted grouping of trees that she was told there was on all of Tantaris, except for maybe the Lypurnen Woods, so why was she so surprised?

Tree Morrigans were solitary creatures, living amongst the deeper parts of the woodlands, and moved about the denser places of spongy moss-laden swamps. Kashandarhh lived within those very borders, and any one of the trees or animals that resided here could be part of the majik of her forest realm. There was a truth to be known that not many Aelfs had seen these creatures in all of their lives, but their mythology was written within the archives of each of the different clans that remained intact, and had been mythologized to be a rarity that actually needed to be seen not theorized.

Coutinnea didn't read those books, they were mostly found in the old majik shops of the old cities, far from where she could travel. It wasn't that she couldn't read, it was just that their village was a working village within the land of the working poor. And most of the residents didn't have any books; for those that did, they were mostly from the larger libraries of Fomor, or the Elemental worlds off planet, none of which she had ever seen anyway. Even Sombreia held a rich library within the village. But she had spent so much of her time in the working of her herbs, that she hadn't had much for anything else, but her lifemate Stephponias.

The Tree Morrigan's mythology was just that, mythology. If you've never seen one, they kind of don't exist in your world on a day to day basis. She needed to get into books more often, it would definitely help in her identification of some of the rarer plants that she had been hoping to find. But for now she was sitting on her butt staring at this creature that was slowly lumbering away, with the very person she had come to see totally ignoring her embarrassment, in the broken branches of a Silvercross-Fillstar bush. She needed to get up now, and quickly proceeded to try and get her feet, moving after Kashha.

Kashha had instantly moved back into the tree's grand branches, as the Tree Morrigan moved away. She didn't need eyes in the back of her head to know that Coutinnea would soon be gathering herself up to do one of two things: follow her and the Morrigan, or leave whatever she was bringing and head back the way she had come. Kashha was betting on the latter. This was a day of firsts; she was wrong a second time this morning. No sooner had Kashha travelled no more than fifty feet ahead, she heard Coutinnea shout from behind.

"Hey, wait up! I've got something here, from your mother." The female Aelf stumbled towards the trailhead, trying to keep her feet underneath her, and not trip on any more vines or leaves that littered the pathway. Kashha yelled without looking backwards at the small footsteps advancing towards her, moving just fast enough they would eventually catch up to her in a short amount of time.

"Just put it on the trail like everyone else does, and say hello to my mother for me." She waved her hand over her head without looking back, and continued moving down the trail. When the junction point at the trailhead appeared, she jumped away to the left, moving in a different direction than the Morrigan, who had lifted a leafy arm to wave goodbye as she disappeared from sight and around the bend.

But still the voice of the annoying Sage continued talking, or at least shouting for the most part, as Kashha had already gone far enough away for the Aelf to detect her presence. Coutinnea stopped briefly at the juncture where the Morrigan was heading along alone, moving slowly into the depths of the deeper forests. She hesitated with the decision, and watched with curious interest as the Fey disappeared, before she turned in the direction she had thought Kashha had disappeared. She now discovered she was entirely alone, with all trace of what just happened obliterated from her view. Damn, she didn't expect this; she took mental note of the directions Kamera had given her, and moved off to where Kashha was said to have built a cottage in the clearing, about five more miles up the narrowing pathway. She still could hear the tree moving about the forest to her right, but as far as the Witch was concerned, every trace of her was simply gone.

If the Witch wouldn't talk to her here, then she'd leave the stone on the stoop of her wards, there. She had gone this far, she might as well continue, even though every bone in her body wanted to flee in the opposite direction, and give Kamera back her little stone. She had heard lots of stories about the Witch, but had mostly taken them for what she had thought they were; just stories meant to scare the undeserving. It never occurred to her that she would become one of the statistics of that very group, and add more fuel to the fire of all the other Sages that had come and gone before her. She hoped it wouldn't come to that, but for now the trail was still a long way away from where she needed to be before nightfall, and she felt in her heart of hearts, that she was at least deserving.

She found the junction and began again, but this time she moved with a little more caution, vowing to stay away from trees, at least in any part of the Damonian Woods. The last time Kashha felt her energy was when she moved from the ground up into the stratosphere, then she cut the tie and moved on.

Kashha didn't stay earthbound for long; instead she went to air and moved into a lighter mode of transportation. She needed to get eyes on whatever was originally hunting in the woods, before it came across the Aelfen Sage again. This time she would have to intervene in its hunting movements, and make herself known in its arrival within her territory. Nothing came into her woods without some kind of permission; all Fey had a code of ethics and this one had directly disregarded decorum; that made her very unhappy.

There were ways that had to be instilled within her realm of placement. It would be unwise for the creature to piss her off, at any time during its stay. She needed to find this creature before it moved from her borders, and slipped her reach to encounter another of her kind. If she didn't deal with it properly now, the next time it came within reach it would think it had a pass to do as it saw fit. That was something she was not willing to give it, and with her mood souring by the minute, there would be no time like the present to kick some creature's ass.

It didn't take long for Kashha to see the long trail of red-edged plant life, all along the area where the thing had been wandering the edges of her woodlands. She took herself a little higher up to see if it was still in reach, or had gone away from the boundaries she owned and protected. But, as she moved into the thinning atmosphere, she could see it just seemed to disappear from sight, not even leaving the red line flowing about in the air for her to visually see anymore. Sometime in the next few days, she was going to have to go and talk with Lugh, and see if the Tuatha had been hearing of anything strange passing along their boundaries. She knew in her heart that something wasn't right, and if she felt that now, who knew what she was going to feel when something arrived within her field of vision again. She did one last circle to check the wards and see if they were still intact and noticed the little annoying sage was still moving methodically, towards her home. She was going to have to have a conversation with her mother about giving the young whelp the ability to come so close to her damn wards. For all she knew, both of them were in it together, and this thing was a by-product of her moving into Kashha's space without the proper protection spells put into place. She began to wonder who the hel this Sage of hers really was.

She was within a short distance of her own home, and could see the smoke from the chimney rising high up in the air. At this altitude she could still see with her mind's eye that the young Aelfen Sage was still determined to head in the direction of her home, so she turned from her borders and started heading for a discussion with someone who, on all outward appearances, looked the part of a runner. It piqued her interest; this female, it wasn't the usual that ran the gambit between her mother and her clan. Seeing the Tree Morrigan should have sent her running for the hills, and yet here she was advancing on Kashha's cabin, which now presented another slew of issues she would have to go and deal with. Damn, she really hated having company, and if she had anything to do with this, it wouldn't be happening again anytime soon.

Meeting up with the Tree Morrigan had been a stroke of luck. She hadn't seen her friend down this end of the woods in almost a full Mauntra cycle; she also knew it would not leave the area with whatever was out hunting earlier. And she could bet there were probably others moving about, since they travelled in family groups. Sometime in the near future, she would meet up with them again, and spend some time with the real reason they had strayed so far from home. But first she needed to deal with Kamera's pet; too bad the Morrigan hadn't scared the hel out of her and she could just go home and have some bloody tea. Goddess in all flying hel, she could really use a good cup of tea. Oh well, time to scare the hel out of the new pet Kamera chose to send. Maybe, just maybe, she could make a good cup of tea out of her. The wind whistled behind her as she moved in the direction of home.

CHAPTER NINETEEN

Entity

Stephponias shifted into Kilren's outskirts, but within the boundary of its shade. The rocks had been placed specifically for this purpose, outside the village wards, and presented themselves as doorways to each of the villages that anyone wished to travel to. It was a precautionary method used in almost every Fey village, on any of the home planets since the beginning of the Dragon wars. It was used primarily to prevent anyone that was an undesirable, from just popping into the protection zone past the village wards, without warning the inhabitants of their impending arrival.

Each citizen that lived within its boundaries carried a specialized mineralized gemstone that was indicative of their clan, which would be visualized within the transfer to the shade. It was immediately deciphered by the shade warriors at each village's entrance points, who would, at that time compare it with the energy signature of the residents within and allow the transit to continue past the walls and into the interior of the village's inner-wards.

Steph, being not of this village clan, would only materialize here after his shift, and would then be presented to the guardians, with his travel plans, and only then would he be allowed to reach the inner sanctum of its walls. If at any time it was deemed unnecessary by the traveller, he would be refused entrance and be force to wait outside until that decision had been terminated and followed through to a higher station.

Steph's shift had been a little more unusual than it should have been when he had entered the doorway. The mountain near his village that had been causing all the commotion had been directly in his pathway, as his shift was first created. In his haste to get to Kamera's village to find his wife, he neglected to recalibrate his forward motion as the mountain violently moved, sending him off course when he had first gone through the causeway. In doing so, it took him a wee bit off course, sending his bearings slightly sideways into the shade's co-ordinance.

He bit his lip as he caught himself falling to the left and felt a tiny shard of the granite rock catching the nip of skin on his left wrist as he tried to right himself, staining the monolith with a single blood-scrape of his Llyach flesh. It was really nothing to look at when it came to injuries, but it stung nonetheless, and as he followed protocol towards the guardians of the shade, a small black organism shifted and settled inside the surface layer of his skin.

The moment he began his movement towards the guardians of the shade, they physically passed him through the crystals of the monolith with their own hands; this then expelled the organism while he moved forward and through, leaving it behind on the pathway he had just exited. It shimmered blood red on the stones for a moment and scuttled away, twisting back into the crevice it had originally been sitting within, claiming a small amount of Aelven chromosomes and bringing that into its own organismic host and disappeared without anyone being the wiser. The guardians would have discovered its whereabouts immediately, had it decided to come inside the walls, but that had not been what it was searching for, and now, having retrieved what it came for, it melted into the background, waiting its next move.

These protectors of Aelven villages lived beyond the realm of what is between, and physically were not on this plane of Fey life. It was an unusual place they lived in, born of Star Nebulae where neutrons and atoms formed the basis of all life forms within this star system of the current Quasar Queen. It was a place where the four elements dwelt and Elementals begin their lifecycles, hatching into their existence, before moving towards their own individual Fey hosts, that become part of the symbiotic joining that we all of Fey become part of. Their movement through the shade dimensions was their access to the fold in time, which opens a doorway to those that continue to offer their duty long past the limits of our individual Fey lives.

THE BEGINNING

Not all Fey choose this path, and very few of them in their lifetimes are even aware that they are chosen; that is until their own life-breath breathes its last, and expels upwards towards the Ring of Souls. At that moment, they have a choice to continue as they are needed, or to be brought through into the other realm, away from the entrance point of this life.

Steph now continued on with his travels as the wards shimmered clear, passing him through with the texture of a shiver, and he headed to the home where Kamera resided. She had been working in the garden harvesting a crop of pickle-pop beets, her hands stained orange from their thickening bodies, as she used her knife to lop off their tops, before placing them on the drying racks she had gotten her husband to build, on one of his many trips to dry land. When he was in his so-called land formulation, it was good to get the list of things she had compiled done, for there would be long times in between when she would not be able to visit his kind, nor even be able to see him if she went to him.

It was during these periods when they spent their time away at sea — that these stretches also prohibited her from joining his kind. Had she any way of changing into something that loosely resembled being part fish, she would have gladly joined him during his kind's time out at the Undinecis reef. The reef swam and spun along the edges of the Selkie Island of Vaukknea and was special to his kind. It was no secret that they spent a great deal of time out there in the waves, as they replenished their energy reserves within the tidal fluxes. However, she was neither part-fin or Shapeshifter clan, and had legs that were useless when it came to the days out at sea, in their endless search for just the right wave in order to harness its power before heading back to dry land.

It was on this day of warmth and smiles that she heard the footsteps as they entered her garden, and moved from the side of the cobbled lane in front of her cottage. So, here she was quietly working, preferring to stay high and dry, when one Llyach male showed up at her doorstep. When he called out to her, the hand with the knife raised to shield her eyes from the Mauntra to get a better look as to the identity of the Aelfan male that had called her by name. As soon as she recognized his face she smiled warmly.

"Ah, Stephponias, how lovely to see you. What brings you here on such a fair day?" Her smile quickly changed to a frown when she seen his face. Stephponias looked extremely anxious.

"Is Coutinnea still here?" he asked quietly.

"No my dear, you just missed her, but," she added, so as not to alarm him any further, "she's just running an errand for me, and should be back before nightfall." Kamera looked a little puzzled, since she was not the one that Coutinnea had actually come to see. Why had Stephponias come this way, instead of heading straight out to her Aunt Freile's house, she wondered? It brought a new question to her mind, which made her wonder further; Coutinnea's aunt lived just up the road, and he would have had to pass that plot of land before he got to her doorstep. Why had he not stopped there, and had these questions answered for himself?

Standing up, she went to greet him, taking in his sense of uneasiness as she got to her feet. "What's happened, my darling? I could send someone for her. You look scared half to death." Kamera moved Stephponias towards the open doorway of her cottage.

"I don't even know where to begin. I think I need to speak with your daughter, Kamera. Do you think she'd come here while we wait on Coutinnea?" Kamera smiled and lit up the minute he spoke about her daughter.

"No need to wait; that's where I sent Coutinnea on the errand. I thought it would be a change of company for my daughter. Someone to see other than her dear old mother." He stopped walking, looking slightly stunned.

"She's with Kashandarhh?" he asked, surprised that his wife would even attempt that trek into the Damonian Woods without having someone pushing her into actually visiting the notorious Witch. Coutinnea was not the self-assured little Sage that Aelves thought she was; in fact she was downright timid. He shook his head and smiled at Kamera. "Good for you to get her to step out of her comfort zone. But, it is something else that I've come for, that I need from her."

"Really! Now that's a first." Kamera smiled moving towards him putting her hands on his back, then dropping the beets in the basket stoop, she placed her knife in the wedge of wood that rested on the edge of the board on her top step. They moved into Kamera's parlour, and still he remained standing, even after Kamera offered him a seat in one of the beautiful chairs that she had decorated the little cottage with.

"I needed to make sure my wife is safe, and I'm grateful for what you have done but it's your daughter that I really have come to see. Kamera, can you shift with me; I can't get through her wards without you?" Kamera smiled but seemed a little worried, no one really went to see Kashha without a damn good reason, and by the look of him, this was something that needed urgent undertaking.

"Let's go, this can wait," she said, pointing to the garden outside and the vegetables still needed picking that were lying along the pathway, she had been working towards. She brushed her hands on the apron and locked her hands on Steph's big arms; disappearing in his shift. She brushed her hands on the apron and locked her hands on Steph's big arms; disappearing in his shift.

"Crap, I forgot my teeth!" She smiled at the look he gave her when she glanced up in the drift. "Just kidding, my friend, don't look so stunned. I just needed a bit of fun so you didn't have to think about moving through her wards." All she heard was his vague mumbled response.

"Sorry, it is necessary," as they slipped together into nothing but the wind, sliding along the shift-point waiting for them.

It had only taken a few moments and both Kamera and Steph were on the trail leading to Kashha's hidden cabin, spotting the backside of Coutinnea just before she had reached Kashandarhh's wards.

Coutinnea was a little taken aback at her mate's sudden appearance and it was more than obvious she was more than a bit relieved that she wouldn't have to be dealing with Kashandarhh's temperaments on her own. Mind you she hadn't thought she'd see her again, having only just spotted the log she wanted to drop the satchel off on, contemplating the logistics of leaving it propped up for the Witch to find.

"What are you doing here?" she asked. She had turned, hearing the rush of wind just as they both arrived on scene. She had been expecting another one of Kashandarhh's tricks, and was surprised to see both her mate and Kamera coming around the corner of the trail. "I don't understand?" she said as Steph opened his arms to hug his wife.

"Thank the Goddesses," he breathed, kissing the top of her head. "I'll explain everything shortly, but first I need to see Kashandarhh." Coutinnea looked questioningly at Kamera, who shook her head in response, as she watched Coutinnea place her hand in his. She moved to unlock an unseen doorway that had been put in place close to the house, then as they shifted with the final opening taking them through a series of corridors, Stephponias moved forward using his own body to protect his wife, should it be deemed necessary during their contact with the energy wards.

All three arrived and headed past the outbuildings on the other-side of the woodshed that still held one of Kashandarhh's axes stuck in the side of the wooden wall. Kashha met them easily, coming around the backside of her own steps as they moved towards the cabin where Kashandarhh was taking up residence on the stoop. She held a mug of hot coffee in one hand and, standing in plain view behind the rail, a knife in easy access to the other. She sensed the shift but didn't expect what came around the corner. She swore when she saw her mother and the Aelven male coming around the barn area with Coutinnea; when she had felt the shift she was hoping the female chickened out and phased home. Kashha would have to give her a little more respect; she'd called for backup, the little freak.

As the travellers approached the bottom steps of the house, Kashha didn't move, except to raise the mug to take a sip of the contents and salute her mother. She briefly raised one eyebrow as the elder mouthed the words '*play nice*,' nodding to the other two who had travelled into the clearing with her. Kamera went to her and kissed her forehead, placing both hands on either side of her child's head, then turned to Steph and spoke.

"Do we have time for coffee, or shall we get to it?" Steph just nodded, still taking everything in. He had never met Kashha and what he saw of the Witch as she stood on the stoop really intimidated the hel out of him. Her status was legendary; it was a little like coming into contact with the Tuatha and their current commanding officer, Lugh. He was a little uneasy, to say the least, but couldn't let his wife know, even though he felt his knees start to shake the moment her eyes went to his face. He turned briefly to break her stare, and thanked Kamera for what she offered as a form of ice-breaker.

"Coffee would be good Kamera; we shall both have something warm if it's not too much trouble for your daughter." He turned his attention back to Kashandarhh, who replied to Kamera's offer with a shrug.

"Help yourself; I'm not playing hostess." She replied calmly without too much in the way of malice, as Steph approached her with his face turned upwards to speak.

"Hello Kashha, I'm Stephponias of the Llyach clan and this is my wife-"

"Coutinnea," interrupted Kashha, "we've met, yes. Funny creature. Doesn't much like trees." Steph looked between the two of them quizzically, as Kashha grimaced and shook her head at the Aelfen female. Coutinnea let out a small groan, catching her husband's questioning look. Kashha carried on as if nothing was out of the ordinary with her former statement. "I wasn't expecting her to call for backup." Coutinnea became flushed in the cheeks again.

"I didn't," she replied, a little taken aback.

"And yet, here they are," Kashha raised her coffee mug, gesturing at Stephponias, directing the statement at Coutinnea, who looked to Steph for support, clutching his arm with just a little more force than she had before.

Kamera had gone inside the cabin while introductions were being made, and came outside to complete silence.

"Bloody hel, now what have you done child?" she exclaimed, whacking Kashha on the top of her head. She carried on, ignoring all three of them and advancing down the steps holding the tray with three more mugs of freshly brewed coffee, into the middle of that awkward silence, and coughed.

"Can't any of you find something that interest all three of you, without trying to mentally kill each other off? Kashha looked with annoyance at the other two, as she drank her coffee, repeating under her breath something that sounded awfully similar to; *'Never, going to happen!'*

Kamera ignored her daughter's rudeness; she was accustomed to Kashha's sharpness around others, and even though she frowned on it happening in front of her, it was inevitably going to occur anyway. She settled herself on the stoop, blowing cool air into the steaming cup, and carried the conversation without having been asked. She was damn sure not going to let this turn into a war, if she had anything to do with it. And since she was responsible for sending the Sage here in the first place, it was now up to her to lighten the mood the only way she knew how. She talked.

"Steph had arrived in Kilren after I sent Coutinnea to deliver a few things, to give you a change in company from the usual seekers that run for me. It would appear you seem to have alienated all the others, and since they won't come within ten yards of the woods that surround your encampment, this is my way of saying I'm not pleased." Kashha smiled an evil smirk while her mother was making her point about Kashha's personality traits.

"I don't alienate them mother, I just educate them a little." Kashandarhh smirked louder into her mug.

"Is that what you're doing my dear child? Well, in that case it would be kinder if you would stop teaching altogether," quipped Kamera as Kashha stuck her tongue out at her mother. "Now, Steph has come a long way to speak to you about something I gather is rather important, so, can you be civil enough to hear him out?" Kashha turned slowly towards the male standing at the bottom of her stoop and pointed to the Mauntra up above.

"Daylight's ticking, dear boy, spit it out I've got work to do!" Kashha really wasn't enjoying these Aelves camped out at her home. Solitary existence wasn't just a craving, it was a lifestyle choice. She hated everyone equally.

"I realize this is hard for you Kashandarhh, but something's wrong," Steph spoke up immediately when it seemed like the conversation was starting to go south. "Our village has been dealing with a lot of earth rumblings of late, and yesterday while I was drawing water from the river, because our wells have all gone sour, I spotted the Undine moving their young out of the calmer pools to the riverside." Kashha looked at him more closely.

"How long have your mountains been active?" she queried.

"It's been about a week, but that is not why I came." Steph put his mug down on the railing and looked her straight in the eye. "I saw something I should never have seen, and truth be known I really hadn't thought existed past story books and legends." Kashha listened quietly, biting her tongue, trying her best to avoid any snide comments regarding the Llyach male who had come into her woods uninvited. However, patience was never one of her strong suits and she continued to point out the Mauntra's continual decline in the morning sky.

"Please continue, but if you don't get to the point soon, I'm afraid I'll have to be off and running, as I bang my head up against this here railing. So, what is it that you saw my friend, that has got you so upset that you come running hel-bent for leather into my woods?" Steph didn't even hesitate, as her snide comment went in one ear and out the other, before he continued with the answer to her question.

"One of the mythical White Dragons of Leberone," he said quickly. He had planned to find a way to lead up to it, but she had made it very hard to find the right time to do that, so he just spit it out in all its lunatic sounding glory. She almost thought she hadn't heard him right, and spat what was left of the coffee in her mouth out on the ground.

"You saw what?" The other two just stood there, staring at him with their mouths open. Kashha finally organized the thoughts she needed to collect; she was used to the villagers sending stupid requests, all of which were neither valid nor needed, but this was completely different, and required another response entirely. She gathered herself enough to speak properly, in her professional manner as the Witch; she called on a tone that she had not used in almost a thousand years. "You've seen one of them? Where? Dream-state or awake, Aelf?"

Kamera watched her daughter's face change immediately into something she hadn't witnessed in a very long time. Finally someone had got through to her, and she realized this was not just some game they had cooked up. Later, Kamera would have to thank him. Kashha lowered her head slowly, listening to what appeared to be nothing out of the ordinary to the others, but to a Witch it spoke volumes as to what she had become since her birth.

Her daughter took immediate control of her surroundings, and those of the others that had entered her field of vision. She found the weak spot working from within her own body, and drew the energy required to continue as it grew stronger and formed into something plausible, for her to work with. The Selkie half had control of the Witch's anger and seized what it needed, and left the rest...at least for now.

"Tell me Aelf, what is it that you were doing that you had time to find this creature in your busy day?" Steph continued on with his tale, as his mate looked on with disbelief, and Kamera took another sip of coffee that had grown cold.

"I was awake and getting water down by the river, for my village; it flew by overhead, along the tree-line to the north. And right along with it, at a distance, you could see a couple of the wild ones, you know, the Greens." Coutinnea couldn't even speak, but Kamera did.

"Was anyone else with you?"

"Not at first; I actually spotted it in the reflection of the water and thought I was seeing things, so when I looked up, I was surprised it was still there. You know those Ferrishyn ponds; they like to make you see things that aren't really there."

Steph nervously laughed, but then grew serious as he continued. "I left everything by the river's edge, and ran to the village to see if anyone else had noticed it, or if it was just a reaction to the close proximity of the pond that made me see it. But when I got there, everyone was still looking up at the sky, and yelling their heads off as the thing flew off into the distance. We had all seen it, and the pond was not any part of the force of its creation. Then the earth started rumbling harder, and I couldn't wait any longer, so I came here to tell you." He pointed to Kashha, who had momentarily stopped being rude as she watched the Aelf move about during his description of her friend Sigrith Kithtar.

Kashandarhh had been listening carefully, mostly holding her breath, so when she finally did breathe she let out a slow whistle surprising even her, as she spoke almost in a whisper mostly to herself.

"They never come into a planet's orbit; something's really wrong if they sent Sigrith." As she was talking, Kamera smacked her on the arm harder than she had her head, catching Kashha off guard and leaving a tiny red hand print. "What?" She turned to her mother. Kamera looked at her daughter and stood up, pacing back and forth.

"How long," Kamera threw up her arms then pointed a finger at her daughter, "did you know that these creatures existed?"

"My whole life, you know that." Kashha smacked Kamera back.

"I thought it was a fantastical world you had created, like all children do; now you're telling me it's real!" Kamera was stunned. Both Steph and Coutinnea just stood there, watching the back and forth banter going on between mother and daughter, not sure if they should speak up or stay quiet. At least Steph had a few questions, and when he could he was damn sure going to tell Kashandarhh what was on his mind, mostly because he may never get an opportunity to come this close to her again.

But as he watched them go at it, it seemed like it was beginning to feel a little easier to be in close proximity to the legend, and with Kamera railing on her it was the perfect time to do just that. Then the conversation turned south, and his hesitation went to hel as something else began its arrival into his unconscious thoughts. Unaware, the others continued.

"You never listened, not any one of you." Kashha pointed to all three of them standing before her. "You," she pointed to Steph and Coutinnea, "are just like everyone else in my village. I may not know you personally, but every one of you, when I was a child growing up, thought I was just some oddity. Well, I'm not some freak that everyone is pointing to. There goes the Witch that lives in the woods and eats Aelflets for dinner!" Kashha got madder as the thoughts just seemed to pour out of her and into the air. "I work with the Tuatha De`Danann for damn sake, everything I do is not up for discussion, you know that. What bloody more do you want me to say? I have done and seen things which make no difference to any one of you, because you'd never believe them even if I wanted to talk to someone about it all. And in answer to your question," she pointed to her mother, "yes, I knew the White Dragons were real. I've seen them up close and personal, and not just in my dreams as a small child mother, I've ridden the damn beasts!" Kamera just looked at her, shaking her head, but Steph stepped into the conversation. It was the perfect moment.

"But I thought you said they don't come into this orbit." Kashha turned to Steph and cocked her head just a little sideways, looking past him straight at Coutinnea, who now took a small step back like she'd been pushed? But, Kashha hadn't touched her and the Sage was easily played with. And as the question still hung thickly in the air, Kashha moved in close and personal to the little Aelf and whispered into her ear.

"Who said I was on Tantaris?" Kamera immediately rolled her eyes at the stalemate. Her daughter was back, and cruelty was everything that she was about, as she briefly exposed the Llyach Aelves to its creation.

Kashandarhh was difficult to talk to alone, but with two extra pairs of eyes on her, it was becoming exceedingly more difficult to just keep her from getting ramped up. Her daughter really was not one for company.

She'd been like that since the time she could walk. Her father, Vallmyallyn, was like that, but his Selkie heritage was a great deal stronger than Kashha's. Kamera knew her daughter had very different abilities than the normal Fey that lived within this realm, but this was the first time she had heard her daughter admit it to others that were not of Witch descent.

Most Fey that lived on Tantaris did not travel beyond the actual land masses or sea-cities that were their homes. Kashha hated others knowing anything about her in the real world. Having heard her speak of something that she had done in her professional capacity, Kamera knew instantly that something else was about to go down, if Kashha had let that pass her guards and come to the surface. But then again, most Fey didn't have Kashha's abilities swaying on their brain-stem, and the moment she had gone into Coutinnea's centre of well-being, Kamera knew she had truly been off-world.

She worked with the Tuatha's highest commanding ranking officers, and was held in very high regard within their ranks. They were whispered to have other strongholds throughout the other planets that surrounded the Mauntra's galaxy of planets. Could it be possible the White Dragons actually lived on Leberone as the legend told? Kamera stared at her daughter for a moment, truly seeing the girl who had grown up so fast, and far quicker than any of the other Witches that lived within their clan's teachings. She hadn't really grasped the severity of what she was still witnessing, when Kashha looked up into the air all of a sudden, and turned towards the barn. "We've got company coming," she told them, ignoring the others and everything that was just said, walking down the stairs and out towards the middle of the grass at her stoop.

Everyone turned at once, to the sound above them in the skies. Kashha separated herself from her mother and the others completely, walking to the centre of her open yard. Immediately above the area where Kashha stood, a band of electrical blue sparks opened the moment she arrived at the centre point, sending them raining down and exposing the circle hidden there, as they exploded into the ground and set the energy burning. The circle lit up with a small reddish hue and followed Kashandarhh as she moved towards the edges clockwise with wide sweeping hands, opening an entrance point that she created before their very eyes.

THE BEGINNING

It hung there, sparkling and beautiful, as they stood on the outside, looking in. Once moving inside it, Kashha planted her feet firmly on the ground and sealed the inner edges shut behind her. Completely enclosed, she followed the shadows that appeared on the outside rings and directed them to the four different corners of her majikal imagery. They appeared as vague outlines to Kamera, who had seen them before, but never with such vivid clarity, as they now seemed to shimmer in and out of sight, each holding the colours of their different home-worlds for no more than a fleeting trilla-second.

Each being seemed to drift towards different areas of Kashha's circle, floating and moving like a curtain blowing in the wind, never quite staying long enough in this dimension for those that are not of Witch descent to visualize their unique grandeur. Their movements shadowed that of mist, as they shimmered in and out of shift, following no actual shape or form of the creatures that they had come to be. Kashha had long since closed any doorways to the actuality of this hemisphere, and could no longer see or hear the others as she opened her arms in a widening motion that sent sparks flying in every direction in the Elemental homeland, as the elements claimed their rights of passage through their individual doorways, and moved out to this world of substance and gravity.

The wind whipped Kashha's hair as it fell all around her face, following the currents of its arrival. With her face turned upwards to the violet colouring, it melted into the molecules of the ritual majikal interference, which now appeared before them and opened her sky to the rider that was just on the outside of her woods.

The air was alive with life, as oak-leaves and grass that got caught within the circumference of the circle to the north, moved about as if pushed along by an invisible force high up in the currents of the Sylphs that careened in the eastern element of air. They floated in the gravitational pull Kashha had created, right behind the stone guardians that stood in the northern sections of her circle's perimeter. Each was followed in by the violence of the Firedrakes, as they roared around to the south and breathed fire into the direction of the west, which now appeared to hold wetness along the clothes of the Water-Nymphs still dripping small droplets of their purest form of Elemental colours, as they steamed the heat into a more vaporous formula.

They danced around each other about thirty feet above Kashha's head, as a single pinpoint of light began to open up, and bring forth out of that small split of atoms, a single black Dragon and his Aelven rider. The arrival was swift and flawless, as Tansar flew out and up with Soren high on his flanks, midway between his shoulder blades and the feathers that ran lengthwise down his spine. The moment that happened, both Llyach Aelfs went down, losing their foothold on the conscious world that clung to the edges of the Damonian Woods.

"Damn it, Kashha!" Kamera scrambled towards them, not knowing whether to laugh or be cross with her daughter. Kashha had learned her lessons well, she'd bet that particular one must have come from Tamerk, it was one of his specialities, except she had put her own spin on its energy transference. This one required the excess energy to go somewhere, and Kashha had dropped it into the only thing not aware of its bite. As Kamera looked at both of the reasons two Llyach Aelfs were laying on the ground, she discovered they had fainted from two very different causes.

She moved quickly to their sides to place a hand to the veins that ran lengthwise down their necks, listening to the heart beats beneath their outer layers of Tantarisian skin. With the initial throwing of the entrance to the Damonian Woods ward, Coutinnea had fainted from the transference of air molecules that lingered thickly in the air, where Kashha had pushed them. She, although unconscious, still breathed slowly deep inside the heartbeat of her body's energy readings, though in time, would undoubtable come awake with nothing more than a simple headache.

But Stephponias was in far more serious trouble than Kamera had initially believed. It was on the secondary search of his body, after he grew exceedingly warm, that Kamera discovered the small wound caused by the initial scrape he had received outside Kilren. This innocent surface wound was anything but, and had gone much further within the skin, than originally he would have seen. That now, was what Kamera centered her attention to, leaving Coutinnea to fight for her own conscious mind, without any aid from her.

Kamera had frowned at the discovery of it on his left wrist. She bent down closer to look him over when he had gone down after having experienced this kind of Selkie-shift variance, that was different than anything he would normally have experienced before. It took a lot out of anyone that had never felt its threads along the upper reaches of their skin, and seeing him go down almost at the same time as his mate only made sense that this is what it was. But she was wrong, as she approached his body, and realized he was far warmer and very flushed all along his face and neck. The moment she had seen the mark in all its putrefied glory, a shiver of fear rippled down her spine.

Coutinnea was not hurt, due to the unusual disbursement of energy particles on her body, and the weak constitution of her Aelfen DNA. Simply put, she would have fainted if a cone bee had stung her while dancing among the Ferrishyn fairs. But Steph's wrist was something a little more serious, and had turned an ugly shade of black, which could be seen moving slowly upwards to his elbow, after entering a direct vein when the Dragon had come through the open-rift.

The electrical charge that Kashandarhh had conjured up within her majikal circle was not one to jump lines, and had never gone outside those boundaries, so Steph had not been touched by that source, Kamera was sure of that. But how did it happen, and where did this bruise come from, that appeared to be quickly turning black, right in front of her face?

The circle boundaries had always been well controlled; Kamera had no doubt of Kashha's ability to do so. The quartz crystals that surrounded the circle that Kashha and her father Myallyn had buried deep within the ground, would have taken any extra load if something had misfired. This was not the case, because Myallyn was thorough in his search to secure Kashha's entranceways from the volatile Elemental worlds and their energy fluxes. They were designed that way, and had come from one of the Bear Crystals in the shape of tiny individual laser quartz called a Druid Sphere, that she had maintained and fed throughout her time here in the Damonian Woods. If she hadn't, they would have swallowed the entire area alive, and dragged it backwards through the void and into the sea.

Kashha would have sunk them facing the smallest aperture towards the centre mainframe, when she had buried them. They required it in that direction so as to not overload their circuitry when keeping any energy partials from expanding into the other world, and creating a wave motion that reversed their polarity and came back to their original exit point. That was always how it was done. Always, with no exceptions. Besides what others might think of her, her daughter would never have purposely caused another Fey harm unless that Fey had initialized the attack. Stephponias had not done that.

How Steph's arm got damaged, she could not know, but Kashha would, and at that moment she was needed for other things far more pressing than an unconscious couple of Llyach Aelves. Her daughter was still engaged in the crossover, and still had to release the particles and dismiss the guardians that had come to her calling, so nothing would rupture the entranceway after bringing the rider through. Whatever happened while she was busy, Kamera would have to deal with it on her own.

Kamera slid forward on the ground, trying to find a more comfortable position, before her legs decided to cramp up and begin to tingle with the numbness that accompanies one that sits for long periods of time. She looked up momentarily, away from the Llyach couple on the ground, just as the black landed on the edge of Kashha's tree-lined clearing, and saw the rider slip down from the large Dragon's back. He started towards her daughter, leaving the Dragon behind in the grasses to feed, just as Kashandarhh's circle of light went out, letting her step through the fallen rings to join the rider and find out why such a beast as one of the black Dragons had entered her clearing in full battle armour. What words were spoken, Kamera could not hear, but she already had her hands full with other things as Stephponias started to convulse and get very, very sick.

CHAPTER TWENTY

Arrival of a Dragonlord

The directions Soren received, had been given in Kilren by the kin of the wilderness Witch Tamerk had mentioned without any of the difficulties he had anticipated. He may not have been as lucky in the endeavour, had he been any other seeker who had not been affiliated with the Dragon clan Fey. It wasn't that Kilren was an unfriendly village, just that the Witch that lived just beyond their doorway was one of their own, despite the fact she was not born of their soil, and inherited the village of Sages only by proxy.

And even though at times she was difficult to get along with — and most of the village steered clear of her, she was important to one that they dearly loved, who lived within their village walls. Kamera was without a shadow of a doubt an enigma. The village elders still did not know the whole story of how she came to live in Kilren when she was Kanoie born, nor the fact that they had allowed one that was extremely high up in the hierarchy of the Kanoie clan of elders to abandon her position amongst their kind to live amongst those they considered inferior.

Kamera had lived in Kilren for a long time now, but no one knew her before she had arrived with a child clinging to her crimson gown, one dark and dreary day in the month of the triple moons, entering the village's inner wards without being invited. How she had gotten in, without anyone knowing, still to this day was a mystery. But the Kamera of then was really no different than the Kamera of now; she just had to let the village catch up with the unusualness of who she appeared to be, and not what they had not been privileged to understand from before.

She was always the mother of the strange child, who lived in the seclusion of the Damonian Woods, when she had arrived all those long years ago. No one alive today remembered that she herself was of Witch decent from Llavalla, and that the child of unusual talents that she had brought with her was any more than just a baby at her breast. Still, she had lain claim to an area of woods just outside of the Kilren border, on the last day of the Mabonistic gathering feast, and before All Souls Day arrived she was well entrenched inside those woods, while her daughter was still yet a very young toddler.

The villagers had come to think of her as theirs, and it hadn't taken long before they claimed her as one of their own, even if her child didn't want that designation. The child belonged to no one, and given what the alternative would be, they claimed her simply as the wild half-Selkie that lived and practised the old ways inside the woods that no longer belonged to anyone but her.

They would have protected Kamera with their lives, if need be; she had given them only loyalty within the village limits, but on the other side of the barrier into the Damonian Woods she became her own champion. She had seen to that without prying eyes, and given over her own soul as the champion of others, and for this they accepted her with open arms.

Her daughter had grown up away from the villagers and their prying eyes, deep inside those woods, and had not adapted well to any intrusion into her life. That was not by design, despite how hard Kamera had tried. Her introduction to the villagers had not gone over favourably any time it had been attempted; to both of their arrivals on this side of the Morphana River. Kashandarhh was not at all like her high spirited mother, and she couldn't stand a single soul that lived within the villages of this planet's vernacular atmosphere, with the rare exception of a certain breed of Dragon. Soren had to laugh at that statement; so much for loyalty when it came to Dragons. He didn't even know she existed, and his bloody Dragon already had an open invitation.

Even Tansar knew the way into her world, and really didn't need him to ask directions inside Kilren. But ask he did, and Soren would bet Tansar had been here many times before, without the escort of Soren's backside on his dusty old scales. But protocol required Soren to ask, and he was damn sure he would not let Tansar get the better of him despite having zero sleep and little tolerance left in his body, for the last two days. Damn Dragon always seemed to have the upper hand in any situation he got himself into lately. That was going to change, once he had time to think about what he wanted to add to that statement, but for now, he was just plain tired.

The moment he had come out of shift with Tansar, the village folk had been only too happy to help. Their excitement was palpable at seeing one of the lost Dragons of Symarr arriving in the sky, as it had flown low over the horizon, then again as they circled the outer field and entered the clearing on the outskirts of the village wards. Tansar soaked up the attention like a Cauper dog too old to hunt. Tansar had always had a way with the village folk that lived inside this planet's little worlds, and as far as Soren could see, this time through the sight of exhausted eyes starting to really sting from over exposure, the Dragon was really laying it on thick, despite the fact that they already had permission to land. He'd have to have a chat with the old boy (or girl as it seemed to be, thanks to Tamerk), when he had time to rest his body sometime next in the coming of days. One of these days he was going to get them all killed with his stupid antics, like taking hay from the village kidlets while Soren was forced to walk into town without him; unnecessarily now, as it happened.

Now, there was never anything said about Dragons being soft. He didn't want anyone to get the idea that these creatures may not be as dangerous as they had been led to believe. And believe you me, they had a ferocity that could only be explained as equal to that of a bull Twicken on steroids. And if Tansar kept up his act of all brave and innocent, for the village folk, one day some Aelflet was going to come too close and get its ass trampled on, and Soren would have to make a run for it before some parent decided it was time to use one of those rusty old swords they kept in the reeds under the mats of their homes. Besides, they were Dragonlords, not bloody circus folk, and Tansar should know better.

The black Dragons were always seen as warriors among all Fey, and to be a rider was to be given wide berth among any of the Fey clans, being of Aelven descent or not. All exceptions aside, this was not the way Soren wanted to be introduced to the Saber Fennone clan of Aelves that resided inside Kilren's walls. Tansar was kidding himself if he allowed the villagers to get within stepping range of his dangerous paws covered in long sharp talons; all it took would be one little misstep and the whole village would be in an uproar when the crumbled form of one of their prize possessions suddenly found itself flat under the destructive force of those claws. Soren shivered, thinking of the pointless thoughts that would do no good even if mentioned to the old lap Dragon. He had to laugh at the word...lap Dragon, and wondered if Tansar would have found it as funny as he did. Obviously he was worn-out, or that phrase wouldn't have had the same effect....

Kashandarhh required their loyalty and not a sideshow freak about to bite the hand that feeds it; that thought brought Soren into the current timeline. But, as one that has a child that has grown up, and who has watched its process of achievement throughout its toddling stage of learning, he truly wondered if she really paid attention to how they had all gone about their lives, with none of them really trying to actually make her a very angry Witch. He had heard the rumours of her personality traits, and how she preferred to never get involved with the Fey of this particular realm. Soren wondered if this was simply by choice, or did someone really tick her off, and now anyone that came within range just got his ass kicked? He was starting to like her, more and more.

He wished he had been given more information as to the reason for his call to duty, and not just about the arrival into the Witch's domain. Had he not been so pissed off with the little Sprite, or whatever that damn creature had happened to be, he would have asked more questions about the reasoning for this mission of gravitational fortitude. Then maybe, just maybe, Tamerk could have given them more information as to the role the black Dragons of Symarr were about to embark upon, without Soren getting his own ass knocked about by some temperamental Witch. Soren groaned again; this was not going to be an easy day. Maybe he should reserve his feelings about her, he thought; if she was anything like he had heard, this was going to be a very long day.

Those that knew Kamera and her Witch daughter, would never have denied a Dragonlord that information; not in fear of the Dragonlord himself, but in the knowing that the Witch that had lived up in the

Damonian Woods for as long as they could remember would be far more fearsome should it come to her attention that they had denied one of her Dragons. He didn't think that extended to the riders and maybe if he sent Tansar in, he would get more information.

Kashha had that kind of reverence all up and down this side of the galaxy, and was also known for her unequaled and just as deadly temper, should someone come to be on the wrong side of it. And an angry Witch was not conducive to a happy mother, and Kamera definitely was that.

Soren could only hope that his clan's lead Dragon-drover Dyareius, would understand the implications if he had not gone in search of the Witch, as promised to Tamerk. He tried to steer his attention back to the passage at hand, but sleep was beginning to claim him, and things inside the rift were feeling all fuzzy as he came through Kashha's chosen energy point, and steered the Dragon towards where they had directed her entrance-point star to be. Tansar had picked it up not long after they shifted out of Kilren, and was already well on his way into its gravitational field before Soren realized just how exhausted he really was. Soon enough, things around him began to fall apart, as far as his vision was concerned, and tiny little particles of flux were passing through him as if he was a holographic image, and not the flesh and blood of an Aelf. He hated this method of travel at the best of times, and having to pass through it when his brain was this fuzzy was even more unsettling. It would definitely make things a little more direct in his flight through the Saber Fennone woodlands, giving his Dragon the invisibility without causing anymore sightings along the way of the black Dragon flying alone out and near the west side of the Sydclath mountains.

That one single cause could instill something Soren wasn't prepared to contribute to his clan, namely the unusual appearance of them flying solo. It was becoming exceedingly more complicated each time they did venture out alone along the western front of Tothray's area, on this side of the Telpphaea falls. There were still enemies out in the hills, and they were well hidden throughout the caverns the Sydclath Mountains held deeply embedded insides their rocks. And at any time, they could launch a full-scale attack on a single Dragon flying without the herd, causing death to either him or Tansar should they decide to fracture the herd and weaken its strength in numbers.

But that was unlikely; in fact the real danger was the possibility of the full herd of Dragons coming this way in search of where he himself had gotten off to. He didn't need a full scale panic should Dyareius try to backstep his energy signature as he had flown onward towards Kilren, and run into one of the hunting parties of the Caubertian Aelves, who would have surely noticed if the whole Dragon war troop suddenly showed up above their woods, heading towards Kashandarhh's territory.

He really should have told Dyareius himself, but Quist would have known through communication with Tansar the moment he had changed his course and direction away from the herd, shortly into the flight. The Dragons having the ability to telepathically communicate with each other during these times of silent travel, meant that Tansar had already informed Quist what they were up to. If he had any doubts as to what was actually relayed in return from Dyareius, and whether it was important enough for Tansar to speak to him, he was sure the Dragon would have long since instructed him on that status. But then again, he *had* punched Quist in the head, not once but twice, and if Tansar held a grudge for his brethren Dragon, Soren was on his own anyway and would soon find out the cost of that.

Tansar mumbled something to Soren about relaying the request directly to Baelf to tell Dyareius not to follow – explaining the urgency of Soren's sudden and unexpected departure and the urgency to reach Kashandarhh before nightfall of the Fieldmarr moon. Damn, Soren had forgotten that Tansar could hear him. He cringed in his tired body. Well, it was too late to take it back. He had faith in Tansar's decision, although he wasn't so sure of the reasoning behind its creation, let alone whether he heard Tansar correctly in this field of transference. But, Tamerk was adamant that Kashandarhh be involved, and that was all Soren needed to know at this time, until she said otherwise or he fell out of the sky from sheer exhaustion, or on the other-side of the coin….Tansar pushed him. Either way he would find out soon enough.

So, he had shifted away from the others, as they went on to Tameron, pushing his endurance beyond what a large shift would normally have exceeded, and found its place. He winced as he stretched war hardened muscles long past their battle hardy endurance records. It had winded him more than ever it had before; he was getting too old for this kind of travel and far too old to fight without getting food or sleep to keep him going. He still had not been able to regain his usual amount of sleep, and was so beyond exhaustion from days without proper rest, inside a head that had only had majik to knock him out cold that he didn't know why, he had actually gone without telling someone he was going.

Well, at least he had been fed. It could have gone the other way and he might still be in chains. He had been lucky the Sprite hadn't taken him through a Dwarf Star when he had tried to strangle the kid. At least Soren had that going for him. Now, if he didn't have Tansar to guide the way, he would not have found the entrance-point to Kilren as he started to slip deeply into a full-on nod and drifted into the beginning recesses of blissful sleep. He had only one thought as he entered the village — find directions and get out quickly. It occurred to him that that was two thoughts, but he was too tired to argue with...himself? Now that was funny. He started wondering about that as well. He was positive that all this movement about within the particles of shift was starting to affect his brain cells. Shifting sort of left one a bit fuzzy at the best of times, as each of the Fey that lived within this realm came out of faze time after glorious bloody-time. He knew when he first started as a boy, it used to be a bit of a hallucinogen, and it would make you loopy. But as the years went by, and you became accustomed to its properties, it just went away, or you were so used to it you didn't notice it anymore.

But being a Dragonlord had its perks; none of which he could think of that would give him an extra punch of energy at the moment. But come morning, after a full night of sleep, he was damn sure he was going to find himself some.

Now, to be honest he'd shifted maybe several hundred thousand times or more. Could it actually be doing damage to his body that he wasn't aware of? He suddenly realized he'd walked to an actual cottage, all the while fussing in his head about the perils of shift particles on his brain. How he got there he only vaguely remembered, and as he had daydreamed what his life would be like after a full on day of blissful sleep, he realized the building was a simple Sage's cottage with dried herbs and flowers gracing its entrance, hanging all about the laneway before him.

It was not even just any Sage's cottage; this one had a certain air about it. It seemed to shimmer in the morning wind just a tiny bit, enough for someone to move on by and not even notice it was actually there. The land around the tiny cottage had encompassed the majik of the Selkie homeworld and wove its spell of Morgauseine Mylornese, one of the most powerful invisibility spells, around the area of the home. He should have known, the moment he smelled its molecules of sulphite back at the edge of the lane they had turned into, that he had arrived at the home of the mother of the Witch. He must have been tired, he hadn't been aware of walking there.

"Hey, wait for me," a tiny voice said from behind Soren. He looked around and realized he had quite an entourage following him along the road.

He looked down to where the voice had spoken, and discovered a small young adolescent staring back at him. The little boy smiled widely at him and pointed, "This is her place." He sounded so proud, for someone Soren couldn't remember meeting until just then. Soren looked around briefly in bewilderment, and behind him a number of villagers had gathered, joining the Dragon-rider as he had made his way completely unaware of where he was going. He really needed to shake this sleep thing out of his brain, he thought. One day the Dragon majik was going to fail him, and he was going to get himself into some serious trouble. "I told you," the child smiled, "I'd get you there." Soren smiled and knelt down to his level and touched his beaming face.

"You were right; so what do I call you?" Soren asked.

The little Aelflet looked to be about five thickals of age, with just the beginning hue of colour to his beaming Kilrenean face.

"Tommarrius Kuamashe," he laughed at Soren. Soren saluted the youngster.

"Master Kuamashe, from the order of the Dragonlords, I thank you for protecting my walking among the pheasants of this here village, and for keeping me," he looked at the others with a twinkle in his eye, "proper Dragon-rider safe!" The child was thrilled and ran giggling back to his mother, who had followed at a distance.

"I'm afraid it looks like Kamera isn't in." She started forward, her son trying to pull her towards the Dragon-rider's side.

"Mama come on, he wants to see you." Soren stood up, as the mother of Tommarrius pointed to the open doorway of Kamera's cottage. Soren went to the doorway, calling her name, but received no answer.

"I think you're right, it would seem I've arrived without an invitation."

"Something tells me Kamera would not have minded, my lord." Tommarrius's mother spoke with grace. "Dragonlords are not our regular visitors, I am sure that form of communication cannot be expected for such an important guest."

She smiled, pointing to her mate who had just come in from the fields, brushing the dried hay from his clothes and stomping the muck from his boots. "Maybe we can be of service. Kamera would be terribly offended if someone did not offer."

"Welcome my lord, I am ..." Tommarrius spotted his father.

"Daddy, did you see the Dragon?" He ran to the Aelfan male, who swooped up his young son, swinging his slight form up into the air and catching him easily.

"I sure did; he's pretty spectacular, isn't he, little one?"

"He's a Dragonlord, papa," the child pointed at Soren, "and I'm Master Kuamashe." Tommarrius pointed to himself.

"You are? Well I'll be, Master Kuamashe," he grinned at his son and wife, tussling his son's hair as he started to introduce himself to Soren. He put his hand out, as he spoke.

"I'm Zheckarria," he said, as he shook Soren's hand. "My wife, Thimelteen, and of course Master Tommarrius you've already met. What can we do for you-" he looked momentarily puzzled, not knowing how to address him.

"Soren," the Dragon-rider added, "I'm from Tameron. And that," he pointed to his Dragon, who was out on the fields that stood by the gateway crystals, "is Tansar. We came to get directions from Kamera to her daughter Kashandarhh's place."

"Ah," said Zheckarria.

"But it appears we've missed her," Soren continued, "so perhaps someone else may be able to help me." Soren smiled.

"Not a problem my lord, everyone in the village knows where Kashandarhh's place is. But I seriously doubt you'd need the directions; your Dragon's molecules will activate her shift particles the moment you enter the Damonian Woods." Zheckarria spoke to the rider with a bit of surprise in his voice. Soren looked in Tansar's direction.

"Well now, that seems to be a tiny bit of information he forgot to relay to me." Soren looked tired.

"Sir?" said Zheckarria, looking questioningly at him.

"We seem to not be on speaking terms at the moment, and I guess that little bit of information was his way of getting back at me." Zheckarria frowned.

"Well it can't be all bad; at least Tommarrius got a chance to meet you, and for this I have to say thank you. Dragons are all he talks about, and today is a day that he won't forget for a long time." Soren smiled at the little one.

"Dragons eh? Well now, what do you know about that." Tommarrius grinned back at him, sending him his best toothy grin, as Soren watched one of the greens off in the distance soar overhead of Tansar, dipping his wings before flying out of sight. "All the Dragons know this?" he asked, pointing at it as it moved off, now finding reason to question Tansar on holding back this information.

"No, I think it's just the black ones. I can't really tell you how, but I don't believe the Greens can do it; their wild nature can't seem to grasp the unique particles. But, since I've only seen your blacks with a rider, I imagine it comes with their unique physiology alone." Zheckarria replied. Soren smiled at the farmer.

"Well that makes it a lot easier; thank you all for being so kind. Please let Kamera know we are sorry to have missed her." Soren shook Zheckarria's hand and waved at little Tommarrius, who was being carried by his mother as they walked behind the two Aelfan males.

"Your status, Soren, allows you to shift within the village; there is no need to walk to the stones if you are in need," Zheckarria told Soren softly, when it appeared how extremely tired he was, and that he would be walking back through the village one more time, through all the crowds.

THE BEGINNING

"Thank you, but that won't be necessary; I'd enjoy the walk if you and your family would accompany me to Tansar. I need the fresh air to keep me awake." Zheckarria nodded and said no more on the subject, keeping his secret, as Tommarrius clapped his little hands while they walked, telling all that they met that he was going to be a Dragonlord just like Soren, when he got big. Soren carried on his conversation about tiny thoughts that the two males discussed as they moved thorough the village, as the farmer pointed out various points of interest, abiding by the Dragonlord's wishes.

When the small party arrived beside Tansar, the Dragon moved his large head down towards the little Aelf and snorted, sending Tommarrius into immediate laughter. Tansar's breath had left his little strands of hair standing straight up and he looked like a Begonin Piglet that had just come out of the muck covered in straw. Everyone roared. Soren said his goodbyes and leaped aboard the black Dragon's neck. Tansar began his preparation for leaping into the air, slowly flapping his wings and stretching their length in the air before gaining altitude. Then, finally achieving enough headway, he corrected the wind speed along his wings and took flight, slowly dipping his beautiful black wings in a salute to Tommarrius and the people of Kilren, then slowly twisted his large frame in a barrel roll just to exaggerate his affection for the youngster who could be heard squealing away with glee on the ground after Tansar sent down one of his feathers towards the little boy as a souvenir. Then they were away, as Dragon and Aelf made their way towards the Damonian Woods on the north east of Kilren's boundaries.

Soren watched the little hamlet disappear as he and Tansar felt the wind flowing with each flap of the huge beast's wings. They continued on their flight forward into the space-between, where the Witch had placed the entrance.

"So, anything you want to tell me, or shall I just say we're even?" Soren spoke rather quietly to Tansar, who didn't respond. "No? Well let's just get this done. I'm too tired to play anymore. So, can we at least hold a truce?" Tansar grinned as he moved along the airways.

"Maybe; we'll see. There is still daylight left, and that depends whether you plan on making it back alive or not." He snorted.

"Yeah, I kind of thought so." Soren whispered. "You know he deserved it right? After all, we thought Symin was in danger."

"You should have known better than to think we'd hurt him." Tansar answered.

"Ok, you've got a point. I'm too tired to fight anymore, can we at least agree to disagree?" Silence followed the question. Tansar flew on without dumping Soren's ass out of the clouds. For the time being, Soren assumed the truce had been called, then set and matched, that is for whatever provisional timeframe Tansar had in mind.

The Damonian Woods lay about five miles north, and half a mile east from Kilren. The day had been so far without incident, which truly surprised Soren, considering how truly exhausted he was. Only Zheckarria seemed to notice, and if not for Tommarrius Soren would have gladly taken him up on his offer of shifting to Tansar, but he only had to look at the excitement in the little whelp's eyes, before he changed his mind and carried on up the laneway.

Most of the village had never seen the likes of one such as Tansar, so he felt it was only fair to allow the little one some extra care, and took the time he needed to spend with someone who might be a powerful ally, one day.

Soren didn't spend a lot of time with Aelflets himself, and other than the Human child called Ryyaan, he couldn't think of another moment when he took the time to actually speak with them. He chalked it up to being overly tired, but for now he had no other thought to the reason why; which was also the reason he didn't feel Tansar shiver as they passed a batch of blacken trees that were just beginning to recover their colour. His scales moved along his back like a deck of cards being shuffled — a direct response to the poisoned molecules it had left behind, then settled back in place without alerting Soren to what was below them. Had he turned around, he would have seen the shade turn to a more greenish hue, and within the hour the passing of the source would have vanished from anyone's view completely. He had missed it altogether, and could not have told Kashandarhh a single thing, being as tired as he was. His body followed suit shortly after, as they reached their altitude and his body could no longer keep his mind conscious. He drifted off to sleep to the constant rocking sensation and thumping of Tansar's wings.

The Damonian Woods could be seen in the distance; Tansar coughed and woke Soren up as he began his shift, and disappeared into the void.

They moved fluidly through the opening that had set itself to Tansar's atoms the moment the Dragon had come in range. It closed off behind them as they moved through where time ran in a direct line, producing several timelines to run simultaneously in this section of linear space. Tansar drew everything from the unseen force that guided him easily through this space between worlds, that seemed to be torn apart with pieces of pure energy, sending signals into his Dragon mind, and guiding him towards the one that would take him directly to Kashandarhh. Pure white meteor lights of long exploded stardust moved and danced all around them, covering everything with the white brilliance of what they had been in younger times.

Everything to Soren appeared to be moving in slow motion, as time began to link itself to both the present and past alike, joining the timelines into one. He had a moment of pure clarity that, should he desire to be, he could be anywhere he wished in the time link this Witch controlled. How was it possible to have this much power? He felt his mind start to shift, and began to lose consciousness.

"*Try to stay focused Soren; let Tansar take the lead and try not to fall.*" He heard Kashandarhh's voice speaking within his own mind. "*I'll guide him through; he's been here before.*" Soren closed his eyes and hung on for dear life letting Tansar have complete control; it was unlike anything he had ever experienced before. He had to admit, he wasn't so sure he could have taken control of his Dragon, even if he needed to. As it was, Tansar moved effortlessly without any encouragement, as Soren's ability to return to the real world slowly began to drift away aimlessly, into the abyss. His desire to explore was too great, and just when he couldn't form his thoughts anymore, between each new idea that began to form within his mind and the one before, Tansar broke free of the in-between worlds; exploding out in a hail of stardust among the brilliant trees and the wide-open mountains.

It was unbelievable to watch; as Tansar drew from the power they had just come through, and soared up through the middle of the Damonian Woods into the world of now. His leathery black onyx wings were covered in the stardust it had created, directly from the worlds of Sopdet's constellations. One that Kashandarhh harnessed from some unknown ritual that belonged to an ancient realm, Soren had never seen.

Soren's vision immediately became crystal clear, and the sleep vanished from his eyes as the stardust that remained on his clothes and body fell away, shimmering in the Mauntra's rays that held the light of Tantaris's afternoon light. Somewhere between when he left and when they had actually arrived, he had lost almost a full two hours.

The stardust glistened one last time, then disappeared from view as they flew in a circle, catching the air that would take them downward. Down below, Soren saw the tail end of brightly rimmed firelight still surrounding a centre ring of energy, from which power still emitted and sparked its last tendrils of majikal intensity.

Tansar circled overhead of the clearing a few times, calling out to Kashandarhh down below, then came to rest in an area that was big enough to allow his girth to feed upon the grasses that lined the meadow where she now lived.

The moment Tansar got himself settled, Soren untangled himself from the scales and feathers that had attached themselves to his legs going through the unusual shift. He slid off Tansar's side, then contacting Tantarian soil, grounded himself from the powerful electrical charge that still radiated from within his very bones. He shook off the extra static and let it fall to the ground, where it landed hard among the soil, producing a sound like shattering glass. He waited for the last of it to fall from his clothing, and then proceeded forward to meet Kashandarhh with the last drags of energy still flickering off his boots and falling harmlessly to the ground. He walked towards the one that he hoped would make things a little clearer in the coming days.

The Witch met him with a formal greeting that her kind was renowned for. Soren bent his head to receive her touch, and she greeted him, forehead to forehead, not more than twenty paces in. To have her hands placed on his face was a little unnerving at first, but Tansar had relayed the information from Quist, as to what to expect when meeting someone of her kind. She moved to his chest, and took everything else that remained from the shift, letting it fall to the ground within the clearing where they met. His heart skipped a beat.

"Welcome Soren, it takes a strong mind to allow your Dragon to lead you in." She removed her hands, and stood back smiling as she tilted her head upwards, looking into his eyes, slightly cocked to his left. He was floored....she was stunning!

"Do all your riders come in this way?" Soren coughed a bit on the dust that was just settling, and had come straight at him from Tansar's wing draft.

"Oh my no, only the black Dragons have that ability." She smiled, gesturing for him to follow her back to Tansar, where she took the lead and led him back in the direction from which he had come.

She reached up to the big Dragon who had lowered his long neck to her hands, and brought lumps of something green out of her pockets for him to eat. "Good to see you again, old soul, how have you been?" Tansar emitted a low growl, almost like a continuous moan of happiness – looked up at Soren and winked. Then without skipping a beat, the large Dragon crouched down low, and then rolled over on his back along the field grass. He scraped the scales of his body along the occasional stones that stuck out of the soil, dislodging them and sending them rolling in all directions. Small animals living within the impact zone went scurrying for cover as his wide girth laid anything within distance flat out along the ground. Both Kashandarhh and Soren roared with laughter at the sight, as one last Rocklerite poked his head out of one of the tunnels it had been sleeping in, and almost lost it when Tansar's tail nearly decapitated the poor soul.

Kamera watched at a distance, as Coutinnea came out of her faint to the sight of the great beast having already landed on terra firma. To be able to see the legendary war Dragons in all their splendour flying by overhead, was a little daunting to most of the Fey on any given day, but to be this close to any single one of them on the ground, was beyond anything she had been able to grasp so far. Kamera quickly took over, and pulled her attention away from the Dragon crunching on mouthfuls of grass and pulling them out by the root stems, seemingly oblivious to her terror; she knew that was not the case; nor was it even close.

Tansar, Soren's Dragon was just as conscious of what they were doing, but simply choose to ignore them. It proved to be more of a challenge than Kamera first thought to move Coutinnea's wandering eyes from Tansar's huge talons, to her fallen mate. And just when she continued to appear mesmerized and stare at the creature with wide-eyes and a mouth opening like a Croptan Frog sucking in his tongue, Tansar for whatever reason turned his back on her and started to forage further away. Bless his six little hearts....

Not many Aelfen females ever got an opportunity to be in such close proximity to one such as Kashandarhh, in their whole lifetimes. So this, was beyond anything that her little world of wild-crafting could draw from. Kamera had to smile, watching Coutinnea moving about as she sidestepped to stay away from the general area that Kashha moved through, trying to not draw attention back in her direction, if there was any way to help it. It wasn't every day that someone from her particular field would believe that she had seen Kashandarhh, let alone visited her in her own backyard. But, for timid little Coutinnea to be squatting in the meadow right beside her daughter's house, let alone trying to ignore one of the black Dragons that was no more than a few hundred yards down in the clearing; that was going to take some doing. She was going to have a bit of a time getting them to believe any part of this story, should she decide to tell it. Those who knew Kashandarhh would have had serious doubt about her tale being nothing more than some kind of fantasy, thereby finding the means to shred it to ribbons before the words came out of her mouth. Everyone knew that being in the vicinity of Kamera's daughter was like a wild windstorm moving through the upper atmosphere, sending rods of lightning down over the entire countryside. Kashha never did do anything half way, and poor Coutinnea was only halfway there at the best of days, so how was she able to pull this one off? No, Kamera thought, their secret was safe...

Kamera watched all of this with great interest; she was, after all, the keeper of souls within this realm. She worked at collecting the fragments from everything and everyone that came into contact with her, like that of an ethereal spirit from that very realm. She reached within the mind to the silent cracks that no one wanted, or needed the use of, and gave them substance, as they re-structured themselves and found their worth. Many were old things that fought with the fluctuations of today's worlds, and couldn't tear themselves away from terrors that had released them into this realm in the first place. And one by one, Kamera was able to find the crack and fill that void, melting from within like warm Wulushian honey, seeping into every pore and filling the void with acceptance and new meaning.

THE BEGINNING

Coutinnea was one of those souls. She couldn't find the trigger point of what was, and what is, that directed her thoughts to form the truth of what she was seeing. She just knew it was strange and unbelievable, so she would shut herself off to the outside world, and didn't function more than the tiny amount that was required to settle within her soul and breathe. There it settled, and presented itself within her mind, to continue the things she needed without her mind being always present. That allowed her to have sustained life within this world of strange and unnatural beauty, and gave her lungs the oxygen they required for her to live.

But she was able, as far as Kamera could see, as all the rolling around the ground from Tansar erupted like an insane Kitten behind them, and Coutinnea helped Kamera lift her husband's head off the ground and onto her lap. Then without further prompting, she shut herself off to the world once more, and retained the look of one that lives within a world that only they can see.

There was too much tactile interference from outside sources that she could not fully comprehend. So she focused on what was familiar, and what was actual; helping the fallen Aelf that was her life mate, and tilting her head back to maintain the balance that was required to keep him from falling back onto the ground. But, that was it; as far as she was able to intervene, and as far as she was willing to go. It was all Kamera needed at the moment, until Kashha returned.

Kashandarhh felt the loss of consciousness of both Aelfs. It was a small matter, which she was not currently focusing on. The female was weak, but she had not the time to deal with the reasoning of the male, until both Soren and she arrived back at Kamera's side and were within sight of the actual event.

Soren was mildly happy to find Kamera here with her daughter, but a little surprised to find two Llyach Aelfs at Kashandarhh's doorstep; one apparently out cold, lying on the ground, while the other moaning slightly with her head tilted back.

"Are we responsible for that?" Soren inquired, half smiling, turning to both females, as the Llyach female Aelf whimpered louder, closing her eyes the closer they stepped towards her. Kamera nodded towards Coutinnea.

"Hum, I'm afraid it is, yes…and for him," she pointed to Steph, "I haven't got a clue." She turned to her daughter, and directed a different question at her; one that was a little more unsettling. "Kashha, look at the mark on his arm." Kamera pulled the cloth away, revealing the ugly blackening welts, which now seemed to be heading upwards towards the shoulder muscle connecting his head to the rest of his body.

Soren whistled, but Kashandarhh didn't hesitate and took off running up the stairs to her cottage, yelling at both Soren and her mother.

"Get his head down NOW, and raise that arm above his damn heart! Soren, if you please," she pointed to the Aelf and directed him to move quickly to Steph's side, "hold him down with all your might, the seizures will be violent, and they will be soon!"

No sooner had Coutinnea arrived back into the current conscious situation, and had just put her arm under Steph's head to lower him down, Soren grabbed him by the ankle, yanked the inert form from her lap, and laid him out flat on the ground out of her reach. Kamera watched Coutinnea's lip begin to quiver, but Kamera had had enough; she moved towards where Soren had dragged the Aelf, to help in any way she could. Ignoring civilities, she yelled at Coutinnea for her to either help or get out of the damn way.

Soren leaped onto Steph's chest, pinning one arm under his left leg, while pulling the infected arm upwards, jamming the fingers under his chin and squeezing them tightly between his jaw and neck, while Kamera grabbed one leg and pushed both hands down towards the ground.

"Coutinnea, for the love of the Goddess, get yourself together and grab that other leg!" Soren didn't wait, his right leg moved in that direction and pinned the other leg to the ground, just as the first ripple of seizures began. "Your husband will die if you don't reach out and ground him with your energy, Coutinnea!" Kamera was shouting now. Coutinnea couldn't move.

Inside the cabin, the crashing of bottles and vials could be heard as all three conscious souls outside waited for Kashandarhh to return. When she finally did, the seizures were in full swing and the Aelven male was thrashing about the ground in any way he was able to move, as Soren rode it out almost single-handedly. Both Kamera and Soren were doing the best that they could to maintain their hold on his convulsing body. Kashha looked at Coutinnea, then to her mother, who shook her head as she came down the steps.

"Coutinnea," Kashha began to speak to her mentally, away from the others in hearing range. "You need to reach out and ground him, or all the medicine on Tantaris won't help him and he will die!" Coutinnea looked up at Kashha, startled.

"How did..." she started to speak. Kashha shook her head.

"Now sweetheart, or I cannot touch him." Kashha told her softly but with a firmness she would understand. Coutinnea responded immediately, and moved toward Steph without hesitation. He was thrashing, and becoming harder for Soren and Kamera to control. She reached out for the leg Soren was starting to lose control over, just as his ability to hold it began to fail. Both Soren and Kamera felt the rush of energy from a pair-bond surge through the circle, and Stephponias started to relax. They loosened their own hold to a fraction of how they held his limbs previously, but did not release the Aelf entirely; giving their own limbs some relief from the spasms that were going through their bodies from holding him so tight.

Now Kashha could approach the Llyach Aelf without having to hurt those around him and sending the whole group into the ground. Something strong had put up a protection ring, to keep her from touching him while he was unconscious. With her energy, she settled alongside his head and called her guardians to come forth and protect the ones that had been helping the injured Aelf, as he started to sink into a deep majikal sedation, releasing the field. With Kashandarhh sitting by Steph's head, the circle was complete and the seizure began to subside. It did not diminish entirely, until Kashha placed the herb gently upon Steph's bare chest, right on top of the heart muscle that beat ever so slowly now that the calming drug had taken affect.

"Llay De Tung Mya Thouce Eh Ell Mack Ef Ffrew, Ce Be Cetu Cere Ata Myya Ffrew." She whispered in the thick dialect as all three beings continued to wonder just what in the heck was going on.

Kashha repeated the syntax of each ancient Aelven word in sequence, to the letters that she spoke. Small white sparks ignited within the heart muscle, following the bloodline towards the darkened area that was now heading towards Steph's wrist. She smiled, knowing the medicine of the

Selkie home-world was far superior to even the strongest entity that lived outside the landslip of Selkie territory. She picked up a hand-blown glass container she had carried outside with her, and placed the jar at the opening of what looked to be the original entry point just above his wrist. The location she applied the container to, held the original injury from outside Kilren where he had fallen against the stones and cut himself. She shifted her weight just slightly, and started to slowly press downwards, applying constant pressure along the mass with her other hand, and moving it downwards. As it started to come down to where the cut originally opened up, the inner muscle and blackened sinew of the wrist were exposed down to the bone.

Out into the vessel two tiny organisms withdrew from Steph's skin, and became trapped inside the glass bottle that she held tightly closed against his skin. Kashha pointed to Soren, who released his hold on the now limp body of the Aelf, and instructed the Dragon-rider to pour lamp oil on a rag and wrap it around the bottle top just about an inch where it comes into contact with Stephponias's skin, then waited for the seizures to come to a complete stop, as she chanted quietly one more time. "Cu dra llaya de tong." She applied more pressure and slid her thumb down the vein again, and immediately out popped a third one into the jar. "Soren, can you hold this," she pointed to the jar now pushed with the tightness of the oiled cloth, "while I close off the exposed area?"

Soren reached his arm across Steph's body, and placed one hand tightly upon the glass jar, allowing Kashha to mix a combination of Amaranth and Althea wax to seal the wound. She coated the outside of the oiled cloth area, careful not to get it onto its surface. "Mother, come and...no!" she yelled at Coutinnea who had started to remove herself. "Stay connected until I've sealed this." Kashha nodded to the injured area, making Coutinnea jump; she re-attached her energy to that of her husband's, frowning. "Mother, can you smear this on the wound, keeping it thick along the blackened area, while I remove the jar?" Kamera moved into position, watching Kashha move things away from the area they had the Aelf secured within, with her fingers ready.

Kashha coated her own hands with the lamp oil, and lit a small candle by Steph's injured hand with her mind. "OK Soren, when I say go, I want you to flip the jar up, then take the rag from Kamera so you can oil the area along the rim. As soon as that's done, I will light the oil to seal them in." She looked up at him directly, making eye contact. "Do not let go of the jar, under any circumstances." She looked at each of them, to confirm their silent nods of understanding. "Coutinnea," she added, "do not let go of the connection, or they will jump into you," she said quickly, unable to help herself, and winked at both Kamera and Soren. The female Llyach Aelf would need that thought in her mind, for Kashha was certain that what came next would surely scare the life out of her, and sure as hel the kid was going to pass out again anyways.

"Do it now!" Kashha yelled. Soren raised up the jar, turning it towards the cloth, running the surface with the opposite hand onto the oiled cloth. Kashha lit the cloth simultaneously and held onto Soren's hands to ground him as the fire seared the rim, popping the seal shut with a sound like fireworks exploding. Kamera pulled the herbs together in a bonding over the wound, and found the suction of live cells damaged by the organisms foaming up like a volcano beginning to erupt and overflow down the sides of his skin.

"Stay focused Coutinnea, don't let go!" Kashha yelled over the popping noises. The jar that Soren held began to bounce violently as the three entities inside realized they could not escape.

"What the helix?" shouted Soren, as the glass began to fly up then down and move around as if it had a life of its own.

"Hang on, the fumes from the lamp oil will knock them out in about ten more seconds." The glass vaulted away from the skin and hit Soren in the face, and just as Kashha's hands moved to help him hold it steady, he saw something he wished he could take back. For at that moment, tiny little heads covered in teeth inside the glass could be seen sneering and snarling away, with spit dripping down their fangs glaring back at him as if they meant to tear him apart, limb, from bloody limb.

"You little bastards," he yelled, "if you think that's going to make me let go, you've-" Soren slammed both of their hands between his knees and held on for dear life, "got another thing bloody coming you bunch of freaks!" Both Kashha and Soren rode the wild wave of energy that bounced between the high pitched screams coming from inside the vessel, as the entities went crazy, hissing and spitting at them from inside their prison walls of glass.

Small electrical charges popped out and tried to zap Soren's knees, but Kashha had prepared for that, and grounded both of them as the entities inside the container began to slow down and sizzle into nothingness.

The violence of a moment ago, began to fizzle, rocking slightly back and forth, then stopped any movement at all, landing right side up. The entities inside became deathly still, completely knocked out cold, as all four of them relaxed tense muscles and looked from one to each other.

"Cheeky little buggers, aren't they?" Soren began to laugh, followed heartily by Kashandarhh, as the jar finally became absolutely quiet and the final rocking motion had found its peace. But Kashha was not finished with her last sarcastic comment of the day, as she looked at her hands jammed in between Soren's knees in a vice like grip; she smiled warmly, winking at the Dragonlord.

"And you haven't even bought me dinner yet," she quipped. Soren immediately released the jar, going red in the face, letting Kashha take it in her own hands before they both burst out laughing. Kamera could only shake her head at the lunacy.

"Trust you two to find humour in this insanity." Kashha opened up one eye to look for Coutinnea, and found her once again on the ground.

"So much for that warning. Something tells me I haven't made a dent in her disciplinary action." They all stopped and looked at the young Sage lying quietly on the ground once more, making Soren and her again roar with laughter.

Kamera couldn't resist and joined them in their well deserved mirth, now that Stephponias was no longer in any danger. "She really does have quite the disposition." She looked from one to the other, and her smile completely turned from one of innocence to one of sheer amusement. It in turn became fits of laughter, as all three fell over in true hysterics and couldn't have stopped it, if their lives depended on it.

Meanwhile, the sound of laughter had rung out all the way to the field where Tansar had for some reason, gone uncommonly quiet.

CHAPTER TWENTY-ONE

Tameronian Switch

Dyareius had moved towards Tameron the moment Soren finished cursing Quist out. At least that is how he perceived it. It had taken a while to finally calm him down and he had gone begrudgingly with Dyareius, who had promised to cause him further harm if he caused the Dragon any more damage. The last thing he needed was a mutiny on his hands, if the other Dragons took Quist's side, and flatly refused to fly the riders back to Tameron.

The molecules of flux drifted in and out of the air as all twelve moved swiftly along, each rider firmly ensconced on their individual Dragon, following the full-shift back towards the Stones of Panthor. As with many times in the past, their flight proved to be nothing more than the usual amount of energy interference and each settled well on their Dragon's back as they began their arrival into Tameron's final dump-point.

The Dragon-riders popped out one by one through the outer-rings of the circle of stones, and then continued slowly in a uniformed movement towards the battlements, with Dragon wingtips floating gracefully along the treeline.

As each of the riders and their mounts got their bearings, they took a singular slow glide over the village, looking at the land beneath them, before landing in the outer-courtyard. Upon touching solid ground, reining Baelf in, and talons raking the stone causeway, Dyareius had only just turned to speak with the others behind him, when he realized that Soren wasn't with them. He swore under his breath.

A third and fourth Dragon landed with thuds to his right, and touched Tameron's solid ground with their nails racking the old cobbles. Dyareius continued to hold his tongue; there would be plenty of time for questions when all were safely down. Bellowing about something that he could no longer do anything about, was all but meaningless.

Quist flew in riderless, and joined the herd of riders, landing as though Symin was not among the missing, acting nonchalant about the whole affair; aliening with Baelf in their decision not to tell him where Soren had gone. Dyareius insisted that he be the first to speak out, giving him the opportunity to get his bearings before going over and demanding an explanation. The moment they had landed the air smelled different, but Dyareius brushed it off as exhaustion, and took a second step towards the others.

He didn't get one. Instead, Quist met him halfway and bellowed that something wasn't right, just as Assha noticed the difference with its structure that was slightly tilted and not uniformly put in place. Each rider came off their mount with swords instantly in hand, battle ready in the eerie silence that awaited, and permeated the air all around them.

Dyareius cautiously raised his free arm not carrying his sword, to warn the others quietly, and pointed at each of them to move to the covered ground below. Each Dragon-rider made his way in relative silence to the stone edges of the battlements, watching each other and Dyareius for any further commands.

The Dragons simultaneously left the ground without their riders, taking to the air to swerve and dip around the edges of what now appeared to be a completely vacant fortress. Not a single whiff of cooking fire drifted on the air currents, where previously when they had arrived, it had been a thriving village full of life. Even the birds that had ducked for cover and dodged the wingtips of the bigger than normal Dragons when they had first arrived overhead, no longer flew wildly in the village's skies.

It wasn't that they had moved away out of the direct pathway the Dragons had descended on, as their riders had come careening through the Stones of Panthor, it was because not one single bird was occupying

Tameron's skyline at all anymore. It appeared that all life within the vicinity of Tameron had quite simply disappeared the moment they had landed, and nothing breathed a whisper as they began to feel the first tendrils of dread inside their bones.

Dyareius signalled for Markus, who held the highest rank next to his own, to follow the air molecules that they had rode in on to see if he could feel where the residence signatures had disappeared. Markus's eyes shifted to another of the riders, called Gantay, who he found nearest him. He needed a touchstone, and Phaetum was too far away for him to reach. In order for him to reach the other Aelf, Gantay would have to get out of the way. Gantay nodded briefly, and closed his eyes to concentrate on the task, before he allowed Markus to move through him.

Markus had the gift to shift his mind within the spaces between the solar winds, to pick up energy signatures that all Fey beings needed to exist within. Phaetum was a touchstone Aelfan warrior from the Caubertian clan. His body provided all who existed within this galaxy of planets, which circled the Mauntra, the safety and polarity of re-fraction. Without Gantay his power would not have the polarity he needed to succeed. Markus needed Phaetum to begin his search, which meant Gantay needed to get out of the way so he wouldn't get burned, and he needed that direct line into Phaetum's energy twist, without the blockage of Gantay's body.

Gantay quickly shifted backwards as he jumped into the rock wall, allowing the silver from his sword to direct the pathway to Phaetum's loop. The connection found the signature, redirecting Markus's airspace into the direct line of Phaetum's full twist.

Markus floated without body and form, searching for the link that would allow him to decipher the in-between world where substance and form would find the line to all that had vanished from the area. Unfortunately, something prevented him from detecting life, and some part of it no matter how small, should have been visible at this molecular level. Nothing he saw made any sense of what was in evidence below him. All trace of resident signatures had been wiped clean. Not one atom remained within the air, and it felt like something or someone had literally sucked the life from Tameron into the jettisons of actual space, and left it bare.

He moved out of the castle that housed his friends and followed the airwaves through the outlying village, which the townspeople had built to be next to their protector and Liege. Everywhere that he went, he was greeted with the same empty hollowness. Things from the air looked very much the same, as if something had moved through the entire village and literally sucked it dry, leaving a hollowed out husk to rot and dry out in the heated rays of the celestial quorums of their own star's heart.

It was the oddest feeling, Tameron had been a bustling township when they had left, no more than five days ago. Now it was a ghost village, consisting of nothing but stone and — then it hit him. This wasn't real. There wasn't even a scrap of paper out of place? It was immaculate, freshly scrubbed within an inch of its life, with not so much as a food scrap lying around or a dung heap seeping with manure flies. Nothing within Tantaris was like this; it was a fake, an illusion made to appear as if it was Tameron. He retreated back into the flowing umbilicus that attached itself to his energy core. He found his airspace within Phaetum's lifeline, and grabbed hold of his twist, unravelling the link to his conscious mind and bringing him fully back to his conscious state.

Phaetum yanked Gantay forward, bringing all three within the space they originally found themselves to be in, and watched Markus catch his breath. His face was a bit ashen in colour, as his lungs took on the molecules reserved more for their own physiology than that of the twist. Gantay gasped and grabbed hold of the wall, taking in huge amounts of air as Markus looked up from his angular position, realizing just how long he had been gone. He always recovered from these transfers faster than his friend. He turned to Dyareius with his hands on his knees, trying to breathe with easier breaths.

Over his shoulder, Gantay continued to gasp for air as Markus spoke quickly over the rattle. "It's not real, it's an illusion; a really good one at that, but they missed a very important part of our true-selves." Dyareius looked at Markus, frowning with the question in his head. Markus caught his breath and turn once again to the group. "Stuff!" Markus spat the word out, as Gantay finally caught up to his own breath.

"What stuff?" Dyareius looked even more puzzled.

"Everything that we own, you know, STUFF!" said Marcus.

"You mean the village is empty?" Marcus looked at him from the level of his knees and nodded rather affirmatively.

"Yup, I mean gone-zo, kaput, and furthermore… arrivederci." Markus stepped back and swore.

"Shit, now what?" He moved, placing his fingers in his hair, and accidentally scratched his elbow on the rock wall behind him. Cassmare swore.

"Everyone, did you see that?" Cassmare pointed to the wall. "Everyone come here, do it again Markus. Everyone watch."

"Do what again?" Marcus looked up, puzzled at him as he rubbed his arm.

"Scrape your arm on the wall again."

"Why? It still hurts from the first time."

"Never mind, just humour us and do it."

"Fine, but I still don't get it." Dyareius watched as Markus slid his arm slowly across the rock-face of the battlements, letting it disappear and then re-enter the place where he had pushed it through. It shimmered slightly, interrupting a basic power link to whatever threw the image onto the rock, and quickly tried to reset itself while the Aelves gasped with an odd sense of tribulation.

"What the Gods is this?" Dyareius swore. "How come we can feel it and see it now?"

"Majik can't be interrupted with force," Assha replied, smiling, "but it can be scratched to punch a hole in its form." Dyareius grinned as Markus once again repeated the manoeuvre, and then removed his arm as the rock wall returned to its former intact form.

"So, what do you think?"

"I think," said Markus, "we now have what appears to be the upper hand." He smirked and pointed his fingers at his eyes, in a gesture of watching everything around them. "So, shall we continue?" Dyareius drew his sword and gestured for all of them to follow him, as he walked behind in the direction Markus was heading.

"We need to talk with Quist first; after all it affects all of us and includes the Dracore more than any of us, if I know anything about rocks."

"Humm," coughed one of the Dragons in the background where it had been listening, before Quist broke into the conversation and voiced his own opinion on the matter of the rocks.

"You may be more right than you know." Quist's voice echoed in the location the Aelven warriors had started to gather in.

"Did you hear what we said, Quist?" Dyareius spoke openly in front of the others, so everyone heard what he said to the Dragon.

"Every word, including the actual movements and sounds you and your men have made since you departed from the field where you first left us." Quist sounded like he was right beside them.

"Where are you?" It was Markus who spoke up this time.

"All of us are up in the air, at various parts of the landscape, searching the sights around the entire city of what appears to have been a complete copy of your village." Dyareius looked up, shielding his eyes from the Mauntra's rays. One of their Dragons flew by, or rather soared by overhead. He was closer to the ground than Dyareius would have liked him to be. He wished they'd try and take more care, instead of going about like a bunch of Flight Monkeys dancing from a Fickletree to the ridge of a Mongolian Ridgemaw.

"Is that you Quist?"

"No, I'm over by the lake; that's Aantare." Assha looked up, shielding his eyes, and yelled at Aantare to take it easy before someone got hurt. Dyareius was a little puzzled.

"Did he say lake?" He looked around at all of them, mouthing the words to them that Quist had said. "What lake? We don't have a lake."

"You do now," Quist growled, a little amused, with a slight slant of sarcasm.

"But that's impossible, why would anyone who has gone out of their way to make us think that this is Tameron, go and put a bloody lake in where it doesn't belong?" Markus looked at Dyareius, then back at the others.

"You would think that the illusion would be better suited to actually follow the guidelines of its realistic environment; especially now, when we don't have one at home." Markus shrugged and moved his hands in a wide gesture, as he was talking to Dyareius. Dyareius seemed to be still stuck in deep thought, on the lake Quist had seen, and wondered why they would make something so realistic, and make a simple mistake of this calibre, within visual sight to the castle walls?

"Have you noticed anything else?" Quist continued patiently, as he listened to the Aelves below talking to themselves, ignoring the obvious as he flew underneath it.

"Why, are you seeing doubles of us as well?" Phaetum chimed in, as the others seemed to be hung up on the lake theory.

"Not of you, but a double of something besides your rocks," Quist answered the other rider.

"You Dragons never just spit it out," Phaetum said under his breath.

"You haven't noticed, any of you?" Quist put in, sarcastically again.

"No, what?" Dyareius finally replied, hushing the group so he could hear what the Dragon had said, trying to ignore Phaetum's sarcasm.

"The sun!"

"Quist, I don't have time for riddles."

"Ah right, you don't call it that, hum….could it be the big ball of heat that you see every morning when you wake up. You know, the hot star that heats your days; that Maun-thingy!"

"What is a sun?" Phaetum whispered to the others under his breath, smirking a bit, while the explanation was still forthcoming, and then choked on it when he realized what he was pointing to.

"You mean the Mauntra? What about it?" Dyareius asked as he stepped out to see what all the fuss was about. "Freaken flipping Coir Kat crap, how did that happen?" He signalled for them all to have a look. They stepped out around the corner and looked up into the sky into the face of what appeared to be not one, but two of them.

"What the … hey, look,"

"Faeman come over here, take a look at that." Something had definitely changed since they had first arrived, and seeing both home-stars hanging rigidly above in the morning sky, was a little unsettling to say the least. They absolutely, unequivocally were not there when they had first come through their shift, or they would have definitely noticed something was indeed wrong before now.

"That can't be good." Assha had been a little quieter than normal as soon as things had started to feel wrong. His calling was sorcery within the group, and his bones could feel its stink surround all of them, as it slowly tried to drag them in. He had worked with majik since he was just learning to walk, and much younger than anyone he had known in his schooling years. He had a very good teacher, and this teacher had been one of the best that this Fey realm had ever heard of, and never seen.

The Aelf master had come from the Island of Tayose, where he belonged to an ancient race of Fey known as the Synotays. A long time ago the legend of this race was written on cave paintings throughout their beautifully sculptured caverns, deep within the Tayoseian Mounds of Tayose's smaller group of off-shore islands. Legend says that they were able to travel through shift-points within those very old caverns, and those very rocks took them to many different worlds in their individual star systems within this end of the Goetutonias Galaxy.

Assha had been raised by them, and was rescued as an orphan, living in the jungles of one of those islands on the planet of Naunas. He had first come to Tantaris through one of those doorways, when the Dragonlords were called into being, back before any of them yet had been selected as riders. The Tuatha had taken each of the best that the Fey worlds could provide, and from those they chose only a special few had made it into the Tuatha's special forces that Dyareius had commanded.

Assha was the first; he had been chosen even before Dyareius had been picked. But his world within his own mind refused to accept their offer as commander of the riders. He didn't want that kind of control over anything, when he had such strong majik in his veins. Assha would only change his mind to join later, after much negotiation and agreement that Dyareius was the one put into that position. It had been the right decision for everyone involved, for now it gave him what he would need to work silently away from the others, without having any interruptions. He could not have fulfilled that destiny to the best of his ability had he been the one in charge.

But right now, during everything that was going on, Assha was worried. Someone had gone through an awful lot to get them out of the way and away from the village that they called home. He didn't think the charade was meant not to be discovered; he thought maybe it just needed to last long enough to get them out of their shift without sounding the alarm. If he had the time to think, he would have caught it sooner; in doing so they could have easily caught the tail end of the molecules and jumped back through to the other side.

He also thought that in staying here for those extra moments after coming out of shift, they were more than likely locked out from returning the way they had come in. He'd have to bring this up to Dyareius soon, but for now, as they all did, he needed to know how strong the majik was. And for that, he needed Dyareius to send him away to check a few things out. He needed that distance to be far away from the others and their questions, which would be running rampant in all of them, and mess up the signals that only he could visually see.

The illusion had been created and set for all of them, but one alone may be able to punch through the barriers that comprised this world of make believe. Well, maybe the others might not have been able to do it, but he definitely would, if he was not among them.

"Can you send me away from the troop?" Dyareius knew immediately who was talking to him. He knew his group of Aelfs like the back of his hand. If Assha needed to ask the question, he had a pretty good reason for doing so. The fact that he spoke within Dyareius's mind telepathically, instead of out loud for everyone to hear, made the urgency of the issue self-evident.

"Assha," Dyareius spoke quickly before it came to be directly linked to the airways of Theiry's attention, "can you join with Aantare and fly over to the west-field to check the strength of the net that's holding this illusion in place?" Assha moved, whistling for Aantare to meet him the moment the words passed Dyareius's lips. He didn't look at anyone except Dyareius, and to him he nodded; had he hesitated for even a moment, or had his timing been off for a split-second ahead of the words, Theiry would have picked it up, and he would have to deal with another way to get around this illusion. He didn't want even a whisper of evidence that someone was looking through their visual effects from another perspective. What he needed done had to be accomplished without anyone being aware beforehand. He couldn't give away the vibrations of the unusual talent that allowed someone of his kind to be looking in through the backdoor of the screen set before them.

On the flip side, Theiry was the Sedger by trade, and was used as an Earth Seer for the Dragon clan of riders he had been chosen to ride with. He could pick up and decipher body movements along with various changing temperatures within their individual moods, then pick up its deception or intended course of action from any being that it came from, alien or Fey alike.

Theiry had been born into a large family of Sedgers from the Kanoie Clan, who were considered to be the gypsy offshoots of the old city of Fomor. His parents used to travel throughout the region and had been asked to take him to Tamerk when he was about six or seven years of age, to begin his formal training. There were only a select few that had ever been designated to be able to train such gifted children within the Fey worlds, and when Tamerk had first arrived he had been sent only the best of the young minds of that group, and the only ones the Tuatha would be able to use as part of their elite grouping of Dragonite lordlings. Tamerk had only taken a handful of those young gifted minds throughout the years; with each of the little ones possessing many different abilities and gifts from their particular Fey hereditary roots — Theiry's being one of the strongest, next to Assha.

Theiry's training may have started earlier than most, but his circumstances were far from ordinary. The Tuatha, who had their sights on many of the young warriors, had tried to keep Theiry's abilities out of the reach of Balor, who at that time still inhabited the Fomor village during certain times of the year. The family had been nervous around the angry King, and had taken the drastic measure of moving away from the safety of the village wards, which was unprecedented in itself, to keep their little one safe.

Balor had contracted spies within his notoriously crooked band of thieves, and they had been getting too close to discovering the young Sedger and his family, living not far from the borders of one of his more entrenched encampments. So, when his family had become known to one of the troops the Tuatha had enlisted to watch the youngsters and their families who had been forced to flee, they had given word that they were coming to retrieved the young Sedger to start his training at an unheard of age.

It hadn't taken a lot of persuading to get the family to allow the Tuatha to bring him to Tamerk at an earlier age than first discussed, to cultivate his gift to a higher level. The night before, Balor had sent one of his thugs into the night to retrieve the boy, and during that raid one of Theiry's younger brothers was badly injured. The family had fought off Balor's ruffian, and had only just taken more water on to move to a higher encampment come daylight, when the Tuatha had sent their best scouts to bring the family into their protection.

His family was to this day, protected by their warriors, even though Balor was long dead and buried. But the past has a way of bringing things back into play, and Theiry's gifts were not something they could well have done without. So his family was still somewhere along the western cliffs of the Telpphaea falls, safely tucked away with others of their kind. It was here that they found themselves living in a much more secluded and safer encampment that protected many of the Dragon-riders' families and their loved ones, from the wandering thieves and raiders of a lost and very insane king of old Fomorian rule.

Theiry had been taken to the Tuatha training academy shortly after his schooling. Then, when he had passed all the Tuatha's elite squadron's highest military training, they incorporated him into their Dragon trials, when their Dracore selections had been chosen. It was here that all thirteen riders had been introduced to each other, and the first time any of them had actually met one another up close and personal. They would be living and working as one within the mind of the one Aelven special forces unit that needed all of them to think as a solitary mind, or at least die in the trying.

So when Assha needed to get away from Theiry's mind, it was something that was never as simple a thing as one might think it would be. Before long, the Sedger would find his signature trail, floating high above in the upper airways of his trace. This time that could not happen; Assha was careful not to leave any part of an inquiring mind pondering why he had left, as he quickly moved out of sight, majikally severing the bond that would show the others where he was.

Assha moved quickly, and disappeared around the corner, hiding his intent from Theiry's field of vision in an instant. Aantare was accustomed to his unusual drift-points, and never hesitated when being asked to do something for his powerful rider. He hovered for a moment above, then landed near the rocks, as Assha leapt aboard in one fluid motion, before taking to the air away from an area that Theiry would be able to link with his body or facial movements.

"Aantare, could you take me to the lake that you Dragons saw from the air?" Assha asked. Aantare moved into the upper air currents swiftly, gliding within a short wingspan of flight, landing by the lakeshore and releasing his rider within the mossy thickets. "Now go quickly, and keep a lookout in the upper fields. Stay within range of my whistle in case I need out of here in a hurry, or as soon as Dyareius calls us back."

Aantare jumped back into the wind, careening towards the others at dizzying speed, letting his wings take the brunt of air molecules that would damage and fracture any of the other Dragon's bone structures in their small grouping of Dracore. His belonging to Assha was not coincidental, he was chosen for this due to his uniqueness alone.

Dyareius watched Assha's Dragon fly high above without his rider, and return to the others at the far side of the Western shore. He noticed that a barrier had gone up, protecting Assha from the mind link that he shared with each of his warriors the moment Assha had got airborne. He looked quickly towards the area that Assha was in, and hoped whatever he had in mind worked quickly, before Theiry picked it up for himself. Dyareius searched briefly to see if something might have gotten through, but nothing could be felt within Theiry's mind that he would construe as a problem, so Dyareius moved on to reduce the chances of that coming into play.

He instructed both Theiry and Markus to move from the battlement, and work towards the wellhead that Tameron used to draw its water from. It would keep Theiry busy for about fifteen microns, and it would be something his men would expect him to check on soon enough. Both Aelfs moved quickly away towards the area, without a second thought as to the reason, carrying their swords at the ready but taking the other hand to their knives, just in case something changed their mood and they suddenly had to fight.

The wellhead was located just past the main barn where the castle kept their prize horses paddocked, off the side of the old stone wall. It had once been used to keep the fortress free of crosswinds, which Tameron was known for. They would suddenly without warning in the colder months of the year, just blow up out of the blue, during the harshest times of the Cailleach Bheur's arrival and the entire village's equestrian race would come running in out of the pastures for protection from her wrath. She was an angry wind, and the barn had not been torn down when another much bigger had been built to replace the old one. It stood as a reminder of days long past, when it carried the weight of several newly born Waterhorses, after their mothers had been blown away from the Island of Mangoesa in a full on hurricane one year, and were stranded after they made landfall out along the eastern shores of Kartouche.

The barn smelled of freshly cut hay at the moment, with tiny fragments of animal dung still clinging to the tufts of grass left to keep the stalls clean along the southern wall, as they moved past the opened stalls within an older enclosure. The horses would have still been out in their summer high pastures at this time of year, but strangely enough, no hay was presented within the haylofts that should have been full to overflowing in the overhead storage lofts.

Dust permeated the hay attic, but nothing could be visually seen that would explain the strong odour of newly cut field grass, anywhere inside the entire area. Where could the freshly cut grasses be hiding, with such a strong binding of the hay smells in an entire barn full of non-existent field grass? The illusion was a worthy one, to bring in smells within the apex of its core of falsified atoms; they would return later to try and figure this one out, along with the others they were sure they would come across in time. They moved on without finding any more trace of the missing bales.

They soon reached the outer-rim of the main rampart's fresh water well, and shoved the lid with its carved engravings, sideways off the top of the low walls, with a hard kick of their boots. It should have been heavy; instead it flew off and landed several feet away, crashing down along the rocks piled high by the old water trough.

Both Aelfs righted themselves at the last minute and came precariously close to falling into the damn thing, knocking their balance off kilter. They looked at each other questioningly, realizing their luck had sustained them from almost falling head first straight down the shaft, with the non-existent resistance of the fake lid. Theiry went and picked it up, banging on its texture as it lay sprawled over in the stones, and found it to be made out of some kind of material that resembled a hardened leather-hide.

He came back, carrying it in his hands, with a questioning look on his face, which he aimed at Markus. The lid was having none of it, squirming easily free from Theiry's grasp, then having gained its freedom, righted itself and tore off into the bush, leaving them looking on with astonishment at Theiry's empty hands. 'What the heck is that?" both looked to the retreating creature, then back to each other.

"Ok, that is just plain weird. Do you think that maybe someone doesn't want us out here?" Theiry questioned.

"Who in the hel knows what's going on. But I'm staying until we figure it out." Markus responded as he watched several trees suddenly move out of the creatures way as it tried to hide. They peered back into the hole, finding not even a trace of water in the basin that had always housed the freshest of water for the fortress since it had first been drilled. Normally, the water should have been about 20 feet down, instead they found the bottom at about seven feet, covered in bare earth, looking as if not a trace of water had ever been in this wellhead in its entire life.

"Yeh, that can't be good." Markus shook his head. Something else was there in its place; something very similar to what looked like the roughened edges belonging to some sort of cave. "What do you think?" Markus looked at Theiry.

"It looks like whoever built this place didn't think beyond the surface above, so unless I'm not thinking straight, I'd say let's go below and find out what its hiding." Theiry answered, and cocked his head to the side, shifting his head towards Markus. "So, shall we?" Both grinned at each other.

"Absolutely, you?"

"Right freaking behind you!" Both Aelfs jumped in, landing easily, not even jarring the armaments that were tucked within reach of their hands.

"Smells like something damp, with a bit of sulphur mixed in with the mud." Markus said, as he rubbed the muck together in between his forefinger and thumb, bringing it up to his nose.

"Majik has that smell; it's even in the walls." Theiry replied, turning to look at him.

THE BEGINNING

"I agree, but come and look at this." Markus motioned for Theiry to join him. "There's light down here, it should be getting dimmer not brighter." He picked up whatever was covering the walls with his knife tip, and lifted the feather-light moss in front of his face and brush it aside. "What is this stuff? The whole area's covered with this algae-like material, which glows in the dark when you move towards it."

Theiry knew what it was, and had not seen it since the last time he had run into one of their cities up top-side of another mound, far away on a different planet.

"This is Ferrishyn moss, Markus. It's best not to touch the stuff." Markus was picking away with the tip of his knife and had dislodged something else off the walls, passing it to Theiry on the edge of his knife. It was one of the mushroom lichen stones that typically accompanied the Ferrishyn moss; interwoven and symbiotic with one another. It was used as a mapping stone, and mimicked the signatures of the clans that owned the tunnels in the area, giving other clans a heads up that the territory was taken.

Theiry picked up the stone Markus gave him, and brought it up to his nostrils to pick up the scent of whatever clan had built the tunnels within the stones of this darkened place. "It only grows near cities of the Dark Sidhe, and this clan is one that I'm not familiar with. Hum, strange?" Theiry said, as he dropped the stone along the edge of the tunnel. It landed hard against the sides of the tunnel walls and instantly grew legs, crawling back into the wall it had just been absconded from, before disappearing. Both Aelves shivered as the thing moved out of sight. Markus motioned for both of them to go back.

"We'd better get Dyareius down here; I don't feel like walking into whatever is waiting for us without backup from everyone topside. Come on, let's go back, this is just getting weirder by the minute." Theiry nodded in agreement and the two of them turned around and started back.

They had just arrived at the bottom of the pit where they had jumped in from the surface world above, when they realized they weren't going anywhere in that direction any time soon. The moment they reached to begin their climb to the surface, an invisible entity immediately started to weave a thin sheet of a clandestine web-like barrier over the entrance, blocking their way from above. They were completely trapped at this entrance point, and would have to find an alternative exit-point through whatever lay in the corridors below. Markus swore as they watched the web form itself throughout the entire rounded drill point of the wellhead, literally removing any chance that anyone would be able to use that exit in the foreseeable future.

The Aelfs were now forced to make their way through the tunnels below, and by the look of things they had already seen from the inside of this strange cave, there was somewhere down below a very clear entrance to an underground city of darkened covenized Shea. Theiry let out a hiss as they moved cautiously back the way they had just come, feeling the hair on the back of his neck stand straight up, as he felt strange eyes on both of them.

"Why do they always have to form a damn coven? It always takes the fun out of finding them." Marcus only growled, as they turned reluctantly and moved back the way they came. What clan was living deep within the soil, and carved their home out of the bare earth right underneath Tameron's main gate, was anyone's guess. But one thing was certain, whatever lay in wait in the tunnels ahead would undoubtedly lead them straight to the home of the resident Sidhe, and its earthen hoard of Faery fangs.

Up on the surface, Assha moved silently around the western part of the lakeshore. He put his hand in the water, and felt the cool liquid slide through his fingertips. He tasted its texture, to see whether it was fresh or salt. It was salty. Assha frowned slightly; Tameron was about nine miles from the sea's actual shoreline, so unless something had recently decided to dig an underground trench into the resident Fireworm's turf, this shouldn't be here. He hadn't heard of any saltwater rivers finding a home in one of the old lava flows, which ran as far back as the backside of the Capourian range of mountains that Tameron was sheltered by; at least none this close to their village. But then again, this lake shouldn't exist either, and he now stood ankle deep in its clear blue salty waters.

He needed to get to work before the illusion took on a more sinister approach and changed again. He moved back onto shore and took a pinch of Muscle Toe Root out of the leather satchel that was strung around his neck, and flung it high above in the air towards the waters of the lake. It turned bright orange and burst into tiny fragments of silver oxide. When the water absorbed the mineral, a single strand of white crystal could be seen weaving itself around the north shore on the far-side of the lake.

He took out the Stone of Kaliea that had been given to him by one of his Earth Elemental friends who used to visit Naunas, and placed it about eye level above the lapping water, and let it hover. It stayed in place, as he watched the crystal move slowly along the far shore, and then dipped its edges into the lake before it vanished into the treeline.

The stone had come from Tantaris's second moon Kaliea, and it had seeker properties that would reveal the true forms of whatever could be seen through its series of centrifuged revolving rings. The matrix worked far better over water, rotating and bobbing about like a replica of the inner workings of a mobile of planetoids and Mauntra's he had once seen on the Island of Tayose. That one had been placed outside in the gardens of their solariums, near the waterfalls where he had spent many hours during times of rest away from his studies, watching it. It had fascinated him, and he had spent many a night taking note of how it moved and shifted around in the air currents, each revolution arriving at the precise conclusion of the answer held before it.

It had been years since he had thought of it, and now as he watched the stone hover in its warbling way, it reminded him of his time at the school and the friends that he had left behind so long ago. He took the leather pouch he covered the stone with, and tucked it into his shirt so he wouldn't drop it into the waters of the lake. When the stone was wrapped up and tucked away within his cloak, it lay flat and pressed itself within a smaller amulet bag which now dangled around his neck encrusted in the covered etchings of lapis-lazuli. The stone had been easy to use, and would instantly expand itself outwards when the proper panels were opened in the right sequence. It used the particles of those panels to amplify the inner rings, giving visualization abilities of whatever it was seeing into something that could be visibly seen by the naked eye of the holder.

Assha stepped forward into the lake about a boot print in length, and looked through the glass. Everything went completely hazy in texture, further obscuring the scene before him, as if something had fogged up the mirror in front of its orbit. He moved a little to the left and re-centred the stone, but got the same result. That was odd; he had never encountered it not being in its crystal clear state before. He slid the rings a bit the other way, and found that he had become slightly elevated. He noticed as he looked down that he had stepped from his original position onto a series of pebbles that littered the lake shore along the shallows. Although he was still in the water, he was slightly elevated and not actually touching the lake's bottom, and the circle wouldn't clear itself until he moved back into the lake's silted soil. He stepped sideways, back into the smaller versions of the stones, and it cleared itself immediately as soon as his boot heels came away from the larger stones. That was new.

He ignored the slight adjustment to his frame, as he re-adjusted the rings to his newly planted height, and tried to step onto the stone's central alignment under his teetering feet — feeling it wobble back and forth. It seemed precariously balanced at first, before he was able to gain his stability back, and sync into the perfect equilibrium of the rock's surface. He slowed the rocking motion along his wet boots to its central pivot point, and fully balanced himself in flawless symmetrical rhythm to the rock beneath him. Most Aelves had that unique ability without even having to think about it; his this morning, seemed somewhat askew, and was quite capable of dumping him into the lake at any moment.

He smiled slowly, thinking about that, and almost fell ass over tea kettle into the damn lake. He needed to focus if he was going to get this right. He redirected his attention to balancing himself, and waited until the stone stopped rocking before he continued on.

He closed one eye and looked with his open eye, millitrons from the central eye-piece, focusing right into the middle section of the rings' newest reference point. That directed him to visualize the blur that he had seen and bring it clearly up in the glass that now focused perfectly across the lake to the north shore. The thing had re-appeared from the woods, and was once again sitting just above the water's surface, undulating away with the surface ripples. Assha held his breath as a single crystallized strand of some kind of fibre remained motionless in the air, like it was caught in the movement of the stone's centre-faced rings, and lay hypnotized by its influence.

It hovered for several minutes remaining perfectly still, with only the wind giving it motion. That gave him time to recalibrate the lens of the eye-piece, and notice it was covered in a feather like mineral of finely honed Tameronian lace. It also had several smaller multi-coloured gemstones of amethyst, aquamarine, and Apophyllited-Larimar flowering outward along its rim. As he glanced further along its frame, he saw sharpened blades of Kyanite protruding from its breath, like blackened spear heads sharpened to a point facing outwards, producing the look of swords poised for some kind of battle.

"What the kip?" he whispered into the breeze that had picked up, watching the image reflect in the last stranded rays of the Mauntra, beginning to disappear through the tree foliage. The light caught it in its awkward dance within the stones, continuously shimmering its fleeting tentacles between the ring's needles, but never moving more than a few inches from one side to another. He sighed and took the rings to the left again to refocus, stepping away from the rocks that threw him off centre. The lens went opaque again.

"What the kiper-figg is wrong with this stupid thing?" he laughed, thinking of Tayose. He had learned that swear word from one of the older Aelves of his clan, who had used it for almost everything. It wasn't until he himself became a Dragonlord that the word had resurfaced and become part of his vocabulary. The other Aelves used an old earth term called hel. He didn't know the meaning of it, but it sounded just as funny to him as he was sure this had sounded to them, and on occasion he used it just because it was there.

It was during this event, that he realized what was wrong with the central lens. Each time he stepped onto a larger pebble at the bottom of the lake, the clarity fogged up. The moment he went down off the elevated stone, everything became clear once more. But still, one thing puzzled him. The Stone of Kaliea had always allowed the thing he was watching to keep moving. It didn't have a pause lever on it, so why was the strand not moving as he watched? The only thing he could think of was that the water must have amplified not only his ability to see better, but his movements as well. If this were true, then the crystal strand was not a majikal projection at all, but a living sentient being, which was very much aware it was being observed by him.

His foot shifted beneath him, knocking his balance sideways, and as he tried to re-balance himself from the rocking motion of the waves of the lake he had kicked up, he took his eyes off the lens for no more than a few seconds and the lens went opaque again. When his eyes came back to the lens, he found the strand had moved into a different position. It seemed to have moved more than one hundred feet away from its original place, and as he re-calibrated its heading he could see it was coming directly away from the north shore, and headed straight for him. Crap!

He needed to get a closer look at this thing from a higher vantage point; one that didn't end in his demise, should it prove to be dangerous. He whistled for Aantare, putting distance from where this creature appeared to be moving in the water, as he quickly moved up the beach area and back to the thicket where his Dragon could land. Aantare didn't come; he waited a while longer, moving further away from the beach into the safety of the hedgerow, and whistled a few more times. Nothing moved, even the airspace felt heavy around him. He watched the skies and would occasionally see one of the other war Dragons flying about, but not even they heard him as he tried to get their attention from far below. He started for the castle on foot.

He didn't get far!

CHAPTER TWENTY-TWO

The Shadow of Aperthan

Meanwhile, Dyareius could feel that something had changed within the various degrees of activity his men around him were starting to react to. He could virtually trace each and every movement they had made since he had sent them off to explore the areas that had held interest to him, in the illusion of this village he had thought was Tameron.

But once leaving his side, and after reaching a certain distance, they seemed to be affected by something just out of reach that was floating in the air of this fictitious compound. After he had sent Markus and Theiry off to explore the well and away from the movements of Assha's deception, he had sent Cassmare, Faeman, and Kaprey to the eastern wall to check that area for deceit of the stones' illusional abilities. His main reason was so that he could have eyes on every part of the village, which had continued to hold up the illusion, and kept repeating itself to him in indirect ways.

He needed Bynffore and Elyizeam to squat at the south gate of whatever this complex was, and sent them on their way. Gantay and Phaetum, who worked together as one mind, had remained beside Dyareius to keep him from being separated entirely from the others. He needed them together here with him, in case the situation changed and he was required to shift out of here quickly, and retrieve the others before something made it impossible to do so. Gantay could do that quickly with his ability, but he always travelled better with Phaetum in tandem, as did the others with their own unique pairings inside their own rider mentality.

Dyareius's ability to pull that kind of load was why he was their Lieutenant, not because of service rendered as others might have thought. Each of his warriors had their unique gifts; his own pulled everyone together mentally into his own, within the collectional mind of each other's mental networking. He used it to give the direction that needed to find the centre of the chaos and control its function, as he fit it efficiently into his level of expertise and modified its placement. That was who he was, and having found the right mixture, it had worked and progressed slightly for each of them, in tandem to his own chemistry.

Assha was different. Only Assha had the ability to throw his voice back to Dyareius. The others could hear him, but only Assha could talk to him. This made for a very unique bonding between the two, and it was one he trusted without question during his time as their leader.

Dyareius could feel the others' whereabouts at all times inside his mind, and right now both Markus and Theiry had just dropped off and out of his link without any warning. He had never had that happen before; something was just wrong about the feel of this whole damn place. He called to the Dragons to see if they could spot the pair by the old well. They didn't respond. It was at that time he truly realized ... they were in serious trouble.

With his call going unheeded, and the Dragons refusing to answer, he felt their molecules shift away and disappear from Tantaris airspace, leaving their energy to dissolve amongst the wind in that flicker of a majikal breath that gets produced amongst nothing more than a Zephyr's wind. He yelled for Dragon and riders alike, without caution or care for who else might be in the vicinity and had eyes on them.

"Assha, you need to come back now!" he reiterated, shouting into the open air.

"I know," Assha said instantly, back inside his mind, "calm down, or whatever it is will know they've been found out, and will undoubtedly cause further trouble."

"I think we've passed that milestone, don't you?" Dyareius yelled back at him, trying to take control of his emotions. However, Assha kept his cool and continued watching the lake behind him while responding to Dyareius's shouting.

"Aantare wouldn't come either. When I called, he didn't answer his whistle, so I tried to get the others' attentions as they flew by overhead. They seemed to be watching something near the treeline, but from my vantage point, I just couldn't see what that was. I thought it very odd they didn't respond to my voice, so I used the touchstone inside my shirt to get their attention. Even that didn't work, so unfortunately I'm going to have to hoof it on foot and I won't get there before the others."

Dyareius didn't need to think anymore; he needed to get everyone together quickly and away from wherever they had landed, and whatever reality they had gotten themselves involved with that had started to circle its proverbial horses and drag them in.

"Can you just hurry?"

"I'm already on my way," Assha said.

"Where were they flying?" Dyareius asked, as an afterthought.

"Over by the lake," Assha responded.

"Damn it, how far out are you?" Assha's link got disconnected and disappeared, as the others in range started to arrive — Dyareius began to swear rather loudly, to no one in particular. "Everyone that can hear me, that can get back, do it bloody now. Something's wrong, and I'll be damned if anyone gets killed on my watch!" Dyareius yelled rather intentionally to anyone who would listen.

Dyareius knew he needed more time here to understand what this was, but not when his riders were disappearing faster than he could call them back. It was at this time that Cassmare, Faeman, and Kaprey ran into his field of vision from the far side of the keep, where they had also felt the shiver of something move towards them as they sidestepped out of its path and it passed them by. He felt it disappear around the corner as several of the others nearby projected their molecules of arrival towards him, but up till now he hadn't laid eyes on them.

The beginning molecules of another transferral came into play as Bynffore and Elyizeam materialized out of nowhere, in the middle of a full out run, towards Gantay and Phaetum. They had been literally pushed into the shift where it directed them onwards and they fell headfirst into the drift. Both Gantay and Phaetum turned to meet them, as they rounded the nearest archway overhead, while something pushed them into another shift and send them stumbling toward the group. But before they even fully materialized towards them, the six remaining Aelfs who had made it to the rampart watched in horror as something claimed them backwards through the drift point. The two vanished from sight, never fully completing the transformation with a look of surprise on their faces. Each of them carried transferral crystals and they should have protected the Aelves from anything that would cause them harm. Those crystals could now be seen lying ruptured on the ground, as the energy inside dissolved into the atmosphere, rendering them useless.

Dyareius stopped the others, who had tried to move towards the Aelfs, as Bynffore and Elyizeam disappeared right in front of their faces. Particles of what could best be described as feathers floated down from the area they had previously occupied, as all the remaining Aelves watched in abject horror, skidding to stop just millimetres from the exit point.

Since the Fey signature was no longer in play, there was nothing to hold anything back from the particles of space that had been set into motion. They quickly reversed the flow, and began to jettison anything within range out into space. The voided space quickly duplicated what was in the area, and was replaced by several more drifting feathers of another foreign waterfowl not belonging to this part of Waters Deep that had rained down in their place, and littered the ground they originally had been standing on. But before they could come to terms with it in their minds, and conceive of the actuality of what had just happened, the ground underneath them began to shatter and break.

The earth beneath their feet at once split wide-open, sending the remaining Dragon-riders to their knees. The ground moved so violently, with the initial wave of what appeared to be the sudden onset of an earthquake, that their swords were magnetically pulled from their hands as if something had yanked them physically from their fingers.

They had been through this before with Tamerk, and were in no mood for a repeat. However, before they were able to connect with the physical aspect of their metal blades moving out of their reach, their bodies were physically thrown and dragged away in the opposite direction. Instinctively they tried to right themselves, as it pulled them backwards, rolling along like a fish caught on a hook in the raging torrent. However, the invisible hands seemed to have them well under their control, as if they were protecting them from being injured by the sharp blades, and took the swords further away out in the back eddies of the swirling current, as the ground roared all around them, bucking and kicking itself into further turmoil. Then, if that wasn't enough, as the earth continued to roll and pitch their bodies in all directions, their swords began moving as if something had changed its mind, threatening to pierce them as they swayed, and dangled, coming dangerously close to impaling them. Majikal guidance lifted each of them into the air, throwing them about in the currents for a while, until they got bored and lost interest in their little play. Something then released the majik they had assembled around them, as the ground continued to rumble, threatening to uproot the trees nearest them, and project them and the swords in an upside-down spiral straight for their heads.

Roots could be heard ripping off from the main stem of the largest of those trees, as whatever hung thickly in the air got caught in the majikal mix. The swords lost their momentum and shot straight into the earth at their feet, burying them completely, while the ground continued to move quite violently. Several huge rocks began to uprooted themselves from the depths beneath them, then changed direction and started to fly overhead in a more lateral direction. One narrowly missed Kaprey, as his head came into contact with Faeman's hand shoving his skull sideways just in time, as the rock made its way past him and the whistle of the stone could be felt inside his eardrums.

The ground continued rocking so violently that, even had they been able to retrieve their swords, there was no way they could have released themselves from their prison inside the earth. The Aelves were taken further away in the other direction, and heaved as if they had no body mass at all, while the ground continued to solidify around the buried swords, virtually encasing them in the solid ground-stone as if they were part of the original soil composition; hiding them from detection. In addition, they could do nothing but watch, as they crashed headlong into one another and any unlikely piece of castle iron workings that had come off from above the buttress in the middle of the quake.

It was at that moment, when they couldn't imagine how it could get any worse, and the ground had begun to settle itself down, that the earth of the village of Tameron gave them something different to worry about. This new threat was something they could fight and they watched it hatch into existence with abject horror, while the ground once again took up the cause for alarm, twisting and cracking below their feet, as it exploded upwards, exposing something best spoken about in hushed whispers.

This new threat growled low and spit rocks upwards, forming a stone waterfall of solidified matter, as the being that lived beneath fully emerged just feet away from where they had been, while they could do nothing but watch it hatch, like freshwater eels caught in a riptide.

As it turned out, this being was known to only come out of the Elemental worlds in times of dire trouble, and those that saw it in its true form were generally those that were about to die in battle. However, that was not always the case; many of this clan simply did this when things had pursued them from out of the planet's core, and in their mad attempt at retreat, had simply arrived without the creatures on the surface who had been living in relative harmony, having been oblivious to its existence several miles below their feet.

This creature was in no terms an ordinary creature, but it became something best known in times of legend as a simple Earthshaper, and belonged to the Snapperhead-Knocktaw clan of Elementals that ran with the northern race of that element. This lone creature rose much more swiftly up out of the ground around them, than it should have arrived. It tore apart the stone walls of the castle in the foreground like something was in hot pursuit behind it, and it made a hasty decision to burst forth out of the bowels of the earth to freedom.

It was comprised of all things related to that northern element of earth, which produced the living breathing being made out of Elemental stone. Now unmistakable in its surefooted arrival, and exceedingly louder the higher up it went, it grew enormous, surrounding the Aelves with its entirety as they were knocked on their asses to the ground, before they could do anything about it.

It continued to rise up out of the earth around them, dragging anything within the vicinity of its reach from the castle upwards, and towards its quantified mass, as it continued to form. Although there wasn't much the Aelves could do to prevent its arrival; it was still in the process of finding its final form, standing hundreds of feet in height and surrounding them from all sides, towering over the entire area. They could do nothing else but wait until the shaking had found its center and stopped, or....*no, I got nothing that could have made this an easier time for them.* For to do anything during, would only cause further injury to each other, so they held on as the creature continued to grow.

Now seriously, how does one react to such a thing? All they could do was stay out of its way, as it took everything within reach of its powerful energy, skyward. What wasn't nailed, glued, or pegged down, was literally uprooted or ripped from the castle battlements into shreds, turning everything in it's path inside out. In simply terms in case one doesn't completely get the drift; it tore apart the molecular strands from the very heart of whatever rock, plant, or tick of soil within its direct vicinity that happened to get or drift into its Elemental way.

The being from beneath the surface, seemed to step out of its own element and conjured up what it could, shoving everything that had previously been the village of Tameron into the mixture and, producing this new creature that now arrived in all its Elemental fury. What became of the village was anyone's guess; for once it left the ground and turned into a living breathing Earth Elemental; the likes of which had never been seen for some time, any semblance of what it used to be, went out the proverbial window and died a quick death.

Meanwhile, as an added visual effect, several wind vortexes were howling above them, procuring a single air Viper into the mix, which seemed to be using its own molecular fields of strength to catapult them forward into the outlying areas of the storm it had created, and transferring them alongside the stone creature's birthing. It blew right through the middle of the maelstrom, allowing the pieces that hadn't become the Elemental's body in its final stages of completion to fly right through the air, crashing outwards to the other side of where the fortress had been situated, as both disappeared into the forest beyond, dispersing anything left into the trees.

That began another situation within the forest itself, as the residing creatures within the perimeter of the castle sedges, sent mammals and Fey animals alike all scurrying away in search of any kind of cover they could find, before they became part of the forest's newly decorated landscape.

All the while, the ground continued to shake violently, causing things to unearth, as the Elemental screamed its newly created-self into this side of life.

The Aelves did their best to hold on to some semblance of order. Still, things did not settle with the arrival of the being; branches and limbs shook loose whatever dirt that had clung to their roots, as it echoed past farms, and fields long gone to rot and decay throughout the newly created storm front. Then it circled back with the creational wave it create, and sent the air collapsing the cleared airspace within the centre of the storm, as it twisted back on itself, and turned into its fully newly formed life of indescribable calibration.

The Aelves began to hear other things around them, despite the violence of the birth. What they heard was the beginning sounds of life shifting in other ways around the stone creature, which apparently had not quite finished its birthing. Loud cracking noises could be heard as the rocks and mortar from the walls of the castle, which lay strewn about and scattered out on the earthen floor, seemed to take on another transformation of this newly formed creature's body. It started to place itself together in rapid succession, by picking up pieces as if fitting them into a jigsaw puzzle, and turning them into what would later appear to be living appendages, similar to that of a Gorgon's head, growing right out of the tree limbs it had replicated and placed around its body like a spear.

On the ground at their feet there had been plenty of tiny pebbles and little stone fragments which had appeared from beneath the ground, shaken loose by the earth's rolling and pitching movements, when the creature had started forming its original shape. It began to utilize them now, making a pair of arms, hands and fingers, each rolled to form the intricate bones that it could use to fit those pieces into its newly made appendages.

The Aelves had no choice but to sit and watch, completely captivated with apprehension and little bits of what, one would call dread, as every piece of the newly formed creature was built from simple rocks and stones right in front of them. Dyareius winced, remembering a long time ago during his early training years, when he had the unfortunate opportunity to witness a Lycanthrope changing from his Fey form into the shaggy beast. It had gone on to destroy an entire blood-line of hereditary born

Jungle-Piper clansmen, during a single night of feasting. Only a handful of those warriors escaped into the night; he and his friend Soren, of the Dragonlords, were witness to that night. Everyone else within the villages radius, including the animals, had died during that horrible night, and he would have only been too glad to have never seen anything again that even closely resembled that night.

He had a bad feeling that someone was not going to live through the night ahead, and drew the energies of those that were closest to him, inside his own heart. Too many oddities among other things, were starting to fall apart, and his riders were far too close to this thing not to be damaged in some way or another, as the ground continued to roll and pitch with the creature above screaming itself into existence.

By now, the Elemental had created seven of those arms; the original one was still moving about and folding the rocks in on themselves, pushing flat elongated rocks in-between to form what appeared to be sockets and elbow joints. It was moments away from completing the eighth and final appendage, when something seemed to confuse the creature, distracting it momentarily. It stopped long enough for the Aelves to grow concerned, shaking its head, seemingly tasting the air around the area they were all in. Finding nothing to prevent it from continuing, the Elemental twisted the final arm into place as the dust from the rocks shifted, and squeezed in-between the stone sockets it had created.

Again, it stared down at them from above, looking from one to the other, then grunted and returned to count their numbers, before growling. The Elemental appeared somewhat disturbed by the six that had arrived, and looked behind and around the remnants of the remaining stones lying on the ground, to see if the others that seemed to have disappeared had been hiding there.

Dyareius' group felt the release of attention he seemed to be paying them, as the creature turned to look in another direction away from them. That was all they needed, and they moved as one to become the warrior clan they had been born into. Dyareius didn't even need to verbalize the command to go, for each of them had already begun to scatter in all directions away from the creature above them.

But they were too late in their timing. Unbeknownst to them, they had had picked up a tag, and the very thing that had been stalking them on the outside-world of the real Tameron had just pushed through the barrier and arrived, bursting through the trees. It flowed in towards them, snapping with jaws not fully formed within its blackened twisted form, vaulting forward trying to get behind the Elemental who had instantly gone into a defensive mode like a mother hen protecting her chicks from a crazed hawk swooping in for the kill. Both creatures met in midstream, full of rage as the fight shattered what had appeared to be an innocent encounter with the accidental birthing of a simple Earthshaper. It positioned itself with the Aelves behind, putting its own body in the direct line of fire. The Aelves changed their minds without a backwards glance about the direction of escape, reversing their forward momentum, skidding in on bended knees back towards their original position and what appeared to be a new ally. Anything was better than coming into contact with the new threat coming through the trees, which now appeared much more dangerous than the simple creature of stone that apparently was doing its best to defend them.

The rumblings of the earth around the trapped Aelves rocked the ground, knocking the remaining Dragon-riders that had just successfully gotten to their feet once more to the bare-ground. The Elemental who now fully assembled, had already rumbled past the Dragon-riders, when he attempted to try and make physical contact with the other form that had arrived for a fight. But nothing connected with the creature, as the thing began to rear itself up and the Elemental stone fist went completely through the creature emerging from the other-side slightly scorched.

The creature looked on smugly and shimmered in its vaporous concoction, gathering the tendrils of its flowing substance inwards, as it made preparations to move right through the stone surface of the Earth Elemental that stood between it and the Aelves it had come for.

It had sought out the whereabouts of this band of Dragon-riders for a long-time, and nothing was going to prevent it from moving through this overgrown stone Troll, and obtaining that goal. He grew larger as he started to pull in other pieces of gaseous elements that were lying about just below the surface, the by-products of whatever Fire Elemental had deposited along the earth during a night of foraging. He could use them to boast his energy reserves; he drew them inward, reversing the polarity of their attachments to the ground, feeding his own energy with something the others had cast off as nothing more than waste.

He was much more dangerous in this form than anything or anybody had initially been aware of, as he had slithered along the barriers of the Dragonlords' hunting grounds, out by the coral reefs on the backside of the Island of Symarr, since he had arrived and been transported inside this creature.

What he hadn't known, was that the Aelves had not been in touch with the Dragons since the old wars, and therefore he had not been able to find them, while hunting for the thing it needed most to survive along the fringes of this universe. But even had he been able to find the Aelves, the thing he hunted for was lost from this world the moment the war had ceased, and these creatures had disappeared into the Witch's protection field. Tamerk had seen to that when he had sent the Dragons away to the deeper sections of the mountains along the fringes of another realm; one, just out of reach of anyone's touch including his own. The old Sprite was stronger than he had been led to believe, and knowing what he did now, he would have surely disposed of the old Sorcerer when first he had had the opportunity, back when the wards had gone down in the Sadllenay village.

Back then, the Seelies had been his lead warriors in the war against the Tuatha, and surely one of them would have been able to find the means, with the old majik of the Dark Queen he had been exposed to during those times. Unfortunately, she had had another clan of Seelies at her doorstep when this had gone down, but the majik he had been able to conjure up from them had given him the edge he had needed to hide himself among the enemies on that side. However, that had not come with a warning label, and he had been left betwixt both worlds inside this body without a way out.

In the meantime, he had been given a lot of insight into the Fey population of this realm where he was born, and knowing things that were best left to the world of the Sirens where this thing he had become had lost its mind, coming through the dark matter star, there was still the small issue of whether it was programed to finish the job it had been hired to do. He often wondered why it was still functioning in this world, so far removed from his own. Whatever the reason for his luck, he hoped it continued in the fight without running out of steam and coming back in a loop and pulling him out by the hairs of what was left of his own mental skin. But was it enough Sidhe energy to keep his eyes on the prize that was still being protected by those of the Elemental race? Neither of them, as far as he could see, knew the real reason why this thing was still coming after them even in today's world, long after the creature that lived inside of him was no longer a threat without him.

Either way, the Aelves had materialized after his search had discovered a hiccup in their mainframe, which he had taken from another that belonged to the Elemental race of the Fire Druids he had procured. He began to pace the forest floor, just out of range of the Elemental and its cumbersome movements, as he changed tactics and whirled within the newly acquired gasses he had completed incorporating into his matrix. He had tried several times to get past the massive stone structure of the Elemental creature, which still for some reason was hel-bent on protecting the puny Aelves behind it while they remained profusely pressed onto the ground virtually protected from him killing them by the creature's sheer mass alone. He wondered where it had come from? When he had first spotted the Aelves signature, they had been alone, moving along the castle exterior walls which now appeared to have disappeared altogether.

The Earthshaper ignored his search of the area, and tried to counter his movements at precisely the same time, but the creature coming at him was full of vapour, and flowed rather than walked, passing closer each time he came within reach. Each time it directed its attack, it would come towards him, turning once again into a gelatinous liquid that soon covered him from head to toe, searing his earth majik as he passed him by. He did his best to counter the effects of the creature's superior speed, but it was soon apparent that this would eventually not be enough to protect the Aelves for long, as the caustic effects of the acid were starting to make his Elemental bones more brittle with each searing pass.

It was obvious that the vaporous creature moved too quickly for one that was so large and made of heavy stone. But Dyareius noticed the Elemental appeared to be thinking much faster than the scene being played out before him. If it could not touch the thing that was made primarily of air and gasses, the Dragon-riders were in grave danger. Time for a change in tactics. However, they didn't get the opportunity before it was decided for them. With a wicked grin, the Earthshaper waited for the creature out on the fringes of the woods, as it slithered in for a final time. The Aelves looked for an avenue of escape, and would try to execute it at the next window of opportunity, despite help from their overgrown champion. It would only be a matter of time before the toxic creature made it through their newly acquired benefactor's body, and then he wouldn't be able to protect them for long.

The wind picked up and brought the black swirling creature closer; it moved in once again for what it believed would be the kill. It had its own strategy, as it as it tried to move in the other direction to get to the back side of where the Aelves were presently lying prostrated on the ground. He went in for the final assault. If he was lucky, the stone creature would step on them and end this battle in one final swoop, and he could be on his way come the second pass around.

He moved in for the kill shot, taking his time as he moved towards the Elemental. But at the last minute he changed his direction of flow, coming up short of his previous assault, and changed compass points, approaching them from a different angle. As he did, he began to spot small little pieces of pebbles and smaller stones that the creature had discarded haphazardly when it had initially begun to create its arms and hands. He noticed them just before he burst through the trees to get to the Aelves, who were still out in the open. The rocks thrown on the ground seemed to be placed in some random pattern, and he had dismissed them as nothing more than discarded rock. It would soon prove to be an error in his calculation to their arrival into his visual cortex. He hadn't simply made a mistake; he had made a severe error in judgement regarding the Elemental's actual ability to out-play him.

The stone creature had anticipated that the vaporous creature would dismiss his Elemental brain as nothing more than vague thought patterns. He had purposely used that very thing to his advantage, within his ability to think things through. He had set things up in this particular linear pattern, before the vaporous creature had arrived overhead in the skies, producing a procured scene of innocence that was far from what it appeared to be. This was how he would win the fight. Disguise something that was complex, with something that is simple and clean.

The Elemental realm was alive with spies in all things Dracore related. The realm of the Goddesses had warned them, it would try again to retrieve those that were responsible for the killing of the one that had brought him into this realm. So, they brought the Dragonlords here to an alternate Tameron to prevent the whispers of the Dracore's signature energy from being detected. They knew it would only be a short time before it was able to find a way through the void, and come for those responsible. Basically, they had laid a trap with proverbial stone breadcrumbs, complete with the matrix molecules of simple stone all mixed together with a spackling of Dragonlord tailings.

Using the time it took to plan his trap quickly, the Earthen Elemental had risen to the challenge that had given the others only moments to get their strategy into play. Then, with a moment of speed, he placed his body of stone over the Aelves, entirely encasing them within its porous core, before the creature could react from outside and find a way to stop him in his tracks.

It was then that the real reason the pebbles had been placed in their particular location came into play. The stones had been placed with precision, along uniquely quadrated angled positions. It appeared that in his error, the alien species that attacked without provocation had been out foxed at his own game.

The Elemental had waited, and pulled everything together the moment the creature tried to attack from the rear to retrieve the Aelves from outside his stone body. He then did something no other Elemental had done in the past, and moved them physically with another element of the Elemental realm. Truculence had been the reaction they had expected from the creature, as his prey had instantly become no longer game. The reaction they received was far greater and much more volatile, and one of the Goddesses had predicted that precisely, as the game came to its full completion.

It would appear the Goddesses were also not playing fair, and when the moment was right they released a fairly large Sylph, who had been waiting on the outskirts of the trees that had helped in the formation of the other's arrival. This particular Elemental had arrived simultaneously

THE BEGINNING

with the Earthen element's attaché, Aperthan; each having their own individual essence in element particulates transferred into the directions of the compass lines, as each of the beings was honour bound to do.

The northern element called Aperthan, having buried itself within the rocks along the castle foundations, was situated in the most northern location of the clearing, using the castle itself as a pivot point, to set itself in rotation to the coming storm. The Sylph was honour bound to the eastern point of the castle walls, and continued on further out along the treeline, staying out of sight. It had watched as the Aelves had shifted in with their Dragons, and remained invisible to the alien creature that had attacked the Aelves, silently shimmering in and out of the treeline, watching the war from an Air Elemental's perspective during the onslaught of violence.

The Goddesses had been very specific that it stay completely out of sight, as it watched silently waiting for its turn, to finish what the Earth Elemental had started. If at any time it had moved slightly, it would have instantly put the majik in jeopardy, and the Aelves could have been taken as payment with the alien creature's silent fury still well intact.

This was by no means an easy thing to accomplish for an ordinary Sylph. These creatures by nature are always moving about the airways, and to have one stay as still and quiet as this one had to, would have taken an army of Sylphs to actually accomplish. But Pipmore was not an ordinary Sylph. She worked her majiks in tandem to the Earthshaper Elemental, and was something they had no knowledge of in the farthest reaches of Tantarian space. She was an enigma, and moved about the in-between worlds away from the others of her species and held no boundaries or affiliations with either side. Her soon to be exposed soul, would come at another time during our visits to the Fey worlds, but for now she moved in without a single echo along the whispers of the airwaves that had moved quite suddenly in the alien creature's direction.

A female voice could be heard calling up the eastern majiks of air, releasing Pipmore from her perch and letting her take control. She flew in gracefully but with deadly intent, allowing each whisper of wind to rise up one by one, and fill in the cracks and larger grooves which had been placed on the far side of Aperthan's hidden interior cavity. The Goddess smiled, knowing she had played her part in allowing the timing of the majik to be properly set; moving the outer entranceway through which the Aelves could still see from within their temporary confinement. It locked the barrier with solidified stone, now kissed by the wind of Pipmore's breath, allowing it to be forever closed from the world he resided in.

Once the Aelves had been taken into the stone sanctuary of the Elemental's body, Pipmore slammed the doorway from the outside, and quickly forced each one of the stones that lay inert upon the ground into action. Once becoming airborne, they quickly turned themselves into a whirling mass of solidified meteorites, circling Aperthan as they laid claim to him as their homemade planet within a star, and using the gravity of this illusion made of some of the stone pieces that had been the full widespread illusion of the city of Tameron came immediately to life. Thus she safely protected the Aelves from anything that would try to harm them from the outside in.

Dyareius and the five remaining Dragonlords had been automatically shoved, rolled, and lifted inside, placing them well within the interior of a stone room. It had virtually and quite suddenly swallowed them up whole, thereby extinguishing their energy patterns from anything, including the alien creature still hunting them from the outside world above.

Aperthan was taking no chances that the creature had brought help, and made quick work while the majik was at its peak, giving him the ability to work faster than he had ever done before. He began to quickly close any gaps, sealing them deeper inside, while Pipmore continued her attack on the creature from the outside, ripping the mist right off its vaporous bones.

The moment Aperthan placed his huge body above the old battlement, right above the Aelves' position, everything suddenly grew quiet for them. Any sounds from the outside world around them no longer held any references to the complete silence that now entombed them.

The ground had momentarily stopped its shaking, although the occasional rumble could be felt underneath them, while they continued breathing inside the Earthshaper's hollow core. At least in the meantime, they were able to get to their knees without being thrown around like a sack of fish. Bruised and battered, they finally found their voice, taking in the surrounding area he had allowed them to be pulled into. They wondered again how the Elemental had known that it couldn't win against something you couldn't touch: It had only been a matter of time before the vaporous being would have been able to reach them, and crush the life from their soft bodies.

That too wouldn't last long. They hadn't seen the Air Elemental, as it sat among the upper branches of one tree, but they had seen an unusually swift gust of wind sweep down along the forest edges, and come whistling in at an odd angle just before the stone creature had physically removed them from the outside world.

The ground once again began to pitch and roll, causing great amounts of dirt and rocks to begin raining down upon their soft Aelfan bodies. Sopdet watched her ladies work their majik from the other realm; giving them an opportunity to see how one of the more unusual guests to her galaxy, could be put to good use for future endeavours. She had known Pipmore could easily dispatch the wind to disperse the tendrils of mist which seemed to keep on growing wider by the minute. But Aperthan needed to get things into position without the knowledge of the one that didn't belong to Sopdet's circle of planets. One day soon, if Tamerk didn't get this one to the other realm, Pipmore would have to use some of her more volatile gifts to shake it loose, and send it running to its home-world. But something told her they had it in full control, and even though it was easy to intervene, she had resisted the urge to show them the easy way out, and patiently waited.

On the outside, all hel had broken loose with the discovery of the Aelves' immediate and sudden disappearance. The creature that had attacked them from the trees knew he had the upper-hand, and it would only be a matter of time before he got through the barrier he had put in place. What he didn't comprehend was why the Earthen Elemental had tried to protect his prey in the first place? These beings made up of the four great elements should never have that kind of emotion, and therefore this was something he had not been prepared to deal with. Now he had something else to contend with as it had banded together with another Elemental to outmanoeuvre him. In future dealings with any of the dark-horde of Faeries, he was going to have to make a point regarding the Queens' deception, and dig deeper inside any further information this particular Seelie gives to him. A small matter, but one that could turn things into a distinct disadvantage for him if he didn't quickly turn it around.

Meanwhile inside Aperthan, Cassmare had had his arm pinned by falling debris. It had happened when they had been unceremoniously diving for cover, and their soft shells pitched and rolled about in the initial encasement of their confinement. Both Faeman and Dyareius had rolled towards the far wall, and were the closest to Cassmare's position. However, none of the Aelves were able to move more than a crawl once the rocks began to fly, and trying to avoid the falling pieces that were still crumbling overhead and breaking apart from above was difficult at best, as the creature outside still moved about in battle.

The shaking slowed to a dull roar momentarily, and they were finally able to reach the position Cassmare was pinned down in. Dyareius found his balance, removing the fallen rocks from atop Cassmare's arm, as Faeman went over to help Gantay pick up Kaprey. Both had sustained injuries from the pitching Elemental above them, as they jockeyed for position along the fallen boulders around them, and righted themselves amidst new stones dislodging from above. They still had to contend with Kaprey having been knocked on the forehead, above his right eye, which continued to bleed heavily. Dyareius ripped open the seam on his shirt to use as a bandage to slow the onslaught of blood. It appeared to be nothing more than a surface wound, and until things started to slow down on the outside of their prison walls, they still could not see what was below the blood, that continued to pour down the sides of his face.

They hadn't got too far with the examination, when a new shower of rocks slid down one of the stone legs of the Elemental, sealing their exit and preventing them from moving forward in any direction. Kaprey had been barely on his knees as it was, and had slipped towards the rocks, when Phaetum's arm arrived to steady his body, colliding on the other side. The touchstone Aelf instantly grounded the other, and gave Gantay the necessary push to move them through the solid rock wall that had not been properly completed; trying to bring them smoothly through to the other side as another series of rocks came crashing down towards them.

Dyareius swore aloud thinking they had just been crushed, as debris continued to fall around them. He only began to breathe a sigh of relief , as one by one they began to materialize on the otherside in one piece, without having gotten more than a few scratches.

"What the hel is that thing out there?" Kaprey yelled, wiping the blood off his forehead.

"Move, another rock's coming!" shouted Phaetum. They all moved in what appeared to be a distorted time dilation, watching with wide-eyes as Gantay threw up another shield and moved them sideways as it crashed down on top of his shield and bounced off its protective wings. Cassmare drew everyone's attention, as he began to scream again in pain. "Where's Assha? We need his healing ability," Phaetum yelled to Dyareius across the room.

"I have no idea, I lost his energy movement just before he disappeared," Dyareius yelled in reply.

"You what?" Phaetum looked back at him, through all the chaos that was falling all around them.

"I said," Dyareius ducked from another barrage of stones that had come loose, and were still falling over top of them, "they all disappeared from my damn senses."

"Who did?" someone else screamed at him from the other side. Cassmare's arm finally came loose, as Phaetum got underneath the rock and pulled him free. The arm had been wedged between two larger rocks, and was growing an ugly shade of blue. It didn't appear broken from the angle they could see, but pain could manifest itself in other ways, undetected by what they could visually see of the shoulder bone. The hand was another story, and as Cassmare screamed in pain with the last of those stones coming loose, it had become very apparent that it was broken quite badly, in more than one place.

Dyareius didn't have time to answer whoever had thrown out the question, and dragged Cassmare quickly to where Gantay had pulled Kaprey out of the rubble. They all sat on the ground panting for the moment, with their backs to the outer walls of the Elemental prison cell, still trying to avoid the occasional overhead showers of rocks, as one of their own started to feel the first tendrils of unconsciousness. Phaetum finally broke the silence, while the others looked towards the ceiling.

"That thing is starting to move overhead, again. What do you think it wants with us?" he said. Faeman ignored him and turned to Dyareius.

"Did they even make it to the well?"

"I think so, but they seemed to be shifting in and out of my senses just before it happened, and then I got nothing farther along wherever they had moved to."

"That means they're underground," Phaetum spoke up.

"How is that possible?" Dyareius spoke quietly, thinking aloud. "Only caves can interfere with the signal." Phaetum returned, as Dyareius turned to make sure nothing else was in the process of crashing down on top of them.

"And only caves that have protection," he continued, unfazed by the other's response to his words. Inside, he was still in shock from what had just happened. He watched the others who were injured slowly start to crumble and slide over, losing the ability to maintain their own bodies in a rigid position.

"We've been in caves before, and that never happened." Dyareius returned.

"We've never been near a Sith cave before." Phaetum looked at all of them when he spoke. But, Gantay wasn't looking at him; instead he was watching a small crack in the stone wall that had suddenly opened up and given him a bird's-eye view of the outside-world. What he was watching, was the black twisting movement of the creature that had attacked them from out there, still trying to make it through to where they were presently out of its reach.

"How come it can't get through?" he pointed to the thing swirling and darting above them.

"Tameron was built out of stone from Naunas. It must have a molecule it doesn't recognize and can't penetrate the structure." Phaetum answered him.

"Ok, another question, what the hel is that?" Gantay pointed above them, referring to the Elemental that had them trapped.

"It's an Earthshaper," Phaetum told him,

"What's it want?" Gantay asked again.

"I don't bloody know, but right now it's keeping us away from that bloody thing." He pointed to the mist that had started to vibrate, as they looked out the crack in the Elemental's body. Gantay yelled for them to watch, as the mist started to turn from black to white.

"Shit, now its changing bloody colour on us." Several of them moved closer to the crack, watching as it began to change the black pigment on its skin to this new colourless shade above them. It had soon lost its entire former shade; now turning slightly translucent and beginning to show several veins peeking out of the almost clear hide, which seemed to show some kind of orange molecular substance trying to pump life through its veins.

The stone creature began to move around, as the other finished its transformation, starting another barrage of rocks coming down from above. This time it appeared to be disassembling itself from the outside in, and shifting the walls inwards towards the place where the Aelves were currently housed. It moved them into a tighter banding, walling the Aelves up closer together. Whatever he was doing, it appeared that he was herding them tighter inside his body, trapping them further within its own building blocks of natural stone.

The black entity now was fully colourless, and had acquired its final stage of development, swirling about like a long band of silk blowing in the wind. It darted above like a hawk, flittering in rotation towards the retreating rock, watching for any flaws in the stone from his vantage point. It completed one full circle before it challenged the Elemental, gaining speed as it dove straight into Aperthan's body, trying to reach the Aelves inside before the crack it had noticed closed completely. It moved down through several layers of stone, fracturing them severely. He had noticed several flaws that had formed tiny fracture lines visibly weakening it, in its initial assault. His downward spiral took out several larger stones randomly placed in his way, as he tried to move directly to the heart of the beast. That was a mistake.

The stone creature had created a hidden space that the Aelves were sitting within, which was made out of parts of the old castle armoury. Its iron works had been purposely put to good use, and had the creature moved inside any further, they would have been protected by its molecular structure. As soon as the walls began to move inwards, the Aelves moved away from the weakened stone sides that had been revealed to the creature above, to entice him in, as the metal plating opened up and slid sideways. The Aelves had heard the grating noise behind them, and had quickly retreated to another chamber, which had suddenly been released for them behind the wall that they had been resting against.

Dyareius and Gantay pulled the others, with the help of Phaetum, through the opening, as the creature narrowly missed each of their bodies. They landed safely inside, and out of its reach. Aperthan had counted on that and all that was left to do, as the entity moved in between to retrieve the Aelves, was seal up the ceiling to the room they had previously been sitting in and close off all avenues to where they had escaped.

Hearing the stones move behind it, the creature turned around in retreat, and realized its mistake. It tried to veer off sideways, to get away from an incoming slab of metal. It didn't make it. The Aelves did, as the Mauntra above showed its face through the rapidly clearing dust of nothing left of the room Aperthan had allowed them entry into; it was replaced by daylight and the stone that had lifted, fitted into place to contain the howling creature now snarling away behind them.

The stone Elemental's final movements were far from fast. But he had help. He had only just completed the last placement of rocks to seal them in, before he completely disassembled himself, and fell into a pile of rocks, allowing Pipmore to push her enormous strength inwards, to move the single remaining large slab of stone down, from on top of Aperthan's last remaining wall.

The creature was trapped in the solid stone casement lined with a thick coating of iron worked metal, as Pipmore went in for the kill and sent all the meteorites moving inward. She moved around in circles sending the vortex whirling about in the air, moving them with her mind as they formed a seal, fitting themselves into place like puzzle pieces.

Dust rained down, settling itself all around where the Aelves had previously been housed. The Earthen Elemental breathed a sigh of relief amid the debris of rocks it had become. The mist had been arrogant in its assumption of what an Elemental was capable of achieving if it worked with others that had similar interests. The giant cube of rock raised one finger bone in salute to the pretty little Sylph, who disappeared into her own realm smiling at Aperthan, leaving not one single crack for the trapped entity to fold itself through and escape.

Aperthan knew it would hold until the Aelves were far enough away from its field of sight. By then, something else would have to find a way to fend it off. The Earthshaper winked once, and then the last remaining stones still standing fell into the pile of rocks that had once been the castle of Tameron, now indistinguishable from the pebbles and other stones littering the forest floor.

CHAPTER TWENTY-THREE

Assha and the Water Elemental

Assha felt the link he had with Dyareius disappear the moment he stepped away from the lake side. He spotted a trail just to his left, and quickly moved towards it, stepping across a few pieces of broken fern, when he felt like he was being picked up through the air from behind and dragged back to the lakeshore. Whatever had him, he couldn't see them, and his body dangled like a sloth on a vine about three foot markings from the ground, moving backwards towards the lake at incredible speeds. No matter how much he twisted and yelled he couldn't feel or see what it was; as if some invisible force simply picked him up with its' hand, grabbed onto his back, then telepathically connected his brain to it's.

This was new; only Dyareius had that kind of mind-link. He had been struggling so hard he didn't even hear it call him by name. He stopped struggling to listen when it became apparent that something had indeed done just that.

"Assha, hurt you I'm not, do you have understanding?" it said again, quickly.

"Yes, I bloody hear you. Why have I been taken against my will?" Assha asked angrily. Assha was not afraid of anything; this was more on the lines of uneasiness, mixed in with frustration at not having control of the situation. He looked down at his reflection still being dragged across the lake, watching several small fish swim along the surface following his shadow, as it made its way from the shore to almost the middle of the lake.

Small ripples bubbled up from below, creating tiny bubbles that rose and fell as he stayed inert for a few seconds, hovering inches above the water, while something could be heard crashing through the trees up on land, in mad pursuit.

"There is much need to go below, I promise safe you keep. Big breath in, Assha." Before Assha could respond, the thing yelled, "Now!" and, as Assha grabbed onto whatever air he could shove into his lungs, the thing dragged him under the surface of the lake, moving him deep into its depths, and away from the surface where he could breathe, as the shadow of something big whizzed by them overhead.

He hit the first level of atmosphere and felt his ears start to pop, as the pressure of the depth began the first of many intrusions into his inner-ear drum. It began to sting and then the pain came on in waves as he struggled even harder to regain the surface atmosphere. He heard another female voice that spoke much clearer than the previous one.

"Use your fingers to pinch your nose, and blow it. You know, like you do when you're sniffing — only in reverse. It will release the pressure and equalize the atmospheres you are about to go through, Assha Aelf, or eardrums begin to die."

Bubbles started to escape from his mouth and nose, making their way to the surface above, causing him to panic slightly. He blew his nose like the new voice said, causing little creatures to skitter away that had stopped to watch the spectacle that had entered their lake. The relief in his ears was short-lived, as it hit the second level of pain within seconds of the first. He released the pressure as he had the first time, while the creature continuously pulled them downwards, reaching one atmosphere after the other, only pausing momentarily for his release.

Now, from the perspective of telling the story, one forgets to give you another side to the thoughts of the one that was being dragged unceremoniously downwards to Goddess knows where. Of course he struggled. He even tried to kick his legs to the surface, much to the unrelenting annoyance of the one pulling him along, but it kept moving him deeper to the lake bottom, uncaring of what Assha was actually going through. He blew his nose a third time and the pain lessened as it had the last two times, but now it relieved him of his last remaining supply of air.

"Still OK, Assha Aelf?" The voice spoke very calmly. Assha couldn't respond out loud, instead his mind was losing consciousness. He only thought the words in his head. *'I am not, bloody OK,'* he began. *'you're trying to freaking drown me.'* As he started to drift away from rational thought, he began to wonder if it was male or female, as one does when things start to drift from conscious thought, not making sense of the reasoning behind the idea.

"Would that be easier for your motion, to know, Assha?" His breathing air was gone, and the air stuck in various parts of his body started to begin another form of release, finding its way out of various areas through the pores of his skin, trickling upwards towards the surface. Panic was beginning to invade the threads of his consciousness; he would try not to let it arrive. He opened his eyes, almost afraid of what he might see, but he wasn't even close in his mind to what arrived in front of his face.

It made his eyes grow wider, as the last bubbles escaped his skin and he began to drift away from reality. He no longer struggled, as quickly deflated lungs that were on the edge of being done slowed his progress and alerted the creature that his metabolism was on the verge of collapse. The fight was going out of him faster than the creature thought was possible, and if she didn't do something fast, she would have a dead Llangera Aelf on her hands when they reached their final destination.

What Assha saw just before he lost consciousness, as the air he had been able to hold onto finally ran out, were two things. The first being: tiny blue lights moving all around the bubbles that he had produced, and stopping them from actually reaching the surface above. Each blue light had a life of its own, and moved along with him towards a group of underwater caverns with two or three air bubbles under ... tiny little arms. They were tiny little Water Faeries moving about the water like bees in a hive, scurrying around his bubbles, collecting them like coins and taking them away to some Faery bank for whatever purpose had entered their crazy little minds.

The second thing, and he was still unsure about this one, as his brain was beyond that fuzzy stage, and he thought maybe at first he was at that dream-state just before someone dies, was a beautiful Water Elemental all covered in the thread he had seen on the farside of the lake. His eyes grew wide as he watched it realize he was about to drown, a wide grin coming around the edges of its face, splitting its mouth almost in two. He felt a small shock run through his body, and felt the strangest vibration begin to resonate from the creature inside his own skin. His eyes grew wider when he realized just what was happening, and with eyes not quite able to fully focus, he watched the creature holding him appear to be reaching around its back and releasing something that floated towards him. It quickly attached itself to the skin of his neck, giving him the oxygen he needed to live, as he stared on bewildered at the face that split like a clamshell before his very eyes.

Assha felt the warm trickle of much needed oxygen filter into his lungs, as he was forced to take a deep breath from the crystalline appendage. He didn't know how it was possible to actually have the energy to take that first initial breath, but somehow the creature knew just what he needed, pushing air into his lungs manually and his brain began to clear as it lifted the fogginess from the inside out.

"My apologies, Assha Aelf, the breathing not so clear. I'd forgotten for the length of swim, to hold a breath was not of your capacity." Assha looked slightly pissed, still taking in big gulps of the air that was being pumped into his body from somewhere inside the creature who held him captive. His vision began to clear up enough for him to see that he was very deep within the waters of the lake, and the light from above was receding in the depths below him. Along the ridge of rocks to his left, he started to see the vague outline of lights coming from far inside a darkened cavern. They moved towards these, as his vision adjusted to the dark environment of the underwater world, while the Water Faeries returned, carrying away the bubbles he was expelling through his skin's pores.

"I don't understand; where are you taking me?" he asked, half expecting the creature to ignore him. Instead he was surprised by the voice once again echoing through the underwater world, shifting the water molecules into language.

"Do you see lights?" it asked.

"Yes, where are we...?" but the being interrupted Assha.

"I'll explain soon enough; breathe in deep, calm stay, and please stay alive Assha, we are almost there." Assha could see the lights getting brighter, then saw what appeared to be a set of black stones forming an archway overhead; they swam underneath it and continued on. The creature didn't stop, instead it moved them further, going deeper into the underwater city and far from the world of the land Fey. Assha could do nothing but float along beside it, and everywhere he looked he saw small shimmering outlines of buildings with the unmistakeable structure of a vast underwater civilization.

He glanced up and saw large dark shadows come into view. He half expected the Merfolk to have arrived to escort him in to wherever this creature was taking him. Instead, they were nothing more than huge oxygen bearing plants resembling lily ferns and kelp fields, floating overhead, as they made their way through and alongside old stone columns on the outskirts of the enormous city.

The further along they swam, the larger the columns became; revealing an older written script of Malachim symbols he had not seen before, carved on their stone bases. They had similar etchings of another race all over them that Assha didn't recognize; created by what he could only image belonged to stone masons of another era he had previously never seen, alongside the larger stone façade of buildings that they moved amongst.

Now larger stone carvings of a lost civilization came into view as he was pulled along, belonging to a race of Fey he'd never seen before on this planet. He was fascinated, and continued to take it all in, watching larger water creatures off in the distance as they made their way towards them. By the time they reached them, animals swam by not fish, as he had first thought.

A female of the species smiled at him, showing tiny fangs with a face that had glistening scales coating its exterior surface instead of skin, with a Human looking torso and fish body behind it. He'd never actually seen Merfolk before of this kind, and judging by their large and exquisite tails these creatures had covering the lower part of their bodies, they definitely were part of that race of Fey. However he had never heard of them being this far inland, and even further puzzling him was the lake that he was currently deep within; it now seemed to have switched its saltwater molecules for those mostly comprised of fresh, and he could not explain that either.

Another creature swam by. This one had the body of a Dragon with a face of...well, a Dragon, but it had gills in its neck where the leathery wings should have been. Its fins were completely transparent, and you could see the fine placement of each bone that grew and made up the skeleton of the animal. It ignored them as they passed, swimming by without paying them any attention; patrolling the grounds like it was some kind of sentry. Assha realized it's body had no real colour, but if Assha were honest, everything seemed to be dark and colourless down here, and the creatures reflected that image as they swam around him and went on their way. Then it was gone.

Up ahead he could see some form of reflective plant surface above them as they swam, or rather as he was pulled in its direction. When they got within viewing distance and he saw his own reflection staring down at him in its surface coil, he now could see that attached to the back of him was a beautiful shimmering ladey as they ascended up from the bottom of the lake. Her body was covered in some kind of long flowing material that was comprised of plants and forest mosses, which dropped behind her as they moved upwards, looking similar to the sentient thread he had first seen up on the surface. Upon closer inspection he could not really see her image very well, she kept moving about, shimmering in and out of his line of focus.

The mirrored surface of the big flower drew nearer as she swam and directed both of them towards it. It was then that he realized they were moving at a good clip, and the mirrored image he was seeing was all of a sudden right in front of his face. He closed his eyes and braced for impact, putting his hands up to protect himself from the oncoming obstacle seemingly blocking their pathway. He hadn't needed to; instead the surface seemed to change texture and majikally they broke through its surface like the image of a single drop of nectar falling into the flowers center.

He heard the splash and the fall of water all around them, but they were not in the actual part of where the water had remained behind them. Gravity took hold of him and he felt her claws grab hold and pull him towards her as they dangled sideways, coming through the strange entrance. She lowered both of them to the ground, as the creature detached the thing from his neck, holding him upright with strong bare hands.

She steadied his arm and shoulders as he got his bearings, and he realized they were now in a chamber filled with breathable air. He looked all around them and noticed many things, but mostly what caught his attention was behind him. For directly where they had entered the room was the surface of a shimmering window that lay inverted, with waves shinning like a school of fish at the edge of a rainbow.

He watched as the strange window changed its molecules and became hard once more, forming a clear barrier of glass that held back the lake, which became part of the interior surface of a functioning wall. "Easy now, Assha Aelf; this will all be here when you get your underwater-legs back, later today." She disconnected her mind from his, leaving him to hear things around him on his own. He tried to shake the sloppy feeling out of his brain that had arrived the moment she had disconnected from him, while she directed them into a beautifully coloured garden of an ancient underwater city.

The air smelled sweet but brought a certain light-headedness quickly to the surface of his brain, as Assha started to stumble and the creature once again placed a better grip on his upper body. She bent towards him to hold him upright, and placed him over by a bench that was designed for one that was much larger and bigger than what he was. "Breathe not so deeply, Assha Aelf, the air is designed for other creatures that have a different physiology than your Aelfan one of land. It may take a few hours for it to become easier, so we shall just take it slow for a bit....right not are we?"

The language she spoke, began to take on a more broken pattern of speech. The last part of the sentence seemed to change direction from the words she had given to him in her head, as they had descended into the depths. These words, as the withdrawal of her telepathy started to dissipate, seem to come almost backwards. He listened to the change and remembered that all Elementals talked that way. It had been so long since he had any dealings with them, that he had forgotten their language. He gave in as the struggle to breathe and balance himself became too much, and nodded as she lifted him and carried his body cradled in her arms, towards the trees that began to arrive within his line of sight. She dropped him gently down once they got there; Assha's body felt the familiar texture of what appeared to be grass beneath his feet. No longer feeling strong enough to stand on his own, her arms helped him to bend down to kneel upon the turquoise coloured grass, with his hands on his knees.

"It's very difficult, I don't think this is going to be as easy as you think," he groaned. "I feel like I'm going to be sick." He threw-up what little he had in his stomach. Assha couldn't speak it; instead they chose another method, and aimed for the one that carried him to the grass where he struggled for air. He simply no longer could fight it; he didn't have the capacity for it. The creature smiled and slowly, so very slowly, Assha started to fall over, losing himself to unconsciousness; all the while the creature stroked his hair and let him fall. Then he was gone, and not in control of anything that happened next.

Images swam in and out of his brain; voices came within hearing then went away. It took a good two hours before he really started to come out of it. Pink began to fill out his fingertips, and he heard the female creature that had taken him down in this lake talking with another quite close by. "I didn't have any choice of it. That horrible creature Balor sailed from its house, let loose about the trees and was moving towards his drips."

"No, right you did; choices easy one. Me it been, he would have not stayed surface bound of it either." The other voice sounded concerned. Assha stirred and moved his hand forward to rub his forehead. He groaned loudly, his head still pounding like it was going to split in two. He felt the creature sit down beside him, and realized he was no longer on the grass but lying on a cot with some form of soft fluid bubble under his skin. It was made of something that felt like liquid, and each time he moved it slowly moved with him, forming a link around his own body like a living cocoon.

He opened his eyes, now fully able to take in deep breaths without so much as a hiccup. It felt great to not have to struggle for each breath, but to move his body it still hurt his head.

"Still lay, Assha Aelf, Azareth is a brewing Withy tea to seed the headache; you can drink it best when it's hot and spicy clean." Assha tried to focus, but his head still lay deeply fixed within the splitting headache.

"What's your name?" Assha asked as he laid there holding his head in both hands, trying unsuccessfully to squeeze the pain out like a sliver of wood.

"I'm named of the calling of Caferish," she answered him slowly, balancing the tea mug and blowing on its contents, her breath majikally bringing it to a boil just by the air alone. He watched as the tea changed colour from the clear side of the mug that seemed to be made out of primarily water. How it was held together was anyone's guess, but Assha assumed it had the same consistency as the mirrored surface they had moved through on their arrival. He watched her blow it into its present formula, as it turned from a clear water into a deep blue swirling substance, as cool water mixed with the hot molecules and blended to its proper sweetness. Assha was fascinated by unusual things, and watched as the female Elemental stirred its contents with only her mind.

"How'd you do that?" he said, looking at her.

"Do what?" Caferish smiled, passing him the tea.

"The tea; how'd you make it hot, and make it go all...well, blue?" Assha pointed to the mug he now had in his hands. He smelled its sweet aroma and tasted it slowly, sipping along the mugs rim.

"Ah," she said, "it's just tea." She shrugged it off and got up to help Azareth with the stone mixing bowl she had been crushing the herbs in, deciding the question really didn't need to be answered.

Assha shook his head and snickered at the female Elemental as he slowly took in the whole mug of soothing tea deep within his stomach, warming everything from the tip of his toes to the outer edges of his eye lashes. He watched the two female Elementals from behind its rim with a bit of awe, as the two continued to shift in and out of time, seemingly unaffected by his presence, going about their morning activities.

Something started to come to the surface of his thought process. The tea began to dissolve the pain in the front part of his skull, and as the pain went away it began to peel away the fogginess of his brain.

"How long have I been out?" He leaned towards both of them, wanting to know and needing to understand the reason he was here. Across the room he looked between both Azareth and Caferish as each Elemental shimmered nearby, stopping only to pause for a moment at his question, and then continued on turning the colours around them to a deep blue colour. Caferish stopped her shifting for a few seconds, in thought.

"Tantaris moves in different time waves Assha, but I would think as long as it took to wake up, I suppose." She returned to her former state, shifting in and out of Assha's line of sight; moving about the room on one side, only to reappear further over on the other.

THE BEGINNING

"What kind of answer is that?" he yelled after her. "One hour, two? More than that?" But both Elementals had moved away, chatting amongst themselves and he was left alone. "How about another question, like where the heck am I?" he yelled, knowing they were already gone, and no longer able to hear him.

He got up, holding his head just in case the headache was actually still there and dropped him like a sack of willow wheat. Finding himself still standing with no ill effects, he wandered through the apartments that he now found himself to be in. The Elemental females had left him alone momentarily and would be back before long, so he wanted to get an idea of where he actually was before they returned to get him and take him Goddess knew where.

He stepped outside the corridor where the living quarters were situated, and found himself in the middle of the trees which seemed to line all the streets of the underwater city they had taken him into. There were many beings living within the underwater city, and it had a great many of the Elementals of different worlds moving about in all kinds of different locations. They seemed to be everywhere, blinking large saucer shaped eyes, looking and peering out at him as they moved about their daily chores. Some drifted in for a small peek, seeming to go out of their way just to see the newcomer that had come into the depths of their world from above and then they drifted off, quickly moving with tiny noises of embarrassment as he caught them in the act of staring.

But mostly they were all around him doing other things, as he moved along the corridor, watching parts of the city shimmer in and out of faze. One moment a beautiful garden lay before him, and then within a mere moment it was replaced with a desert like setting, complete with triple moons and landscapes of sandy dunes. He stopped moving, afraid to breathe in case he was accidentally sucked through the void, as the occasional corridor would open just steps away from his own movements. Each time this occurred he would see one of the various factions of Elementals drift past his shoulders without touching him, as they ignored his presence and moved towards their home-world. Once he even spotted one of the outer islands from Naunas, and watched as several tribes of the locals seemed to come into focus before they too disappeared, and were replaced by another world.

He stayed for a moment, while he watched the hallway that led into the gardens shift through a full gambit of different worlds that the Fey inhabited, seeing that most seemed to be situated along the edge of Faden Corpeous's biggest star shift-points. But every now and then he recognized a familiar place he had once laid eyes on, and the markings of one of the outer galaxies would appear before his eyes. That made him homesick for travelling, but being a Dragonlord had its benefits and it wasn't something he was ready to give up on yet.

At times he would see creatures moving about him in the corridor, and then they would walk through the shifting curtains without even hesitating, into the places he could see appear on the other side. He could see that it wasn't random, and that these Fey that moved between these worlds seemed to be made out of pure energy, and their individual umbilicus would set itself within the various worlds they resided in, letting them enter without having to wait. Assha laughed; he wished he had used this kind of transportation when he and Moraig were still at school. They wouldn't have had to ditch most of their classes with this method. Even their teachers would not have taken an issue with how quickly they would have been able to return to their present location. Mind you, that may have set a new set of rules for both of them to break, had this method of travel been implemented. He was absolutely sure that either he or Moraig would have had a field day, racking up as many miles as they could in a single Moon-day, just to see if it could be done.

He continued to watch as Elementals from other worlds made their way from this part of the city to that. He finally figured it out as each in turn would only have to think where they wanted to go, and the corridor would absorb that thought and become that which they had envisioned in their minds. The whole city was covered in this kind of perpetual flux, and constantly changed with each of their movements, as they walked down their own hallways across the expanse of inner-space under their own feet. How it was held together in one place was anyone's guess, for all of them sort of just seemed to be in both places at the same time.

But if Assha felt a little at odds with everything that swam or flashed by him, he soon found himself staring in remembrance as an Elemental flashed by that he recognized from his adopted world of Naunas. It kept on moving past him, and disappeared around the corner.

"Quickly, Assha, do not make a scene. Follow me without causing the bother." He heard it as plain as if Dyareius had spoken it to him from within his own mind; a command that meant only one thing. Moraig was also here.

He turned around in mid-step, keeping his eyes averted as the Elemental directed his movement away from his own, and led him down another corridor he had not seen before. Assha slowed his footsteps and strolled slowly towards the courtyard that held shops and what appeared to be a market of some sort. It was difficult to pin that one down, as the shifting wall of curtain like material these Elementals caused with their very presence, made it very hard for any other Fey to really see it clearly.

Elementals always had that way about them, and it was with this motion that he rounded the corner, and found himself to be in an old cobbled street covered in small workshops, smack in the middle of Alchemist territory.

Small particles of different coloured metals greeted his nostrils, and floated among the cobbles that now seemed to form and fit under his feet, as he walked along. They disappeared into the ground as he passed over them along the pathway behind him, and formed into something else for those walking in different directions around him. Majik was all around him, and he remembered how much he loved working in the cities of the Elementals for this very reason. Nothing about the Fey worlds was ordinary; however the Elemental realms were marvellous, and you never knew what was about to happen — he just wished he had a plausible explanation for why he was here among them.

He moved slowly, taking in the scene before him, smelling wood fires bubbling up with the aroma of cooked food, making his mouth water from the smell of dried meats and Potter-pudding. He remembered it well, as he followed the scent and found what he was looking for amongst the marking on the old store fronts that lined the walkway.

The open doors were there right where he had left them, in what seemed like only a moment ago since he was here. It was far more time than that, and was probably pushing about a full two centuries since he had actually set foot on the bare stoop, but it was all too familiar and he grinned at the sight. His home city was covered with these carvings; on Tantaris he had seen similar markings, but had found them sparse compared with those of his own planet. He went up the stoop and opened the door, only to be met with a stone wall....a dead end? He was puzzled. Why had he been led here?

Moraig was an alchemist who studied ancient metalworks and lore, and according to anyone that knew him, one of the best. Assha had trained with him back on Naunas when they were students within the old walled city of Finias. Finias was one of four main Fey strong holds within the Galaxy of Faden Corpeous. Each stronghold was built on a different planet, and linked together through shift-points in huge caverns built within the bedrock of each of the cities they had been carved out of. The directions of the Synotay's master builders had included certain contingencies that only the elements of each of the factions would be able to function with; this wasn't one of them.

Assha knew of the city on Naunas, and each of the builders that more than likely had a hand in creating this place. It was deep within the jungles off the main coastline of the southernmost continent Naunas had — above ground. The Islands of Tayose were well known for their teachings of Fey knowledge, and hosted one of the biggest universities around since the times of the Lemurian race.

Moraig had been his friend since he was a small child, when Assha had been rescued from the jungles off that group of distant islands. Assha didn't know much about his past, nor did he really know how he had come to be alone at the young age of six. They didn't keep records of things like that in the smaller villages across the other Fey realms. But he had come across the record keepings of the ruling Sage clan that raised him briefly, before he was sent along to be taught at the University of Tayose with the others. They had a complete library of everyone within their own clans, but all they had said of the foundling known as Assha was that he had been rescued from some unnamed Aelven clan, before they had left the island and disappeared into the night.

He had made fast friends with Moraig, and spent the better part of four hundred years in and out of classes with the Fire Elemental. It would be quite difficult for him to be here in this world of water, so to see Nomae scudding through the streets of ...? He realized he really didn't know where he was. Caferish didn't answer him because he hadn't formed the question in a way she could reasonably answer it.

"What is this city of the calling, Nomae?" he asked Moraig's young attendant.

"Does not that they give you, all that you need?" he returned back to Assha.

"Not as of yet, they did not of the telling. But, tell do, do you answer, quite with?" Assha replied. He had missed what it was like to be around an Elemental. Their understanding was always posted a bit sideways, and sometimes formed as a question of life, first. He had to be patient, he had at least that to give.

"Ah, a city needs truth to the right of its making." Nomae smiled even though Assha could not see him in his true form. But, smile he did, as he sparked into rivulets of flame dropping the occasional piece of ash for Assha to follow behind. He turned around and followed the young apprentice who had spent many years as Moraig's faithful attendant.

The ash floated and moved about the air molecules, like feathers blowing in a small breeze. But down there under all the water, no breeze would be present from the wind in any form. Assha moved through the stone buildings of the alchemist town quarters, and found himself at a dead end. He seemed somewhat puzzled in his arrival, seeing nothing at all to suggest that anyone was running a bustling shop, let alone a window to peak through to see if he had entered the right area.

He back tracked within his mind to see if he had indeed taken a wrong turn, and was greeted with a slight mimicry of morose laughter. The lopsided twisted kind of childhood prank laughter, that only Moraig would be able to create. The barrel laughter that an old friend had been able to make, as Assha watched the stone wall in front of him re-form itself into the doorway of Moraig's shop. However, it was not just a replica of what was on Naunas; it was actually Naunas itself that he was on.

"How in the Klifferdesh?" Assha still could not find the correct words, as the doorway swung fully open, and he stepped into Moraig's study with all its Elemental grandeur. The smells and aromas of his home-planet brought memories he hadn't thought of in hundreds of years. Moraig's attendant came through the stone wall firepit shrugging off his cloak, freeing both molecules of his hair and arms at the same time, and letting the ash lightly float to the floor. The light from the fire danced throughout the interior walls of the shop and with his body free from the restraint of the cloak, Assha could see an amazing resemblance to Moraig himself. Nomae grinned at his responsive thoughts, and spoke briefly.

"A smaller version that I am to be, and certainly a few centuries younger, than what is before his pipe."

"You look so much like him," Assha responded as he looked through the shop admiring certain touches Moraig had made with the interiors old structure.

"That he should, being an offspring of his own choosing!" Moraig spoke loudly. Assha turned towards the voice to find a smiling Moraig coming through the back of the shop.

"You found joining." Assha returned the smile, "I am pleased of heart."

"Heart? Maybe, better of actual mind," Moraig added, heartily dancing around as if he found it amusing, almost causing the lamp to tip as he came dangerously close to the edges of the table. They were back once again, amid the chaos of their friendship, and both laughed heartily at the near upset.

Moraig gestured for Assha to sit on the pillow near the rounded fireside alcove, as he shimmered in and out of the room finding the right molecules that would allow him to join him for a short while, as he moved in and out of the placing of his fire-flux. He reached above the firepit mantle and retrieved an amulet of silver wrapped Merlinite; placing it around his neck. The stone instantly stabilized his Elemental flux, bringing his ethereal body into the present world that Assha now sat within, and stopped the faze from shifting him back and forth.

"Ah, I see you haven't lost it yet." Assha smiled before punching the Fire Elemental in the arm.

Moraig laughed and punched him back.

"No, not yet of the taking, but time is young and the day could ignite the lava field and we could freeze of the time." Both laughed as Moraig had simply put, they still had time to do so.

All Elementals have a similar amulet, some find different stones work better for their needs. Merlinite is an alchemist's stone, and Moraig used it to support that, notwithstanding the fact he liked its lustre and sparkling shimmer.

"I see you still carry it with you." Assha spoke quietly, pointing again to the amulet.

"Would be mindful, with the sum travel be, that I find my heart in." Moraig laughed. "But yes it be with me, till the blending. Which is to what, the reason of it is Assha." Assha turned to meet his friend's face.

"Do you know its beginning reason as to the why?" Assha asked him.

"That would be, as to the understanding of it." Nomae interrupted the sequence of the conversation, bringing with him two steaming mugs of Jaboorian Fire-Whiskey.

"I well hope it not be as deathly cinder for your speaking voice. The mouth of the stomach is but ten paces of walk to you." he smiled, passing it to both Aelf and father.

It had been many years; Assha had missed their language greatly. On Tantaris it would just have been kitchen over there, sorry I fried it being a Fire Elemental and all, sorry about that, hope you don't mind. It made him laugh as he blew on the edge that had begun to find its flame. He had missed his friend.

"So we, as talked," Assha continued, "what is the why?" He looked to see what his old friend would add, but wasn't expecting the answer Moraig gave.

"It is of old King, that be named so, to enemy of the great race of who is you." Moraig was watching Assha through veiled eyes.

"You mean to Naunas or Tantaris?" Assha stopped blowing on his mug, to pay attention to Moraig's story.

"Many worlds, but Aelven race to be of attention to."

"So, should heart be worried?"

"Your heart is safe in water." Moraig paused "Be full of water, by looks, being without heart, thinks Loch Na Sul is death Soul."

"So that's the name of the lake?" he looked up to see Moraig looking puzzled. "Oh sorry Moraig, that be lake to name."

"Yes, friend too. Lake of an old King, be that village, given to Cian." Assha had been away from Elementals for a long time. He knew it would take time to extract enough information to piece it all together. He also knew it would be difficult for his old friend, but more important was the danger he had risked in sending his only son to a Water Elemental stronghold. Assha would have to be patient, no matter the time it would take. So he pieced together that the lake where he was taken underwater was Loch Na Sul.

Legend had it that it was supposed to have been created by Balor, when he was killed by Lugh in battle. Throughout time, various theories had surfaced in the telling of the tale of the old vicious King of Fomor's death rites. This was one of the more fanciful versions, as Loch Na Sul had never materialized within Tantaris as a whole. But Assha also knew that dimensional shift lines could be crossed, and what was able to appear to be here could also be there, but with several small differences. He needed to find out just how small this one was.

He had found out that the underwater city was Murias, from Nomae earlier. He had never been to one of the famous cities of old Lemurian culture. They were held in the Elemental realm on four different worlds, three of which he had not visited in his learning years. Then, when the Dragon wars began, he hadn't the time. He just never quite understood the fuss until now. To have had the opportunity was unbelievable, he just hoped there was another way out of this one, than the way he had arrived earlier.

He would have to ask Moraig about it, along with what he said about the enemies of the Aelven race. He also mentioned a being without a heart, and that he was safe while in water. Too many missed meanings would cause unnecessary worry; Assha would have to find another way to clarify for both parties. Then it dawned on him, Nomae spoke quite clearly when he spoke with the linking. He wondered if it would offend his old friend if they changed format and brought his son into the medium.

He couldn't remember when they were at school, if Moraig had trained in that field of the mind. He only remembered the important things. He laughed, remembering blending the robes of the fire Goddess Pele into that of the phoenix, and having her set it into a spiral of early combustion that

THE BEGINNING

almost fried them both as it sent feathers, lava, and living atoms sailing outward-bound in all directions.

At least Pele had laughed at the prank as she had hiccupped hot fire, sending both of them running down the stairs, only to find themselves shifted into the home world of the Manitae Trolls. Good times. However it was truly amazing, as he looked back at its creation, that they actually learned anything. No wonder, they were separated shortly after into two different realms of schooling; with memories such as these. They must have driven the teachers quite batty.

He really needed to spend some time with Moraig when time was not of the essence, in their present state. Which reminded him, he now had to worry about what Dyareius must be doing, with him disappearing as he did. He would ask Moraig if there was any word on the matter, and if he had heard.

"Old friend, that to which is mine, can you task that of my Dracore family and co-kin?" Moraig had been stuffing the flames of the candles with more molten wax that Nomae had given to him, while Assha had gone silent.

"So, you find peace with knowledge?" he looked at Assha. "I move Nomae to seek the movement to your mind thought." He motioned to his son to come forth. "Be there quick Nomae, to search his task." he said, to his son.

"For Assha." Nomae said, bowing towards both of them, leaving quickly to find what Assha had asked. He had only just left the room when Assha heard Nomae loud and clear, calling to him.

"The answer is yes, Assha. I will speak to you of all, much more clearly than what my father can do for you of then," he said to Assha. "I also can follow rules that do not allow me to find your mind, while father is within the vicinity. So what else should you ask while this link is attached, out of his range of speak?" he added to Assha's mind link. Assha grinned; the little Taglow had heard him. He liked this child; he had more of Moraig in him than he knew. "I do not answer to my father's likeness, which cannot be what truth is."

"You are his child, my friend that is young, and yes please tell me about the being without a heart and his water issue causes."

"You speak with tongue of old rule Assha, but I will tell you in plain speak that to which I know. Fair?"

"Yes, fair my friend, as we," Assha said figuratively pointing to himself then to Nomae. "Fair."

"Good to hear, but it was a very hard time for the father, when he heard that you had been taken into water city of Murias by Caferish, in her way of the doing." He had started to move further away from the quarter of his father's shop, but Assha still heard him speak as if he were sitting across from him in the same room. "She took you hard, and it was not by accident to the telling," he carried on.

"Why?" Assha asked him.

"She saw the being without a heart, stalking the Dragonlords of Tameron the Quick." Assha needed to stop him once more.

"What does the Quick mean, Nomae?"

"The Quick is of the world of the true Tameron. There are many worlds of each that find their flux within the depths of the old maps. You move different in your world Assha, the planet of Tantaris that you know moves in a different Quasar of time movement than the others of the dimensional shifts. Those are the ones that we visit, and see in our ways. But your Tameron has a different pattern of old and young blending together, so that time moves sideways, not up and down. We call it the Quick, and it is to this world that, when you fell through your Dragon shift, you broke through just slightly out of faze and entered the other world of movement."

"I still don't understand. How can we be here, are they not also the others that follow us in duplicate, also living in this world?" Assha needed to know where they might be located, so as to possibly make them also aware of this situation and warn them to stay away.

"They must have been transported and got lost in the Quick, when you came through. It was to this happening the Elementals of this world felt the loss of their energy, and moved to find the meaning of its nature. When Tameron was empty of those souls; we ghosted the city to that of the Earth Elemental Aperthan to watch to the markings of the region. But it seems your Aelven troops of the Dracore warriors had a Sling follow through the gap, when you entered without following the protocols of the movement." Nomae slowly pronounced the word Sling.

"A what?" Assha asked, not having heard the expression before.

"A Sling," Nomae repeated. "It's a dark matter form that is created with malevolent intent; sent on a purpose to destroy or maim."

"Sent for whom?" Assha accidentally raised his telepathic voice to within, Moraig hearing. Moraig asked him again.

"I said to that Nomae, will seek the kith, for to your hearing mind that ask." Assha, caught between the two, fired his mind in two directions. His ability to keep Moraig away from the conversation was strong enough, but he needed to pay attention to his outer voice, and stay within the boundaries of the quiet speaking inner-self. He forgot how easily Moraig could pull the mess apart for his own childish amusement. Nomae returned to the question Assha had asked.

"Sent for you, and the Aelven race that carries the child."

"What child?" Assha listened to the words carefully; Nomae now had his full attention.

"The child that you take and the child that you hunt." Nomae continued.

"We haven't hunted, nor have we taken any children. The Dragonlords don't do that," Assha said to Nomae, incredulously.

"You have, and you did, but both are taken in safety away from harm, because of the Sling that hunts them here, and there." Nomae pointed and replied calmly, with purpose.

It made no sense, Assha tried to wrap his brain around the words. He hadn't been around children in a very long time. In fact, Assha kind of stayed as far away as possible from the offspring of even the villagers. He had always found the high pitched squeals grating to his majikal nerves; to be honest, he'd always feared they'd cause him to lose his control, and turn them through another dimensional shift-point accidentally-on-purpose, sending them into some world of an obscure nature. He raised an eyebrow at the amusing thought.

It was as the whiskey had begun to warm his toes that he remembered the Human child Ryyaan. He hadn't spent more than five minutes around the boy, and had not even got a chance to see him up close before the Great White Dragon whisked him away, along with Symin.

"You're meaning the Human child then?" he asked Nomae. "We didn't hunt him or take him, Nomae."

"You understand too literally Assha; the Sling has hunted those children of mystery for a very long life of its making. It was created to destroy three. When the Dracore came into being, they were sent as guardians, but the children had different pathways that the Elementals could not care for with too many doorways within reach. So they separated, causing energy to bounce around through different walls and the Sling was unable to differentiate the movement of both. Your involvement and the calling back of the Dracore fractured that bond; they allowed the source world to be seen, and the Sling just followed you in when you opened it up."

"Why was I taken to Murias?" Assha posted the question to him, afraid now of what the answer was going to be. "The Sling had descended too close; your majik would have been absorbed and made it very powerful Assha, we could never let that happen. Caferish was on the surface, watching within her element breath, and came between the moving and the water. The Sling would not follow to that substance."

"Why, what's in the water?" Assha asked.

"Not what, but why. Water belongs to the creature's destruction; it was afraid.

"Enough, child, the Aelfan mind is unfound to your quickness, find kin that seek his energy," Moraig cut in. "GO!"

"You heard us speaking?" Assha asked, watching Moraig hold his amulet in his hand. He had become so involved with Nomae that his lack of attention on the right answers to Moraig talking, had given Moraig time to realize he was only half aware of his surroundings. Taking his amulet off gave him his Elemental shifting molecules back, and he was able to follow why his friend was no longer making sense. He shimmered now within the vestige of the room, replacing the amulet, becoming once again solid, as he cuffed Assha on the side of the head.

"My son," he laughed, "is too loud." Assha couldn't help himself, before he knew what to say the two of them were laughing so hard Assha started to choke on his whiskey. Suddenly Moraig reached right through Assha's body with his hand and extracted the contents onto the floor, frying its essence into dust from the fire within, and leaving Assha yelping from the sting.

"Stop that, you bloody fool. You could have scorched me!" he hiccupped, laughing.

"Should anyway have, damn waste of good whiskey be," smirked Moraig, which took both of them onto the floor; Assha from the sting which brought him to his knees, and Moraig after Assha knocked over the bottle and he went to retrieve it as it rolled towards the fire.

Both missed their mark. Assha never made it fully to his knees, as his legs tripped Moraig in the process, who then missed the actual bottle as it rolled on by. All hel broke loose. Moraig, in a flash of brilliance, tore off his amulet thereby allowing his form to return to its flux. The bottle had then reached into the far side of the stone hearth where the fire was burning its hottest, giving Moraig the ability to find his mark and blend with the fire and retrieve its contents.

In theory anyways, that is what they had been aiming for.

Well, that's not what happened, or anything even close. Jaboorian fire-whiskey doesn't really do well in the hottest of flames for more than a few seconds. No sooner had it begun the process of expanding outwards with the intensity of the element of fire itself, the bottle molecules blew outwards just as Assha had started to move into position. He stopped its destruction with his mind, taking on the majik to its fullest intent. But only for a moment, as it started a chain reaction that would soon turn into something much bigger and way more dangerous.

It wasn't that his spell didn't work; it was just that dealing with fire and a Fire Elemental, is far more versed in the elements of its true making. But it would be enough of a head start before the momentum could pick up speed, destroying everything in its pathway, and return them to real time liquefaction.

The sudden movement of time to one thousandth of a second ticked by, allowing both himself and Moraig to get out of the way, as the perfectly beautiful brown glistening orb of liquid fell and then slowly splashed down and came to life. It began to pick up speed in a slow downward spiral, and changed into the very active fire that Moraig still momentarily reside within.

Moraig moved like a Kaulfarrier flare towards Assha, thereby shielding him as the first droplets of super-hot liquid hit the once beautifully warm and soothing firestone. The little drops got caught in some form of time dilation, then began to ignite as they fragmented outwards, moving slowly at first like a match slowed down as it was captured at the moment of ignition. Starting slowly, it travelled as it dripped into the fire and soon ignited into a spectacle, causing all hel to break loose within the room, and turning everything within range into a full fireball of roaring flame.

Moraig moved quickly, using his body as a shield, rolling Assha with him as the explosion picked up speed. It extinguished the majik Assha had laid out, and blew both beings backwards through the door of the shop, and into a windowed archway that was currently in a state of forward flux, returning them instantly back to Murias. The archway shattered, collapsing the structure, and transported the pair through its fractured medium to the centre of the rotational windows, moving them immediately to the next shifting window that opened. They disappeared amongst the atoms that sucked them into its centrifuge, to wherever it was headed to next.

The alchemist section of the city dissolved in on itself, returning the image back towards the realm of the home world of the Fire Elementals. Alarm bells began to ring throughout the city of Murias, sending Water Elementals in all directions, to plug the now vacated space with a gravitational vortex that immediately went nuclear and tore a hole into the sides of the city inner wall. The entire outer-lake that was being held back by its force field began to pour into the now vacated space, sending the entire city into a state of emergency.

Nomae closed his eyes and fazed into the next shift-point, getting the hel out of the way, as his father had almost single-handedly extinguished one of the four most important home worlds of the entire Elemental worlds. He was mortified. It would be a long time before the fire beings would be allowed anywhere near this Elemental home world, let alone the other two worlds that existed on this side of the Faden Corpeous branding. He would have to find the Aelven warriors another way. His atoms dissolved from Murias' field of existence, and then he too was gone, as the Water Elementals ran for their very lives in the chaos that followed.

CHAPTER TWENTY-FOUR

The Unexpected Meeting of Lugh and the Fire Elemental

Shifting to the stars, or to any planet normally, would have been an enormous feat. Rolling with a Fire Elemental into a shift-point doorway, Assha would not ever recommend favourably, anytime soon. Elementals on their own can disassemble their molecules on a molecular strand, far better than an Aelf. To have an Elemental actually attached to your epidermis might not be too bad, if they were any of the other three of the four main houses. However, fire was designed to burn, and as he came through the otherside his entire outer body that had contact with Moraig, had the makings of what could only be described as burns constructed out of something that might have climbed out of the primordial soup of any planet in its infancy.

He hurt everywhere. As they came through the flux Assha rolled to one side of the archway, falling through the stone walls, and didn't move. Moraig had protected him the best way he could, and taken the two of them through the gravitational pull of Leberone through the airless environment to first put out the flames, then landing them just outside the Tuatha stronghold that the Aelves housed their garrison in. The luck of the draw was not a coincidence, as they fell into the still breathable back section of the southern point of entry along its most favourable rotating axis, primarily directed by Moraig to keep Assha alive.

Moraig's entire body started to flicker on and off as it became more starved in the thinner oxygen of the moon world. However, as it was he still had his wits about him, and he was able to crawl towards an area that had a more direct line of oxygen flow, for both his life force as well as that of his friends, which he now could be seen dragging behind him. His contact with the Aelf did not go unnoticed. Assha groaned in pain with each movement that Moraig made to drag him towards the better levels of Leberone's air supply, which they both needed, despite what one would think of the Elemental structure of Moraig's DNA. He needed to get Assha to higher levels to saturate his body's energy forces quickly, before one or both of them fell over and died.

He had only made it halfway, when he realized he and Assha were no longer alone. His Elemental form, showing definite signs of fatigue, could no longer maintain form and started to revert to his corporeal state, shimmering between his world, and that in which they had arrived, while he continued to drag Assha towards the buildings he could see in the distance. If he hadn't been in such dire circumstances, and in a hurry to pull the deadweight of his friend through the thinning atmosphere, he would have realized his aim was off, and that his eyesight had gone mostly fisheye. The creature that looked to be standing off in the distance, was actually closer than he knew. As he tried to drag both his own body and that of his companion into the safety zone, the warrior hollered to the others coming over the rise, and all he could see was the glowing reflection of gleaming steel blinding him further.

Tuatha warriors have a very strong sense of presence. Alarms going off within their own defences sent warriors scattering in all directions. No scheduled travellers were due on their radar as far as they had been made aware of, so finding two life forces moving somewhere along their southern wall was completely out of sorts with the regular workings of this northern outpost. No one should have been able to breach the walls, let alone shift in their entirety without the proper safeguards put in place for their defence.

It didn't take more than a few moments on foot for them to find the two travellers who had come unannounced through the exterior shielding. The Tuatha soldiers surrounded the two on the closest side to the encampment, not being able to cross the barrier to surround them entirely without doing serious damage to their soft outer shells. The sight that they came across, when they located the two struggling forms lying prostrate upon the ground, was chronicled shortly after in the book of histories.

The records would say: Two beings were found on the ground, one dragging the almost unconscious form of an unusual Aelfan male, by the arm. The other was a Fire Elemental, one that was familiar to the garrison, doing the best it could before it could no longer maintain its form in the hostile environment that surrounded the Tuatha mooned garrison.

But that had been enough to send everyone scurrying towards them, in defense. So you see, as the tale continues, when they had built the outpost on this moon with the knowledge of its extremely thin atmosphere, it was for the sole purpose of preventing outsiders like those who lay before them from arriving without warning. So in retrospect, they had not considered that it was possible to actually achieve its probability. There was virtually no atmosphere on most of this entire moon, and no one should have been able to breach the rings set into place that prevented those outsiders from even trying. Yet here they were, concluding, they were either very stupid in attempting such a feat, or very unlucky in their intellectual proclivity.

The history of the Aelven encampment, I shall try to put into words that you as Humans can understand. A long time ago, when the Tuatha arrived, they had built the stronghold on a plateau of sheer rock that has naturally occurring canyons on all four sides. It was completely cut off from any external ability to infiltrate its defences, had anyone chosen to arrive on any other part of the planet to lay siege to the Aelfs within.

The plateau itself was made out of Silica Glass, hardened from the Tektite that was ribboned throughout it. Leberone has been riddled by meteorite strikes throughout its history, and the canyons themselves supported nothing that could be construed as a threat. That did not mean that it did not contain life, which it did, just nothing that any of the Fey had a problem with, when they moved to this remote and foreign location.

Life on this world was just as alien to the Tuatha Warriors as they were to the indigenous life that lived here since the moon could sustain life, at the beginning of its time. The inhabitants of this small moon lived in extremely thin gravity, with very little oxygen; sustaining themselves on other gases that drifted within its rocks, as they found themselves within the confines of whatever atmosphere came into being for each particular moment.

This was a way-station Cazern for those creatures that had been seen fleetingly at best by the Humans that once lived on the planet that was called Earth. This race of beings was a single group of entities that Humans, having never really decided what they actually were or where they came from, made up another name to suit their unusual behaviour. To the Humans they had a simple name, 'The Rods'. But to the Fey they were known as the Selmathens. Their translucent bodies shimmered incandescently, moving about like a curtain in a breeze as they travelled from one place to another through solid rock or anything else that got in their way.

They at first appear translucent to the unsuspecting traveller, but upon closer inspection it is revealed that their bodies do have the ability to change into the creature that has the same formula of limbs as the resident Fey of the area. Those of you that see them from afar, only glimpse the outer sails they have, that propel them through the air along the molecular strands of the planets rotational drift. It is only when you take the time to meet with them, that the true nature of their beings comes into focus.

They may not have had limbs like the majority of the bipedal Fey living in this realm, but that did not mean that they were anything like the insects, as the Humans once thought. For these creatures lived in high standing with the Goddess realm, deep in the confines of Leberone's small gravitational pull, as well as numerous other planets with similar gravity wells, alongside their surrounding moons on this side of the galaxy. But it was this moon known as Leberone, which most of them established themselves on and found their first settlements away from their home-world.

They were highly skilled at moving through the rock masses when changing shape, as they glided between the solid formations like a ghost walking through a solid wall. Their cities were deep within the depths and twists of this moon, and littered the interior core through unusual tunnels that warped and turned, leaving the whole outer surface a moonscape of dust and rocks, constantly changing with the impacts of the meteor season. It suited them well to live deep within their fortified castle walls, far below the surface world, unaffected by the constant bombardment during that time of year.

The Tuatha had been first introduced to this species when coming through the stones, which had been built by the ancestors of these creatures when first they had set foot on Leberone, almost five hundred thousand years ago. In the generations that followed, the Tuatha De`Danann were able to come up with a sustainable endeavour that was beneficial to both themselves and the Selmathens, and exchanged trade willingly and frequently amongst each other.

In agreeing to the new designs that the Tuatha brought forth to them, the Selmathens asked for two things that could not be changed for the history of their lifespan upon this moon, or until the Aelves decided to leave for other locales. The first being, that they would only use the one plateau — regardless of the nature of things to come. And the second, and more important of the two, they would allow the Selmathens to travel alongside the Tuatha, piggy backed with their own molecules, as they travelled to other worlds that might be unavailable to the Selmathens' current way of life.

This would grant them the opportunity to get off world from time to time, to see the galaxy without the chances of getting trapped again without a ride home. And with this in place, both species lived in harmony together for many thousands of years, alongside the other local resident that had been part of the original written agreement of laws.

Having the Plateau as his own private residence, Lugh, who was the current military leader of the Tuatha De`Danann, had lived quite peacefully within the small cluster of structures that housed the secondary military garrison. It was situated here on Leberone, far away from their main mound on Tantaris, called **Aggulf Elkcum**, to give the Tuatha an outpost closer to the outer-edges of Tantaris's rotational drift. This was used primarily, for those Fey species that could not withstand the atmosphere associated with a planet-based gravity.

He had enjoyed the relative peace and quiet that living on one of Tantaris's moons gave him, and the location of the home on Tantaris was beautiful beyond anything that Lugh had ever known. But up here he simply enjoyed the alien aspects of Leberone's sheer desolation, and the vast expanses of outer-space. He didn't kid himself that trouble could not find him here upon this moon. But it seemed to give him more of an edge, if it did come looking; or at the very least made him feel like it did.

His warriors also enjoyed their own stay here, while on a kind of a time out from the mainstream of the mound; as did all the Fey that came under his command. They were a working outpost situated along the outer-edges of Tantaris's rings and the first line of defense, in case something strayed into their realm on a collision course with the planet below. Most did not stay here for any length of time, moving instead where the numbers were needed, as his own command dictated to that aspect of senior authority.

But dictator was not what he was; if at any time any of the soldiers felt that they could do a better job than he was doing, he would have welcomed the change, as it would give him more time with other endeavours, that always sat by the wayside while he ran and took charge of one of the biggest garrisons this side of the Tuatha De' Danann's holdings.

He had decided a long time ago, he would not become what his tyrannical grandfather had become, but that did not mean that he was soft. Balor had so much evil inside his Fomorian mind, that had he lived, Lugh felt that Tantaris would have been in dire trouble within the community of other planets that existed within the Faden Corpeous cooperative.

But that time faded away with Balor's death from a blade in his skull, and Lugh truly believed in the destiny of the Aelven race as a whole, and although the Fey had many things that the Aelfs had no part in, he would always try his best to help any one of them within their many friends and allies to achieve what was best for the community as a single tribe.

With that being said, it was no easy feat. He knew there were still some factions of his grandfather's minions, quite active within this realm, and they had tried on numerous occasions to murder him in his sleep. Their hatred of the leadership of the new Tuatha De' Danann, which the old King of Fomor had tried so desperately to steal, meant they would go out of their way to cause as much mayhem in retaliation for Balor's death at Lugh's hands. They would in time try again, as they had in the past, but nothing would come out of the little skirmishes they continued to wage along the border towns that lived in the outskirts of his reach.

So with this knowledge at his advantage, he needed to keep the troops in constant movement around the areas he deemed to be at risk, based on the intel he had been given by none other than the Dragonlords themselves, who mysteriously had been set into play once again — not may I say, by his hand.

He took time to watch one of the huge beautiful White Leviathans fly overhead, finding the freedom that it seemed to also find within this moonscape they both shared. They were the second of the group of creatures that had been living here among the moon's thin atmosphere, when they had first arrived. Most Aelves planet-bound today cannot explain to the current Fey race of worlds, how the doorway had come to be wide-open, beckoning the Tantarian Aelves to explore this planetary body and all it had to offer them. It had just suddenly shown up on their shift-point world window. When they had gone to investigate, they had been only too keen on exploring what it had to offer them, after so long being denied access to its spacial frame-workings.

They had been stunned to find that the legend of the White Dragons, that had been told to them in Faery stories as small spits, had come to life. The window that had opened had caused them a bit of a dilemma, discovering that it was very difficult to breath within the moon's atmosphere. But once having arrived, they had found unparalleled beauty and did their best to use other methods to help them with their oxygen consumption.

It was soon after that moment that they had met the Selmathens and their unusual mode of transportation. They directed the Whites to move them to a more suitable breathing environment, to begin the talks of getting them to possibly stay, and have the window left open on a more permanent basis. With a proposition that was too good to turn away, they had soon found out that they had opened the window just long enough for the Aelfs to see that life was here on Leberone, and that they were indeed part of a plan that had been in the workings longer than what was told to them previously.

The Selmathens had been stranded on this chunk of rock when one of Balor's kinfolk had first taken power, to keep them from turning the tide at the moment he was thinking he would be able to strike at the Aelves and gain his kingdom back from the hoard of gypsy warrior-caste that had overthrown him previously. Their knowledge in key aspects of the Dragon wars, that would arrive in the coming years, would have spelled disaster for the new up and coming race of Fomorians. It was due to this information that the old chieftain had the address removed from the moving windows, trapping the Selmathens on this side of the doorway to wait out the war. It was this thought that brought the alarms within his daydreams to the surface.

Booted footsteps moved in all directions towards the two beings that without warning appeared to be moving through the old section of the garrison. The alarms brought Lugh out of his daydream, jarring every bone in his body into battle readiness mode, as he grabbed his sword and headed out into the yard.

The midnight glow of the evening sky, that shone through the orbit that Tantaris was currently on, highlighted his guards standing over two beings fighting for their very lives just metres out of coming out of a shift-point module that had not been used in over 10,000 years. Both were burned by something other than the second's Elemental body; the same body that looked vaguely familiar now, dragging the first towards a pair of Lugh's warrior's booted feet.

That one seemed to be losing the ability to hold his present form steady, and had reverted to his Elemental form, which could best be described as the most dangerous of the four Elemental groups that lived in the Fey worlds. Those that arrived could only watch as the Fire Elemental struggled to maintain the bare essentials of his form and structure, as he steadily moved towards the Aelfs, dragging the blackening form of the other creature towards them.

It only came to rest when it was finally able to pull the stricken Aelf to safety, and it was only then that they realized that it was an Aelf, and not a Shapeshifter, as they scrambled to grasp the stricken creature. The other stayed well out of their range of touch, and returned to the boundaries where the Tuatha could safely stay out of harm's way, and quietly burned his Elemental form into a hot seething fire-storm.

As the warriors reached the injured creature, the Elemental that had just passed through the toxic atmosphere which had been set up previously by the Tuatha, proved to be none other than the one Elemental Alchemist that had helped set up the area with Lugh. Moraig flickered in and out of his life force, keeping his distance from the warriors who had come to aid his Aelfan friend. Lugh was floored when he realized just what he had done, and watched the Elemental who was dangerously close to fazing into the surrounding and causing irreparable damage to himself, only to save one of their own.

Lugh shouted to Bendamere to bring the fire chalice that resided within his chambers, moving towards the now fully engulfed curtain of swirling flame, as several of his warriors rushed the burned and injured Assha into the infirmary. The Elemental wavered in and out of the time-shift, staying well out of his way, as Lugh advanced with his sword hilt out towards the roaring flames — the heat from the blade beginning to sear his own skin. He placed it in the air as it hovered around where the Elemental was floating in the space before him, offering it as a token of respect to let him know Lugh was honour bound to help him through what he was now experiencing.

Bendamere returned in a clattering of stones, with the chalice in hand, and passed it willingly off to another. The offering between Elemental and Aelf was accepted; though those that witnessed it could not explain the verbal agreement, as no one but Lugh heard its response in the sound of the rushing flames which had just begun a more sinister outward expansion.

Boot heels could be heard as they skidded to a stop, and Lugh turned to retrieve the chalice from who he thought was Bendamere. Upon turning, he discovered Symin grinning at him and handing him the fire chalice.

"What can I do?" Lugh didn't get much time to respond to his question, as Moraig's essence started to change colour, producing a brilliant white light in the final stages of the Fire Elemental's life. Lugh quickly lit the chalice and slid it towards where he thought would be the easiest point of entry for Moraig to reach.

"Don't go anywhere; I have a feeling that we will require your services if this doesn't work." Lugh turned to shield his body as Moraig had reached the pinnacle of what looked to Symin like the eruption of a rather active volcano, ready to burst through its central plug. He had seen some rather stupid things from Elementals by and large, as far as their inability to understand the frailty of Aelven physiology. But Moraig always seemed to be able to outdo even their standards, by leaps and bounds. There had been many instances that Lugh would probably like to forget, but he thought maybe it would be his warriors that would prefer to have that chance. Moraig had done a lot more devious things to them, than to any other group of Fey that probably lived within this realm.

Had it been any other Elemental that had breached this garrison, they would more than likely have been lead away in chains, rather than been given the opportunity to live within a specialized vessel that had been made for them. Especially one that had been sitting within the chambers of the leader of the current Fey race, waiting on his next excursion into the stars, after he had been told to construct it all those years ago. How odd was that, in the grand scheme of things?

Lugh often brought things that were in his possession on Leberone back with him when he returned to Tantaris, when he planned to stay for an undetermined amount of time. This was not one of them. Instead, he had prepared a specially contained housing chamber to hold him there, should he decide to grace the Aggulf Elkcum mound with his presence down there. At least there, no matter where he came in from, Lugh could shift him out of there into the more stable atmosphere of Tantaris's inner rings, should he decide to burst into flames. But out here they would never have the time in their smaller contained bubble of life, which they had built especially for the small community that was housed here.

He brought himself back to the present, realizing Moraig had not moved in to house himself within the container. The Fire Elemental was beginning to show clear patches and missing parts of his Elemental matrix, and was still not advancing towards the chalice which should have been able to house his degenerating form — to keep it from dissolving completely in its current state. The movement to his right caught Lugh off guard, as Symin's whole body moved past him and shifted in towards the area where Moraig should have been moving.

"What are you doing? You're going to get yourself killed!" Lugh called after him, but it was too late. Symin had already moved within the boundaries of the toxic atmosphere. "Why would you do that?" Lugh looked shaken and a little stunned, shaking his head as his own men began to move in, pulling Lugh from the dangerous gasses that had started to change colour the moment Symin had reached the barrier. He had almost gone in after him, forgetting the actual danger that had presented itself. If it had not been for Bendamere forcing the issue, he would have lost consciousness within about a fourth of a second. It was then he noticed something else, just before they led him away.

"Stop, wait a minute," he said, shoving one of the pairs of arms off his own before looking over his shoulder. "How is **that,** possible?" He turned to look at Bendamere, who had not totally let go of his arm, and pointed to where Symin was still standing. He should have gone down instantly, but instead he was still moving upright within Moraig's flame, and not actually affected by the heat.

"Symin are you able to hear me?" he yelled, shielding his eyes from the intense heat, moving back towards the area, but this time staying within the boundaries. Symin kept moving away, not outwardly responding to his call, until he reached his destination.

"Lugh, do you see the crack in the stones along the far-edge, by the south wall? If you can, you should find a safety net set deep inside the stones designed for those of us who belong to my race. If you can spot them you'll understand why I'm here, and why anyone else would perish in my stead." Symin had heard him, and was talking to him as he continued to move towards the Elemental, with the chalice tucked under his arm. No one had seen the fine hairline cracks that had been sitting idle for so many years without activity, along the edge of the old entrance doorway.

When the Fire Elemental had shifted just a little to the left, Symin had noticed the beginning stressors move. His eyesight was a lot more advanced than the Aelven race of his brethren Aelves, and far superior to their normal physiology. Symin's DNA was a little bit different than his adopted clan of Dragonlords. Dyareius had knowledge of this long ago, and he would not have flinched at Symin moving within the area that he now stood. However, Dyareius wasn't there.

The other Aelfs that had been in the vicinity were unaware of Symin's extraordinary gift, for Symin had not only been used by the Tuatha, he had been recruited and handpicked to join the Dragonlords from where he had come from, by none other than the Selmathen's. His kind was in appearance very similar to the Aelfs, but that is where his similarities ended. Lugh knew some of it through Tamerk, although to what degree he was uncertain: However, for now, in this capacity, Lugh had been very aware of what he was capable of doing, the moment he seen the cracks in the stone that Moraig was standing in front of.

At first glance, it had not appeared to be more than a simple ball of intense flame — one that he knew even his unique physiology wouldn't be able to stand for long. Symin however, would prove him wrong, and in the next few seconds was about to blow that theory right out of the proverbial sky. Symin had an audience who, barring any who didn't believe what Lugh had already known, became willing participants in this new identity and instantly found out, the moment Symin continued to stay alive in the middle of that inferno. Symin ignored the warriors starting to gather outside the protection field, letting Lugh answer any questions that arose from the situation at hand. He let go of the chalice, moving it towards Moraig with his mind. He would not fall victim to the burning as Assha had. Assha's burns would heal in time, his could destroy this whole damn moon!

The chalice arrived within the safe distance it required for Moraig to complete his transfer. The moment it did, the Fire Elemental raced into its matrix with a puff of what could only be described as relief — then absolutely nothing. I mean no sound of any kind, just blankness all around for at least a full twenty seconds. Everyone looked at each other in complete astonishment, waiting for something to transpire. Then, just as they were starting to feel at ease, the far off sound of thunder rolled in. The chalice hung still in mid-air, hovering like a ball that had lost a bit of its roundness, and then it moved with a bit of a wobble, slowly gaining speed. At first it looked like it was going to slow itself down as it started to decelerate, but that quickly changed as the thunder started to move towards the plateau.

Huge peals of that sound rolled into the cliff face, as the warriors scattered, trying to make it to cover as the mineral began to pelt down hitting rock and searing skin alike on anyone stupid enough not to find cover. Many did not, and remained rooted in place watching the phenomenon unfold, finding themselves fighting off the hissing minerals that moved to eat the clothes right off their bodies, with something smelling like sulphur. Symin gained control of the situation for them. It was astonishing to watch, as huge fire globules began to assault the entire plateau. Had they put it in writing, it would have been the strangest sight that they had ever seen.

From the moment that Assha and Moraig had landed on this strange landscape that was full of amazing and wonderful things, Lugh had never

THE BEGINNING

seen it behave in this manner. It's not that Leberone was barren of storms; it was just that Leberone was incapable of having anything but dust storms, in whatever shape or form.

You see, Leberone did not have any climate like they did on Tantaris, or any of the other worlds that the Fey currently occupied. Even Naunas, that had all the best climate conditions in the entire region, did not have weather of this magnitude. What was falling was what from the outside looked like meteor's, but the illusion held by Symin controlling it, holding off the true nature of what it was. It wasn't until the last of them scrambled for safety, and had reached it, that the illusion was broken and a brilliant shade of the most vibrant of reds within the history of written text, came forth out of the mist. It would apparently be known as the day it rained fire from the skies, and the day the Fire Elemental made it bleed tears. Then, as the illusion came crashing down and all were undercover, the reality of the situation changed into something that made them move to an even more secure location.

The remaining few who still continued to be awestruck ran, looking for anything that would sustain them, as it rained pure undulated fire all around them. Moraig's chalice had taken the essence of the Fire Elemental, and exploded itself within the atoms and molecules of the gasses that perpetuated the very existence of anything that could give it life, and let the mineral take it down from every available space and spread it outwards towards the ground. It was like watching time restart its existence in the beginning of another much younger galaxy, back when the bang of perpetual birth exploded into the metamorphism of creativity.

On the edges of all reason, Lugh watched the world in slow motion, as the flames rained down into the silence of the edges of the field where Moraig had been hanging in limbo, and gasped at the vision that assaulted his sight. The chalice was moving so fast, rotating with the pure essence of the flames that completely surrounded its entire vertical mass, that it actually created a storm. Not to further confuse the situation, for there wobbling within a substance that currently housed the volatile Fire Elemental, who was renown for creating havoc – the chalice still remained hanging in mid-air without falling. Not to be outdone by the creature that seemed to be anything but a simple Aelfan male, who continued hel-bent for leather on keeping the population on this moon from getting itself wiped off the face of Sopdet's flipping map.

So it wasn't surprising when, all hel broke loose within the compound, but it would only take a second in actual time for everything to settle itself into the reality of what was transpiring. Lugh took that time and pulled back his troops into the buildings which had not been affected by the flames. With that in motion, he realized that nothing outside the ring of flames that remained intact was actually on fire. The blast that had been slow in coming never materialized past the event horizon, which currently housed the essence of both beings, fully engulfed in the Elemental world of its molecular fireball.

He realized that when the Selmathens had given the Tuatha this piece of land, they had incorporated a small slice of razor thin crystal, which now lay exposed within the cracks of the stone wall that had drawn up the boundaries of the garrisons, and all that had been eaten by the fire was only that which had not been part of the original walls.

Someone had added an extra rock wall that duplicated the original barracks out on the fringes of that boundary; one that from the angle the fort was located in, could not be seen. Lugh had no idea when it had been constructed, or even if it had been done on the site during his own command. It was immediately incinerated upon contact with Moraig's energy and nothing was left of the origins or makers of its construction, or why it was there in the first place.

Someone had driven a crystal shard into the actual bedrock of the original foundation — that had been formed with Tellurite, and altered the original agreement, they had all decided was to never be changed. Someone had known that, and taken precautions in allowing this to happen. Apparently, someone had foreseen a disaster of this magnitude happening, inside the outer-walls of Leberone's thinning atmosphere, so for whatever reason, they decided to mask the wall that could hold the essence of any Fire Elemental — not knowing which of the creatures would be the one to breach its walls, therefore preventing any exposure to the lethal atmosphere that happened to execute itself into the mainframe, allowing the being to function on another plane of existence, until its form here could be stabilized.

Lugh was stunned once again. How had the Selmathens known a Fire Elemental would be coming through into this particular gateway today, more than 5000 years later, and one that would reveal what another had done behind the Tuatha De˙Danann's back. But, his astonishment would last only during the few seconds it would take for him to see Symin still moving within that part of the wall, which had been the housing unit for most of the toxicity that fell on this side of the moon. Yet there he was, with no apparent repercussions with the levels he was breathing in, as he continued to thrive in its lethal environment, all the while completing what they as a species were unable to do.

Symin moved towards the edges of the field, and then with the crackling of flames he shifted his energy through the barrier and dissolved the curtain of flames with a single movement of his hand. He emerged through the veil of the Elemental shift-world and came through with no trace of toxicity on any part of his outer-skin as the fire particles turned into dust.

When Symin emerged from the flames, he passed Lugh the smouldering fire chalice that held Moraig's energy, smiled, then carried on walking out of sight as if nothing out of the ordinary had happened. Lugh shouted after him, smiling.

"Symin, we will have to speak about this, at some time." His answer drifted back.

"I'd like to say we will, but I seriously doubt it would make you happy." The words floated on the air currents and disappeared just as fast as Symin did. Lugh moved towards the buildings, with the chalice deeply seared with blackened soot tucked safely under his arm.

'That damn Elemental is going to get us all killed one day, for sure.' Lugh whispered into the wind. Taking the chalice, he shook his head in stunned disbelief at Symin's abilities, muttering away to himself. He soon disappeared out of sight into his own quarters, to secure the Elemental and place his essence back into his own body, while Bendamere called the warriors who had watched the insanity unfold, to record the event the others had seen...

...To be continued in book-two, In-Between...

BOOK·TWO OF THIS TALE

A brief glimpse, into that first Chapter.

Tansar heard their laughter as the battle with Stephponias's demonistic particles of foreign substances had been deemed to be dealt with, done, and finely baked, leaving him to graze along peacefully for the moment. The present danger was far from over he well knew, but if they could deal with it one small battle at a time, they would be that much further ahead of the coming conflict.

Nonetheless, the battle would have to be more on the relevant plane, before those that were involved would find its end. As it stood now, they were only just becoming aware that it was even going to be fought here upon their own world, among the enemies that were just beginning to show themselves like little dots on the landscape of a minefield.

Only Kashandarhh, he knew, could feel its stink, as it slithered through the atmosphere. When it became known to the others, it would take most of all of them to put it down for its final assault. Unfortunately, someone within this clan would not make it through to remain here within the realm of the current Tuatha De`Danann's family of elders. The clan would have to surrender one of their own and that Fey would have to die in order for the others to live. That was why Tamerk had sent his rider Soren here in the first place. Soren was crucial to this fight; one that would only be revealed in days to come. However, with Quist's request to find Kamera's daughter within Kilren's mountainous hillside, the Witch Kashandarhh would have

Soren's help to try and get it started, before someone else became a little more on the dead-side, this time around.

Tansar knew she really didn't need any help, and would be already working on it; Tamerk had called when they were out in the trees, while Soren and Symin watched their young friend Ryyaan come over to meet the real creatures that were hidden inside their Dragon bodies. The Dryads held this secret for a long time, but the boy had needed reassurance before he even attempted to go with their Dracore counterparts.

She recalled how Tamerk had started the ritual to change both her and Quist into their Dryad forms and how he had also sent word to Kashha using the same airwaves, linking the two simultaneously at exactly the same moment, while his majik was still at its peak. No sense wasting perfectly good majik when the waters are running deep. He just popped Horae (his little time Goddess) into the mix, and Tuffaa... time stopped for a brief microsecond, while all around the glen everyone momentarily moved in different threads of life with none having been the wiser, nor having hadn't a clue that he had done it.

Mind you, no one really knew most of the things Tamerk did anyway; it was just his way. A little quirky at best, and I would think he was more of an enigma to most of us that lived inside our little Fey lives. However, for those of you that have seen the small things he has done in the past, I would hope you'd understand when he pulled the memory from you and made you lose its particles to another memory he slid in its place, that it was not done in malice. That is what he does, when it comes to his kind. The malice part comes later, when you have done something that cannot be repaired. For the most part he simply pulls the things apart, selects what he thinks you need to remember and puts that memory back in its place. Strange creature, a little nuts, and dangerous as all hel. Tansar snorted with the thought. Malice was an odd word, once only used in the darker regions of the Sea of Contentious Souls, having it resurface on the continents was disturbingly familiar to the war Balor had almost created when the Humans had first arrived. But the thought dissolved and disappeared in place of another.

He couldn't help himself; he smiled thinking about Soren's reaction when he had found out what he didn't know about the Dragons. In her female character, she had been somewhat offended when he had reacted like a spoiled brat the moment he had found out they were not the Dragons he had believed they were. But, as the male persona took over, he had to think what it was like to have something you thought you knew inside taken out from underneath you, and replaced by another train of thought entirely out of the context of what you were lead to believe was true.

Males just couldn't switch alliances that easily. It wasn't in their inherent makeup, and Tansar could smell a rat in the cook-fire. And that proverbial rat, was about to make a huge blunder in the coming weeks — stirring up that pot. Having done so, it would soon expose the one that really doesn't belong to the hierarchy of elders coming together for the Gathering; the very one that has remained hidden in someone that should not be here!

He also knew that someone else, who still resides on this plane of existence, had not done their job in its final stages with placing this thing within the restricted zone. Its very existence within the galaxy of planets on this side of the Goetutonias Nebula's vast network of planetoids, was proof enough that someone had really screwed up, and not just royally!

It set his feathers on edge, just thinking what this could mean for the Fey race here on Tantaris. It couldn't possibly think that it was absolved of what it had been called to do in the first place, without some kind of retaliation coming from those that had planned their line of defence out to perfection, only to have one tear it down in a matter of seconds. Its very nature would not have been that easy to restructure and the hardwire having come through the black star it had journeyed through when Balor had evoked its essence into the denseness of its crushing forces, should be showing some form of weakness by now.

But then again, that should have been severed the moment Balor had been killed; instead it still flew without restraints, remaining free to continue the revenge of a now dead master. Surely Kashandarhh would have the means to find the key to its destruction by now. It was after all, more than a thousand years in the making, and that in itself should have given her a heads up on the situation at hand, as it spun out of control and landed once again in their proverbial laps.

This was how things were done in this world of Fey regulations, to prevent something such as this from taking on a life of its own. This kind of thing was always brought into the world with safeguards put in place. However, nothing seemed to have been allocated for just such an occasion, especially when one is hatched without requesting provocation.

With that still very much on his mind, Tansar still fussed about who that person would have been that could be so inept at a job that even a bornling that lived in the primordial sea could have done blindfolded, or at the very least bloody web-toed and sucking on a Starfish. Balor had been a very cruel man; so it could also be that once the creature had been raised, Balor was unable to reverse his own majik, and his own ideologies of himself as this super Wizard would have taken a tremendous hit, especially given the actuality of how little he did know.

It had been rumoured some time back, that he had executed the one who had witnessed its birthing, thereby preventing any further action in its retaliation and his defection when things had gone sideways. But, Karma does work in mysterious ways and when it eventually makes its way here, it sometimes bites you in the ass and spits you out cold. Truth be said, his reign had been one of pure hatred from the get go and all that had lived through his insanity could only imagine what his mind was truly capable of dreaming up. He was after all, born with a Vermorbian mean streak that carried on through to his adult life. By then it had tripled in replication, and anyone that got in his way had their own throat slit come nightfall and lay dead where they fell by the following morning. Yes, I would say that is more the definition of the word…. Malice.

It would be a long time in coming, with regards to the reason that the Dracore had been first implemented into the protection of the chosen three. That journey was quickly coming to fruition, and would in the coming days have the clans stunned at its outcome. But first, for that to take place a series of events had to have occurred. And for that to happen, it had to be in the correct order.

First off, Tansar and his twelve friends would have to give over their essences, to become hidden from the directional shift-point they would need to maintain their identity. And that, thought Tansar, was not going to be an easy task. He licked his paws and spat out a piece of Fever-pitch he had picked up during the skirmish in the field back when Ryyaan had met the sky Leviathan.

He shook his head and cleaned the scales on the back of his left side, finding the source of an itch and continued on with the next thing on that list, as a Ticktisaid jumped free from his feathers and scurried into the undergrowth. He hated the wingless insects, always trying to undermine his cleaning routine and jumping in where they didn't belong.

Second, and just as important as the first, he thought, they would need that completed in order to hide the children from that which Balor had created to kill them. If even a whisper of where they were was to leak out, all would be for naught and the Queen that would be born would fold up this world never to let it rise again.

There had been a time when their own chance at survival was directed towards this, but that was not to be in its own completion. It would seem that something else had been in the works for an entirely different set of circumstances, and had it not been for the unexpected arrival of Tamerk in this Spriteish formulation of drift, that would indeed have taken place, and the Dragon wars themselves would have never been fought in the first place.

So the story carries on, with Tansar needing to get those involved to move towards the time when they would find themselves at that arrival point; to accomplish just that very situation, and remove this hunter from the world of Sopdet's constellations and back to his own time-line.

He shook his head and flattened the area of grass, just as another Ticktisaid tried to free itself from his scales, and dove back in. This time he shook his entire frame and watched a whole colony of the creatures fly outwards into the woods and he returned to his field of grass unharmed by whatever section of downy feathers they had decided to set up shop in.

Tansar shuddered to think what might have happened had they dug their teeth in for the long haul. But before he had time to consider that thought again, another memory arrived before the making of its actual germination, and the Sling attained and turned what was already into the mix up on its heels, as it tried to move through the motions of thread towards them. That call sent Tansar's attention to more immediate matters, which drifted on the atoms of this other world; one that ran alongside the places of in-between somewhere far out there, to where it continued to hammer it's way inside. It was getting close; before nightfall someone from the old guard would feel it sting, as it crossed through over to this side......

SPECIAL NOTE

from the Author to the Readers

I'd like to take this time, to explain to the readers why this single novel has ended this way. I tend to be one of these long-winded Authors that simply like a story to last as long as it can without the reader going, *'what the, come on... it can't end here, give me more!!!'* Unfortunately, there wasn't a way for it to be put into one book, without it being outrageous on the pocket-book let alone the dimensions of the novel to be too big to hold in one's own flipping lap; so here it is-for what its worth...and the reasons for what I came up with.

Bookstores now days, seem to be full of Trilogies, but the truth of the matter, they are simply stories where the Author didn't have any other recourse than to split the larger novel into three individual books, so you could afford them and still be interested enough to read them.

This tale, has been split up into three sections; two being still too big, and four being way too small. For me, it was not the original intension of my writings to have this final copy formatted in this formula, but I had no other choice if I wanted it to be available for you in paperback. This is not a trilogy: Apparently, since the novel is over sixteen hundred pages, and no way to split the story-line effectively without damaging the final outcome, I have had to listen to others to bring it to you differently than it was initially intended...

The tale that is set before you, is complete in its long form through eBook, should you decide to do it that way, and it has not changed for that medium. Nonetheless, I did have to put in the ' what happened in the previous novel retiary' and did my best to fight tooth and nail to have it released in the one go — but that only got me behind in releasing anything at all, while I fussed and fretted with the final design of the digital version.

Now, I have my doubts on this and truthful, I was also a little leery to do this at all. At first after mulling it over for a very long time; almost a year in the making; I finally had no choice but to let the book go to an E-Book only format — for the time being, but in the end had far too many readers that had asked me to get it into paperback. For this, I revisited the whys and wherefores; split it up and continued with the chapters as is, just like it would have been if you hadn't closed the one before it and cracked open the next one. That is, except for a shiny new re-write from the digital version; now dedicated to my readers who still feel the need to have an actual book in their lap. Well my darlings, this one is for you; so enjoy the additional words that I have adjusted, making it smoother around the edges and adding a lovely new look to the cover.

However, the actual format I came up with might be unusual and therefore may have the cynics slightly out of sorts, but I persevered despite the naysayers frowning at something they would have liked to have squashed; in turn I put my foot down, and made it exactly as if each book had not been stopped in the one before it and the three shorter novels take you down the same curvature of the road I had originally intended.

This is a new approach and maybe a slight gamble: But, they do lead you along the path set amongst the Fey Worlds, without you having to get lost along the way. I hope it will work for all you avid readers that just want to sit down with some huge novel, while you fuss and ponder over where I am going to take you next along this journey.

...I hope it gives you as much enjoyment, as it did for me writing it...

FEY DICTIONARY

Aelf... Fey creature that has characteristics of modern man in this novel. Some of the clans have majikal powers and others not so much

Aelfan... male inflection of the name

Aelfen... female inflection of the name

Aelven... this is the name for the species as a whole

Aelf-fledge... little child

Aelfling... older child, not yet full grown

Ahseekah... to move forward

Alraun... a herb for nightmares

Ambertine Glow... this is the colour of warm browns, infused with bits of yellow light

Anapher... one of the falcons of the Goddesses

Anforian Sugar Maples... one of the larger maple trees growing on the land of the Water's Deep continent

Anthrodeans... crystalline Fey from the planet of Anthros, belonging in the Goetutonias Nebula

Arns... a measurement of time; this one specifies it to be on the one year timeline

Astraltarian Waters... waters that keep the in-between worlds from colliding into each other

Attwicks... to stay still

Auick... these Elemental creatures were born in the Trench of Talon and live among the wide-open oceans. They are the protectors in the Selkie energy fields out in the ocean currents around Vaukknea Island. They run with pure Narn molecules during the storm waves and guide the Selkies to their shedding grounds out around Undinecis Reef

Axenic Knives... sharpened blades used by the Fey clans

Bairn... a small child of the Fey

Begonin Piglet... a pig that has feathers coming out of its head the colour of its own skin

Blood Fire... the fire that spews out of a Dragon's mouth

Bornlings... pure creatures born into that race of beings

Bowl of Kalmayta... water bowl of the ancients, to see through to otherworlds

Bragna... another word for hel

Branding Times... a time in Fey history that claimed the ownership of those that walked with the spirits and used their council to protect the village from majikal assaults

Bull Cathor... extremely cumbersome animal with bad behaviour

Bull Twicken... an animal that looks something like an old bulldog with fangs

Bumblefied Insects... Tantarian insects that resemble bees

Buttercup Katerpillar Odessa... a plant that grows near any kind of waterfall

Byanadorian Moon... moon of August nights

Cabrofairious Tabers... a measurement of hours

Cammond Berry Bush... a bush that has thorns on the end of the fruit

Caorunn Tree... a certain kind of tree; used for making the strongest of wands

Capilictic Period... the time in the beginning of the formation of Tantaris

Capourian Canine Pack Wolves... fierce wild Wolves that are known for their kill ratio

Cartouche... naming a Fey royal elder carved in stone, with a Celtic circle knot engraved around it

Caspian Beaverclaw Net Fungus... a type of mushroom

Catacombs of Naunas... a doorway to Leberone used by the Selmathens for travel

Cateferious Disease... this can attach itself to the Fey, when they shift into the in-between realms of Provenance

Cauper Dogs... village dogs of Sombreia

Centaur... Fey creature that is part-Aelf and part-horse in this rendition, and comes from The False Galaxy of the Crystal Horse Nebula

Clactonian... the age that moves between the interglacial era and the Acheulean period, of time

Cloud People... Goddesses, Gods, and celestial beings

Cobbledwebs... nesting material from the Minerarious Katwalk Fleas

Cone Bees... stinging insects that store their poison in their duo cone-shaped bodies

Crabiolouses... newly formed pieces of currently dead pieces, that are re-animated

Daunt... track or trace of molecules left by a Fey being

Death Monkey Barb... poisonous plant used to kill

Declivous... sloping downward

Deiseal... moving in a clockwise direction of flow

Digs... measurement of weight

Doubl`on... currency that is something similar to that of the Doubloon from Earth

Dracore... a Dragon being that moves between both worlds of Dryad and Dragon

Draggert... a sum of money

Drymiais... Fey creatures which resemble mist; they are the nature-spirits of the Fey

Each Uisge... this Fey creature is a member of the Water Elemental family and resembles a wild looking horse, and tries to lure smaller and more docile creatures into the water to drown and consume them. It is extremely vicious and tends to be wilder than its kelpie cousins

Elderkat... older version of matriarchal indifference

Elestial Crystal... a multilayered crystal that folds itself among other terminations when it is formed. This also comes enhydro; meaning, some have fluid inside them

Embryous... the molecules belongings to anything, via the embryotic threads

Energy Bees... a burst of energy in waveform, which is aimed towards someone to calm them down

Energy Sting... a single strand of conjured central contained energy that moves as one being, outwards towards an intended target

Enhydronated... to hold some form of water or liquid inside the container

Ereton Ages... an ancient era of time within the Fey galaxy

Euphoria Issadalfae... a calming drug produced by the Anforian Sugar Maple tree

Farmian Coir Kat... lives in the caves of the ancestors

Fascuin Centurian Hug... something that knocks you over

Faunt... the energy thread of someone's molecules

Feast of Colours... celebration of light festival found in the cold nights of winter

Feldabob... freaking

Felldakat... Fey creature evoked away from her home-world, by the Sidhe Priestess. She has two tails and looks like the cross between a Dragon, and a flying Cat

Ferrishyn... old name for Faeries

Ferrishyn kidlets... children of the Sidhe

Ferrishyn moss... grows near cities of the Sidhe

Ferrishyn Ponds... inhabited by the creatures of the Water Faeries

Fey Lines... similar to Ley Lines of earth, except these ones are shallow cracks within the upper surface layers that hold the energy of the planet's signature core

Feynominal... play on the word phenomenal

Feytonian... the race name of all the Fey

Fickle Tree... member of the monkey wart plant

Finical Spideranthemaous... entity that entered Leonae's atmosphere

Finings... another name for the Selkie race in their Seal form

Firebrands... Elemental fire creature; usually small

Firecript Water Spits... tiny sea creatures that live in the depths of deepest underwater caves, and are the young of the Octtipede

Fires of Falias... a wave of fire

Fires of Osiris... a ritualistic fire festival

Flagnard... three boot lengths long

Flight Monkey... creature that spends its life in the air

Flocculating Forms... coming out of suspension into another formation

Florafied... a sentient creature made up of the chemical structures of flora

Formediso... highly concentrated metallic coating growing on the skin of the Sirens to prevent the temporal flux from occurring

Fracklesteen... a swear word

Fragged... wrecked

Fragmire... a swear word

Friar Monkeys... cave monkeys that reach out to travelers in times of illness, giving a boost to depleted energy reserves after being lost or disorientated in the darkness

Fringusha Swallows... cave creature that flies out into the daylight around fields and farms

Fulgurations... to emit major fluctuations of energy, changing it into a form of lightning

Ganmole... Coutinnea's falcon

Garthenon Tree... Earth Elemental city fixture in Gorias

Genesis Planting... planets that are seeded into life by artificial means

Geode... a hollow sphere that contains an inner structure of crystal termination points growing in all different directions within a cave-like appearance

Gillified Bark... this a term for the Rayoola Tree's outer-exterior when it lives beneath the water near the Selkie home-world. This strange tree has the remnants of gills to breathe underwater and uses them to fish in the shallows

Glyph... highlighted graphics done in carved stone

Glutinous Restaferious... a formed mass, made up quickly by transmorphication

Gorgon... lives within the Capourian mountain range, outside Tameron

Great Boors... lives in the caves of the ancestors on the far side of the moon

Gryphon... a mythical beast with the body of a lion and the wings of a Dragon

Guttering Shifter... a creature that can take on the forms of things that are not alive, and can form it into a living sentient body as it comes to life. It was thought to be long extinct, and no longer part of the Fey worlds

Gwadrafed... feathered bird that belongs to Coutinnea's aunt. His kind is used to protect the sages of the Fey clans

Gwraqedd Annwn... Water Elementals called Undines, they live in tiny pools near larger sources of fresh water

Hakerling... a swear word

Hebradines Race of Aelves... one of the old ones that lived before

Hel... This is not a misspelling; it is the Fey and pagan spelling of the Christian word hell. Although this manuscript has neither the religious connotation, nor the use of its dogma it is used fluently throughout the story and will not be capitalized

Helical Period... in reference to the age of the planet

Hobbernaut Stones... a swear word

Hot Barbery Sage... leaves of this sage plant, is used to dissolve circle nasties

Is`lantic homes... water based fauna that bond together, to make up a living island

Jaboorian Whiskey... Moraig's concoction of spirits

Jacobien Camiforean Elm Tree... this species also known as the Rayoola tree. It is also one of the sentient flora species, that can move from place to place

Jadquoius Oysterus... brilliant green and blackened colouring

Jellyfishcals... slimy creature of the sea without any skeletal system

Joie Giun Bear... dangerous mammal living and hunting in the forest

Jump Jaw Crickets... an insect that uses its large legs to sing by rubbing them over its jaw

Kaulfarrier Flare... meteor flares that are part of the Kaulfarrier asteroids

Kendoffalous Ale... fermented drink brewed on the planet Naunas

Kepet... another word for hel

Kidlet... young Fey are called this just after they pass the infant stage

Kiffersnitt... young Goddesses' name before they come of age

Kip... sleep

Kiper-fig... swear word

Kit... a young Shapeshifter or Selkie

Kitwicks... island based homelands of the Selkie clans

Klifferdesh... helish

Kraken Moth... cave insect that has a poisonous stinger not unlike that of a box jellyfish from planet earth

Krugs... small warring pictish Faeries that live among the Tryilamore's landslips. These small Faeries have taken it upon themselves to be the ambassadors of the Island of Vaukknea

Landasticlly... sworn to be land bound

Landfish... animal living on, or within the soil

Liquidine... this term is used when a water source is part of a formula of liquid and brine

LucreousTree... a majikal tree that resides in the village of the Kanoie clan of Witches

Lycanthrope... Werewolf like creature

Mabonistic Gathering... one of the last gathering festivals before the end of the growing season

Malachim Symbols... derived from the Malachim alphabet from the 16th century Earth, consisting of Hebrew and Greek letters maintaining a mystical feel to them

Mathura Tree... this tree is highly sought after for its fire resin that are used in Selmathen Fire rituals

Mauntra... the hot star within the Faden Corpeous Galaxy, resembling our sun

Mercorian Death Blade... swords made within the village of Sombreia's forges

Metalrats... an Aelf that specializes in metalwork in tunnel building

Micro-Arn... a measurement of one hour

Micro-second... a measurement of minutes

Micron... a measurement of inches or feet

Miladram... a molecular measurement in the velocity of placement

Millisecond... a measurement of seconds

Millitrons... a measurement of centimetres

Miraclouscitity... meaning miracle

Moondogs... reflection of light that circles the moon during times of changing weather systems. This occurrence, can be simply having an unusually warm day and a cooler night clashing away in the atmosphere high above

Moon Mansions... these are intervals that separate the phases of the Moon and Mauntra's rotational times, giving them a much more defined working time for a precise spell or ritual

Morgauseine Mylornese... this is a Selkie majikal invisibility spell. It is used to hide things that others cannot see

Muscle Toe Root... allows one to see distances

Mushroom Lichen Stone... this stone accompanies the Ferrishyn mosses. They are always interwoven, and live symbiotically with each other. It is used as a mapping stone, and can mimic the signatures of the clans that lay claim to a particular tunnel system they are found in

Mycorpian Thread... this runs in the families of the Lemurian line of Fey that lived within this galaxy, thousands of years ago

Naiads... water creatures that resemble Faeries, but are residents of a freshwater environment

Narcan... a reclusive loner

Narn... solitary Selkies that live their lives out at sea and never set foot upon the land

Nest Tree... host tree that houses many different creatures

Newbornling... infant offspring of the clans

Orb Blowers... subterranean Spiders of the Sidhe home-world

Orealis... Elemental sheen

Oxymorpheeis... oxymoronic

Pandora Berries... berries similar to pomegranate and blueberries

Pantherous Succubus... mythical creature of dreams

Penndersnagen Game of Flagernutt Tuttle Cards... a Fey card game

Phases... pertaining to time. Mostly in the hourly quadrants of our clocking systems

Pickle Pop Beets... a vegetable beet that grows in Kamera's garden, and is used in her herbal remedies for pushing things into motion

Pizenean Jellyfish... large looking creatures about three feet across with all the makings of the earth Jellies. They live out and around the Water Elemental city of Murias

Plagasfear Majik... this ritual is known on the earth worlds as zombie animation, but here in the Fey realms it has been practiced only by the Sidhe tribes of the old world of Faeries. Its properties more or less animate simple flora or fauna into an animated creature, that is given a directive to move forward towards its fruition

Polarlithic Flow... movement going in either north or south direction

Potter Pudding... a food that is similar to meat pies

Pyaan... a creature that is similar to the mythical Pan, and has the personality of a trickster

Pyckadyes... cave creature that lives in the bark of the madder tree

Pyriticle Scapolite Octtipede... giant creature that lives deep in the ocean, similar to an octopus. However, these can reach proportions far exceeding their Earthen cousins

Quadpoolings of Flux... energy harness; used to fit something into place

Quadra... a measurement

Quadrafed... sent in secret

Quadramass... final resting place after something snaps

Quadrapitions... a measurement of inches

Quadra-second... a measurement of half seconds

Quadriplunket Saberious... a herbal remedy for severe mystical poisonings

Quantum's Body... the minimum amount of any physical entity involved in an interaction that allows one to enter another creature into its core

Quick's Bottom... this is a natural depression in the Dells around the Lypurnen Woods

Radiating Pulse Worm... earth creature that lives underground near active volcanoes

Rathskeller Gold... currency trade with higher than average sums to the simple Fey barter

Ratterfellen... a swear word

Red Dragon Salamanders... a member of the Fire Realm that breathe fire, like a Dragon

Red Tide... a large concentration of algae, blooming within the salted waters of an ocean

Ritual of Shedding... Selkie and Merfolk use the storm seasons for purification rituals of cleansing, to perform this rite. It is also for feeding their energy reserves

Rocklerite... Earth Elemental that lives inside the burrows that it digs. They are usually found near a Witch's homestead

Rokh... means one of the hidden animal colonies of the forest

Runenitic... designs made from the ancient art of runes

Runner... one that fetches things

Salamander Oxenberry Dust... herb used to cleanse one of anything hidden

Salamendrium... tiny Fire Elemental horse with wings

Sangrinine Butterfluncal Trickells... sea creature living near the reef worlds

Santarian Brandy... a special blend of spirits that Cian and Tamerk endeavoured to brew

Santherian Religion... an old world order that was used in helping all the new Quasar Queens to move smoothly into their transition, with the full understanding of their abilities

Sarcophagus... enclosed container to house the dead

Sea Tucker Fish... beautiful and very expensive, well sought after fish

Sea Woraninthias... a large sea creature

Sedmires... land of the Protection Goddesses

Seeker... runner

Seer Stone... helps to slow speed or time down, so one can visualize its properties

Seliki... Selkie amphibious state, when they become a water bearing creature of the waves

Selkie... Fey creature that resembles a Seal in the sea, and changes to a creature similar looking to an Aelf on land. However this one is much taller with unusual features

Selkmordian Miracle... Selkie miracle of words

Setti... life beyond living as a Corporeal Fey

Shade... a life force that sits just on the edges of peripheral vision, and can be visualized by those with the sight to see. Also known as a village shade

Shadow Fey... Elemental beings used by the factions of the individual Elemental tribes

Shadowlands... the place where darkness lives among the light worlds, and everything is not solid in its touch

Shadow Land Horses... huge Water-Horses that belong to the old world royalty

Shee... The word Sidhe, is usually pronounced this way. But here is pertains to the Dark-Faery or Seelie beings

Shippels... Shapeshifter youngsters

Sidhe... Fey creatures that are Dark-Faeries; not to be confused with the Light-Faeries

Sigg... creatures of opportunity living deep within the vastness of deep space

Silvercross-Fillstar Bush... silvery bush that have flowers that resemble small stars

Slips... measurement of time in Fey language. One slip constitutes one hour of their day

Sliverstone... mirror

Sitorer`ay Demon... this creature is part of the venomous Gargoyle family

Slaugh... Wild Boar

Sling... entity called Symbya, originated in the Star of the Sirens

Small Spits... young Fey child

Soft Landers... any Fey creature that lives on land

Sopdet... an Egyptian Goddess that lives and resides in the star cluster Sirius. In this novel she is the head of the Goddess race of Fey that controls the constellations around Faden Corpeous

Sopdet Fly... one of the insects that live along the spacial fields of the Goddess Sopdet

Speleothem... stalactites and stalagmites are a form of this mineral deposit in the caves

Sphere Line Dust... a description of measurement

Spitlet... Shapeshifter child, not yet a fully grown adult

Standing Mirrors... these are creatures of opportunity called the Sigg. They become the standing mirrors when they reach maturity, but till then they live and breed out in the confines of deep space as a spectral juvenile without solid form

Star Point Collision... a collision of spacial molecules spit out by a revolving star

Stingers... dream tendrils that seem to cling to one's mind during the waking phase

Stone of Kaliea... this stone has seeker properties. It searches for what you ask, and shows it to you

Stony Mason Bees... Fey creatures that are conjured by majik

Suter Plank Cat... a ferocious feline that lives within the old city of Jaborria

Sylph... an Elemental creature of the element of air; rides the wind during huge storms

Taber Owl... a pet of Ryyaan's whose species lives in the Lypurnen Woods

Tacknea Spinder Spider... found in the caves of Almalta

Taglow... means simply, a little bugger

Tagmar... name of Sibrey's Wolfen Owlley – her pet dog

Tambergeen Fickle Fly... one of the fastest insects that lives on Tameron

Tameron the Quick... the village of Tameron's essence; one that the Elementals and Sky Goddesses see

Tameronian Elkhound Rock... a very beautiful and sturdy rock that has veins of minerals in it, that give it the look of fur from an Elkhound dog

Tantarian... language spoken on Tantaris

Tantaris... planet where this race of Fey is centrally found

Tantarisian Skin... simple way of saying the creature that belongs to this skin, is from Tantaris

Tantarisian Space... area of space around the planet Tantaris

Tantorian Space... the spacial inflections that the Air Elementals see around Tantaris

Tantry Snakalofous... underground protector of the dark Faeries, living in the Sidhe tunnels

Taper Deer... one of the wild deer that roam along the tree-lines, out near the far eastern ridges of the Sydclath Mountain Ranges

Taps... measurement of footprints; equaling one, for about every two of your boot steps

Tayoseian... people of Tayose

Terrand... all seeded land on the planet's surface

Thickals... used as a measurement to judge age; or in place of the word 'years'

Thunderstormation Waves... giant wave action during Selkie energy storms

Tidal barriers... a set arena of space that has been limited to another creature's movements

Time Link Crystal... a programed crystal's safety area; always used in the making of ritual spells of protection

Time Star Circle... protection sphere that works in conjunction with the Time Link crystals

Transdental Factions... beings, that belong to a certain race of caretakers

Transmorphication... to change into something different

Transquadrated... shifted from one body, to another

Travelational Point Module... a moving point of transportation

Tree Morrigan... a creature that is one of the forest inhabitants that resembles a tree, and has skin reminiscent of bark

Trenchers... wooden bowls used for food

Trilasecks... a term used like an old earth exclamation of factual thought

Trilla-second... a measurement of time — one billionth of a micro-second

Trumpet Ivy Vine... a big vine that has leaves the shape of trumpets

Trysector... a measurement of what ten miles in the Human language, would look like

Tuffa... means something that is instantly happening

Undines... this Elemental creature lives in any source of water. But the creatures of the same species that live primarily in fresh, are also called Gwraqedd Annwn

Valkyrji... a Fey creature that is the chooser of life or death and the dying, as it escorts you through to the other-side

Vermodious... a Fey swear word

Vermorbian... this creature from the Carthanthien Nebula has a nasty temperament, and is known for its resistance to dark star matter

Vermorbian Craklenock... a creature of the imagination

Viper Spanger... a creature with paralyzing fangs

Visinean Jars... holds a Fey Queen's inner Elemental rites for the four directional quarter guardians. They are given back to her, when she comes of age

Volcanic Glowerites... creatures that infiltrate and live in the Tuatha De` Danann's volcanic structures of pumice stone

Wailing... newborn Fey of the Witch clan of Kanoie; or a sound sent out in warning

Wards... majikal locks placed on things or places to prevent anyone from getting inside

Watermite Kind... waterfolk

Whenshi Rites... calling of this rite makes something forever

Wick... a name for an area resided by only those of Witch clan; all of which live within this area of the energy field they call the wick possess majikal molecules needed by those of that race of Fey

Widderschynnes... moving in an anti-clockwise direction to the sun or celestial objects within the sky; always keep the object to your left while in motion

Willow Wheat... a Fey root staple, used in making bread

Windistic Rhythm... tide of spacial movement

Winged Fire Fox Flies... Elemental creatures that look like small flying foxes

Witchnical Testing... a Witch school that blends all Fey learnings into the highest degree of passage

Wolfen Owlley... a dog-like creature that the Fey have as guardians and pets

Wulushian Majik... ritual majik founded within the old cities of Wulusha

Yardlens... measurement of inches

Zedfrens... the Fey name for hours of the day

LIST OF CHARACTERS IN
THIS NOVEL SO FAR

Elementals, their Homes and Druid Elders:

The **Earth Elementals** live in the Home city of **Gorias** with a Druid Elder called **Esras**...

The Earth creatures in this novel are: **Aperthan** and **Japonagus**

The **Air Elementals** live in the Home city of **Finias** with their Druid Elder called **Uiscias**...

The Air creatures in this novel are: **Agramon** and **Pipmore**

The **Fire Elementals** live in the Home city of **Falias** with their Druid Elder called **Morfesa**...

The Fire creatures in this novel are: **Nomae** and **Moraig**

The **Water Elementals** live in the Home city of **Murias** with their Druid Elder called **Semias**...

The Water creatures in this novel are: **Azareth** and **Caferish**

Goddesses in The Stolen Child Book:

Hexe... Goddess of Healing

Horae... Goddess of Time

Nina... Goddess of Dreams

Sopdet... Goddess Queen of all the constellations around Faden Corpeous

THE BEGINNING

Nature Spirits:

Arddhu... protector of ancient tree groves

Drymiais... nature spirits of the Fey

Triduana... protector of sacred water sources

Coloured Dragons and their significance:

Black Dragons... these particular Dragons are from the Island of Symarr, and are known as the Dracore

Green Dragons... these are the wild ones

Red Dragons... these belong to another world

White Dragons... these huge Leviathans belong to the outer reaches of space. Sigrith Kithtar is the name of the Dragon that took Symin and Ryyaan to Leberone

---

Black Dragons:

Aantare... His Dragon-rider is called **Assha:** He is considered a Synotay Aelf; though he is not. He is actually a Llangera Aelf that was found on the Island of Tayose on the planet Naunas. He has strange majik full of mystical powers and his true heritage isn't revealed until the next book; *Circle of the Fey*

Baelf... His Dragon-rider is called **Dyarius:** He is the lead Dragon drover, and the joiner of their minds and can go in-between realms

Causeey... His Dragon-rider is called **Theiry:** He is an EarthSeer from Kanoie; he reads minds and picks up thought patterns

Fauler... His Dragon-rider is called **Cassmare:** His gift to be determined in the next novel

Kiptitt... His Dragon-rider is called **Bynffore:** He can change things into other things

Quist... His Dragon-rider is called **Symin:** He is not an Aelf, though he looks like one. He is extremely dangerous and incredibly powerful

Reely... His Dragon-rider is called **Phaetum:** He is a Touchstone Aelf, from the Caubertian clan; you can touch him to ground yourself

Salmin... His Dragon-rider is called **Kaprey:** His gift is to be determined in the second novel

Sienn... His Dragon-rider is called **Elyizeam:** He is a language theorist; knowing languages in both written, and spoken formulas. He was born off World

Tansar... His Dragon-rider is called **Soren:** He is a Tracker from Tameron

Tayto... His Dragon-rider is called **Markus:** He's a mind Shifter; one that has the ability to make people do things not of their own volition. He also can go in-between realms when he calls up a phenomena known as The Twist

Toomae... His Dragon-rider is called **Feyman:** His gift is yet to be used in another novel

Toupoe... His Dragon-rider is called **Gantay:** He is a Directional Quantum Phaser; one who has the ability to allow something to shift through anything, without the need of a shift stone or a Dragon

---

List of Fey in the first Novel, Stolen Child:

Annagmore... Selkie friend of Vaal's

Balenas... one of Lugh's soldiers

Balor... married to Ceithlenn, father to Eithne; deposed king of the Fomorians

Balorfynn... great, great, grandfather to the current Sibrey

Ballynamullan... Vaal's Selkie best friend, that accompanies him to the underworld

Bendamere... one of Lugh's officers

Caberaana... one of the Shapeshifters who traveled with Daniel to Tameron

Carpathious... head Druid of Balor's court

THE BEGINNING

Cian... father of Lugh, lives in Fomor as their Chancellor Regent, married to Eithne

Coutinnea... wife of Stephponias

Daniel... Shapeshifter's father from the village of Sombreia

Eithne... mother of Lugh, daughter to Balor; married to Cian

Eurgerus... first Aelven warrior trying to reach Sibrey in her dreamstate, belonging to the Capourian Mountain Wolf pack clan

Freile... Coutinnea's aunt who lives in Kilren

Gabriel... Cian's father

Gelmeg... one of the Tuatha warriors who saw Eithne in the mound when it exploded

Horse... a Centaur that befriends the Shapeshifter clan when they go to Tameron. He is the Gatekeeper to the space In-Between that is on the lower level of the Goddess Realm

Jazmyyn... headmistress and keeper of Cian's estate

Kamera... Witch's mother; she is of the Kanoie clan of Witches from Llavalla and now lives in Kilren — banished for producing a daughter with a Selkie and making the prophecy come true

Kashandarhh... daughter of Kamera and Vaal, she is of Selkie and Witch heritage

Kaber... clan leader of the Llyach Aelfs

Kronn... Selkie healer

Llathieria... Queen of the Aelfs

Llyemyllan... King of the Aelfs

Lugh... leader of the Tuatha De`Danann; first son of Cian and Eithne

Lunesa... wife of Kaber

Morgan... Shapeshifter; son of Daniel

Muijalaa... third Aelven warrior of the Capourian Mountain Wolf pack clan

Nymphatious... young Aelven male that befriends Ryyaan at the Tuatha mound

Pharonis... second Aelven warrior of the Capourian Mountain Wolf pack clan

Sibrey... Shapeshifter from the Village of Sombreia — also known as Ree, single Shapeshifter member of the Panther clan of Shapeshifters

Ryyaan... Human child found in the Lypurnen Woods — also known as Ryy

Selmathens... rod entities that are creatures of both vapour and substance, belonging to the Siren race

Sercovious... married to Jazmyyn; main metalsmith of the Tuatha mound

Siian... previous mate of Kashha's father Vaal; she is the mother of Kashha's brother

Stephponias... Llyach Aelfan medicine elder from Clan Sylmoor

Tamerk... Wood Sprite living in Lypurnen Woods

Thimelteen... mother to Tommarrius

Tommarrius Kuamashe... little Aelflet from Kilren

Tuatha De`Danann... ruling Military Army of Tantaris

Vallmyallyn... Witch's father; he is a Selkie from Vaukknea Island — also known as Vaal

Zheckarria... father to Tommarrius

Sea Creatures and Deities:

Each-Uisge... these creatures are the cousins to the Kelpies. They will be amalgamated with the Kelpies should one of them break their promise of sworn protection, and cast out from the safety of hiding in the space in-between

Manannan... Sea God

Selkintramblay Capatofic Tryilamores; the true name for the species known as the Selkies

Shalimar Ridiculous... this Sea Witch is one of the strangest you will find in the pages of any of my books, being born into the water world of the Elementals. She has both tail and legs that are twisted and malformed from birth; changing her into a very angry creature

Snickann-Freymyi... a Venomous Valkyrji that can be a very deadly being, known for her cruelty and violence within the Sidhe home-world

Tailtiu... wife of Manannan, she is a Sea Goddess

Planets, Moons, Nebulae, and Galaxies:

Anthros... wandering planet with no fixed address, living somewhere in the Star Nebula called Anthros Major. It is the planet that is home to the crystal caves, and gave birth to the large pillars of stones that are outside the Tuatha De˙Danann's mound, and the village of Tameron

Bulgapher... planet in the Crystal Horse Galaxy

Carthanthien Nebula... home of the Vermorbian Race

Centarraura Nebula... home of the race of storm planets that harness and manipulate the weather with unusual energy fluxes

Faden Corpeous... the Galaxy that these planets and moon exist within

False Galaxy of the Crystal Horse... hosts the Rings of Brodgar in a future novel

Goetutonias Nebula... sister galaxy that rotates around Faden Corpeous

Hydrous Secular Nebula... out past the Goetutonias Nebula

Kalieas... second moon of Tantaris, that disappeared into the space in-between

Kepet Minor... this is where the Bagorin race of Aelves live

Leberone... first moon of Tantaris

Leonae... first moon of Hydrous Secular; it hosts the Finical Spideranthemaous – the very thing that can detect the Dragons wherever they are currently hiding

Mauntra... the sun

Naunas... second planet in Faden Corpeous Galaxy

Northern Rings of Goetutonias... constellational reference point that hangs just south of the main system of shift-point doorways, in this arena of space

Pin Nebula... this nebula has vast energy strands; used for the removal of memory by the Selkie Priestesses

Star of the Sirens... Selmathen home-world

Star Nebula... home of Anthros the roaming planet

String Nebula... worlds connected by energy strings and threads of light

Suedamorphay... Gargoyle home world planet

Tantaris Suppramorphis... home planet of this storyline, and first planet in the Faden Corpeous Galaxy

Tuworg Nebula... a drifting Nebula that comes into contact with the Galaxy of the Crystal Horse at a certain time of the year

---

Comets and Meteors:

Angagan... this comet was known for its vast tail debris that could knock a planet out of its rotational path, and cause incredible damage to anything out in the open, as it passes along its way

Dark Star Meteor... Balor pulled Symbya through this when he brought him to Tantaris

Lyra... this is a fast moving meteor that occasionally comes into range with some of the planets

Starshaper... this meteor was the center of the largest of all the seed formations, and each of the comets or meteors were born from this gigantic field of stardust

Zedrith Mordea Kippsen... this comet is the one that caused the formation of both Naunas and Tantaris

THE BEGINNING

Moons Phases for now and future:

This is a list of Moons and their festival names for both of the Moons during certain times of their year. The months of the year are not used and will be called Moon times, with reference used simply in referring to the names of those Moons, instead of referring to an Earth month. Not all have been used and will continued to be used in the series to give the reader an idea what time they might coincide with — in the human schedule of their Solar-Festivals.

Leberone's festivals:	Coincides with Your Earth Date, of:
Dynastic Moon... Arthuan Season, renewal festival	*December 21*
Quladah Moon... Oimealg Season, purification festival	*February 2*
Sithka Moon... Earraigh Season, beginnings festival	*March 21*
Fenoria Moon... CalinMai Season, fire festival	*May 1*
Percide Moon... Alban Heruim Season, Mauntra festival	*June 21*
Byanadorian Moon... Nasadh Season	*August 1*
Fieldmarr Moon... AlbanElued Season, remembrance fest	*September 21*
Twintaea Moon... Samhuinn Season, fire festival	*November 2*
Kaliea's Moon Phases:	Coincides with Your Earth Date, of:
Calmystic Moon... Modranicht festival	*December 21*
Zepheragulous Moon... Lubercalia festival	*February 2*
Incubus Moon... Caisg festival	*March 21*

Twiggglemarr Moon... Roodmas festival	*May 1*
Zahkorbial Moon... Samhraidh festival	*June 21*
Sandnostic Moon... Lughnas festival	*August 1*
Soleus Moon... Fomhair festival	*September 1*
Mantorian Moon... Deadnuaght Festival	*November 2*

Villages and Towns of Water's Deep:

Aggulf Elkcum Mound... Tuatha De˙Danann stronghold

Fomor... Fomorians clan of Aelfs

Kilren... Sayber Fennone Clan of Aelfs

Llavalla... Kanoie Clan of Witches

Sadllenay... village of the Dryads; overrun by Seelies; used to be the home of the Kyafth clan

Sombreia... Shapeshifter village; Togernaut clan

Sylmoor... Llyach clan of Aelfs

Symarr... home of the Dracore

Tameron... Syann-Clan Aelfs

Tothray... Caubertian Clan of Aelfs; Gypsy offspring of the Sage clan of Fomorian Aelves and ostracized Llavalla Witches

Woods, Forests, Lakes, Islands, and the occasional Rocks:

Beletruxe Island... this island is situated in the North, just south of Toraigh Island and is full of sea-caves along its beaches. When the surf is just right — during the high-tides, the sea can be seen exploding through the blow-holes with life, as they produce huge water geysers at the tidal flats

Damonian Woods... Kashandarhh's home faunt

Dead Monkey Rocks... place where Kamera met Vallmyallyn for the first time. It is situated on the mainland, northwest of the Island of Vaukknea

Esoyat Island... is on the Planet of Naunas; there is a shift-point doorway here that was build by the Synotay's and is one of the main doorways used by the Selmathens to move between Galaxies

Kartouche Island... between Tameron and Sylmoor villages

Killchurn Lake... lake doorway that leads to the Other Realm of the Cloud People

Loch Na Sul... Balor's lake near Tameron's other realm

Lucidity Lake... water near the Sombreian Village; home of the Naiads

Lypurnen Woods... Tamerk's home

Mangoesa Island... island in the North Sea, above the Tuatha De' Danann Aggulf Elkcum mound

Symarr Island... home of the Dracore

Tayose Island... is situated on the planet Naunas and hosts the largest university of the Fey clans in this galaxy. It is also the home of the ancient race of Synotay Fey

Toraigh Island... Fomorian's Stronghold

Tryanafie Bay... body of water that is inside the barriers of Vaukknea Island

Vaukknea Island... home of the Selkies

Fields:

Fields of the Cauldron... sacred Fire Elemental grounds

Fields of Odisias... underground within the Symarr Dragon Range

Seas, Rivers, and Oceans:

Morphana River... snakes its way from the north across the Zarconian Falls at the Tuatha De`Danann mound, as it passes on its way south over the Telpphaea Falls at Dragon Claw Drift, then comes out the south-eastern shore of the continent by Kartouche Island

Ocean of Souls... home of the Merfolk

Saltwater Trench... runs between the continent in the south and the Island of Symarr

Sea of Contentious Souls... body of water that rests above the North-east of the continent around the area of Fomor and the Damonian Woods

The Old Sea of Hioroques... this ocean runs around the Earth Elementals' city of Gorias

Plains or Lowlands:

Plains of Sheymoar... piece of land northwest of the Telpphaea Falls, that runs in the area of land where the Morphana River snakes its way around the village of Llavalla and crosses the continent to the outskirts of Sadllenay

Reefs and Trenches:

Trench of Talon... a deep trench where the mystical waves of gigantic proportions are seeded, from deep beneath the ocean floor; the area is home to the majikal beings called the Auicks. These creatures come to life as sentient beings, to direct the vast contingency of sea creatures to the world of the reefs during the times of the shedding

Undinecis Reef... underwater reef world just north of the Island of Vaukknea; this is the shedding grounds where they feed on its energy to live and grow strong

Saltwater Trench... this is new land found between the Island of Symarr and the continent

Mountain Ranges, Hills or Canyons:

Capourian Mountain Range... lies to the south and cradles the Stones of Panthor, and mostly circles the village of Tameron

Copper Canyon... situated north of Sylmoor, and rests along the western flank of the Sydclath mountains, south of Kilren

Cydclath Mountain Range... runs from just north of Capourian Mountain's Pickle Canyon; west of Morphana River, and ends at Dragon Claw Drift North of Tothray

Dragonclaw Drift... this piece of land is part of a huge plateau that is near the Morphana River that winds its way through the Cydclath and Sydclath Mountain Ranges. In the middle of both mountains is a huge waterfall that splits the two ranges in half. The drift is part of the Sydclath's northeastern cliff-face and runs sideways through the gulch that forms one of the two sides of these mountains, which come together at this juncture – transforming the surrounding rock into the shape of huge Dragon claws

Pickle Canyon... deep within the Capourian Mountain Range, bordered on all sides by huge cliffs of red jasper and hematite

Sydclath Mountain Range... starts at the east of Sylmoor village, runs past the tail of Morphana River and ends at Dragon Claw Drift, northwest of Kilren

Symarr Dragon Ranges... this Mountain Range is situated on the Island of the Dragons and literally surrounds the entire Island of Symarr leaving the Island impenetrable to outsiders

Fault Lines:

Panthorian... this fault line runs from the middle of the two main mountain ranges in the centre of the continent and makes its way to the North near the Tuatha's Aggulf Elkcum mound

Waterfalls:

Telpphaea Falls... these falls separate the Sydclath and the Cydclath Mountain Ranges at Dragon Claw Drift

Zarconian Falls... these double falls are part of the head-waters of the Morphana River, as it travels from the north to the Aggulf Elkcum Mound and splits the river in two — just as they go over the edge into the depths of the mound

Stone Circles and Leylines:

Ley Lines of Kalmaskis... certain points of energy leading towards the home-worlds of all Fey

Shivonian Ley line... sits high in the north-east of Tantaris's main Aelven Aggulf Elkcum Mound

Standing Stones of Anthros... the stone circle that was a gift from the Selmathen race; its currently standing guard at the Aggulf Elkcum mound

Stones of Panthor... shift-point stones at the entrance to the village of Tameron

Ley lines of Lemarr... very similar to the Ley Lines of earth, except these ones run deep within the planet's crust near the Standing Stones of Selmathen origins

Covens:

Ka`afrey Coven... is an elite group of individuals that look after the well-being of those inside this realm

Kashandarhh's light... Kashha's newest coven of Witches

Synatarrae... one of the old Faery Queen covens in the next book

Clans and their Destinations:

Bagorin... this is a colony of space faring Aelves that live in the Kepet Minor Star system

Capourian Mountain Pack Wolf... clan of mystery and legend used to protect those of significant importance

Caubertians... adopted name of the clan from Tothray

Flambosa... Centaur clan

Kyafth... clan of Dryads from Sadllenay

Llavalla... clan of Witches from Kanoie

Panther... clan of felines that have adopted a Shapeshifter from Sombreia called Sibrey

Saber Fennone... clan of Aelves from Kilren

Snapperhead-Knocktaw... Earthshaper Elemental clan

Syann-Clan... clan of Aelves from Tameron

Togernaut... clan of Shapeshifters from Sombreia

Trithogeans... coven of warriors primarily used to protect royal patrons along the edges of the rings of space.

Trolladites... clan of Gargoyles from the planet Suedamorphay

---

Cities belonging to other worlds:

Finias... Fire Elemental city that is on the planet Naunas. It is deep in the jungles off the main coastline in the southernmost part of its largest continent

Sairog... this is the home city of the Sidhe elders and their hordes; its location will be included in future novels

Lemuria... city of the ancients

Wastelands of Paramour... gathering place found on the Siren's Home-Star

---

Temples:

Temple of Paracleese... this ethereal temple belongs to the Witch kind of Kanoie

Mounds:

Aggulf Elkcum... this is the main Tuatha De˙Danann Mound here on Tantaris. It is situated in the north of Water's Deep, beside a series of hidden Traveler Stones set deep inside its walls — given to them from the Selmathen race of Fey. It also hosts the Standing Stones of Anthros, which are set above the Zarconian Falls up on the surface

Caves:

Caves of Almalta... home of the Tacknea Spinder Spider

ABOUT THE AUTHOR

Adele DeGirolamo was born and raised on Vancouver Island, on the West Coast of British Columbia and spent most of the later part of her school age life living on sailboats and sailing the Gulf Islands in British Columbia. Now, living in an isolated small community on the Island, the Author has found the peace and tranquility that allows her to create the epic sphere of the Fey, drawing on the animals that visit her gardens to fuel the creatures that inhabit Tantaris and the other planets she creates in her writing.